Anne Douglas, after a v_____
her home in Edinburgh, _____
She very much enjoys life in the modern capital, but finds its
ever-present history fascinating.

She has written three previous novels, including *Catherine's Land*, also published by Piatkus.

Also by Anne Douglas

Catherine's Land

As The Years Go By

Anne Douglas

PIATKUS

For more information on other books published by Piatkus,
visit our website at *www.piatkus.co.uk*

First published in Great Britain in 1999 by
Judy Piatkus (Publishers) Ltd of
5 Windmill Street, London W1P 1HF
email: info@piatkus.co.uk

This edition published 1999

The moral right of the author has been asserted

A catalogue record for this book is available from the British Library

ISBN 0 7499 3125 6

Set in Times by
Phoenix Photosetting, Chatham, Kent

Printed and bound in Great Britain by
Mackays of Chatham plc, Chatham, Kent

Author's Note

In writing this novel, I found the following of particular value:
HARRIS, Paul *Edinburgh, the Fabulous Fifties*
REEVES, Thomas C. *A Life of John Kennedy*
SKED, Alan & COOK, Chris *Post-War Britain: a political history*
The files of *The Scotsman* newspaper

As my novel is set in a real city, obviously some of the streets and buildings I've described in my text are also real, but I should like to stress that Catherine's Land, the tenement that becomes Catherine's Hall, is purely imaginary, as are the S and G Bank and Logie's store. It is true that there is a real University of Edinburgh hall of residence in the lawnmarket, but Catherine's Hall has no connection with it, and my 'man from the university', John Mains, is as imaginary as all my other characters.

For Dorothy Lumley, friend and agent, with gratitude.

Part One

1952–1953

Chapter One

Goodbye, Catherine's Land. This was the day. 6 February, 1952. Kate Rossie, speeding up the Royal Mile towards the house, had been thinking of nothing else. Until she heard the wireless news. The announcer's voice, broadcasting to the world. That voice still rang in her ears, solemn as a passing bell. *Der König ist tot. Le roi est mort.* The King is dead.

George the Sixth dead? She still could not believe it. He had been ill, it was true. A lung resection, the doctors said. Cancer, said the rumours. But he was supposed to have recovered. Kate was only twenty-one; she could remember no other monarch. Now Princess Elizabeth would be Queen and she was somewhere in Kenya, watching wild animals. Lord, thought Kate, this was going to send the paper hopping, she'd better ring the desk as soon as she'd seen Will.

It was only three months earlier that she had landed the job of junior reporter on a Glasgow left-wing newspaper. She'd asked for special leave today to say goodbye to Catherine's Land, but now of course she'd have to go into work and wanted to, for who'd want to be away from the centre of news at a time like this?

She had reached the Lawnmarket. Next stop, the Castle. Behind her lay the long historic thoroughfare that stretched down to the Palace of Holyroodhouse. These were the stones of Edinburgh she had known all her life. She had been born in the tenement that was Catherine's Land, she had gone to school in the Canongate. It had always seemed to her that nothing could change, yet here was change happening before her eyes. Even though her pulse was racing and her heart beating fast, sadness gripped her at the door of her old home. Just for a moment, the news about the King had

3

sent the other significance of the day from her mind, but now it returned in full force. This was the day the last tenants were to leave. This was the day that Catherine's Land closed its doors. Until the builders moved in.

Kate stood looking up at the six storeys that had been home. Every window was known to her, every blackened stone, every tile, every leaning chimney. Her beautiful eyes moved slowly down to the front door hanging open and the steps where children, herself included, had played down the years. Here were the empty shops. Donnie Muir's grocery, Will's mother's dressmaker's, her father's newsagent's that had once been the sweetie shop. Ken Rossie had been a boy in Catherine's Land, along with the Kemp boys, the Muir boys, the Ritchie girls, the Finnegans, the Pringles, the Craigs, the Erskines, so many people Kate had known only as grown-ups. All gone now, except for the Gilbrides, who would be up the stair waiting for the removal van. At the thought of Will Gilbride, Kate pushed open the front door and went sprinting up the worn stone steps calling, 'Will, I'm here!'

And Will came thundering down the stair to meet her.

Chapter Two

Catherine's Land had been built by a merchant in 1701 and built to last. In its early days, it had included quality among its tenants. Later, it had become a slum. Restored to respectability at the turn of the nineteenth century, it had soldiered on to survive two world wars. By 1945, however, it was obvious that the years had finally taken their toll. The landlords, their hearts failing over the repairs, sold the house to the university for conversion to students' accommodation.

No tenant at the time was worried. Why, the university would niver get planning permission! You couldna get the bricks for housing, niver mind digs for students, and who cared a toss for students, anyway, when there were families with nowhere to live? But eventually the university did get planning permission. By Christmas 1951, most of the tenants had been dispersed, some to council estates, others to lodging houses or other tenements, anywhere they could squash themselves in. By this significant day in February 1952, only the Gilbrides were left.

There were four of them. Madge, Will's grandmother; her daughter, Jennie, and Jennie's sons, Will and Hamish.

Madge, still sweet-faced, still pretty, had come to Catherine's Land as a young widow when her mother-in-law had brought her back from Southampton with her three little girls, Abby, Jennie and Rachel. That had been in 1912. Madge had been Madge Ritchie then. Jennie and Rachel had married brothers, the sons of Jim Gilbride, a widower. Years later, Madge herself had married Jim. Rachel's Malcolm was still alive, but Jim was dead and so was Jennie's Rory. Will and Hamish rarely spoke of their father.

'Oh, Kate!' Will strained her close, then released her to look at

5

her, taking his usual delight in his Renoir girl as Rachel Gilbride, a painter, liked to describe Kate. Will knew nothing about art, but he knew that Kate, with her velvet dark eyes, her peachy skin and tawny hair, was beautiful. Folk said she and her sister were like their mother, but Ivy Rossie these days was a spent match to their flame. That was what life did to you, eh? Why, even Biddy, older than Kate and married with three children, was showing signs of wear and tear. But Will couldn't imagine Kate's looks ever fading. She wasn't the type to let life grind her down. Just let it try!

Kate was taking pleasure in her Will too. He and Hamish had Jennie's blond good looks, even though their father's extravagant handsomeness had passed them by. At one time Jennie used to say she could just see a look of Rory in Hamish, but after Rory left her for Sheena MacLaren, Jennie never mentioned that look again.

'No uniform?' Kate teased. 'Why, I was looking forward to saluting!'

'Ah, come on!' Will protested, not wanting to be reminded of the row they'd had when he'd taken a National Service commission. Kate didn't approve of differences in rank and thought it crazy that anyone from Catherine's Land should want to be an officer. But then Will was a university graduate and had already been promised a post in one of Edinburgh's most famous banks. Kate knew he didn't think of himself as belonging any more to Catherine's Land. After all, two of his aunts and his uncle had long ago escaped. Well, everybody's escaped now, thought Kate, if you wanted to put it that way.

'I'm on leave,' Will said softly. 'I've got ten days, if you remember.'

'I remember.' Kate, her lower lip trembling, didn't have to be reminded that he was bound for fighting in Korea. She swallowed her tears and took Will's arm to run up the stair to his mother's flat.

'Have you heard the news?' she cried, greeting everybody.

'What news?' asked Jennie Gilbride. 'We've packed the wireless.'

Jennie, Madge and Hamish, surrounded by boxes, were in the living room that still showed signs of early grandeur in its long windows and handsome cornice. The ceiling over the old range

6

was blackened, Jennie had never been able to do anything about that, but elsewhere everything was clean as a new pin for Jennie was a good housewife and liked things tidy. The gas was still connected, the kettle had not been packed but was singing in the little scullery. Soon Madge would make tea for everyone, the removal men as well, when they arrived.

'What news?' Jennie repeated, taking the top off the milk bottle.

'The King is dead,' said Kate.

There was a stunned silence. Everyone stared at Kate, who couldn't help enjoying her moment of attention.

'Aye, I thought you might not've heard,' she went on. 'I heard it on ma portable. He died in his sleep, his manservant found him.'

'Oh, the poor King!' whispered Madge. 'Only fifty-seven!'

Kate and Will exchanged looks. Seemed to them, fifty-seven wasn't very young.

'And the poor Queen, too.' Madge shook her head. 'A widow. We know what that's like.'

Jennie said nothing. She had gone rather pale. Remembering, perhaps, thought Will, the time she had found his father dead. He had just returned to them from London. Would he have stayed? They would never know. Death gave no answers.

'What'll happen now?' asked Hamish. 'Will they have to get Princess Elizabeth back?'

'Of course,' Madge answered. 'She's the Queen.'

'That'll be funny,' Will commented. 'Having to sing, God Save The Queen.'

'I remember when we thought it strange to sing God Save the King,' said Madge. 'I was only seventeen when Queen Victoria died. Everybody said it was the end of an era.'

'So's this the end of an era,' said Jennie. 'I mean, for Catherine's Land.'

'Listen, is that the van?' shouted Hamish.

They rushed to the windows to see. Three storeys below, they could see a large furniture van manoeuvring itself into a parking place. Three men jumped out and began to fling out cartons and sacks, then there came a thundering blow on the downstairs door. Everyone exchanged glances.

'Nineteen twelve,' Madge said huskily. 'That's when we first came. Of course I had Jennie's flat, then, that's where we all lived,

7

then when Jennie got married, I moved up the stair and let her have more space. Nineteen forty-five, Jim and I moved across the landing—'

'Yes, Gran,' Hamish said patiently. 'I'll go down and tell the men to come up.'

'Will,' whispered Kate, 'I'm sorry but I'll have to go to work.'

'Why? I thought you'd taken the day off?'

'Yes, but now the King's dead I'll be needed. You know what it's like when a big story breaks, they'll be sending everybody everywhere.'

'OK, I'll come with you to the station.'

'No.' Kate flattened herself against the wall as one of the removal men marched past with an armchair. 'You stay here and help your mam. She's going to be feeling pretty blue, leaving here. And then she'll be needing you at the bungalow.'

Abby, Madge's eldest daughter, had bought the family a bungalow in Corstorphine, a part of the city that had once been a village but was now a large residential and shopping area with the Edinburgh zoo on its fringe. Abby was the clever one, dark and spirited, full of energy. From being a housemaid, she had risen by self-education and brains to the top post at Logie's, one of Edinburgh's most fashionable Princes Street stores, and had married her childhood sweetheart, Frankie Baxter. For years, she had wanted to transplant Madge to a little house with a garden and an apple tree, just like they'd had so many years before in Southampton, and for years Madge had resisted. She was happy with her friends in Catherine's Land, Peggie Kemp, Joanie Muir, Jessie Rossie. Even when Jim had died, she still hadn't wanted to leave and Jennie, whose life was part of Catherine's Land, had also refused to go. Now, of course, they'd had to accept the inevitable, aware that they were in fact luckier than most. Still, it was an ordeal, leaving their homes, moving into the unknown.

Will sighed. 'Suppose you're right, I'd better stay.'

'See you tomorrow night, then,' said Kate, as they ran down the stair. 'For Bobby's welcome home party.'

'Oh, God, what a waste of an evening.' Will brightened. 'Hey, maybe they'll cancel it, now that the King is dead.'

'Nothing in this world will make your Aunt Rachel cancel a party for Bobby,' laughed Kate. 'Speaking of angels, here's Rachel now.'

A small car had squeezed itself in behind the furniture van and out of it stepped Rachel Gilbride, Madge's youngest daughter. Still very attractive, with dark Ritchie eyes and delicate features, she was a gifted artist who had seen her image change from innovator to establishment figure and wasn't sure she liked it. Still, her pictures sold well and that pleased not only her but Malcolm, who was an accountant. Their other shared interest was their only child, Bobby, who had just completed his National Service. Will knew that Kate was right. Rachel would never cancel a party for Bobby.

'They've come, then!' she cried, greeting Will and Kate. 'The removal men? Oh, isn't this a sad day? Seeing the end of our home?'

Will said nothing. Everyone knew that his aunt had never been so happy as when she married Malcolm and moved to a fine solid house in Morningside. Like Abby, Malcolm had made his way by his own efforts. 'Doesna want to be a house painter like his Dad,' Jim Gilbride used to say, and Malcolm always quite sincerely said Amen to that. He and Will were of a mind, whereas what was in Bobby's mind, nobody knew. Nothing sensible, thought Will.

'Your Aunt Abby's tied up at a meeting,' Rachel told Will. 'She'll be coming round to the new house this afternoon.'

'OK,' said Will, his eyes on Kate's retreating figure. 'There's some tea on the go up the stair if you want it, Aunt Rachel.'

'Always tea on the go if Ma's around,' said Rachel with a smile.

Chapter Three

It didn't take long to dismantle Jennie's flat or Madge's; didn't take long to dismantle their homes. The family stood around, watching in melancholy as the piano went, accompanied by much groaning and swearing, then the chairs and washstands, the beds where people had been born and died, the kitchen table where the girls had sat in the old days, eating meals, cutting out patterns, adding up weekly bills.

'I did my first drawings at that table,' Rachel said softly.

'Yes, and wouldn't budge when I had to lay the cloth,' Jennie reminded.

'Well, where's all this stuff going now?' asked Hamish. 'I mean, will it all fit in to the bungalow?'

'What doesn't fit can go in the garage.'

'Keep forgetting we've got a garage.' Hamish grinned. 'Supposing I want to get a car?'

On the strength of being a 'poor fatherless bairn', Hamish, like Will, had been lucky enough to be given a place at Heriot's, one of Edinburgh's fine old schools, but he had refused to go to university and as soon as he finished National Service had declared he wanted to be a tailor.

'Like mother, like son,' Jennie said proudly.

'Like grandmother,' said Madge, for she too had trained as a dressmaker, though had worked most of her time in Edinburgh at Mackenzie's Bakery.

Will had not been pleased.

'Doesna want his grand friends to be measured for suits by his brother,' Jessie Rossie had shrewdly commented.

But Madge would have none of that. Will was no snob. What

10

grand friends was Jessie talking about, anyway? Will's girlfriend was Kate, Jessie's own grand-daughter!

'Aye, it's funny, that. Chalk and cheese, eh? Canna see how they get on.'

'Opposites attract, Jessie.'

'True. Look at you and your Jim.'

Madge had not replied, but everyone knew about Jim's fiery temper that had kept him and Madge apart for too many years.

'When are you going to have enough money to buy a car?' Will asked Hamish now, his tone a little acid, but Hamish only laughed.

'Why, when you get me a loan from your bank!'

If only Will were going to work at the Scottish and General now, thought Jennie. If only he were not going to Korea. Why did the British still feel they had to send troops all over the world, fighting battles that weren't theirs?

'Have to defend South Korea against the North's aggression,' Will had told her. 'Have to protect the weak.'

But Jennie felt quite weak herself at the thought of her son in a fighting zone. Why couldn't he have been as lucky as Hamish or Bobby who had never even left their own country? She knew she must look on the bright side. Will could well come home safe and sound, probably to Kate Rossie. It wouldn't surprise Jennie if those two slipped quietly out one day and got married. There was no doubt that they were very much in love.

'That's it, then, hen,' said the foreman of the removers. 'That's us. We're away.'

'You've got the new address? Nineteen, Brae Street?'

'Aye.' He waved a roughened hand. 'See you there, when we've had a bite to eat, eh?'

'Oh, yes, there's plenty of time.' Jennie's voice faltered. 'We want to have a last look round, anyway.'

'And then we have to wait for the man from the university,' put in Madge. 'He wants to lock up.'

They smiled their sad smiles again. When had Catherine's Land ever been locked up? People had always walked in and out through that hanging door, moving aside children to go running up the stair. There was never anything to take, nothing that would be missed, anyway.

* * *

11

John Mains, a stooping figure with greying hair and moustache, arrived from the university as the removal men were leaving.

'Timed it nicely,' he said, politely touching his hat.

'We were just going up for a last look,' Jennie said quickly.

'Certainly, certainly. Just take your time. I know this will be a sad day for you. A sad day, anyway, of course. Who'd have thought the King would go so quickly?'

'I don't know that I want to look round,' Madge said, tears choking her voice. 'I don't need to, I can see it all in my mind. I think I'll always see it in my mind.'

'We could wait down the stair, Gran?' suggested Will, but Madge, clutching her kettle, said she'd wait for the others on the landing, they would all leave together.

'I just want to look in at our old room,' Rachel whispered to Jennie. 'I know it's different, I know you split it, but I'd like to see it again.'

'Everything will be split up soon,' said Jennie.

She was gazing at the old range in the living room, remembering all the hours it had stolen from them, all the sweeping and raking and washing with soda it had needed, all the blackleading and filling up with coal and starting all over again. Poor Ma! How hard she'd had to work, even after a full day at the baker's. And then wouldn't she want to go and start washing the stair! At least, things were easier for her now.

'Come on!' called Rachel from Jennie's bedroom, one half of the original room the two sisters had shared. 'Remember when we got dressed here for our weddings? You in blue, me in cream? We thought ourselves the bee's knees, didn't we?'

'Seem to remember we did look pretty good.' Jennie's eyes were fixed on the spot on the floorboards where her marriage bed had stood.

'Oh, Rachel,' she said, sombrely. 'Let's go. Ma's right, there's no point in all this.' But when Rachel had gently touched her hand and left her, Jennie still waited a moment.

'Goodbye, Rory, darling,' she said softly.

For the last time, they walked down the stair, and the ghosts went with them. They all had their special ghosts and did not speak of them, except that Madge said she could still hear the boots of the Kemp boys, the Rossies and the Muirs, ringing on the stone.

'Lucky to have boots,' muttered Hamish, feeling ashamed of the lump in his throat.

'That's true,' said Madge, remembering all the barefoot children of the not so distant past. 'Here's Mr Mains waiting for us.'

'Ready to go?' he asked kindly, swinging a bunch of keys from his finger.

Yes. Now they felt they couldn't go fast enough.

But when Mr Mains locks this door, thought Jennie wildly, who'll go running up the stair?

They moved into the February cold and stood shivering on the steps, while Mr Mains slammed and locked the door of Catherine's Land behind him. More than anything else, that locking brought it home to them: this was the end.

'The end of Catherine's Land,' Rachel whispered, but Mr Mains looked his surprise.

'Why, no, it's not the end, it's a beginning. Tomorrow the builders arrive to start on Catherine's Hall.' Mr Mains rubbed his thin hands together. 'Sad it had to be at this time, though. I mean, with the death of the King.'

'Shan't forget this day,' said Will. 'Goodbye, Mr Mains, and thanks.'

'Goodbye and good luck.' He tipped his hat and walked away down the Lawnmarket and they stood watching him go. Rachel said they should go to the car and be on their way, but two people were hurrying towards them, a narrow-shouldered man and a young girl. Donnie Muir and his daughter, Nina.

'Oh, what a shame, Donnie!' cried Madge. 'The man from the university's just locked up. Did you want to have a last look?'

Donnie Muir, one of those whose boots had thundered past Madge's door, gave an asthmatic cough.

'Och, it doesna matter. I thought on about it too late. It was all the news about the King, put it out o' ma mind, then Sally says you nip round now, I'll mind the shop.'

Donnie and Sally, who had kept the grocery at Catherine's Land, now rented a smaller shop in the Haymarket, close to Ken Rossie's newsagent's. Their only surviving child, Nina, had just left school and was helping in the shop and studying book-keeping at night school. Now, standing with her father in the chill wind, she did not look at any of the Gilbrides, but kept her eyes

13

cast down. It was generally accepted that Nina was a clever girl, but shy.

'I wish we could give you a lift back,' Madge was saying to Donnie, for she had a soft spot for the son of her old friend, Joanie, who had died the previous year. 'The thing is, Rachel's taking us to the new house.'

'That's all right, dinna worry, we'll get the tram.' Donnie shook hands all round. 'Glad to have seen you, though, and the best o' luck, eh?'

'I'll come and see Sally!' called Madge, as the two rather woebegone figures turned away.

'She'll look forward to that!' Donnie called back.

'Come on,' said Rachel again, 'Let's go.'

DEATH OF THE KING was on all the placards, as they drove down the Mound. Above them, the flag on the castle drooped at half-mast.

'Oh, don't you feel sad?' cried Rachel. 'Everything seems to be sad together, doesn't it? At least we can cheer up tomorrow at Bobby's party.'

'You're still having it?' asked Madge.

'Oh, Ma, you don't mean I should cancel, do you? I can't, I've done all the food!'

Will, stuffed between his mother and Hamish in the back seat, remembered Kate and smiled, but the smile soon faded. Now was not the time for smiling.

Chapter Four

Rachel, striking in full-length black, was checking the buffet table in the dining room of her house in Morningside. It was a handsome room, Victorian, of course, not Georgian, which was one step down the scale in Edinburgh, but Rachel was proud of it. She was proud of her buffet, too, which was all her own work and very hard work at that, considering the rationing problems still around, but she had wanted it to be a thank-you for Bobby's safe return from service. Having the caterers in would not have meant the same.

'All set?' asked Malcolm, joining her.

He had put on weight recently and lost most of his sandy hair, but he thought he looked well, looked what he was, a successful accountant. He had never had his brother's good looks or his fierce desire for social change. The only social change Malcolm desired was his own and he had achieved that by hard work and application. If he appeared dull to some, he wasn't going to lose any sleep over it.

'Looks all right?' asked Rachel.

'Looks fine.' He kissed her cheek. 'And so do you.'

'Better check the drinks,' she told him, with a pleased smile.

'Your ma and Jennie still coming?' he asked, moving to the trolley of bottles and glasses.

'Of course, why not?'

'Thought they might be a bit low, leaving Catherine's Land.'

'Well, of course it was sad, saying goodbye. You might have come over for a last look yourself.'

'I hate goodbyes. Only upset you. Anyway, we were never so

very fond of Catherine's Land, were we?' Malcolm pulled the cork of a bottle of red wine. 'Damned glad to get away.'

A grandfather clock chimed seven and Rachel gave a start.

'I do wish Bobby would come down! People will be here soon.'

'Don't nag him. He's straight out of the army, he's had enough of worrying about time.'

'I'm not going to nag him, Malcolm. When have I ever nagged him?' Rachel's eyes lit up. 'Anyway, he's here!'

As Bobby, in a dark suit, stood looking in at the dining room, Rachel ran to him and kissed his cheek. She thought he looked wonderfully handsome, with the dark Ritchie eyes he had inherited from her and finely chiselled features. Oh, but why had the army ruined his sandy-blond hair? Cropped so close to his skull, it made him seem a stranger. The good thing was that it would grow and then he would seem their Bobby again. Not for a moment did she allow herself to remember that Bobby had not been their Bobby for many a long year.

Malcolm suggested a quick drink before the guests arrived and fussed to give Bobby a gin and tonic, as Rachel lit his cigarette.

'I can't tell you what a relief it is to have you home,' she told him. 'No more worries about where you might be sent!'

'To be honest, I'd rather have been sent where there was some action,' Bobby replied. 'What's the point of doing military service if you only stay in the UK?'

'You're not saying you wanted to go to Korea?' Rachel shivered. 'I'm just thanking my lucky stars that you're not Will.'

'He'll be all right. Probably won't be in real danger.'

'But he's an officer, Bobby!'

'Bully for him. I never wanted a commission. Look, can we talk about something else?'

'Such as what you're going to do now,' said Malcolm cheerfully. 'Back to university, eh? You'll want to get your degree out of the way.'

It had been Bobby's decision to opt for National Service half way through his history degree course. Malcolm had thought it unwise, but provided Bobby completed his studies on his return believed there would be no harm done.

Bobby studied his cigarette. 'I don't think so,' he said quietly.

16

Malcolm's eyes stared glassily. 'What do you mean? Of course you'll be going back to university!'

'No.' The monosyllable was flat. Final.

'Oh, God.' Rachel slumped in her chair. Here it was, here was what she always half expected with Bobby. Trouble.

Malcolm's fleshy face had turned a dusky red. 'If you're not going to finish your degree, what are you going to do?'

'I'm going to London. I intend to become a professional musician.'

Malcolm and Rachel turned to each other. They didn't know whether to laugh or cry.

'A musician? You mean a pianist?' Malcolm ran a hand across his brow. 'Who in hell put this idea into your head? Frankie Baxter?'

Frankie, Abby's husband, was Bobby's idol. His mother had kept the sweetie shop at Catherine's Land, he had had no formal training but had earned his living as a pianist all his life. Pubs, cinemas, ocean liners, American radio, he had played anywhere, and was now running his own band in London and doing very well. But of course he had talent.

'No, it wasn't Uncle Frankie,' Bobby retorted. 'It was my own idea, because I play jazz pretty well, everybody says so.'

'Everybody?' repeated Rachel.

'All the fellows I met in the army. I used to play wherever I could find a piano and they thought I was terrific. That's what made me realise playing piano was what I wanted to do.' Bobby's eyes glinted. 'All I wanted to do.'

'Bobby . . .' – Malcolm was hesitating, searching for the right words – 'what you're suggesting, it just isn't practical. I mean, to succeed as a professional pianist, you have to have more than just – '

'More than just what?'

'Well, you know – you have to be able to do more than – play a tune or two.'

'You're saying I haven't enough talent?'

'I mean you should just think of playing as a hobby. And earning your living some other way.'

'Like you?' Bobby's lip curled. 'Working in an office all day? Thinking about money that isn't even yours? I'd rather do anything than that. Drive a van – dig coal.'

17

'Go and dig bloody coal, then!' cried Malcolm. 'You have the nerve to sneer at the way I earn my living? When it's paid for everything you've ever wanted? I ought to knock you down!'

'Malcolm!' cried Rachel.

'Oh, don't worry, I've got past that sort of thing. But when I see a son of mine turning down the chance to go to university, something I'd have given my soul for, it sticks in my throat, Rachel, it makes me sick!' Malcolm turned his glassy gaze back to Bobby. 'You go to London,' he hissed, 'you try to keep yourself on what you earn, playing your damned piano, and see how far you get. But don't look to me for a penny piece, or your mother either!'

'Fine!' shouted Bobby, turning white. 'That's all right by me! I don't want anything from you, I don't need anything, I'll leave this house now, so you won't need to feel sick a minute longer—'

'Bobby, what are you talking about?' Rachel screamed. 'You can't go like this, you can't!'

'For God's sake, have a heart,' groaned Malcolm. 'Can't you see what you're doing to us? Your mother's arranged this party for you, the guests are due at any minute—'

'I don't care about the party, I don't care about the guests,' Rachel whispered. 'I just don't want you to leave us like this, Bobby.' She put her hand to her brow. 'I don't understand, you see, I don't understand where we've gone wrong.'

'We haven't gone wrong, Rachel.' Malcolm put his arm around her shoulders. 'We haven't done one damn thing that hasn't been for that boy's good and don't you forget it.'

Bobby stood with lowered eyes. 'I don't want to hurt you,' he said hoarsely. 'Please try to understand. I have to make my own decisions. I have to lead my own life.'

'We do understand,' Rachel said eagerly. 'We know you have to make your own decisions now, but there's no need to go rushing off to London without thinking things through, there's no need for that at all.' She tried to smile. 'And think how you'd manage on your own, Bobby! Why, you've never so much as washed a pair of socks!'

'Mum, I've been in the army,' he said wearily. 'You don't know what I can do.'

'Just tell us,' Malcolm said curtly. 'Are you going or staying?'

Bobby slowly raised his eyes. 'If it's all right with you, I'd like to stay on for a while, till I've made my arrangements.'

As Rachel gave a long shuddering sigh of relief, the doorbell pealed.

Chapter Five

The party was not going well. The guests, mainly older people, friends of Rachel's and Malcolm's, seemed subdued. The few who had television at home described for the rest the arrival of the new Queen at London Airport, so young, so vulnerable in her mourning, it had brought the tears to their eyes. Rachel, white-faced with chagrin, hurried about with drinks and crisps, murmuring that it wasn't her fault if the King had died and what was she supposed to do with all this food it had cost her so much effort to find? And this party was a welcome home to Bobby. Was nobody remembering him?

'Never mind, Rachel,' one of her friends consoled her. 'We'll think of it as a welcome to Queen Elizabeth the Second.'

'Queen Elizabeth the First, if you please,' someone else corrected acidly. 'I hope the government remembers that there has never been another Queen Elizabeth of Scotland.'

'Aye, we mustn't upset the nationalists,' Malcolm agreed. 'Or they'll be taking the Stone of Destiny again, or something of the sort.'

Everyone remembered Christmas Eve, 1950, when a group of audacious students had removed the ancient Scottish coronation stone from Westminster Abbey. Centuries before, Edward the First had brought the stone to London. All they were doing, claimed the students, was taking it home. They kept it hidden for four months, then returned it. No harm had been done, a grand gesture had been made, but now the stone was back in position in the Coronation Chair, ready for the Queen's crowning.

Kate, eye-catching in black sweater and full skirt, moved restively, trapped by the chat. Somehow she had become separated from Will and wanted to find him. Being with these arty friends of Rachel's and business colleagues of Malcolm's depressed her. She felt they distanced themselves too far from the sufferings of ordinary people, would probably have screamed aloud if they could have seen some of the sights she had seen in Glasgow, yet wouldn't lift a finger to change things. Thank God the Welfare State had shouldered responsibility! Something was at last being done. People needn't starve if they lost their jobs, they could go to the doctor's if they were ill, they could live without fear. But with the Tories in power again, how long would it all last?

Sometimes Kate worried about Will. She knew he was entitled to his own views, but you would think he would join the Labour Party when his father had been a party worker all his life. Was he a secret Tory? He always laughed when she tackled him and said his politics were his own affair. As though politics could ever be your own affair! How you voted affected everyone else. If folk hadn't made the wrong choice at the last election, the country wouldn't be stuck with Winston Churchill as prime minister again, a man of seventy-seven, who had already had two strokes and might well have another.

'How are you, Kate?' asked Will's Aunt Abby, coming up with her husband, Frankie, a cheerful-faced man, with curly greying hair and dancing blue eyes. Like most people from Catherine's Land, Kate knew that these two had had a pretty tempestuous marriage at one time, but they seemed to have reached calmer waters now. Cynics might say this was because Abby worked in Edinburgh and Frankie worked in London, but Kate thought it was probably just because they were getting old. In their late forties, at least. Surely love had died down for most people by that age?

'How's your family?' Abby asked kindly. 'Settling in well to the new shop?'

'Och, they're managing, thanks, Mrs Baxter.' Kate shrugged. 'Havena much choice to do anything else, have they?'

'And you're enjoying your new job on the Glasgow paper? You know, I've often wished you'd come to Logie's. We could do with people like you.'

'Come to Logie's?' Kate smiled. 'When I try for something else, it'll be politics. That's really what I want to do.'

21

'A tough life,' Abby commented.

'Plenty worse,' retorted Kate. 'In this very city, too.'

'Guess you're right,' said Frankie in the American accent he'd retained from his US radio days in the belief that it impressed his public. 'If you'll excuse me, I'd better find Bobby. Somebody said he was looking for me.'

'I'm looking for Will,' said Kate.

Bobby was in the study, talking to Lindsay Farrell; she'd been at university with him, they'd had something of a relationship. An attractive girl, with high cheekbones and rich brown hair, Lindsay was now on a management training scheme at Logie's and tipped to go far, which was not surprising. She and her sister, Sara, were the adopted daughters of the late Gerald Farrell, who had been chief executive of Logie's and a member of the founding firm. Abby in her youth had been his protegée; there were rumours that there might once have been an affair. Though Frankie was certainly the great love of her life, she had suffered when Gerald had his fatal heart attack. Bobby wasn't too interested. This stuff was all in the past. Abby was chief executive herself now and on friendly terms with Monica, Gerald's widow, who was at the party tonight. So was Sara, blonde and bubbly; Bobby could see her out of the corner of his eye, smiling up at his cousin, Will.

'Would you excuse me?' he murmured to Lindsay. 'I have to go and find my Uncle Frankie.'

'I thought he was in London?'

'His playing engagements were cancelled till after the King's funeral. He came up last night.'

'OK, I'll see you later,' Lindsay said coolly, for her technique with Bobby was never to let him see that he mattered to her. She had been devastated when he suddenly left university for National Service, but had kept her feelings to herself, even when he never wrote to her. There was only one thing to do and that was bide her time, but she had done that for so long and here he was back and wanting to find his uncle! She sipped her drink and concentrated on keeping her iron control.

'What's so important about seeing your uncle?' she allowed herself to ask, with a laugh.

'I want his advice.'

'He's a pianist, how can he advise you?'

22

'I want to be a professional pianist myself. I want to go to London.'

'London?' Lindsay's control was not iron, it was like a band, stretching, aching – at any moment she felt it might snap. 'I – I think that's a very good idea.'

'You do?' Bobby's eyes shone. 'You're the first person to say that, Lindsay. Keep your fingers crossed Frankie says it too.'

Kate was looking in at the door of the study. Her eyes picked out Bobby talking to some girl she didn't know. Moved on to Will's mother talking to some man she didn't know. Found Will.

He too was talking to someone she didn't know. A girl with blonde hair and blue eyes framed in dark spiky lashes. Expensively dressed, expensively at ease, a 'have' if ever there was one. No doubt she called her mother Mummy and had been presented at Holyrood. No doubt she didn't have a job but did little courses, filling in her time till Mr Suitable came along.

But Will was smiling down at her. Listening to her. Looking at her as Kate had never seen him look at anyone else except herself. She couldn't believe it, couldn't believe he wasn't aware of her eyes burning into him, her heart crying out to him. Something thin and painful buried itself in Kate's breast and held her fast so that she felt she couldn't breathe. What was happening to her? Was this jealousy? She had never had the need to feel it before.

'Would everyone like to come through and eat?' called Rachel Gilbride's voice. 'Oh, there you are, Bobby – could you give Daddy a hand with the wine? Kate, dear, would you mind moving? You're in the way.'

The hours passed, the party ended. Will and Kate left together and waited in sleeting rain at the tram stop. When a 23 came in sight, Kate turned to Will.

'You want this?'

'What do you mean, do I want it? I'm coming back with you.'

'I think you might as well go straight home.'

The tram had drawn to a halt, the rain glittering in its lights. Kate leaped aboard, her fare ready. Will followed and when she climbed nimbly to the upper deck, so did he. It was late; there were only themselves up there, no one to see her flinch as he sat next to her and grasped her hand.

'Kate, what are you playing at, for God's sake? You've been impossible the whole evening —'

'I've been impossible?' She snatched her hand from him, staring at him with outraged eyes. 'You can say that to me, after the way you behaved?'

'What did I do? Just tell me what I did!'

She withdrew her gaze and sat pleating her ticket, gazing out from their swaying vantage point at the city moving by.

'Oh, I see.' Will groaned. 'This is to do with Sara Farrell, isn't it? I spend a bit of time talking —'

'A lot of time talking. And laughing. Right through supper, talking and laughing, I didna get a look in!' Kate's eyes filled with angry tears. 'How do you think that made me feel, Will? You take me to Bobby's party and spend all your time chatting up somebody like Sara Farrell!'

'Kate, darling.' Will tried to take her hand but again she snatched it away. 'It was nothing, honestly, it didn't mean a thing. You've no reason to feel jealous —'

'Jealous? I'm no' jealous. I just canna understand why you'd want to waste your time with a woman like that.'

'The only reason I talked to her at supper was because you were sitting there like a thundercloud and wouldn't talk to anybody. Snapping our heads off, no matter what we said, God knows what Sara thought.'

'I dinna give a damn what she thought! She's no' in ma world, Will, and shouldna be in yours.' Kate shook her head. 'But you canna resist anybody like her, can you? Somebody born with a silver spoon stuck in her stupid mouth? Somebody who's no' had to struggle like the rest of us?' Kate gave a strangled sob. 'But maybe you're no' like the rest of us yourself. No' like me, anyway.'

'Kate, none of that is true. It's not even true what you're saying about Sara. She and Lindsay were adopted, they were probably illegitimate, they weren't born with any silver spoons in their mouths.'

'Soon got them, all the same.' Kate stood up and grasped the hand rail to the stair. 'This is ma stop, Will, I'll say goodnight.'

'I told you, I'm coming with you!'

'Hey, you two, watch yourselves!' cried the conductor, as they leaped off the tram before it came to its screeching stop, but they

24

paid no attention and went running through the rain to the door of the terraced house where Kate had her bedsit. But here Kate turned.

'I'm no' letting you in, Will. I feel too bad, I feel too hurt. OK, maybe I am jealous, but it's no' just that. It's seeing all those people tonight who dinna care about the things that matter to me. It's seeing you making up to that girl who's like them, who doesna care, and wondering if you're the same. Och, Will, you dinna even talk like me! We canna go on, we're just too different.'

Rain mixed with the tears on her face as she fumbled for her key. 'Too different,' she said again. And then her door banged.

Will was stunned. He couldn't believe it. Kate had really shut the door on him. For a long time after he'd heard her feet running up the stair, he stood in the rain, looking at her door and thinking, she'll come back, she'll come back and let me in. But she didn't. He saw the light go on in her room, then go off. It dawned on him that she had meant what she said. Slowly, he walked away.

He remembered that there was a piece of paper in his pocket. At the end of the evening, when thunder-faced Kate had gone for her coat, Sara Farrell had put it there.

'What's that?' he had asked her.

'My telephone number.' Her blue eyes sparkled.

'Who says I'll need it?'

'You never know.' She smiled. 'Weren't you ever a Boy Scout? Be prepared, Will Gilbride.'

He looked at the paper now, as the rain slanted down, blurring the numbers she had pencilled for him. Then he tore the paper into shreds and let them fall to the gutter, where they swirled away to a drain and disappeared.

'Goodbye, Sara,' he murmured. 'Truth is, I never was a Boy Scout.'

25

Chapter Six

The day after the party, the Gilbrides in their new bungalow were still surrounded by packing cases and furniture yet to be put in place. It all looked like chaos to Jennie, but at least she had found her pots and pans and had been able to make the breakfast. Eggs and fried bread, but they'd finished the bacon. Now wasn't it a piece of nonsense that there should still be shortages and rationing so many years after the war! Probably the Tories would be no better than Labour at getting things back to normal, but there was no point in complaining, folk just had to endure it, as they'd learned to endure so many things.

'Oh, but I wish we were straight!' she cried. 'When are we going to see the end of these boxes? Where are we going to put everything?'

Hamish, on his way out to his tailoring class, said Will would do everything. When he'd thrown off his hangover.

'What hangover?' asked Will, from behind the pages of *The Scotsman*.

'Well, something's up with you.' Hamish clicked his tongue. 'Talk about a bear with a sore head! And what was wrong with Kate last night?'

'Nothing. Give it a rest, will you?'

'Better get off to your tram, Hamish,' advised Madge. 'You're going to be late.'

As Hamish departed whistling, Will, to deflect attention from himself and Kate, read a piece out of the paper. Apparently, Catherine's Hall was to be larger than first intended. The university was buying its two neighbouring tenements to incorporate them into the finished hall of residence.

'I don't think we're interested in the university's plans,' Madge said coldly.

'No point in being an ostrich, Gran. You can't put the clock back, you know.'

'I'm not saying you can. I just don't see why we should ever have had to lose our homes, that's all. Think of our friends, having to take what they could get. We were lucky, Abby bought us this place.' Madge glanced around the cluttered room. 'Even if it is too small.'

'Too small?' Will laughed. 'You had two rooms at Catherine's Land, Gran!'

'Two BIG rooms, that's the point. I'm used to big rooms and high ceilings. I feel sort of shut in here.'

'Had no garden.'

'That's true, but I didn't miss it after the early years.'

'Well, now you'll be able to sit out in the summer and have all your pals round, give 'em apples from that tree Aunt Abby thinks so much about.'

'She just remembers the tree we had in Southampton in the old days.' Madge turned her head to look at Jennie, who was clearing the table. 'That reminds me, Jennie, did you tell Will about that man you met last night?'

'What man?' asked Will.

'A friend of your Uncle Frankie's, they were in the navy during the war. Now he's in the merchant navy, just like your grandfather, Will, and based in Southampton where we were. Isn't that strange?'

'So what was he doing at Bobby's party?' Will was also looking at his mother, who was not looking at him.

'Frankie'd asked him to stay for a day or two before he went over to his brother's in Fife. Rachel said to bring him along.'

'Certainly seemed to be enjoying talking to you, Jennie,' Madge remarked, carrying away plates. 'It must have made a nice change for you to have someone new to talk to.'

'You mean, a man?' Jennie asked wryly. 'Yes, it was nice. I liked Mr McKendrick. Mac, he's always called.'

'Going to see him again?' asked Will.

'No, he'll be off to Fife soon and I told him I'd just moved house, didn't have time to —' Jennie stopped.

'To go out? He did ask you out, then?' Will looked astonished.

'What if he did?' Jennie flushed. 'Not so amazing, is it?'

'No. I've always thought you should go out more.'

'Haven't I told her that over and over again?' cried Madge.

'People do what they want to do, Ma.' Jennie was putting on an overall and tying a duster over her hair. 'Come on, we've a lot to get through.'

The problem was the surplus furniture. Jim's chair, Jim's wardrobes, Madge's sideboard, the big scrubbed table, so many pieces that had fitted easily into the flats but now would fit nowhere. The thing was, they didn't want to part with any of them.

'We'll have to try the garage,' said Will. 'But I'm going to need some help.'

'I can help,' offered Jennie.

'Come on, don't want you putting your back out or something. We shouldn't have let Hamish go.'

Into their considerations, the doorbell rang.

'Will, go and answer that,' said Jennie who still hadn't got used to having her own bell. 'If it's a neighbour, don't let them in, I don't want anyone to see me like this.'

It wasn't a neighbour, it was Frankie Baxter. And he wasn't alone.

'Frankie!' cried Jennie, snatching the duster from her hair. 'You've brought Mr McKendrick!'

He looked like somebody's shipmate. It was the weathered face, perhaps, or the sea-green, far-sighted eyes, but mainly, Will thought, his way of standing, as though he couldn't trust the floor. As Frankie introduced him, he looked as embarrassed as Jennie, but Frankie, who could carry off any awkward moments, slapped him on the back and said they'd come to offer their services, knew there'd be heavy work to do and maybe only Will to do it. How about it?

'You're an answer to a prayer,' Will said fervently, and watched Madge hurry away to put her kettle on, smiling like a cat at the cream. What was she thinking? Here was another man in his mother's life at last? A man based in Southampton? Will felt a little unsteady himself at the idea of his mother forming a new relationship, perhaps moving away. Ah, what was he thinking,

28

marrying his mother off on the strength of one guy asking her out? Even if he were interested, she might not be. After all these years of carrying a torch for a dead man and one who'd let her down, she might not want to get involved.

'The idea is to decide what goes where and push what's left into the garage,' Will said aloud, watching Frankie's old shipmate warily. Those sea-green eyes were certainly following his mother around, but then Mac was off to Fife soon. Maybe he'd stay there.

It was a relief to hand the tea and biscuits Madge had brought in, but as soon as Will put his mother's admirer out of his mind, Kate moved in. He felt again the dull ache in his chest that came when he thought of her closing her door on him. They were too different, she'd said. Had she meant it? He could scarcely bear to wait till the evening when he could see her again, but she was in Glasgow anyway and he was moving furniture. With his uncle and his uncle's friend.

The three men worked steadily, while Madge and Jennie fussed around, making decisions. This to stay? No, wait a minute – the garage, I think. Settee along this wall? No, maybe opposite. Canna shift the piano, it'll have to be where it is – OK, Mac, that's fine – Ma, what about Jim's cabinet? Oh, I'd like that. No, there isn't room – well, try it –

When the rooms were finally arranged to their satisfaction and the garage filled to bursting point, they started on the pictures. Jennie said they couldn't all be put up, the place would look like an art gallery, but Madge said she must have her favourites, or she wouldn't feel at home.

'Have to make you feel at home,' said Frankie, cheerfully blowing straw from one of the pictures he'd just unpacked. As he looked at it, his expression changed.

'Where'd you like this, Jennie?' he asked gently.

Everyone looked at the picture in his hands. It was the portrait of a young man, dark-haired, blue-eyed, unsmiling; so handsome, he might have been called beautiful. Only Mac did not know who it was, but he could guess.

'Is that – ' He stopped.

'That's Jennie's husband,' Madge said quietly. 'That's Rory.'

'Rachel painted it,' Frankie said, after a pause. 'It was a good likeness.'

'Aye, somehow you can tell,' Mac agreed.

29

Before the handsome painted gaze, he lowered his own eyes. It was Will who took the picture from his uncle and carried it away.

'Your room, Mum?' he called.

'Yes,' Jennie answered huskily. 'Yes, please.'

The little house sprang into action again, as the last jobs were completed. Mac, an engineer, said he'd check the plugs and electrical fittings, while Frankie and Will folded cartons and stacked boxes, then sank into chairs in the living room.

'Think that's it, folks,' said Frankie, stripping off the gloves Jennie had made him wear to protect his hands. 'We'd better be on our way.'

'I'm so grateful to you,' Jennie murmured, her mind moving frantically round the contents of the kitchen cupboard. Madge was looking at her meaningfully, she knew she should ask Frankie and Mac to stay and have something to eat. But what could she offer them? There was tinned soup, tinned beans, bread and butter, and a few tomatoes, they'd finished all the eggs. Jennie had been planning to take their ration books to some new grocer that afternoon, now that they could no longer go to Donnie's, but at the present moment she felt like old Mother Hubbard. Hadn't even a bottle of beer to give the poor thirsty fellows. Should she send Will to see what he could find?

Oh, Lord, there went Ma, asking recklessly if they wouldn't stay and have something to eat just as Jennie had known she would. She held her breath, then let it go, as Frankie said thanks all the same, they'd better not, Mac had to catch his train to Fife.

'You're going today?' Will asked in surprise.

'Aye, ma brother's expecting me.'

'Well, I want to thank you very much for all you've done, we couldn't have managed without you and Uncle Frankie.'

'No more thanks,' said Frankie, rising and moving to the piano. 'Let's just see how the old piano's borne up, eh? We've got a few minutes.'

He ran his fingers down the keys, smiling at Madge, as he played some of her thirties favourites, 'Smoke Gets in Your Eyes' and 'Love in Bloom'; nodding to Jennie over hits from 'Oklahoma!' and 'Annie Get Your Gun', finishing with his own beloved jazz. Even in that little living room, on that worn old instrument, he showed his professionalism, and it did them good, raised their spirits, to recognise his excellence.

'Remember how I used to play this old joanna in your flat?' he asked Madge. 'My old ma couldn't afford a piano, Mac, I used to play at school and sometimes practise at Madge's. Good old days, eh?' He leaped up and closed the lid of the piano. 'No, we're all a damn sight better off now, is what I say.'

'Except that we had to leave Catherine's Land,' said Jennie.

'You'll be better off here, I promise you. You'll get so you won't even remember a time when you weren't here.'

Will she? wondered Will. Will Mum be here to think that?

Frankie and Mac were moving to the door and Will could hear Mac asking his mother if she was on the telephone.

'Sorry, we're not. It's very difficult to get a phone these days. Anyway, it's an expense.'

'Aye, it is.' Mac looked away and Will thought, OK, OK, why don't you say you'll write? But Mac just went out to Frankie's car.

There were goodbyes and more thanks, then the car was on its way and Madge and Jennie were following Will back into the house.

'Wasn't it good of them to think of helping us like that?' remarked Madge, putting coal on the fire.

'A very nice idea,' Will agreed. 'I wonder whose it was?'

In the car, Mac said cautiously,

'Handsome guy, that Rory, eh?'

'Handsome is as handsome does,' Frankie retorted. 'Led Jennie a dance. Don't worry, she won't mind me telling you. Everybody knows he went off with a girl from Catherine's Land.'

'What happened?'

'Och, Sheena dumped him. He might have guessed she would, she'd done it before. Before he married Jennie.'

'I dinna ken how a fella could do that,' Mac murmured. 'Leave a good wife and bairns.'

'Aye, and Jennie adored him.'

'Suppose she would.'

'Never forgave him, though, until he came home to die. Might have taken him back then, but it was too late.'

'Poor lassie.'

Frankie gave Mac a darting sideways glance. 'Taken with her, Mac? Come on, you can tell me.'

'Cut it out, Frankie. I've only met her twice.'

'You wanted to see her again today.'

'All right, I did.' Mac moved uneasily. 'But she wouldna look at me.' He laughed. 'I'm no oil painting.'

'I'll let you into a secret. Jennie's had enough of oil paintings. And it's time you had a woman in your life again.'

Mac was silent, remembering his own broken heart. As Frankie knew, the girl he'd loved before the war had died of TB. The girl who might have taken her place had married someone else.

'You can't go on moping for ever,' Frankie told him. 'Can't go on being afraid to take the plunge.'

'If I'd lived in Edinburgh — '

'There are such things as trains.'

'And I'm thinking of ma train to Fife,' said Mac, and would be drawn no further.

'Know what I've got to do when I get back?' asked Frankie, handing out Mac's case at the station. 'See Bobby. He wants me to hear him play.'

'Have you no' heard him play already?'

'Sure, and I'm just wondering what the hell is in his mind. Knowing Bobby, nothing good.'

Chapter Seven

Punctually at two o'clock, Bobby arrived at Frankie's flat with Lindsay.

So that's on again, is it? thought Frankie, showing them into the drawing room where his baby grand piano waited. He knew that Abby had been relieved when Bobby had gone into the army and there had been a break in his relationship with Lindsay. Though both were favourites of hers, she had never thought they were right for each other. Frankie rather agreed, but took the view that the young folk must work things out for themselves. Looked like they were intending to do just that.

Bobby's eyes lit up when he looked at the grand, which had been an anniversary present from Abby to Frankie, but he made no move to take his seat at the instrument. When he turned his gaze on his uncle, he seemed very young, very vulnerable, glad of the support of Lindsay, who stood close to him. Her eyes on Frankie were full of appeal.

'Well, now, what's all this about?' Frankie asked heartily. 'You said you wanted me to hear you play, Bobby, but I know how you play. What's new?'

'I want to go to London,' Bobby said quickly. 'I want to be a professional pianist.'

Frankie blinked his blue eyes. 'In that order?'

'No! It's just that London is where it's all happening. I feel I'd have a better chance there.'

'I'd no idea you had this in mind,' Frankie said slowly. 'You've always enjoyed playing, I know that, but to do it for a living – boy, that's different.'

'Yes, I only got the idea when I used to play for the chaps

33

in the service. I realised then that I wanted to be a musician.'

'Kind of late, Bobby. Most of the guys I know never had to make a decision like that. I mean, never had to say, I want to be a musician.'

'Why not?' Lindsay asked sharply. 'You must all have had to make choices at some time.'

'No, I guess we always were what we were. Music chose us, not the other way round.'

'OK, so it chose me later than you,' Bobby retorted. 'That doesn't mean it can't be my life now. All I want is for you to hear me play, Uncle Frankie, and tell me if I'm in with a chance.'

Frankie waved a hand towards his piano. 'I'm listening,' he said quietly.

Bobby sat down at the piano, took a deep breath and began to run his hands up and down the keys, took another breath and sounded a few chords.

'You've heard Bobby play before?' Frankie whispered to Lindsay.

'Yes, but I'm not musical.' She gave a shame-faced smile.' I'm afraid it doesn't mean very much to me.'

Bobby was beginning to relax now and moving into the kind of jazz that always seemed to Lindsay to be going nowhere, wandering over the keys aimlessly without any particular tune. Yet she knew she must be wrong in her opinion for other people raved over it, and they probably knew more than she. If only Frankie would rave over Bobby's playing! She stole a glance at him, saw his eyes were closed, but couldn't decide if that were bad or good.

Oh, please, she begged silently, be kind to him, Frankie! If he's no good, please, please, let him down lightly!

It occurred to her that she was the same as Bobby's mother, couldn't bear to think of his being hurt. Yet if he were to enter the world of professional music and run the risk of disappointment and failure, perhaps it would be as well if Frankie hurt him now, so that he might abandon his idea of going to London. Supposing he didn't abandon it? Supposing he still went? It came to her like a lightning flash that if he went to London, she could go with him. Of course! Why hadn't she thought of it before? Her heart leaped up, then sank. Bobby had finished playing and was swinging round to face his uncle.

'Well?' he cried.

Frankie rose from his chair.

'Wow, Bobby! You didn't tell me you'd switched to cool jazz! What happened to traditional?'

'Dave Brubeck's quartet happened,' Bobby answered breathlessly. 'I met a fellow in the army who had some of his recordings. Hit me like a sandbag, sent me spinning. I mean – new rhythms, new harmonies – I just took off. That's when people began to tell me I was good.'

Lindsay was watching Frankie's face..It seemed to her that they were like puppets waiting for their puppetmaster to pull their strings. But the puppetmaster didn't know what to do.

'Do you think Bobby's good?' she cried in desperation.

'I am good,' said Bobby softly. 'I know I am.'

'Yes, you're good.' Frankie ran his fingers through his hair. 'You're right about that. But – the thing is – it's a tough world out there, Bobby, it's a jungle. I'm not sure you can survive, however good you are. What you have to remember is that there are a lot of guys who are good.'

'And I'm no better than the next one?' Bobby turned back to the piano and let his hands drift down the keys.

'That's something you'd have to find out.'

'All I want is to be like you,' Bobby said carefully. 'Make a success as a performer. I'm not aiming to be original, a composer, anything like that. I just want to play the hotels, maybe form a quartet. Why shouldn't I do that?'

'You make it sound so easy, Bobby. For me, it took years.'

Bobby stood up. 'I wish you'd give it to me straight, Frankie. You don't think I've got what it takes, do you?'

Frankie didn't answer for some time. 'I guess I don't know,' he said, at last.

There was a long silence. The puppets are collapsed, thought Lindsay, the puppetmaster has cut the strings.

'Thanks,' said Bobby. 'Thanks for listening to me.'

'I'm not saying you shouldn't go to London. I mean, I could be wrong. You could hit the jackpot straight off. It happens.'

'Yeah.'

'And I'll do all I can for you. Set the ball rolling. Introductions, auditions, that sort of thing. Just give me a call.'

'I'm very grateful.'

They moved to the front door, Frankie clearly ill at ease.

'I never asked, what do your folks think of this idea, Bobby?'

'Not much.'

'I guess they wouldn't. Listen, don't quote me, eh?'

'That's all right.' Bobby's face was deadpan. 'I won't pretend you've given me the OK. When you haven't.'

'What do you want to do now?' asked Lindsay.

'I don't know. Go for a drink, maybe.'

'It's far too early. We could have tea.'

'Tea, then. I don't bloody care.'

They found a restaurant where there were white cloths on the tables, metal-plated teapots, vases of flowers and ladies in hats. Also, a musical trio, working away at 'songs from the shows'.

'Typical Edinburgh,' Bobby grunted, eyeing the buttered scones. 'Why don't we have shortbread as well? Why don't we ask the trio to play "Annie Laurie"?'

But the musicians were departing for their own teabreak. The piano stood waiting, its sheet music at the ready, next to the stands for the violin and the 'cello. Lindsay laughed.

'You could give us a tune,' she suggested. 'I'll bet that's what your uncle would do!'

'Well, I'm not him. He made that pretty clear.'

'He did say you were good, Bobby. That's what matters, isn't it? And he's going to help you when you get to London. I think it's all looking very hopeful.'

'Maybe.' Bobby shrugged. 'Might as well have one of these scones, I suppose. I don't know why, I feel hungry.'

Lindsay busied herself pouring more tea. 'You know what I've been thinking? I might go to London myself.'

Bobby's head shot up, his gaze on her instantly suspicious. 'Why would you do that?'

'Well, it's like you say, there's nothing here. Edinburgh's run by lawyers and people like my mother. What school did you go to? Who are your people? I'm tired of it. I'd like to see something else.'

'I thought you had a career all lined up at Logie's?'

'That was Mummy's idea and your Aunt Abby's. They think my father would have wanted it.'

'But what would you do in London?'

'I've got a degree, I'll be sure to find something. And I've a little money, too. My godmother left me a legacy.'

'You'll be all right, then.' Bobby sat back, relaxing the intensity of his gaze. 'My folks are not going to support me, you know. I'll have to start earning straight away.'

'If I took a flat, I could let you have a room,' Lindsay said casually. 'Until you could afford something.'

'Would you do that?' Bobby reached for another scone. 'You know, it's not a bad idea, your coming to London. Can you imagine what it would be like? Being free? Just the two of us?'

'Just the two of us.' They put their hands together across the white tablecloth and each smiled a secret smile. Lindsay, savouring the moment, put from her mind the interviews she would have to have with her mother and Mrs Baxter. She was so close now to having what she wanted, she only knew that nothing was going to stop her taking it.

Chapter Eight

Madge, tired of unpacking, had taken the tram to the Haymarket to see Jessie Rossie. Jennie had gone out with the ration books, Will was mooning around, probably thinking about Kate. Suddenly, Madge wanted to be out of the house and away.

She was already missing Jessie. They'd known each other since they were young mothers together in Catherine's Land. Both had had their share of sorrow. Jessie's husband was now dead, her second son had moved abroad, her youngest boy, Billy, had been killed in the war. She still had Ken, of course, but Madge knew that Jessic was none too happy sharing the flat over the newspaper shop with Ken and Ivy. Poor old Ivy with her smoker's cough wasn't much company and Ken was always working in his 'gold mine', as he called his new shop. All that trade from folk on their way to the Haymarket station! Ken reckoned he'd fallen on his feet. Leaving Catherine's Land had been a blessing in disguise, but Jessie couldn't see it. Couldn't see any gold either.

'Och, it's that small,' she groaned to Madge, waving her chapped hands around the living room of the flat. 'I'm used to a bit o' space!'

'Just what I say about the bungalow!' cried Madge. 'You'll see, when you come over.'

'Aye, but you've got your garden, you've got your apple tree.'

There had been a certain amount of envy shown among Madge's neighbours when it had become known that she was moving to a bungalow with a garden.

'There'll be no bungalow for us,' Peggie Kemp had sniffed. 'No apple trees, no bit of grass.'

But then the Kemps had been given a council house, so envy

38

had shifted to Peggie, then had faded altogether when the reality of leaving Catherine's Land had sunk in and the time had come to say goodbye.

'Och, things'll niver be the same!' the tenants wailed, clinging together in a riot of tears and promising to keep in touch. And here was Madge, doing that.

'You're a good soul, Madge, to come so quick,' Jessie told her. She cleared away their tea-cups, pushing aside the washing hanging sullenly in the kitchen, and heaved another sigh.

'No drying green here, Madge, like at Catherine's Land. Och, what's a body to do, eh?'

'Maybe Ken could find somewhere else,' Madge suggested. 'I mean, somewhere separate from the shop.'

'Are you joking? How'd he find another flat wi' the housing like it is? And think of the expense!' Jessie shook her greying head. 'No, I've been given this bed and I'll just ha' to lie on it. One thing's for sure, I'm no' going into no home.'

'Of course not!' cried Madge. 'We're not of an age for that yet!'

'I sometimes feel I'm of an age for ma grave. I'll no' be sorry when ma time comes.'

'What a thing to say, Jessie! You've your family to think of, you've Biddy and Kate!'

'Aye, Ken's girls are very good. No' like Stewart. He's out o' sight, out o' mind. It's like some say, your son's your son till he gets him a wife, your daughter's your daughter all your life.'

'I never had a son,' Madge remarked, 'but Jennie's boys have always been good to her.'

'No' married, though, that's the point.'

Madge smiled. 'I'm thinking that Kate will marry Will.'

Jessie picked up some knitting and began to count stitches. 'Maybe.'

'She's a lovely girl, Jessie.'

'But flighty.'

'Flighty? I'd have said Kate was quite down to earth.'

'Got flighty ideas.' Jessie shrugged. 'Och, she'll settle down, like we all ha' to do. Once she's wed and the bairns come along.'

'I'd love a granddaughter,' Madge said mistily.

'Great-granddaughter, you mean.'

'Oh, yes, of course.' Madge blushed. Was she old enough to be

39

a great-grandmother? Inside, she felt no different from when she was young, but Jessie would never understand that.

'Any tea in the pot?'

Ivy Rossie, Kate's mother, came up from the shop and sank into a chair by the fire. Her likeness to her daughters could still be seen, but her tawny hair had dried, her face yellowed. Some said it was the smoking that had withered her, but Madge knew better. Ivy had lost two children in infancy, her only son, her favourite, had moved away and rarely visited, her husband spent all his free time down at the pub. Madge had seen it all before so many times, and now there was talk that Biddy's Ewan was following in Ken Rossie's footsteps, neglecting his family, spending what he had on drink. But things would be different with Will, Madge comforted herself. If he married Kate, they would know how to live.

'Just look at your legs, Ivy,' Jessie said fretfully. 'All they scorch marks! Away and put some stockin's on.'

Ivy looked down at her thin legs, disfigured by marks from the fire.

'I've no stockin's dry,' she murmured, lighting a cigarette. 'But I could do wi' some tea. I'm freezing!'

'Here.' Jessie lumbered up and threw across a pair of thick lisle stockings from the fireguard. 'Take mine, Ivy. they're no' nylons, but they'll do for now.'

'Thanks,' Ivy said without enthusiasm. She picked up the teapot from the hearth and shook it. 'Looks like I'll ha' to put the kettle on, that tea's cold.' She gave Madge a tired smile. 'Like some more tea, Mrs Gilbride?'

'No, thanks, I must be going.' Madge stood up. 'Still such a lot to do.'

'Your Will away yet?'

'Not yet.' Madge put on her hat. 'We were saying when he gets back there might be wedding bells.'

'For him and Kate,' said Jessie.

Ivy made no comment. She put back her stringy hair and went to fill the kettle. It seemed to Madge that she was not anxious to hear wedding bells for her daughter Kate.

On her way to the tram, Madge looked in at Donnie Muir's grocery, an old-fashioned little shop with a jangling bell and a counter rubbed with age. Here, as in Catherine's Land, Donnie sold everything he thought anyone might ask for; not only the usual foodstuffs, but drawing-pins, soap, aspirin, toothpaste, gummed labels, candles, firelighters – even a few seeds in packets and long bamboo canes for tying up plants, though who did any gardening in the built-up Haymarket was a mystery. Over all these things hung the pleasant smell of Donnie's fruit and vegetable selection and the few bunches of flowers Sally liked to offer, though again it was hard to think of who might be their purchasers.

As soon as the shop bell rang for Madge's entrance, Sally came running to greet her. She was small and wiry, her dusty-blonde hair cut short, her grey eyes constantly watchful for Donnie and his asthma.

'Och, it's grand to see you, Mrs Gilbride! Somebody from Catherine's Land! Have you been to see the Rossies, then?'

'Just had a cup of tea with Jessie.' Madge was looking admiringly round. 'But you're all straight, Sally, and you've not been in five minutes!'

'Seems like five years . . . Now, you'll take another cup with us, will you no'?'

'No, I can't stop, Sally, must get back, there's so much to do. I just wanted to see how you were managing.'

'Appreciate that. Donnie! Here's Mrs Gilbride!'

Donnie and Nina came out from the back of the shop, Nina carrying a roll of black ribbon, Donnie a large photograph of George VI. This was one of Donnie's good days, for he was not wheezing. When he saw Madge, his eyes grew bright and he looked quite well.

'Mrs Gilbride, what a surprise!' He set down the King's photograph and took Madge's hand. 'How are you doing? Settling in well? Nina, pet, tie the ribbon on the photo and we'll put it in the window. A mark of respect,' he added in a hushed voice to Madge. 'Just a small sign.'

'Very thoughtful,' Madge commented, smiling at Nina, who was deftly making a bow from the ribbon and attaching it to the photograph. Such a nice, useful girl, and pretty, too, with a composed little face and shining fair hair. Unlike Bobby, it was plain her parents' devotion was no burden to her. If she was the light of their lives, she didn't mind being that light, was happy to do what she could for them.

'Tell Mrs Gilbride about your book-keeping, Nina!' Sally called, when Nina had placed the King's photograph in the window beside the jars of sweeties and piled up tins of fruit. 'Tell her how you got top marks last week, now!'

'Dinna go on,' Nina murmured, turning her head aside. 'Mrs Gilbride'll no' want to hear all that.'

'I certainly do,' said Madge warmly. 'I'm very pleased to hear how well you're doing, Nina. You know, you remind me of my Abby.'

'We say the very same thing!' cried Sally eagerly. 'Of course we're no' looking for Nina to follow her to the top, but I say she should definitely apply to Logie's when she's older.'

'I'm no' keen,' protested Nina. 'I'm happy working here!'

'Och, your Dad and me want you to do something better than helping in our grocery!' Sally shook her head at Madge. 'Young folk – canna see what's best, eh?'

'Well Hamish is trying for Logie's,' Madge told her. 'Soon as he's finished his tailoring course, he's writing in.'

'There you are, then! Are you listening, Nina?' Sally dropped her voice. 'And what about Will? Has he gone to Korea yet?'

'Not yet.' Madge moved slowly to the door. As a customer came in and Nina stepped forward to serve her, Madge said quietly, 'We're trying not to think about it.'

'Aye, put it out o' your mind till it comes,' said Donnie. 'That's the way.'

Ah, but it was coming too quickly, thought Madge, making her goodbyes. It could not stay at the back of her mind for long.

Chapter Nine

Will was in a pub. He had a beer in front of him and was watching pictures of the King's lying-in-state on the television above the bar. A sombre scene. The draped bier, the soldiers with bowed heads. Waves of gloom swept over Will as he contemplated death and Korea and Kate. His eyes moved to the clock. Would she be home yet from Glasgow? He would have gone to the station but had no idea which train she would take. For all he knew she would stay there all evening. Journalists didn't work office hours.

He finished his drink and left the pub to walk the streets in icy rain until he dared arrive at her door. At the sight of the light in her window, he shivered as though with fever. Then he rang the bell.

Kate had been looking out for him. When she saw him below, when she heard her bell, she stood motionless. The bell rang again, pealing desperately, and this time she jerked into action, racing down the stair and along the passage to open the front door and fling herself into Will's arms.

'Oh, Will, I didna think you'd come!'

'You knew I'd come. Oh, Kate, Kate, why did you put me through such hell?'

'Why did you do the same to me?' She ran her hands down his coat. 'Will, you're soaking! Come on up, come up!'

She took off his sodden overcoat and hung it on the back of her door, then switched on another bar of the electric fire and turned to him, her face very serious. He took her in his arms.

'You knew that girl meant nothing to me, why did you try to make out she did? Making us both suffer?'

'I told you, it wasn't just her I was upset about.'

'You said we were too different. What did you mean?' Will shook her gently. 'Too different to be in love?'

'I do think we're different, Will. We believe in different things.'

'Plenty of folk are like that, doesn't stop them caring for each other. And I care for you.'

They clung together, not kissing, just resting in each other's arms.

'I do love you, Will,' Kate whispered.

His eyes went over her shoulder to her divan. It was stacked with objects she had put down out of her hand – her bag and gloves, some folded clothes, two or three magazines, apples in a paper bag.

'Havena had time to tidy,' she murmured, following his gaze, but Will smiled indulgently. He knew Kate was no housekeeper. No Rossie woman had ever been one for dusting and polishing. Yet when Kate stepped from her clutter, she was as fresh as a flower, her sister the same.

'Come on, let's clear this stuff,' he whispered. 'No, no, not like that, Kate! don't throw it all in a heap!'

'For God's sake, are you made of ice or what, Will Gilbride?' Kate was quickly stepping out of her clothes. 'What's it matter what I do with it?'

'Nothing,' he answered, trembling. 'Nothing at all.'

They had never actually made love, never 'gone all the way', as people said, because Kate was frightened of having a baby, and Will was frightened she might. The fear was the thorn in their happiness. Kate said women would never be free while the fear existed. There was always a risk whatever you did, you could never be sure, and they wanted to be sure. Yet that evening, though no words were spoken, each knew that they had reached a turning point. They had almost parted. In a few days' time they would really part, when Will left for Korea. It seemed right that Kate should whisper, as Will slipped naked into her arms, 'It's OK, Will, dinna worry.'

'What do you mean?'

'I've got maself fitted up.'

'How? You always said you wouldn't, you said you couldn't be sure — '

'A girl at the paper told me about this doctor – doesna care if you're no' married – I went to see him – he said it'd work – he said no' to worry.'

'Oh, Kate!'

She had often dreamed of what it would be like and had been told it wasn't so good the first time, you had to get used to it, or maybe put up with it. But none of that was true. Put up with it? I'm no' complaining, she thought, looking radiantly into Will's handsome face.

'Well?' he asked gently.

'Well, what?'

'You know what I'm asking. Did I make you happy?'

'Will, some things you canna put into words.'

'And you a journalist . . .'

They laughed and kissed and finally got up, dressed and made instant coffee, never taking their eyes off each other for fear of losing their joy.

'I did make you happy,' Will whispered. 'Didn't I? whether you can say so or not?'

He was horrified to see her dark eyes fill with tears.

'Kate, what is it? What's the matter? Tell me!'

'Have you no' forgotten?' Her tears were flowing fast now down her stricken face. 'You're going away!'

Chapter Ten

These were dark days, with the state funeral for King George VI dominating people's minds. A new age might be on the horizon but it was not here yet, and the pictures of the royal ladies, in deepest black and heavily veiled, served to deepen the general feeling of melancholy. Will's family also had to remember that his leave was running out.

When the time finally came for him to join his regiment, everyone, except Frankie who had left for London, came to see him off from Waverley. Even Malcolm, who said at least Will was not travelling by troop train. Oh, how he remembered those dismal scenes during the war, with everyone hugging and weeping and trying to find a bit of privacy!

'I'd say this was bad enough,' Abby said, lowering her voice.

'And Will is still going to war,' Rachel added. 'Even if it's not our war.'

'He'll be all right,' Malcolm said confidently.

He took Will's arm and looked into his face, so youthful and solemn beneath his officer's hat. 'Will, I know what you're feeling, but what you have to remember is that you're going to come back safe and sound. I did.'

Will nodded, patiently submitting to the embraces of his aunts, not looking at Kate, who was standing a little apart.

'Good luck, Will,' Bobby whispered, shaking his hand. 'You'll be OK.'

'So everybody tells me,' answered Will.

He thought it strange that Bobby's sympathetic gaze should seem envious too.

'We'll leave you, Will,' Abby told him. 'Let you have a few minutes with your mum and gran. Now you write to us, you keep in touch!'

Looking back to wave, Abby and Rachel, Malcolm and Bobby, moved slowly out of the station. Will turned to Jennie:

'I wish you wouldn't wait, Mum. I hate goodbyes.'

'We're not leaving until we have to,' Hamish told him.

Will sighed and stooped to kiss Madge, who dissolved into tears. He looked again at his mother.

'Oh, Mum,' he whispered, and as Jennie folded him into her arms, unable to speak, Kate bit her lip.

'Come on, Kate,' Hamish said softly, as Jennie finally released Will. 'Your turn.'

'I'm no' going to cry again,' Kate whispered, before Will's lips met hers. 'Just come back to me, Will.'

'I'll come back.'

He still said he didn't want them to wait, but they did wait, watching to the bitter end the train pulling out of the station and his hand waving. Then they moved away.

While Kate, very pale and resolute, marched off to the Glasgow train and Hamish dashed for his tram, Madge and Jennie wavered along, uncertain what to do with all the time that lay ahead until Will came home. There seemed nothing to say or do; at least until they got used to the idea that he had gone.

'Mrs Gilbride?'

Both their heads went up, but the young blonde woman in their path was looking at Jennie.

'It's Sara Farrell,' she told her, with an engaging smile.

'Oh, yes.' Jennie put her hand on Madge's arm. 'You remember my mother?'

'Of course!' Sara shook her hand. 'Will's grandmother!'

'We've just been to see Will off on the train,' Jennie said dully. 'He's away to Korea.'

Sara's face froze. 'Korea? He never told me!'

'You know Will?' Madge asked politely.

'Not really. Only through my sister, they were at university together. I – I talked to him at Bobby's party.'

And you liked him, thought Jennie. So that's what was wrong with Kate that evening.

'I must dash,' said Sara. 'I have to meet some people from the

47

London train, coming up for talks on the Festival. I've just got a job at the Festival Office, I'm thrilled.'

But as she left them, saying how nice it was to meet them, she didn't looked thrilled, she looked stunned.

'Nice girl,' Madge commented as they left the station. 'And very pretty.'

'But not as pretty as Kate.'

'No one's as pretty as Kate.'

'Sara's sister is working at Logie's,' Jennie remarked. 'Doing very well, I believe.'

'I suppose she would, being Gerald Farrell's daughter.'

'Adopted daughter,' said Jennie.

Abby, rising from her desk, greeted Lindsay warmly.

'Lindsay, come in, my dear, take a seat. Like some coffee?'

'No, thanks, Mrs Baxter.' Lindsay's eyes were everywhere except on Abby. 'I just wanted to have a word. Well — ' she laughed nervously. 'It's a bit more than that.'

'Oh?' Abby sat down, her gaze suddenly wary. Lindsay seemed uneasy. There was nothing new in that. Though she had known Abby all her life and was aware that she was something of a protegée to her, Lindsay never relaxed in Abby's presence. Sometimes Abby pondered over her attitude; mostly, she ignored it. Now she felt a certain unease herself. Something was up.

'What's all this about?' she asked pleasantly. 'Everything's all right with your work programme, isn't it?'

'Oh, yes everything's fine, and I'm really enjoying my time in Accounts.' Lindsay cleared her throat. 'The thing is, though, I want to give in my notice.'

Abby's dark eyes flashed, then became expressionless.

'Seems hard to understand. If you're enjoying your work.'

'It's not the work, Mrs Baxter, it's not Logie's. It's just that I feel I ought to see something else before I settle down. I mean, look around a bit. Make sure Logie's is what I want.'

'Logie's was what your father wanted for you. I thought you wanted it too.'

'I do. I mean, I did.' Lindsay's gaze finally meeting Abby's was wretched. 'But what I've decided to do is go to London.'

'Ah.' Abby sat back, a wry smile playing at the corners of her mouth. 'This wouldn't have anything to do with Bobby, would it?'

'No, of course not. I thought of it myself.'

'Lindsay, look at me.'

With obvious effort, Lindsay raised her eyes to Abby's.

'Tell me now that you are not going to London because of Bobby.'

Lindsay, still staring at Abby, could not speak.

'It's one thing to try to deceive me,' Abby said gently. 'It's another to deceive yourself.'

'I know what I'm doing,' Lindsay said hoarsely.

'You're going to London with Bobby because you're in love with him?'

'Yes.' Lindsay was suddenly defiant. 'I suppose you think that's stupid?'

'No, I think it's easier to understand than your wanting to look round London before you settle down!' Abby jumped up and put her arm round Lindsay's shoulders. 'Oh, Lindsay, you won't be the first person to do something crazy for love, but this is crazy, don't you see that?'

'Yes, only there's nothing I can do about it. I have to go, I couldn't bear to stay here and say goodbye to him.' Lindsay shivered under Abby's encircling arm. 'All the time he was away doing National Service, I was thinking how it would be when he came back. When he told me he was going away again, I just couldn't believe it, I wanted to die.'

'We all feel like that at times, Lindsay, but we don't die.'

Lindsay, shaking off Abby's arm, leaped to her feet.

'But, Mrs Baxter, don't you understand, this is my way out? It came to me, out of the blue, that I could go with him! I could go to London too! I've got my godmother's money, I could rent a flat, find a job—'

'And what does your mother say?' Abby asked quietly.

'Oh, God.'

Lindsay stared up at the portrait of the founder of Logie's hanging behind Abby's desk. He had been her father's great-uncle, a steady, respectable moneymaker. Why could she not have been someone like him? Someone who never felt as she did now? She gave a weary shrug. How did she know what had been in his heart? People were not always what they seemed.

49

'Mummy's devastated,' she said, bowing her head.

'Does she know about Bobby?'

'I've only told her what I told you. What I first told you.'

'You must try to understand how hard it is for her to see you go, Lindsay. She loves you so much.'

'And I love her! I know she's not my real mother, but she's been like a real mother all the same.'

'Of course,' Abby said blankly. 'No one's arguing.'

'I'm just saying I do understand what this means to her, but it's the same for Bobby's mother – they have to understand we have our own lives to live.'

'The only thing is, Lindsay, that Bobby seems to me to be a very confused and unhappy young man. I love him dearly, but I don't honestly think there's room in his life for anyone but himself.'

'I know what he's like. I'm not seeing him through rose-coloured spectacles. That's why I think it may work out, because I'm not expecting anything wonderful.'

'Oh, Lindsay!' Abby laughed. 'What a way to embark on a love affair! Oh, please, won't you think again? Consider all you have here, all you're giving up — '

'Mrs Baxter,' Lindsay broke in. 'Will you give me a reference?'

At the door, they shook hands. Lindsay said she would be leaving Edinburgh very soon, she would be in touch, she was very grateful for all that Mrs Baxter had done.

'I keep thinking of your father, Lindsay. He was so proud of you, so looking forward to your taking his place.'

'You took that,' Lindsay whispered. 'You know I could never have done as well as you.'

Chapter Eleven

On the morning of her leaving, Lindsay was up early, not because she had anything to do – she had finished her packing the night before – but because she couldn't sleep. It was still dark when she looked out of her window. Beyond the mellow glow of the street lights, the neighbouring houses were in shadow. This was the Victorian West End, solid and prosperous. Bobby's Morningside was the same. Lindsay had the feeling they had both been brought up in fortresses; strongholds that would protect them for life. Yet here they were, breaking out. Going on the run. Leaving behind comfort and safety and ever-loving mothers. What were they thinking of? They had their own lives to live, she had claimed, which was surely true, but as she let the curtain drop and turned back to the haven of her room, Lindsay's hand was shaking. She hoped to God she was doing the right thing. There would be no turning back.

'What's up?' asked Sara, padding in without knocking. She was wearing a shortie nightdress and matching wrapper, her blonde hair scraped back from a clear shining face. 'Can't wait to get going?'

'Something like that.' Lindsay shivered, though her radiator was heating up, making comforting clicking noises. She moved to her dressing table and ran a comb through her hair. 'Haven't come to persuade me not to go, have you?'

'Of course not.' Sara flung herself on Lindsay's unmade bed. 'I think it's terrific what you're doing, I really do. I only wish I'd the nerve to make the break myself.'

'I thought you were quite happy here. You've got your job, got your boyfriends.'

'Got Mummy.'

'She's not so bad.'

'Keeps such tabs on us, though. I mean, I get a bit tired of having to give a *Who's Who* entry for every chap I go out with. You won't have to do that in London.'

'Mummy already knows Bobby's *Who's Who* entry,' Lindsay said dryly. 'I don't see myself going out with anyone else.'

'Are you really going to have separate flats?' Sara's blue eyes were knowing. 'I heard you saying that.'

'What do you think?'

'Lindsay!' Sara leaped off the bed. 'Honestly, I never thought—' Her expression changed. 'Listen, you will take care, won't you? I mean . . .'

'I know what you mean and I will take care. Now, come on, don't hold me up, I want to get ready.'

'It's going to be so strange without you.' Sara hesitated for a moment, then caught her sister to her. 'Oh, Lindsay, I'm going to miss you! There's always been the two of us, and now there's only me.'

'You'll have to keep Mummy happy,' Lindsay murmured, sniffing a little. 'I feel bad about her, to tell you the truth. She's lost Daddy, now she's losing me.'

'That's life,' Sara said solemnly. 'One of these days I'll be going too.' At the door she looked back. 'Did I tell you that Will Gilbride has been sent to Korea?'

'You told me.' Lindsay gave her sister a little push. 'I'll see you downstairs, OK?'

'For your last breakfast?' Sara grinned. 'Be sure to make a hearty meal!'

Monica Farrell's housekeeper did not arrive until ten, but Monica was happy enough to prepare breakfast herself. In her youth she had scarcely seen the inside of a kitchen, but now had made the echoing basement of the Selkirk Street house into a place of comfort and efficiency. When Gerald had been alive, she had taken pleasure in preparing good Scottish breakfasts, with porridge and kippers, whatever was available, but now of course the girls only wanted orange juice and toast. Everything had changed.

A statuesque woman with golden hair that needed only a little colouring from time to time, Monica sighed as she took oranges from a bowl and began to squeeze them. Until recently her life had been little touched by adversity. There had been the fact that she could not have children of her own, of course, and that had been traumatic. But then the girls had arrived, bringing fulfilment and sweetness, and all had been pleasant for her until Gerald's sudden death. Oh, what a blow that had been! She had thought she would never recover. Now, as she was slowly beginning to rally, Lindsay had sent her reeling again.

Monica placed the jug of orange juice on the table, her fine eyes moist with unshed tears. What was that phrase about ungrateful children? 'Sharper than a serpent's tooth . . .'? Whoever wrote that knew a thing or two. And Lindsay was an adopted child. Shouldn't that have made a difference? No. Monica felt a little ashamed. It was wrong to expect more from Lindsay because she was adopted. But then, one shouldn't expect less. Why should any child be cruel to its parents?

The door opened and the girls came in, sliding quickly into their places at the table. Each murmured good morning, then Sara poured the orange juice. Lindsay's eyes were on her plate.

'Oh, Lindsay, you're really going?' whispered Monica.

Lindsay heaved a long sigh. She put a slice of bread into the toaster.

'But why? I simply don't understand. Why London? You have your post at Logie's, your career all mapped out —'

'We've been through all this so often, Mummy. There's no point in saying any more.'

'Your father was so happy in Logie's. It was the family firm, he took a pride in it.' Monica dabbed at her eyes with a lace handkerchief. 'I'm glad he's not here today, to see you throwing everything he loved back in his face.'

'Lindsay's not doing that, Mummy,' Sara put in. 'She just wants to look around before she settles down.'

'If you think about it,' said Lindsay, 'all I've done is go to school in Edinburgh, go to university in Edinburgh, go to work in Edinburgh. There must be something else.'

'Bobby Gilbride, it seems,' Monica said acidly.

'I'll see Bobby in London, I'm not going to deny it.' Lindsay was carefully avoiding Sara's eye. 'But he's going to be pretty involved, trying to get a start with his music.'

'And what will you be doing? Some silly temporary job? When you could be moving up the ladder at Logie's?' Monica shook her head. 'It's perverse, that's what it is, foolish and perverse.' Suddenly, her expression of baffled woe changed. 'Unless you're doing this just to get away from me? As Bobby Gilbride is getting away from Rachel and Malcolm?'

'Of course not!' cried Lindsay. 'That's not it at all, honestly it's not!'

'Oh, I don't trust him, Lindsay, I don't trust Bobby Gilbride. How could anyone trust a man who's treated his poor parents as he's treated his?'

'Mummy, he only wants to lead his own life,' Sara said quietly. 'That's what Lindsay wants too. It's only natural.'

'So you'll be leaving next, I suppose?'

'I didn't say that. I'm only trying to explain why I can see Lindsay's point of view.'

'And Bobby's. Anyone's point of view but mine!'

Monica rose, stood for a moment looking at her daughters like a wounded goddess, then ran from the room, banging the door behind her. Lindsay and Sara winced. Such a show of emotion from their mother was unprecedented. It hit them hard.

'I knew it would be bad, but it's been worse than I thought.' Lindsay stood up. 'Oh, Sara, why is it such a crime to do something I want to do?'

'Because parents never want you to do what you want to do.' Sara drained her orange juice. 'And we're adopted, aren't we? We should be specially grateful and careful not to make trouble.'

'I am grateful,' Lindsay said slowly. 'But that doesn't mean I can give up Bobby because Mummy wants me to.'

'Better keep your voice down,' Sara advised. 'She doesn't know the truth about you and Bobby.'

Lindsay wasn't listening, her eyes were on the kitchen clock.

'Sara – it's time for the taxi!'

The driver had already stowed away Lindsay's luggage when Monica, red-eyed and composed, appeared at the front door. Without a word, Lindsay ran to her and flung her arms around her, pressing her face against her mother's smoothly powdered cheek.

'Don't think badly of me,' she whispered. 'I do love you and I'll always keep in touch, I promise.'

'There's my girl, there's my Lindsay!'

As Monica managed a watery smile, Lindsay pulled herself away to hug Sara and say, yes, yes, she would take care of herself, she knew what she was doing. But she still darted back to give Monica one more kiss, before finally climbing into the taxi, shielding her eyes with her hand.

'Waverley?' asked the driver.

'Waverley,' Lindsay repeated, and did not look back as the taxi drove her from the house that had been her home all her life, though she knew that Monica and Sara were still at the door.

Bobby was by the booking-office as planned. At the sight of his cropped sandy head standing out from the crowd, Lindsay's heart rose, but she felt no rush of happiness. It was too soon for that.

'Was it bad?' he asked, taking her cases.

'Pretty bad.'

'Same for me. Why do they have to make things so difficult, do you think?'

'I suppose because they love us.'

'Love . . . If I had any children, I'd never make a thing of loving them. They'd be a damn sight happier, I can tell you.'

'Bobby, that's a terrible thing to say.'

He shrugged. 'Look, I've got the tickets, let's find a porter – the London train's in.'

It was a corridor train and had the usual smell of dust and stale cigarette smoke, leather and plush. The porter put their cases on the rack, Bobby tipped him and they took their seats. There were other people in the compartment, a middle-aged couple and a young man reading *Punch*. So we won't be able to talk, thought Lindsay, and was relieved. She felt drained by the scene she had had with her mother, and consumed by a guilt she felt should not be hers. While Bobby opened a newspaper, she lay back against the upholstery, then instantly sat up again, remembering Monica's warning never to rest one's head against seats in public transport, as one never knew who might have done that before. Oh, how ridiculous! But she did not lie back again. Instead, she looked out at the platform with its familiar sign of Waverley. And something tugged at her heart.

'Shall we have lunch on the train?' asked Bobby. 'The parents slipped me a few quid. All I'm going to get, says Dad.'

'Yes, let's do that.' But Lindsay was grasping Bobby's arm,

oblivious of the looks from the other passengers. 'Bobby, Bobby!'

'What is it?'

'We're moving, the train is moving!'

'Good God,' he said, laughing, 'isn't that what we want it to do?'

Chapter Twelve

As soon as Bobby left for Waverley, Rachel drove to the bungalow to tell Madge that he had really gone. Right up to the very last moment, she had been hoping he would change his mind, but of course he had not.

'And never will!' She dashed angry tears from her eyes. 'All he'll do is what he wants to do and the rest of us can go hang!'

'He'll come back,' Madge said comfortingly. 'If it doesn't work out, he'll come home, you'll see.'

'No. He's away and he'll stay away.' Rachel, beneath her anger, was forlorn. 'Didn't I say he does what he wants to do? What he wants is to be away from home.'

'Poor Rachel,' Madge said, when she had left them to drive to the College of Art. 'There's nothing you can say.'

'I don't know why she has to make such a fuss,' Jennie muttered. 'I mean, it's not the end of the world, if Bobby's gone to London. Not exactly Korea, is it?'

They looked out at the weather, which was dismal, with scudding grey clouds and an icy wind. Not worth putting the sheets out, that was for sure, but Jennie suggested they should put their coats on and look round the garden, get a breath of fresh air. Blow Rachel's gloom away.

The garden at the back of the house was a good square plot, with a lawn and flower beds, a patch for vegetables and the famous apple tree. On that late February day it was not of course looking its best and to Jennie, who had no experience of gardens, it wasn't much to write home about. Still, there were already snowdrops spearing up through the grass under the trees, and everywhere small golden flowers that Jennie didn't know.

'Ma, what are these?' she called, 'These little yellow things?'

Madge stooped to look. 'Winter aconites, Jennie. They're like the snowdrops, always come out first. I haven't seen them since Southampton days.' She blew her reddened nose and looked around, her eyes suddenly bright. 'It's exciting, isn't it? I wonder what else is here? There'll be sure to more things coming up, the people in this house were keen gardeners.'

'I suppose now you'll be feeling glad we left Catherine's Land,' Jennie asked a little bitterly.

'Now why talk like that?' Madge was crestfallen. 'You know I didn't want to leave Catherine's Land, I'll never feel happy about the way we all had to go. But the garden makes a difference, you have to admit it.'

'Well, just don't make too much of it when the others come today,' warned Jennie. 'They haven't got gardens, remember.'

'I'm not likely to forget it.' Madge, looking beyond Jennie, gave a start. 'Why, Jennie, look who's here!'

A man was coming round the side of the house. He was wearing a raincoat and carrying a hat. His sea-green eyes were fixed on Jennie.

'Hope I didna startle you?' he asked quickly. 'Couldna get an answer at the front, so thought I'd try the back. You dinna mind?'

'Of course not, Mac,' Jennie said warmly. 'Of course we don't mind.'

'I've borrowed ma brother's car. Thought you two ladies might like a lift somewhere? Mebbe pick up something you need?'

'Why, how kind!' Madge was all smiles. 'I've got some old friends coming this afternoon, but I'm sure Jennie would like a drive.'

'I'll get my bag,' said Jennie.

'Well, is this no' grand?' asked Peggie Kemp, looking round Madge's living room. She was a fierce little woman with a helmet of grey permed hair and narrow dark eyes. With Jessie Rossie and Marty Finnegan, she had been invited over to see Madge's new house and to have a bit of a chat over a cup of tea. 'You've done well, eh? You've fallen on your feet!'

'So've you fallen on your feet, Peggie,' Jessie retorted. 'Did your Jamie no' get a council house, then?'

'Aye, when them as should've got one were after getting

58

nothing!' added Marty, the Irishwoman who had lived on the first floor of Catherine's Land. In her prime she had been known to terrorise strong men with one look from her flashing blue eye, and was still not one to cross. Her husband was dead now and her children scattered, except for Nancy, who was married with children of her own. It was to Nancy's crowded flat that Marty had been persuaded to go when she finally left Catherine's Land, and she had taken some persuading. It would not have surprised Madge to find Marty stretched out across her front door when the removal men came, but her family brought the priest to her, who said it was her duty to go and the Lord's will and she had finally departed, clutching her holy pictures, still outlining what she would like to do to the university folk, whether it was against the Lord's will or not.

Peggie sat down with a toss of her head and took out a packet of Woodbines.

'You'll no' mind if I smoke?' she asked Madge, who shook her head. 'Anyone else want one? No?' She lit up, blowing smoke and frowning.

'I wouldna say I'd fallen on ma feet, Jessie. What's a council house, then? It's no' like Catherine's Land. It's no' like home.'

Madge passed a plate of shortbread. 'Aren't you happy, Peggie? I thought it would be nice where you are. Isn't there a bit of garden?'

'No' like yours. It's a bit of earth, that's what, and the green's full o' kids that shout and swear when you try to put your washing out. I tell you, it's like a foreign country, it's a place I dinna ken and we all say the same.'

'At least you've your own room, eh?' said Jessie. 'Now me, I've only got the sofa bed in the living room. Ken doesna see that that's no' enough. I want ma own things around, I want something I can call ma own. And the walls is that thin, I can hear Ivy coughing her head off like she was in beside me, and then Ken gets up and makes a cuppa tea and stamps about like an elephant.' Jessie shook her head. 'I get that sick sometimes, I dinna ken what to do with maself. Nothing, eh?'

''Tis the same for me, I'm telling you,' Marty said. 'I get Nancy's little ones crying, and Nancy and Col rowing, and if I try to interfere, they're saying it's their place and I know what I can do if I'm not liking it!' Marty's eyes sparkled with anger. 'Saying that to me, fancy! Me that had my own flat since I was coming over from Dublin forty years gone! I'm not one for putting up with that!'

'Have some more shortbread,' Madge quietly urged. 'Had to use margarine, not butter, but it's not too bad.'

'Got fixed up for the messages, have you?' asked Peggie. ''Cause that's another headache where we are, you ken. No Donnie now, to slip us a bit o' this or a bit o' that. We're stuck with the Stores and they're that snooty, just because you want your dividend – anybody'd think it was charity, eh?'

'I'd like to see anybody getting snooty with me!' Marty laughed dangerously. 'If I want my divi, I'm getting my divi, so I'm telling you!'

'Well, Jennie's found a nice little shop in Corstorphine that's taken our ration books,' said Madge. 'Not the same as Donnie's, of course, but I think we'll manage all right.'

'Where is Jennie?' asked Jessie.

'A friend with a car offered to take her out.'

'Why, who'd that be?' asked Peggie. 'No' some fella?'

Madge hesitated. 'He's an old navy pal of Frankie's. On leave in Fife.'

On leave in Fife and he was taking Jennie for a drive here? The visitors looked at one another, exchanging smiles.

'Well, I niver thought Jennie'd look at another man after Rory,' said Jessie. 'But that's grand, that is.'

'Oh, I don't say there's anything in it,' Madge said quickly. 'I mean, he's in the merchant navy, he's based in Southampton. When would he see Jennie?'

'Been wondering?' asked Peggie. 'Where there's a will, there's a way. If they're keen, they'll get round iverything.'

'Ah, Madge,' Marty said solicitously. 'What would you be doing then?' Madge was a favourite of hers, for Madge had helped to deliver two of her babies, Madge had always treated her with respect. 'You'd not be wanting to live here alone?'

'I've got Hamish, I wouldn't be alone.'

Hamish? Again the visitors exchanged glances. Everyone knew you couldna count on a young fella to stay put with his gran. Poor old Madge, losing her daughter and her companion, but you couldna blame Jennie, she had her own life to live.

'I'd like Jennie to marry again,' Madge said quietly, 'But the fact is, she's only gone for a drive.' She jumped to her feet. 'Look, it's still light. Let's go outside for a minute and I'll show you my garden.' Remembering Jennie's warning, she added hastily, 'Not that there's much in it at the moment. Only snowdrops and a few aconites.'

Chapter Thirteen

Jennie directed Mac to a store on the edge of the city where she bought tins of paint and packets of distemper. As soon as the better weather came, she told him, she planned to start on decorating the bungalow; Hamish would help.

'Wish I could have given you a hand,' said Mac, loading the tins into the boot of the car. 'I'm a dab hand at decorating.'

'You've been a grand help as it is, helping me get this heavy stuff home. I'm very grateful.'

'We need no' take it back yet.' Mac opened the passenger seat. 'I thought we might drive somewhere first.'

'It's pretty wintry, Mac.'

He cast a sailor's eye to the sky. 'We'll be all right. We won't go far.'

They drove to Cramond, a picturesque village which had the feeling of being on the sea, though the flats of dark sand and the wide sweep of water were only the mouth of the River Almond. In the summer this was a favourite place for picnics and sailing and it was great entertainment to cross on the tiny ferry to Dalmeny, Lord Rosebery's estate. In February, though, it was better to huddle into one of the little teashops, warm themselves at the open fire and talk.

'You're such an easy person to be with, Mac,' Jennie told him, as they settled again into his brother's Ford Anglia.

'You're pretty easy yourself.'

'I used to be, I used to be calm like Ma.' Jennie stared out at the steep winding street Mac was negotiating. 'But I've changed.'

'You've had your troubles, Jennie.'

She gave him a quick glance. 'Frankie told you?'

Mac nodded. 'I wish you'd no' been hurt like that. I've been hurt maself. I know what it's like.' As they reached the main road to Edinburgh, he said, huskily, 'But it's over now, eh?'

'Rory's been dead a long time.'

'That's no' what I asked.'

Jennie was silent, her eyes on the long lines of traffic ahead. It was the rush hour, not the time to be talking like this. But they must take what time they could.

'It's funny,' she said at last, 'I've never let myself think about it. What you're asking, I mean. Is it over?'

'Well, is it?'

'Mac, I think it is. I think, maybe I haven't loved Rory for a very long time.'

He gave a long satisfied sigh and made the turn for Corstorphine.

'Soon be home, Jennie.'

They both hoped, not too soon.

Brae Street was not well lit and Mac driving slowly towards the bungalow suddenly drew up in the shadows between street lamps.

'This isn't the house,' said Jennie.

'Aye, I know that.' Mac took her hand. 'It's a place to talk.'

'We've talked all afternoon!'

'I think you know what I want to say.'

'Mac —'

'We've just met, OK, OK, but you can tell, eh? I've fallen for you like a bag o' hammers. These things happen, even to a guy like me.' He laughed uneasily. 'No chicken.'

Jennie sat quite still, only her hand in Mac's trembling.

'Are you no' going to say anything?' he asked gently.

'I – don't know what to say. We've only just met.'

'Dinna need time to know what I feel. What do you feel?'

'Stunned. I'd no idea —'

'Come on, Jennie, dinna think you have to talk like that. Dinna tell me I'm wrong.'

'Wrong?'

'Is it no' the same for you, then?' He drew her into his arms and kissed her on the mouth with a long sweet kiss that sent her memories stirring. No one had kissed her for so long, she had forgotten the feelings that rose and took over, but she was remembering now.

'Is it no' the same?' he asked again, and Jennie put her hands around his face which she could see only indistinctly in the darkness of the car. For a while she gently caressed him, then put her lips to his.

'It's the same, Mac, it's the same.'

'The thing is, I'm not free,' she whispered, sitting back in her seat. 'There's Ma.'

'Jennie, she'd want you to be happy.'

'Yes, but I couldn't leave her. Not when we've just moved. If she'd still been in Catherine's Land with all her friends, it'd have been different, but she's a stranger here, she doesn't know anyone. My sisters visit, but they're so busy. I'm the one she needs.'

'You're saying we have to wait? Till she's settled? I couldna wait too long, Jennie, dinna ask me.'

'We don't really know each other,' she said quietly. 'When you're back in Southampton, you might change your mind.'

'You're right you dinna know me, Jennie. I'm no' one for changing ma mind.'

'Well, let's think about it. Let's keep in touch and think about it.' Jennie stroked his hand. 'I've got to go, Mac. Hamish'll be home for his tea.'

'I bet you've spent your life making some fella his tea,' he said with a smile. 'I'll let you into a secret, I could make tea for you. I'm handy, I can make tea, iron shirts — '

'Don't need anyone, then?' she asked teasingly.

For answer, he pulled her close again and kissed her with passion.

'Oh, no, Jennie,' he whispered, breathing hard. 'I need you, all right. But no' for ironing ma shirts.'

Hamish was already home when Jennie slipped into the house, feeling as guilty as a young girl coming back late with her boyfriend's kisses burning her lips. But she wasn't really late and her mother had everything ready.

'Nice drive?' asked Madge, smiling.

'Yes. We got some paint first — Mac's put it in the garage — then we had tea at Cramond.'

64

'Thought that Mac fellow was staying over in Fife,' said Hamish with unusual coldness.

'He had his brother's car, he thought we might need things we couldn't carry.'

'But then you went to Cramond? Why didn't he take Gran?'

'He asked me, but I had Jessie and the others to tea,' Madge told him quickly. 'Oh, I feel so sorry for them, all missing Catherine's Land.'

'Are you going out with him again?' asked Hamish, looking only at his mother.

'He has to go back to Southampton.' Jennie was tying on her apron, not looking at anyone.

'So, you're not going out again?'

'Yes, tomorrow. That's his last day. If it's of any interest to you.' Jennie was suddenly angry. 'Why shouldn't I go out with Mac if I want to? Or anybody else, come to that?'

Madge, listening, turned away. Didn't they say history repeated itself? Hadn't she once said words like that to her daughters? 'Why shouldn't I go out with Jim Gilbride?' But they had stared at her as though she were a criminal, they didn't like to think of their mother with another man, as Hamish didn't like to think of Jennie with Mac. Oh, Jennie, prayed Madge, don't give up Mac for me or Hamish, as I gave up Jim for you. Things had gone so wrong, she and Jim had wasted so many years. Don't make my mistakes, thought Madge.

'When's tea ready?' asked Hamish, opening the evening paper. 'I'm starving.'

'I've done the potatoes, there's just the fish to put in,' Madge murmured to Jennie, and saw that her anger had died and her eyes were alight. She was thinking of tomorrow.

Chapter Fourteen

As spring slowly followed winter, a new mood began to be felt across the country. It was as though the nation were waking itself up to find that the time of mourning was over. The young Queen was seen smiling again, playing with her children, Prince Charles and Princess Anne, or attending functions, carrying flowers, the Duke of Edinburgh at her side. Although it would not be until 1953, plans for the Coronation were already in the air and people were looking forward to it as one grand party, a holiday for everyone from anxieties over trouble abroad and shortages at home. Even in Scotland, where the Scottish Nationalists were complaining over postboxes marked EIIR, there was the feeling that a new spirit was stirring. The new Elizabethan Age was not just for England: Scotland could look forward to the future too.

Along with everyone else, Kate felt the excitement of the time, although she resented the way Korea had faded into the background and social progress seemed to have been put on hold, while the magazines debated which young lady from which great family would be selected to attend the Queen, or whether it was correct to say that the Queen would ride to her Coronation or drive. As though any of it mattered! And there was still at least a year to go.

In truth, Kate was like Jennie, her life revolved round letters. Will scribbling that he hadn't won any medals but was still in one piece; Will telling her to take care of herself; Will warning her not to take herself off to Fleet Street or any nonsense of that sort.

Now, why would I do that? asked Kate. Why would I go to London? Well, Westminster was in London. But Westminster was a long way off in the future. While Will was in Korea, even her politics had to go to the back of Kate's mind.

Monica and Rachel went to London, but only for a weekend in the summer. They had decided they should see for themselves what Bobby and Lindsay were up to, but had made the mistake of announcing their visit. It would have been better just to arrive and surprise them, Rachel thought, but Monica said that that might look as though they were expecting to find something amiss.

In the event, they couldn't be sure whether there was anything amiss or not. Bobby had booked them rooms in a hotel in the West End and said it might be easier if he stayed there too, so that he could 'look after them' as he gallantly put it.

'The whole point is, Bobby, that I wanted to see your rooms, to see if you are looking after yourself,' Rachel told him sharply.

'I'm sharing with a chap in Dulwich, Mum. No point in your going over there, it's just a couple of rooms, nothing special. And of course I'm looking after myself. Don't I look all right?'

Rachel didn't like to tell him that she felt quite ashamed of the way he looked. His sandy hair that had been too short was now too long, and he looked as if he was trying to grow sideburns, like some sort of Teddy boy.

'Never mind how you look,' she said hastily. 'Tell me about your music. Is it working out for you, being here? Has Frankie found you any engagements?'

Bobby was evasive. Yes, Frankie had been very good at getting him introductions and he'd had one or two offers. Well, not exactly offers, but possibilities. Things were quite hopeful. Now, what about dinner? He and Lindsay had found a very nice place where you could get real steak and it wasn't too expensive – no, no, it would be their treat.

The dinner was not too bad. The young people seemed in good spirits, appeared to have no regrets, but afterwards in the privacy of her hotel room, Monica told Rachel that Lindsay's flat was dreary, very badly built, and very expensive. Also, Lindsay wasn't happy. She was missing Edinburgh.

'Has she said so?' asked Rachel.

'No, but I can tell.' Monica was looking tired and defeated, her golden poise temporarily in retreat. 'She's taken on some dreadful office job that only pays buttons, she seems to have no idea about a career, she's just wasting all her money on the London cost of living. So much for seeing places better than Edinburgh! I knew all along it was only Bobby she wanted to see!'

'You can't be sure of that, Monica. They're not living together, anyway.'

'And can you be sure of THAT?' Monica countered.

Before returning home, Rachel arranged a meeting with Frankie. He gave her lunch at the hotel where he was playing, but she took no interest in the menu or the wine list.

'You choose,' she said impatiently. 'All I want is the truth about Bobby. Are things going well, or not?'

When she could see Frankie trying to think of something comforting to say, her mouth turned down in the way her family knew so well.

'They're not, are they? He's had no success?'

'I wouldn't say that. He's had one or two offers.'

'Possibilities, I believe is the word.' Rachel drank some wine. 'And it all looks very hopeful, I don't think. Oh, it's all so stupid, Frankie! He should be back at the university, he should be planning a proper career. Why is he doing this to me?'

'He's not doing anything to you, Rachel. He's just trying to find his own way, be a success at something that matters to him.'

'He'll never make it, you know he won't.'

'Give him time. Give him time and space. Just – leave him alone.'

'And tell Monica to do the same with Lindsay, I suppose? You don't know what it's like to be a parent, Frankie. Having to stand by, watching your children take the wrong turnings.'

'The point is, Rachel, Bobby and Lindsay are not children any more. You have to let them make their own mistakes.'

'And mistakes are what they're making!' cried Rachel.

Bobby and Lindsay saw their mothers off from King's Cross, watching the long train pulling slowly away, handkerchiefs waving from the windows.

'Thank goodness that's over,' Bobby said.

'Yes,' Lindsay murmured, but her eyes were full of tears.

'Hey, what's up?' Bobby looked down at her in surprise. 'Not missing dear Mummy, are you?'

'Sort of.' Lindsay blew her nose. 'Missing Scotland, I think. It's just – you know – seeing the train – going north.'

'Wishing you were on it? Nothing to stop you buying a ticket.'

'Oh, don't be silly.' She put her arm in his and they strolled down the platform. 'You know I want to be — ' she was about to say 'with you', but stopped herself in time. 'Here,' she finished.

'Yeah, I think we made the right decision.' Bobby looked down at a handful of change he had taken from his trouser pocket. 'Think we've enough for a taxi home? I get sick of the bloody tube.'

'We are supposed to be economising, everything's so expensive here.' Lindsay relented. 'All right, maybe just for once.'

In the taxi, she leaned against his shoulder. 'It'll be nice for you to come back to the flat, won't it?'

'You bet. Cost the earth, staying in that hotel.'

'Worth it, though. At least, it stopped them worrying.'

Bobby laughed. 'You're an optimist. They're never going to stop worrying until we book the church.'

'Book the church?' she repeated faintly.

'And we're not likely to do that!' He kissed her lightly. 'Hell, I don't want that any more than you do. I think it's terrific that we can share a flat and make love without getting involved. It's the way things should be, but there aren't many girls can see it like that. I suppose it's because they haven't got proper jobs.'

'Oh, really?' Lindsay asked tightly.

'You're the exception.'

'I haven't exactly got a proper job at the moment.'

'You've got the right attitude. You're special.'

Looking out at the mass of people crowding the pavements, everyone unknown to her, Lindsay felt Bobby's words like a dagger in her heart. Special. Sounded so wonderful. Meant so little.

Chapter Fifteen

The godmother's money was not going very far. As well as the rent to find for the gimcrack flat, which Lindsay had only managed to obtain by paying out what was known as 'key money', there were upkeep charges and gas bills, there were high rates, high fares, and even Bobby's beer cost twice as much as in Edinburgh. Throughout the summer, Lindsay hunted for something better paid than the job at the printer's office where she did the accounts, but her degree didn't take her as far as she had hoped; for anything really well paid, she hadn't the required experience.

As for Bobby's prospects, Lindsay had stopped asking about them. None of Frankie's introductions had led to permanent engagements, the BBC audition had been unsuccessful. He had managed to play the pubs a little, but his kind of jazz was not always popular and he hadn't Frankie's easy rapport with the customers. As the summer turned to autumn and then to winter, neither he nor Lindsay spoke of the future. But on a day in December, the future hit them like a bombshell.

It was foggy that afternoon when Lindsay returned to the flat, a peasouper that caught at her throat and streaked her coat with lines of smut. She didn't notice.

Bobby was already home, for the lights were on and the gas fire lit, but he was in the bedroom and did not appear. Lindsay hung up her coat and sat down by the fire, holding out her thin hands. On the third finger of her left hand, a ring gleamed dully. It was a wedding ring.

'Hi,' said Bobby, from the doorway. 'Didn't know you were back.'

He looked pale and depressed, had clearly not had a good day. Not for a moment did Lindsay expect him to have done anything towards the supper. That was her job, of course.

'Aren't you late?' he asked, yawning.

'I've been to the doctor's.'

'Doctor's? You didn't tell me you were ill.'

'I'm not ill.' Lindsay held out her left hand. 'I had to wear this, Bobby. I had to call myself Mrs Gilbride.'

Bobby looked at the ring, then raised his eyes to Lindsay's face.

'What are you saying?'

Lindsay pulled off the ring and set it on the shelf above the gas fire. 'I'm going to have a baby.'

'That's not possible. We've taken precautions.'

Lindsay smiled. 'It's a mistake. I'm going to have a mistake, Bobby. Next June.'

Bobby ran his hand across his face. His eyes against his pallor seemed almost black.

'I can't take this in, Lindsay. You know how I feel about children. How did you let it happen?'

'How did I let it happen? Don't you think you had something to do with it? As I say, it's a mistake. It's nobody's fault.'

'A mistake all right . . . you'll have to find someone quickly, Lindsay. You shouldn't leave it too late.'

'You want me to have an abortion?'

'You're surely not going to keep it? That would be terrible. An unwanted child. You'd never be able to look after it.'

Lindsay's face was white. 'You're not going to be involved?'

'I told you, didn't I, that I could never be a father? I couldn't bear to be responsible for another human being. Ordering its life, telling it what to do.' Bobby's lips were trembling. 'It's the way I am, Lindsay. I'm not proud of it, but I can't help it. I can't be involved.'

'So I'm supposed to find some backstreet old woman – some horrible doctor – I can't! I don't know anyone, I wouldn't know where to look!'

'There are way and means,' he said eagerly. 'There are always ways to do things if you can pay, and you've got the money.' He came to her chair and knelt down, taking her hand. 'Come on, Lindsay, it would solve everything. A few quid, a few hours, or whatever it takes, and you'd be free! Think of it.'

She freed her hands from his. 'My mother had me, Bobby.'

'Lindsay —'

'I've made up my mind. I'm going to have the baby.'

'And put it up for adoption? OK, that's fine. As long as you don't expect me to play mothers and fathers.'

'I don't expect anything from you, Bobby. I never have.' Lindsay reached up and took down the ring. 'This was the cheapest one I could find, I knew I wouldn't be wearing it long.'

Bobby was sitting with his hand over his eyes. 'Aren't we happy as we are, Lindsay? I thought we were. I thought we wanted the same things.'

'No, I might as well tell you now, I never wanted what you wanted.' Lindsay turned the ring in her fingers. 'I'm not putting the baby up for adoption. I'm keeping it myself.'

Bobby leaped to his feet. 'I need a drink!' he shouted and crashed to the kitchen.

'Do let the neighbours know!' snapped Lindsay. 'You know what these walls are like.'

'Do you want anything?' he roared.

'No, but will you please keep your voice down?'

He came back with a beer, his face now flushed and moist.

'You're crazy,' he said, drinking deeply. 'How the hell do you think you'll manage?'

'I'll manage. People do.'

'In a place like this? I can't imagine a worse start for a kid.'

'Of course I won't stay here. I'll go back to Edinburgh, I'll find a place there. My mother will help me.'

'Your mother? She'll collapse when you tell her, she'll crumble away.'

'No, she's done things you'll never believe. I think she'll understand.'

'And what about the baby? Will that understand? Being a bastard? Going through life without a name?'

As Lindsay stared at him, unable to speak, he added quietly, 'You know the world, Lindsay. You might give this child everything it needs, but it will be illegitimate and that's all anyone'll see.'

Great tears began to roll down Lindsay's cheeks. She fumbled for a handkerchief. 'Oh, what a mess – what a mess!'

Bobby watched her for some minutes without speaking, then he leaned forward and took her hand again.

'If you're really set on this, Lindsay, I think we should get married. No – don't look at me like that, hear me out. I know what I've always said, but the kid's got to have a name. It's my kid, I'll give it my name.' Bobby drained his glass. 'I want to do that.'

'And supposing I don't want to marry someone who doesn't love me!' cried Lindsay.

'Never mind about love, think of the baby.'

'You said you didn't want to be involved!'

'I don't. That's the deal.'

'I bring the baby up alone?'

'That's it.'

She wanted to scream, no, no, be damned to you! But then the light still shone on the cheap wedding ring in her fingers. She thought of being able to call herself Mrs Gilbride without lying. Of not having to face her mother's shock, her friends' reactions. Even if Bobby never appeared, she would be married and her child would be legitimate. The whole thing was sickening and hypocritical, but the child would be a Gilbride, it would have the Gilbride name.

'Done!' she cried.

It seemed incredible that Bobby should take her in his arms and begin to kiss her, but to her surprise she found herself kissing him back. Why am I so weak, she asked, despising herself, but then was taking off her clothes and making love as though everything was just the same as it had always been. Only it wasn't. Even in the grip of passion, when she and Bobby seemed to reach new heights of desperate bliss, she knew it wasn't. Things would never be the same for herself and Bobby ever again.

A few days later they were married by special licence, with two girls from the printer's office as witnesses. Afterwards, they bought a single ticket to Edinburgh and Lindsay telephoned Monica and said she would be returning home alone for Hogmanay, Bobby had an engagement to play at one of the hotels. This was in fact true and provided their only good news.

'We can have Christmas together,' Lindsay told him. 'I'll get a chicken and a pudding.'

He nodded, although Christmas seemed to be only for other

people that year. They couldn't imagine joining in with any kind of celebration. It was a relief when New Year's Eve came and they could go to King's Cross.

'You'll keep in touch?' asked Bobby.

'What a fatuous remark! Of course I'll keep in touch. Will you?'

'I will. I'll do my best for you. I'll send you what I can.'

'You'll have enough to do, paying the rent on the flat for the next six months.'

He shrugged. 'I'll manage. Better get in, Lindsay. The guard's got his flag.'

They kissed hurriedly and Lindsay went stumbling to her seat. Another train, more goodbyes. Only this time it was she who was going north. The platform was gliding by, they were already on the move. She could see Bobby standing, watching, but it was too late to wave.

Chapter Sixteen

Kate had been hoping against the odds that Will would get leave for Christmas or Hogmanay, but no such luck, he wrote. He would be having Christmas dinner courtesy of army cooks, he would be seeing the New Year in on the other side of the world.

'Never mind, pet,' said Ivy, encircling Kate with a bony arm. 'He'll be home in the summer, eh? You have your Hogmanay with us at Biddy's, she's asked us all.'

Hogmanay at Biddy's. Kate gave a deep sigh. She said she'd bring some wine.

'Can you no' get us a nice drop o' port? Or whisky for your dad?'

'Mam, you know I'll never find any whisky!'

'Well, do what you can. All they newspaper folk drink like fish. Dinna tell me they canna find a bottle or two o' something good!'

'They'll find a bottle or two, all right, but no' for me,' Kate answered laughing.

'Come on, a lovely lassie like you! I bet you have the lot of 'em eating out o' your hand!'

Kate laughed again, but there was some truth in the remark. She knew she was popular on the *Glasgow Call*, not just because of her looks but also the strength of her views, which matched everyone else's. Their brief was social change. Kate was one of those who could make it happen, she was going places and might take them with her. Of course, some of the men took a more usual interest, thinking because Will wasn't around, she might be open to temporary offers.

'Can't live like a nun because your man's away,' Moray Chalmers, one of the senior reporters, told her on New Year's

Eve. They were having drinks in their local with the crowd. No paper tomorrow. This was a time to celebrate. 'Isn't that the truth?' pressed Moray, fixing Kate with a deep, dark gaze. He was a Scot who had been brought up in Surrey, which he used to say had given him the right perspective on the class struggle, and liked to talk politics, particularly with Kate. Sometimes he would outline the steps she should take towards a political career of her own and she would listen, but had already worked out the way she wanted to go. The time was not yet right, she was still too young, but that was something that would take care of itself.

'If I'd a girl like you, I'd not be expecting her to be locked up in a chastity belt till I got back,' Moray now told her teasingly.

'It's no' what Will wants, it's what I want,' Kate retorted. 'And the way I live is none of your damn business!'

'You're wrong there, Kate. I care a lot about you.'

'Doesna give you the right to tell me what to do.'

'Sweetheart, I make suggestions, that's all. Can't bear to see you so lonely. I mean, it's Hogmanay, for God's sake! The one night in the year when the Scots can do what the hell they like!'

Kate kissed him on the cheek. 'What I like is to go home, Moray. With Will away, I dinna give a damn about Hogmanay. I'm just going through the motions.'

So were others going through the motions. Christmas had never meant much to the tenants of Catherine's Land, but Hogmanay had been the time when the building fizzed with special feeling that they had all shared. There'd been sing-songs and people gathering on the stair, dancing in the big old rooms, bairns crying or sleeping through it all, boiled ham, black bun and beer that they'd all tipped in to pay for set out on somebody's table. When the clock struck twelve or the wireless told them it was time, there'd been kissing and joining of hands, singing of Auld Lang Syne, and the darkest-haired man sent outside to first foot back again, carrying the traditional bit of coal and all the promise of good luck for what was to come. Good luck, eh? Well, they hadna had much of that. Scattered all over the city, with strangers for company, the old folk gone, the old memories lost.

'Och, it's no' the same,' moaned Peggie Kemp as the evening began in Jamie's small, square living room where there was

76

always something missing, she didn't know what, but it might have been soul.

All over the city that cry was being echoed. Things were not the same for Marty Finnegan, for the Rossies, the Muirs, the Pringles, the Adairs, the Craigs. Hogmanay brought it home, eh? What could you do? Have a drink and hope for better things, a better life. Well, have a drink, anyway.

Jennie, seeing in the New Year at Rachel's, met Mac's eyes and smiled. It had been good of Rachel to invite him over, she thought, good of Frankie and Abby to put him up, so that he needn't drive back to his brother's. Good, wonderfully good, to have him at all, though her thoughts were so much with Will. This was his first Hogmanay away. But, so far, thank God, he had been safe.

'Oh, wouldn't you think Bobby would have come home for the holiday?' Rachel whispered furiously to Abby, who wouldn't have thought it but who looked suitably sympathetic.

'What makes it worse is that Lindsay is coming,' Rachel went on. 'And Monica's making such a fuss. Bobby's supposed to be playing somewhere, but even if that's true and I'm not sure it is, he could have given it up, couldn't he? To come home?'

'Roll on midnight,' Malcolm groaned. 'Let's see the end of nineteen fifty-two.'

'Now where's our Kate?' asked Jessie, fanning herself in Biddy's living room, where the fire was putting out a good heat and Ken and Ewan were already half asleep.

'Train must be late,' offered Ivy, cutting the remains of the Christmas cake Jessie had brought. 'Hogmanay, eh?'

Biddy shook her beautiful head. 'Bet you she's gone to some party. Should've been me, eh?'

The pub celebrations had gone on longer than Kate expected. She had to accept a lift from Moray to get to the station in time for her train.

'You're sure I can't come over?' he asked, as she leaned out of the carriage window. 'Take you to the Tron, eh?'

'I told you, I'm going to ma folks.' She gave him her lovely smile. 'Thanks anyway.'

'Why do I get the feeling that I'm not on your agenda?' He

77

stretched up to whisper, 'That fellow of yours in Korea, he won't want to go your way, you know.'

Kate glanced round to see if the other passengers were listening, but they appeared to be slumped in blissful New Year's Eve repose.

'You dinna know one thing about Will, Moray, so leave him out of it,' she whispered back.

'Lined up for banking, isn't he? Now when have you ever known a banker on our side of the fence?'

'Goodnight, Moray. Happy New Year!'

'Oh, and I wanted another kiss!' he called, running at the side of the train that was beginning to move. 'I'm not giving up, Kate!'

All he got was a last sight of her slamming down the window and laughing.

At Waverley, the London train was just in, disgorging passengers, among them a young woman in a long black coat with two suitcases she could hardly manage.

'Can I give you a hand?' asked Kate.

'Oh, that would be kind! I was hoping to find a porter.'

'At Hogmanay?' Kate laughed. 'Want the taxi queue?'

'Well, the clock, actually. My sister's meeting me.'

And I know who your sister is, thought Kate, with sudden recognition, but she said nothing.

'Haven't we met?' Lindsay asked, as Kate easily swung her cases along. 'I'm sure I've seen you before.'

'I'm Kate Rossie.'

'Oh, of course. I'm Lindsay Farrell.'

'Yes, I know.'

Sara was standing under the clock, twirling her car keys. She looked as pretty as Kate remembered her, and as well fed and cosseted. Scratch, scratch. Kate could feel her claws unsheathing and wondered at her own envy. She should have nothing to fear from this girl, she knew she was just as good-looking, just as confident. Only, her confidence came from herself and Sara's came from Selkirk Street.

Kate resolved not to think of how much that might mean to Will, of how much he was impressed by position and background. She knew he loved her, and she came from Catherine's Land, with

78

no more advantages than he had. Didn't that prove he had, after all, the right values? Kate felt able to smile at Sara Farrell.

'Lindsay!' Sara flew at her sister and hugged her. 'Oh, it's so lovely to see you! But why did you have to come so late?'

'Am I holding you up?' Lindsay smiled apologetically. 'Sorry, this was the only train I could book a seat on. Sara, do you remember Kate Rossie?'

'Of course.' Completely at ease, Sara put out a hand and Kate shook it. 'We met at Bobby Gilbride's party.'

Kate, rather regretting her casual clothes, said boldly, 'Yes, I was with Will.'

'And how is Will? Is he still in Korea?'

'Still in Korea, but well, as far as I know.'

'Thank goodness. When you write, do remember me to him, won't you?'

I will not, thought Kate, but found her eyes drawn to something flashing on Sara's left hand. Why, she was engaged! At the sight of the fine solitaire diamond Sara was showing to Lindsay, Kate's spirits soared. Thank God, thank God, Sara was engaged!

'You never told me!' cried Lindsay, examining the ring. 'It's beautiful, Sara. Who's the lucky chap?'

'Nick Ainslie. You know him, he's one of my crowd. A lawyer.'

'I didn't even know you were interested in him.'

'One thing led to another.' Sara glanced at her watch. 'But we'll have to get you home, Lindsay. You look awfully tired. I'll get a porter.'

Miraculously, of course, because it was Sara who was looking for one, a porter appeared and piled Lindsay's luggage on his barrow.

'Can I give you a lift?' Sara politely asked Kate. 'I have my car just at the front.'

Where she would of course have found a parking place, thought Kate, but couldn't keep up the prickles. Not when Sara was wearing that ring.

'No, thanks.' She smiled warmly. 'I'm going to my sister's, she's a long way out. I'll take a taxi.'

Chapter Seventeen

'Lovely girl,' commented Lindsay, in the car. 'No wonder Will is crazy about her.'

'No wonder,' Sara agreed. 'Oh, don't worry, Lindsay. I'm not interested in Will Gilbride. Nick is much more my type.' She darted a quick glance at her sister. 'But how are things with you? Has Bobby really got a job?'

'Just for the holidays. He's standing in for someone.'

'But things are working out? You're happy?'

'Do I look happy?'

Sara was negotiating traffic in George Street. 'As a matter of fact, you look a bit under the weather.'

'Yes.' Lindsay shifted her position and sighed. 'Some women bloom, they say, others fade. I'm one who fades.'

'What on earth are you talking about?'

'I did take care, Sara, but it happened just the same.'

'Lindsay! Oh, God, you're not!'

'I am. But don't worry.' Lindsay gave a cool smile. 'I have a ring too.'

Monica's welcome was so ecstatic, Lindsay's heart sank. Her eyes met Sara's in warning and Sara nodded in understanding. No saying anything to Mummy.

'As though I would!' Sara whispered, as she took Lindsay's cases upstairs. 'I'll be glad to leave that to you!'

'Sara's going to a Hogmanay Ball,' Monica told Lindsay happily. 'There'll be just the two of us, darling, so we can have a nice quiet chat together. Have you had supper?'

'Yes, I had something on the train.' Lindsay sank into

a chair. 'I'd like some coffee, though.'

The doorbell rang and it was Nick Ainslie, a solid young man with smooth light hair and horn-rimmed spectacles. Lindsay could vaguely remember him, knew he was a partner in his family's prosperous law firm, thought him really rather nice. But for Sara? It just showed one could never be sure of what someone else wanted. Nick was certainly no Will Gilbride.

There was cheerful chat until Sara wafted downstairs in full-skirted tulle and a fur wrap, and was reverently escorted away by Nick, whose eyes on her were like a child's looking at his presents on Christmas morning.

'Oh, don't they make a handsome pair!' cried Monica, bringing in the coffee tray. 'Aren't they so right for each other? I couldn't be happier about the engagement. Of course, I know Nick's parents well.'

'I'm sure he's ideal in every way,' said Lindsay. She drank some coffee quickly. 'Mummy, I have something to tell you.'

'I wish I didn't know what it was.'

'What do you mean? You can't possibly know.'

'Well, I may never have been pregnant myself' – Monica measured sugar into her coffee with great deliberation – 'but I can recognise the look, you know.'

'So much for me thinking I wasn't showing,' Lindsay said blankly.

'It's not a question of showing. More, as I say, just a look. One can't pinpoint it.' Monica blinked a little as she drank her coffee. 'It's true, then, is it?'

'Yes, it's true.'

'You're going to have a baby.' Monica set down her coffee cup and put her hand to her brow. 'When?'

'Early June.'

'Oh, Lindsay . . .'

'It's all right.' Lindsay reached for her bag. 'Look, here's my wedding ring. I might as well wear it now.' As Monica sat like carved stone, Lindsay said bravely, 'Bobby and I are married. I'm Mrs Gilbride.'

Monica went white. 'You're married, and you never said a word? You're married to Bobby Gilbride? Oh, Lindsay, how could you?'

'Obviously, I had to.'

Monica winced. 'When I think of how you tried to fool Rachel and me! Of course, I knew all the time it was a charade. I had this feeling – oh, I can't believe you could have been so stupid!'

'These things happen.' Lindsay bit hungrily into a chocolate biscuit. Always starving . . . sometimes she could hardly think straight.

'Look, we did take precautions, but they didn't work. It wasn't my fault.'

'You shouldn't have been sleeping with him in the first place!' cried Monica. 'Now you have had to marry him and he couldn't be more unsuitable. A wastrel, who thinks strumming a piano is work, a boy who has broken his mother's heart!'

'I love him. Doesn't that count for something?'

'But does he love you?'

Lindsay hesitated. 'I think he might.'

'Might? That's a fine start, I must say.'

'We're not making a start. He doesn't actually want anything to do with the baby.'

'What?' screamed Monica. 'He doesn't what?'

'He's always said he didn't want to be a father, didn't want to be responsible for someone else's life. He's willing to help me financially, if he can, but we won't be living together.'

'This gets worse,' moaned Monica. 'Just what are you going to do?'

'Well, I thought I'd find myself a flat here.'

'While he stays down in London?'

'We'll just see how things go.'

Monica heaved a deep sigh. 'The only good thing in all of this is that you didn't try anything silly.' She gave Lindsay a sharp glance. 'You didn't think of it, did you?'

'No, I didn't think of it. My mother let me live.' Lindsay shrugged. 'Seems right for me to let my baby live too.'

'But your mother gave you up for adoption,' Monica said quietly.

'Yes, and I can understand why. I think it was marvellous of you to help her out, I really do. A lot of wives wouldn't have done it.'

'A lot of wives?' Monica stared. 'What are you saying? I don't understand you.'

'Come on, you may as well admit it. I even look like her, don't I?'

'Who? Who are you talking about?'

'Abby Baxter, of course. I guessed ages ago that she was my mother.'

'Abby Baxter?' Monica repeated faintly. 'You think Abby Baxter is your mother?'

'I know this must be painful for you, but I couldn't help working it out. Everyone knows there was something between Daddy and Mrs Baxter. You couldn't have any children, so when I was born, you offered to take me. Isn't that the way it was?'

'My poor girl, that was not the way it was.' Monica's voice was shaking. 'Why did you never come to me and tell me what you were thinking?'

'How could I? You never told Sara and me about our real parents, how could I have said anything about Daddy?'

'It's my fault,' Monica muttered. 'I should have made it clear. But please listen to me, my dear. Abby Baxter is not your mother. She did have an affair with your father but it was over years before you were born, and it only happened because I was silly enough to leave Daddy for a while. He couldn't give me children and at first I found that too hard to accept. But he and Abby could never have had you, or any other child.'

It was Lindsay's turn to sit like stone.

'Oh, God, what a fool I feel . . . I was so sure . . . oh, I shan't be able to look her in the eyes the next time we meet! But I always thought she specially cared for me and I thought I knew why.'

'She does care for you, Lindsay, but not because she's your mother. I don't know your real mother, or Sara's. I chose you through the Adoption Society. They told me you came from good backgrounds, but the girls in question had just — '

'I know – made mistakes?' Lindsay asked wearily.

'As you say. But let's not talk any more about mistakes. You're home, you're going to be looked after, then we'll both look after the baby.'

'I did say I'd take a flat.'

'Which would be ridiculous. When Sara marries, I'm going to be alone in this big house. I want you here.' As Lindsay hesitated, Monica added quickly, 'It's no easy matter, bringing up a child on your own, and you know you'll have no help from Bobby.'

Lindsay sat back in her chair. She felt exhausted, completely drained.

'All right, Mummy. If it's what you want. Thank you.'

'Now – do you know something?' Monica glanced at the carriage clock on the mantelpiece. 'It's nearly midnight. I'm going to bring in the champagne!'

She hurried away, to return with glasses and a bottle in an ice pail. 'I had this ready, I thought we'd have our own celebration. Of course, I'm getting more than I bargained for!' She drew the cork and laughed as the champagne bubbled into the glasses and overflowed. 'Oh, to think of a baby in this house again, even if it is Bobby Gilbride's! Come on, dear, make the toast. To the baby and to all of us. Happy New Year!'

'Happy New Year,' said Lindsay dazedly.

Chapter Eighteen

All over the city, the glasses were being raised to the sound of the chimes of Big Ben from the wireless. 1953 had arrived.

'Och, I feel a bit better, now I've had ma dram,' Peggie Kemp murmured, after the family had exchanged kisses and hugs. Aye, even though the kids outside were running round the houses, whooping and calling, letting off fireworks, frightening everybody to death. It was Hogmanay, after all, you had to live and let live. Just for once, eh?

'Jamie, I'll take a wee bit more in ma glass,' she called to her son. 'Betty, where's your mince pies?'

'Kate, will you wake up Ewan?' asked Biddy. 'See, he's slept through the bells again. Ivery year, he's in that chair and doesna ken a thing that's going on!'

'Your dad's asleep and all,' said Ivy. 'Still, they're no' down the pub, eh?'

'Not long back.' Biddy herself leaped to her feet and shook her black-headed husband awake. 'Och, I hope you've better luck with your Will, Kate, than I've had with this one here!'

'What's up?' asked Ewan, sitting up, spluttering. 'Biddy, give over knocking me!'

'Come on, you're the dark one, get yourself doon the stair,' she said imperiously. 'Be our first foot and bring us some luck!'

'Oh, God . . .' Ewan staggered to his feet. 'Where's ma coal, then? Where's ma bread and salt?'

'Come on, Frankie,' Malcolm said, pushing him towards the door. 'You're the nearest we have to a dark-haired man, so you're nominated first-foot. Out you go!'

'My hair's pretty well grey,' protested Frankie. 'I'll be no good.'

'Oh, what a piece of nonsense it all is, anyway!' cried Rachel. 'Why must it be a man? My hair's still dark. I'll go myself.'

'No, no, we need all the luck we can get,' retorted Malcolm. 'Frankie, here's your coal.'

'I don't need any luck,' Mac whispered to Jennie. 'I reckon I've struck lucky already.'

'I need some luck for Will,' she whispered back, under cover of the laughter as Frankie solemnly let himself out of the front door and crossed the threshold back again.

'He'll be home for the Coronation, Jennie,' Mac went on, watching Rachel cut the traditional piece of cake for Frankie. 'And that'll be grand, eh? Double celebration!'

'Can't say I'll be thinking of it.'

'Och, it'll cheer us all up. She's a bonny young queen and we can all wish her well.'

'We're ordering a stack of televisions,' Abby announced. 'If the ceremony's televised, there'll be a tremendous rush to buy sets.'

'Fancy folk being able to see it at home!' Madge exclaimed.

'I could get you a set, Ma. Would you like that?'

'Oh, I don't know, dear. I seem to have so many new things.'

'I know what you're thinking,' Abby said softly. 'You're thinking of Catherine's Land. Old things and old days. Shall we drink a toast? To Catherine's Land?'

'No,' Madge said sharply. 'Catherine's Land is dead and gone. You can't drink a toast to it now.'

'To memories, then.' Abby stood up. 'Malcolm, I'd like to propose a toast. To the old days, to memories.'

'To the old days, to memories,' they echoed, and Rachel asked if anyone else would like cake. But Hamish, gloomily studying his mother still in conversation with Mac, was her only taker.

The telephone rang in the hall.

'I'll go,' said Rachel. 'Probably some drunk.'

She was away some time.

'Not a drunk, then,' murmured Abby.

'Well!' Rachel was standing in the doorway, holding herself as tightly strung as a bow. 'That was Monica! Do you know what she's just told me? I can't believe it, I absolutely can't believe it!'

'Tell us what it is, then,' groaned Malcolm.

'Bobby and Lindsay are married. Married! Without a word to any of us.' Rachel came into the room, staring round at the company with wild dark eyes. 'Can you believe it? Married!'

'Married?' Malcolm's face was dark red. 'Why? Why like that? Keeping it a secret from everybody?'

'Oh, why do you think?' Rachel snatched up her drink and drained it. 'Because there's a baby on the way, of course!'

'I've been afraid of this all along,' said Abby. 'Frankie, had you any idea?'

'Me? No idea at all. I've scarcely seen Lindsay.'

'The poor silly girl,' sighed Madge. 'People are always saying that girls know so much more these days, but it seems to me they're just the same as they always were.'

'I think Lindsay has trapped Bobby into marriage!' Rachel cried dramatically. 'She's the one who wants it, not him, it's the last thing he'd ever want, he can't support himself, never mind a wife. Oh, why didn't they tell us about the baby? Why didn't they let us help them?'

'What could you have done?' asked Jennie. 'It was Bobby's duty to marry Lindsay. Would you have wanted her to struggle on by herself?'

'I'm thinking of her as much as him. I know him, you see, I know he doesn't love her.' Rachel flung herself into a chair and stared desperately into space. 'He doesn't love anyone, and that's the truth. It will all end in disaster.'

'A fine New Year this is turning out to be,' muttered Malcolm. 'We're all supposed to be celebrating in nineteen fifty-three. What have we got to look forward to now, I ask you?'

'A great-grandchild,' Madge said quietly. 'Isn't that something to celebrate?'

Chapter Nineteen

June the second was the day announced for the Coronation.

'That's the date the baby's due,' said Lindsay, who could think of nothing else.

'Don't worry, it won't come on time,' Monica told her. 'First babies never do.'

'I hope you're right. Don't want to spoil your day. Specially since you've bought a television set.'

'Spoil my day! You think your baby's coming would spoil my day?'

'Don't get to see a coronation very often, remember.'

'My priority would be seeing my grandchild. Lindsay, I can't wait!'

'Neither can I,' said Lindsay.

Propped against pillows on her bed, she studied her thickened ankles that she had been told to put up every single day. Her pregnancy was not going well. There was a risk of toxaemia, the doctors were talking about bed-rest in the maternity home. Meanwhile, Bobby was as free as the breeze in London, eating what he liked, going where he liked, demonstrating as much connection with the baby kicking Lindsay as the man in the moon. That was the nature of things, of course. What wouldn't I give to change it, thought Lindsay.

As Monica left to do some shopping – she was constantly adding to the baby's layette – Sara looked in, fresh as a daisy in a little suit with nipped-in waist and a hat that was a few flowers perched on her fair hair. She was going with Nick to some reception for visiting lawyers, then on to dinner somewhere, just wanted to say Hi, how was Lindsay feeling?

'Same as usual. Tired of looking at these elephantine legs. Wishing I could be you instead of me.'

'Oh, come on.' Sara laughed uneasily. 'You needn't wish that.'

'You mean your turn'll come? You might not have my problems, you know. Some people sail through it.'

'Watch it, I'm not even married yet!' Sara stood at the door, laughing, but still to Lindsay appearing uneasy.

'That's true. You know, I thought you'd have set the date by now. I'm sure Mummy's wondering.'

'No, she's not, your baby's taking all the limelight, thank God.'

Lindsay sat up and gave her sister a long considering look. 'Sara, everything's all right, isn't it? Between you and Nick?'

'Everything's fine.' Sara adjusted her little hat of flowers in Lindsay's mirror. 'Where's the rush to get married? It's nice just being engaged. Must dash – take care, Lindsay.'

'Don't get the chance to do much else, do I?'

'So, when's this great-grandchild due, then?' asked Peggie, plying Madge with swiss roll in the living room of the Kemps' council house. They were alone, Jamie and Betty being out at work, their children grown up and away. Peggie said she got that lonely sometimes. And what was there to do, 'cept look out at nothing?

'June the second, Coronation Day,' Madge answered, cutting her dry swiss roll into small pieces in an effort to make it easier to get down. 'We're all getting excited.'

'Och, it'll no' come on the day. First babies never do.'

'I suppose it would be a shame, if they missed everything.'

'I'm no' bothered maself.' Peggie lit a Woodbine. 'But our Jamie's talking of hiring a telly. Says it'll give me something to do. I ask you, Madge, do I want to spend ma time goggling at a box?'

'I feel the same, but Abby's getting me one too and I don't like to say no.'

'Was better in the old days, eh? When we'd plenty to do?'

'A bit too much, to be honest,' Madge said with a smile. 'Life's easier for everybody now. All these washing machines! Do you remember doing the washing in the basement at Catherine's Land? That great copper? And the mangle?'

'Aye, then getting everything dry and doing the ironing with flat irons!' Peggie smiled. 'That reminds me, Madge, do you know what they've been doing to our old place? Concreted over all the green! Aye, I'm telling you! Where we had the street parties for the kids, where we hung the sheets, it's all been made into a courtyard for they students to sit, wi' plants in pots and trees growing out of nowhere! Would you credit it?'

'Yes,' Madge said darkly, 'I would.'

'You've no' been back to see it?'

'No, I've not been back. And I've no intention of going, either. I don't want to see it. Jennie looks in sometimes, I never thought she would.'

'Jennie still seeing the sailor fella?' asked Peggie.

'They keep in touch.'

'Was somebody telling me she'd been down to Southampton?'

'Just the once.' Madge was defensive.

'Well, why not, eh? Maybe they dinna want to get wed?'

Madge shrugged. 'She might be waiting for Will to come home.'

'Might be a double wedding, eh? Him and Kate?'

'We'll have to wait and see.'

They finished their tea and Madge said she must go, she'd come again soon. Peggie insisted on walking with her to the tram stop through the lines of stark houses, where no trees broke the monotony of the overall greyness, where no flowers lined the stretches of flattened grass. Of course, Catherine's Land had borne no flowers, either. Why did Madge feel it was different? Perhaps because there had been a sense of community in Catherine's Land that was lacking here. Maybe it would come. It would take time.

'Do you sometimes think they could have done more?' Madge asked Peggie, as they stood near a group of raw little shops, where papers blew and women hauled children in and out.

'It's rehousing, Madge, it's better than a slum. That's all you can say.'

'People should expect more. So Kate says.'

'Kate'll learn,' Peggie said dourly. 'I expected more. Now I put up with what I've got.'

'Still, we should look on the bright side,' Madge said, feeling more cheerful as her tram hove into sight. 'I mean, folk are getting TV sets now, when they used to have no shoes.'

'Madge, you're a tonic. If you find something good to say, you say it!'

90

The two women hugged again and Madge told Peggie to get her knitting needles out and make something nice for her great-grand-child.

'Wi' Mrs Farrell for a grannie, it'll no' want for a thing,' said Peggie with truth, as Madge climbed creakily on to the tram and was borne away.

Chapter Twenty

June the second came at last, the day of the big switch-on. If you had a television set, you were glued to it. If you didn't have one, you visited someone who had. If all else failed, you listened to the wireless. But most people didn't want to miss the spectacle, the chance to join in a ceremony hitherto confined to the 'nobs', to take part in the biggest outside broadcast of all.

In Edinburgh, the Princes Street decorations that included EIIR ciphers had been given an all-night guard, in case the Scottish Nationalists should try to carry out their threat to tear them down. But all was tranquil. The dull grey light of morning showed the streets to be deserted, with everyone at home tuning in. Only people such as Kate, who had to help prepare the paper's souvenir edition, were at work.

'What a fuss, eh?' asked Moray Chalmers. 'Must be something more important happening in the world.'

But word came through that the troops in Korea were firing red, white and blue smoke shells, and the men were all giving three cheers for the Queen. Kate's eyes filled with tears at the thought of patriotic Will.

'Och, I'm no' a red,' she told Moray. 'I wouldna want to see the royals go. Just want to even things out a bit, eh?'

'Even things out a lot,' said Moray with feeling.

Across the capital, people were joining together. It was rather like Christmas, no one wanted to be alone. Abby, Rachel and Malcolm had gone to Madge's, to watch events on the fine set Abby had insisted on presenting to Madge. Frankie, in London, had earlier telephoned to say he'd never been so busy, had been playing everywhere for Coronation parties and dances. Bobby, too, had finally made his breakthrough, with engagements to play at several big hotels throughout the celebrations.

'But Lindsay's baby is due today,' Abby told Frankie. 'You'd think Bobby would have come up, wouldn't you?'

'No,' Frankie retorted. 'I wouldn't.'

All the Rossies, including Biddy and her family, had been invited to Donnie Muir's, Donnie having hired a TV set after long persuasion from Sally. All the Finnegans had been invited to the Kemps. Only Nick Ainslie, however, had been asked by Monica to join the Farrells. Too many people might tire Lindsay, who must conserve her strength, who was lucky indeed not to be in the maternity home at that very moment, the doctors having only lately decided not to bring the baby on.

'It's always better to do things the natural way,' Monica decreed, as she made sure that Lindsay had her feet up and a cushion at her back. 'And the doctors do think you are a little better, dear.'

'How can they say that?' cried Lindsay. 'Look at my ankles! They're like tree trunks!'

'It's only fluid,' Sara said knowledgeably. 'That'll all go as soon as the baby is born.'

'Know all about it, do you?' asked Lindsay, trying vainly to make herself comfortable. 'Anyway, this baby will never be born.'

The TV set was showing pictures of the London crowds, bravely enduring their wait in the rain, ready to cheer anything, even a street sweeper pushing his broom. Then came views of the Abbey, peers and peeresses taking their places, grand clerics standing around in splendid vestments, the organ softly playing.

'I've got coffee and sandwiches all ready,' Monica whispered. 'And when the Queen is crowned, Nick's going to open the champagne.'

'Quiet, Mummy,' ordered Sara. 'Here she comes!'

At the sight of the monarch leaving Buckingham Palace, everyone fell silent. The young woman, already so familiar, seemed at the same time a stranger, a Sun Queen from history, her face pale beneath her tiara, her dress so stiffly embroidered, it might have stood by itself. In her left hand she carried a trailing bouquet of flowers. Footmen held the rich length of her train. Waiting to carry her on her journey to the Abbey, under the triumphal arches that spanned the route, was her coach, so wonderfully decorated it looked like a three-dimensional fairy-tale.

'Oh, I've never seen anything so beautiful!' cried Monica.

'Never,' gasped Lindsay, pressing her back against her cushion.

'Pity it couldn't have been in colour,' murmured Sara. 'That'll be the next thing to come.'

Through the cheering crowds and the rain, the horses drew the Queen's coach to the great west door of Westminster Abbey, and as she entered to the music of Parry's psalm, 'I was glad', ten Queen's Scholars from Westminster School made the traditional shout of welcome: '*Vivat*! *Vivat Regina* Elizabeth! *Vivat*! *Vivat*!'

'Oh, God,' whispered Lindsay, rising. 'I think the baby's going to be on time.'

That afternoon there were street parties for the children, and at night scouts carried a flaming torch to light the bonfire on Arthur's Seat. There were firework displays and open-air dancing. Crowds, released from their viewing, roamed everywhere, drinking, laughing, greeting strangers as though it were VE Night all over again. And at two minutes to midnight, Elizabeth Monica Abigail Gilbride was born, a beautiful baby weighing seven pounds, three ounces. As her mother's ankles miraculously dwindled and a sense of euphoria gripped the family, Nick opened the champagne they'd all forgotten about until then.

'To the Queen!' cried Monica.

But Sara said, 'No, no, to the baby! To little Gail!'

'Come along darling,' Monica said to Lindsay, in her private room, 'the nurse will let you have a tiny sip of champagne, I'm sure.'

But Lindsay was asleep.

Chapter Twenty-One

The Korean War ended on 27 July, 1953. Nothing much had been gained by either the Communist North Koreans or the non-Communist South Koreans, but a great many people died anyway. Will Gilbride, thanking God for his good luck, was not one of them. All he wanted now was to get home, and August was his date. There was general rejoicing in the family and the hope that he might even make Baby Gail's christening, arranged for the middle Sunday of the month. But Lindsay wondered, would Bobby make it?

She knew she was foolish to expect anything from him, but then he had surprised her by turning up to see the baby when she was still in the maternity home. As soon as she saw him, her hopes had rocketed. He would see Gail, he would hold her, he would have a change of heart. It hadn't happened.

'Don't you think she's lovely?' she asked, as Bobby gingerly held his daughter for the first time. 'Look, she's got your eyes, the Ritchie eyes!'

'The Ritchie eyes are dark, her eyes are blue.'

'All new babies have blue eyes, but Gail's are changing. Your mother said that only yesterday. She thinks Gail is going to look just like her.'

'Trust Mum to get in on the act.' Bobby carefully replaced the baby in her cot and sat down with a sigh of relief. He briefly touched Lindsay's hand.

'Bet you're glad that's over, then?'

Lindsay stared at him stonily. 'Haven't you anything at all to say about Gail, Bobby? I thought, when you saw her, you might feel differently.'

'Remember our deal? It still stands.'

'How can you be so hard? Talking about deals! That's a person there in that cot, Bobby, a person we're responsible for!'

'You're responsible for.' Bobby shook his head. 'I'm sorry, Lindsay, I'd like to feel differently, but I can't. And things are just taking off for me in London. I'm getting the work, I'm getting known. There's just no way I could take on a family.'

Lindsay was silent, watching Gail squirm in her sleep, small fists doubled, Ritchie eyes squeezed.

'Will you at least come to the christening?'

'I don't know. You know I'm not religious, what's the point?'

'It's something I'd like you to do for me. Be there, on our child's special day. It would mean a lot to me.'

'OK, I'll try.'

Perhaps she shouldn't have been surprised when he rang to say he couldn't make it, he had an engagement to play in Brighton with a saxophonist who was top notch, but the hurt was suddenly more than she could bear. She put Gail in her pram, threw on her jacket and slammed out of Monica's house, intent on going anywhere or nowhere, she didn't care. For some time, she pushed the large expensive pram across hot pavements, refusing to let her angry tears fall, murmuring to the alert young baby for some kind of comfort.

'There's just the two of us, Gail, just you and me. That's what he wants, that's what we want. From now on, we forget him, all right?'

'Why, hello, Lindsay!' someone said, and it was Nick, dressed in his city clothes, yet not at work.

'Going to the Botanics?' he asked kindly. 'Just the day to feed the ducks.'

'The Botanics?'

To her astonishment, Lindsay saw that she was outside the main gate to the Royal Botanic Gardens. Subconsciously she had brought herself here, to a place to walk in and be alone in. But here too was Nick, walking alongside the pram and looking terrible.

'Is anything wrong, Nick?' She had the feeling she knew already what it was.

'Let's go to the tearoom,' he said quietly.

* * *

96

So, they'd split up, Sara and Nick. No reason. Just wasn't working out.

'For her,' Nick murmured, staring into his coffee cup. 'It was working out fine for me.'

'Nick, I'm so sorry. Sara hasn't said a word.'

'Probably doesn't want to tell your mother.'

'Oh, no, I'd forgotten Mummy!' Lindsay pushed the pram to and fro, watching Gail's eyes finally close. 'Nick, she's going to be so disappointed. Sara's was going to be the wedding of the year for her, all stops out.'

'I know. My parents feel just as bad. They like Sara so much.'

'Maybe she'll change her mind?'

'No, I'm not going to hope for that. I'm just not the one for her, I think at the back of my mind I always knew that. I'm what you'd call dull.'

'Not dull!' cried Lindsay. 'Dependable. Someone to be trusted. If you don't think those things matter, let me tell you that they do!'

He pressed her hand. 'Ah, Lindsay – do I take it Bobby isn't coming up for the christening?'

'He's not coming to anything ever again. I've had enough.'

'If there's anything I can do – '

'Thanks, Nick, but we're fine, Gail and me. We have everything we need. More than we need. We're very lucky.'

'Gail is lucky,' Nick said seriously. 'To have you.'

Lindsay stood up and released the brake of the pram. 'I'd better get back, or I'll be having to feed Gail in the Ladies'. People seem to treat you as a criminal if you try to nurse in public places.'

'I'll walk back with you, then.'

'No, there's no need. You stay on, have another coffee.'

At the door of the teashop, she turned to look back at him and he waved and smiled, but she thought he must look rather as she looked herself, as though he were progressing through some unending ordeal.

Why do we hurt each other so much? she asked herself, hurrying home, as Gail woke up and began to stuff her fingers into her mouth and twisted her face, ready to cry. At least I have something else to think about. I can put Bobby right out of my mind.

But feeding Gail in the peace of the little nursery Monica had created for them, Lindsay found Bobby still very much with her.

* * *

97

The christening, organised by Monica, went off with machine-like precision. The godparents, Abby, Frankie and an old school-friend of Lindsay's, performed their roles perfectly. Gail, in a family christening robe, did not cry. Following the cathedral service, everyone went back to Selkirk Street, where the tea, of course, was delicious.

Only Madge and Jennie were not quite at ease. They told Abby they found Monica just too overpowering, and so very grand. Abby said robustly that she was kind, not grand, and they shouldn't look for slights that were not there.

'Oh, there aren't any slights.' Madge said hastily. 'And I'm not saying I really feel out of place.'

'Not like when we used to go to Rachel's and she had that awful maid,' put in Jennie. 'The one who knew we came from Catherine's Land and never let us forget it.'

'It's just that Mrs Farrell comes from a different world, that's all,' said Madge. 'We realise it here.'

'I'm sure she's always made you very welcome,' Abby replied.

'Very welcome,' Madge and Jennie agreed. But stayed close together, nevertheless.

Sara, working hard to help her mother as hostess, was looking strained and pink about the eyes, but was certain, as she told Lindsay, that she had done the right thing in giving up Nick. She did care for him deeply, but only as a friend. Marriage would have been a terrible mistake and she was glad she had found out in time.

'He's so upset,' said Lindsay. 'Asked if I'd mind if he didn't come today. Couldn't bear to see you, I suppose.'

'Well, I'm upset, too.'

'You're the one who broke it off, it's easier for you.'

'These things happen, there's nothing anyone can do.'

The doorbell rang and a new guest was ushered in, a stranger. Or so he seemed, until Jennie screamed, 'Will!', and ran to take him in her arms.

Monica's guests looked on in amazement as all Will's relations gathered round to hug and kiss him. Who was this tall, bronzed young man in a dark suit that seemed too small for him? Another Gilbride, it was explained, who had just returned from Korea, where he had gained a second pip on his shoulder and was the nearest thing to a hero.

'Oh, Will, I can't believe you're here!' Jennie breathed. 'Hamish – Ma – can you believe it?'

No one could believe it, but there he was, in the old interview suit he had put on after arriving at the bungalow, where he had found Jennie's note, telling him where they all were.

'I knew you were due any time, so I left the note just in case.' Jennie kissed Will's cheek again. 'But I never thought for a minute you'd actually come, not for a minute!'

'Glad I made it before the end. Where's the guest of honour?'

When he had admired Gail and congratulated Lindsay, stooping to kiss her and tactfully not asking about Bobby, Hamish told him in a whisper that he ought to know that Mum was practically engaged. In fact, acting as if she was married already.

'To that merchant navy chap?' Will raised his fair brows. 'Well, why not, Hamish?'

'Seems funny to me, she'd want to marry again.'

'What I've learned since I've been away is that folk should do what they want, before it's too late.'

As Hamish shrugged and moved away, Will turned to find himself looking at Sara.

'Like some tea?' she asked jauntily, though he thought she didn't look well. 'Or will you wait for the champagne? We're just about to drink the baby's health.'

'I wouldn't mind some tea first. And some of those sandwiches.'

'They're so tiny, you'd better take half a dozen.'

He laughed as she piled his plate. 'And how are you, Sara?'

'Fine. Well, I would be, but I've just broken off my engagement.'

'I'm sorry to hear that.'

'Let me get you some tea.'

The housekeeper and a hired waitress were serving champagne. Frankie was on his feet, making a short speech, the guests were applauding, then raising their glasses to Baby Gail. Lindsay was responding, thanking everyone, trying not to look as though there was a void beside her as big as a crater, knowing only too well that people were missing Bobby and blaming him. A fact that made Rachel's face take on its dark frown and Malcolm to stare glumly at his well-polished shoes.

'Thank goodness that's all over,' Sara's voice observed at

Will's side. 'Now I suppose you'll be wanting to be off, won't you?'

As he gave an enquiring stare, she said roughly, 'To see your Kate, of course.'

She despised herself for being so obvious, but Will seemed to think it the most natural thing in the world that she should speed him on his way.

'Oh, God, yes,' he agreed, and at the stark longing in his blue eyes, Sara had to look away.

Chapter Twenty-Two

He had already telephoned her, he knew she would be waiting. She was in the street, in fact, pacing up and down, ready to meet, melt, so they were as one before they'd even reached her divan. But there they made love as though the furies were after them, as though they would never be satisfied, never have enough of each other's bodies, never make up for the long, long time apart.

They parted at last.

'It's like a dream you're back,' gasped Kate.

'You're the dream, Kate. I've thought of this moment so often, lived it over and over again, wondering if it would ever happen —'

'Is it happening? Is it?'

They made love again, then laughed and gloried in each other, lying back, too spent to move.

'I'm hungry,' Will said suddenly. 'Got anything to eat?'

'Not a thing. I was too superstitious to buy anything. In case you didn't come.'

'Superstitious? You? I don't believe it.'

'You'd be surprised what fear can do. I've never walked under a ladder since you went away.' Kate sprang up, finding her clothes. 'Let's go out to eat.'

'On a Sunday? Will there be anything open?'

'Have you forgotten? This is Festival time! I know just the place – it's new – below the Castle – you'll like it.'

'So, who's taken you there?' asked Will, dressing quickly.

'Taken me? No one's taken me. I take maself to restaurants, I pay ma own way.' Kate's beautiful eyes were serious. 'There's been nobody for me since you went away, Will. If I need to tell you that.'

'You don't, I'm sorry.' He kissed her swiftly. 'There's been nobody for me, either.'

'Aren't we virtuous?'

'Yes. You were worth waiting for, Kate.'

She caught her breath. 'Oh, Will —'

They held each other quietly, kissing with sweet relief.

'This won't do,' Kate said, drawing away. 'We'll never get any food at this rate.'

'You're hungry, too?'

'Starving.'

'So am I.'

As she closed and locked her front door, Will took Kate's hand.

'I suppose the next thing you'll be wanting is a ring?' he asked fondly.

'A ring? When have I ever said I wanted a ring?'

'I thought all girls liked rings.'

'Dress rings.' Kate looked intently into Will's eyes. 'You're far too young to be worrying about an engagement, Will. You've your career to think about. So have I.'

'But – what'll we do?' he asked blankly.

'See each other, have sex, be happy. Doesna mean we have to tie ourselves down.'

As Will seemed struck dumb, Kate caught his arm. 'Come on, what are you worrying about? Most guys'd be only too pleased not to have to get involved.'

'I am involved,' Will said huskily.

'You know what I mean. Let's get going.'

As they walked slowly up the Royal Mile towards the Lawnmarket, merging with the Festival crowds, Kate smiled and said there was something she wanted to ask him.

'Did they really fire red, white and blue shells in Korea for the Coronation?'

'Now how did that get out?'

'A message came through. Well, did you?'

'Yes, it did happen. Why not? It was a bit of fun.'

'And did you all give three cheers for the Queen as well?'

'Of course. Queen and country – they mean a lot when you're in a place like Korea.'

'I know. I cheered too, in ma own way.'

'A patriotic red?' he asked, laughing.

'Pink.' Kate took his arm. 'See what's ahead, Will?'

'I'm looking.' His eyes were on the mass of scaffolding covering the building to his right. 'Good God, Kate, is that Catherine's Land?'

'Catherine's Hall. It's nearly finished.'

'With all that scaffolding?'

'Due down soon, they say. First students should be in by October.'

The summer evening was still light and people strolling past were stopping to look at the new building taking shape from three old tenements. Some were even venturing under the scaffolding, though builders' notices were everywhere: No Admission – Keep Out. Kate said she'd kept a regular eye on progress, which had not been quick because of shortage of materials and various other problems. Around Christmas time, work had stopped altogether, but had speeded up again during the summer. Now, though it didn't look like it, the end was in sight.

'Can't make out, really, just what's left of our place, can you?' asked Will.

'If you put your head under the scaffolding, you can see the windows are the same, they've just been given new frames,' Kate told him. 'And they've kept the ornamental bits on the roof that say the date. It's the inside that's going to be quite different. Completely carved up into study bedrooms.' Kate scowled. 'Well, we saw the plans, eh?'

'Door's new. Remember the old one, always hanging open?'

'Do I not?' Kate moved forward to peer through the sheets of polythene hanging from the scaffolding. 'You can see the new shops,' she called back. 'There are notices – looks like there's going to be a coffee shop and a book shop. And a grocery – poor old Danny! Remember his shop, Will?'

'Come on out of there!' he ordered. 'You haven't got a hard hat.'

'Wish we could have seen the old stair,' Kate said, scrambling back. 'Wonder what they've done with it. All the dear students will be using the lifts, of course. No running up the stair for them.' Kate's lip curled. 'When I think what we could have done with a fraction of the money that's being spent on this place!' She grasped Will's hand. 'Let's go through the wynd at the side. That'll be safe enough and you can get to see the new courtyard from there.'

'Courtyard?'

'Yes, they've got rid of the old drying green. It's all beautifully paved now and there are going to be tubs of flowers and God knows what.'

They moved through the narrow passage that had once run by the side of Catherine's Land's neighbouring tenement. In the old days, this had been a way of reaching the back green without going through the basements of the tenements. Now it led to a fine paved courtyard, from which the newly plastered walls of the houses rose to the sky.

'Will you look at this?' breathed Will. 'Remember our mothers hanging the washing out here?'

'And us playing in the shelters when the war came?' added Kate.

A group of young people, probably students, had followed them into the courtyard and were looking round admiringly.

'Gee, isn't this great?' asked a ginger-haired man with an American accent. 'Say, if we get any sun in Edinburrow, you girls'll surely be able to sunbathe here!'

'I can't wait to move in,' said a girl, gazing up at the darkening evening sky. 'I think it's just beautiful.'

'I wonder who Catherine was?' another girl said. 'I mean, why is it called Catherine's Hall?'

'Catherine was the wife of the merchant who built one of the tenements that's been converted,' Kate told them briskly. 'It was the middle house, it was the best. He called it Catherine's Land.'

'A Land is a tenement,' explained Will. 'A building with several storeys and a common stair.'

'Only you'll be using lifts,' said Kate.

'Say, that's interesting,' said the ginger-haired man. 'When would all this be, then?'

'You'll be able to see the date on the roof. Seventeen hundred and one.'

'Wow! do you think she walks?'

'Walks?'

'This Catherine. Think she haunts the place?'

'No, she doesn't walk, she doesn't haunt.'

'No ghosts?'

'No ghosts,' Kate said firmly.

'I'm not so sure that that's true,' Will commented, as he and Kate left the courtyard and continued up the Lawnmarket. 'My mum thinks there are plenty of ghosts in Catherine's Land.'

'Catherine's Hall, Will. There'll be no ghosts in Catherine's Hall.'

'You don't think the students'll see a little Kate and a little Will running down the stair to school?'

'They won't even see the stair. Not from their super lifts.'

'Don't be too hard on them, Kate. They're only young, like us. It's not their fault that their new hall was our home once.'

'It's just the unfairness.' Kate groaned, then gave a sudden laugh. 'Och, it always is, but let's no' get started on that tonight. Let's go and get something to eat.'

They began to quicken their steps towards the restaurant, while in the courtyard where sheets had once flapped and children played, the young people still wandered, looking for ghosts they would never see.

Part Two

1956–1958

Chapter Twenty-Three

Madge said she didn't want to see the last tram go down the
Mound. It was just another nail in the coffin of all she knew and
was used to, just another change for change's sake. Why should
buses be any better than the trams that were a part of everyone's
life? No one could remember Edinburgh without its trams! She
herself had used them since 1912. They'd been cable cars then, of
course, the Corporation didn't bring in the electrified lines till
1922. Couldn't the girls remember the excitement? And now the
trams were to go, pushed on the scrap heap, like everything else
that had to give way to modern times. Well, the girls could go to
the so-called celebration on the Mound if they wanted to, but they
could go without her.

'Celebration?' She shook her head. 'It should be a wake.'

On that bleak November evening in 1956, the 'girls', Jennie
and Rachel, didn't try to persuade Madge to change her mind.
Usually so easy-going, on the rare occasions when she took a
stand there was no moving her.

'You stay by the fire, Ma, and and watch the telly,' Jennie told
her. 'Have a nice quiet time.'

'I think I'll just do my knitting, Jennie. The telly's been very
depressing lately. So much bad news.'

That was true, the sisters agreed. There'd been Suez, when the
British had nearly gone to war over the nationalisation of the
Canal and had only just stepped back from the brink. Then there'd
been the attempt by the Hungarians to rise against the Russians,
and the Russians had simply rolled their tanks into Budapest and
crushed the whole thing. Everyone had seen the pictures,
everyone knew the fear. If this was peace, what was war? Hardly

seemed worth worrying over the trams going, did it? On the other hand, the trams were here and so far, thank God, the Russian tanks were not.

'I know what you mean, Ma,' Jennie agreed. 'In the old days, we didn't know what was going on.'

'Ought to know what's going on,' said Rachel. 'But come on, Jennie, if you're coming.'

'Rachel has to find a place to park, Ma. Are you sure you'll be all right?'

'Of course I'll be all right.' Madge looked at them over the top of her reading glasses. 'Take care now, and we'll have a nice hot drink when you get back.'

'Stubborn as a mule,' Rachel commented, as she drove through Corstorphine. 'She might have enjoyed herself if she'd come with us.'

'No, she wouldn't have enjoyed herself. It's one more change and she's had enough of change.'

'Some changes are for the better. Look how you moaned about leaving Catherine's Land, but you're quite happy in the bungalow, aren't you?' Rachel snatched a sideways glance at her sister. 'Well, you would be, if you weren't dreaming of Mac all the time. Why don't you just marry him?'

'We have our arrangements,' Jennie answered with a small secret smile.

Rachel's smile was knowing. 'Your little trips to Southampton? Well, I suppose it's a good compromise. But I think Ma would be happy for you to make it official. I really don't think she'd mind being on her own.'

'She says that, but I couldn't leave her. Will and Hamish have their own places now, and you and Abby are too busy to spend much time with her.'

'We do what we can.'

'I know, but Southampton is just too far away. Mac will be leaving the service one day, we don't mind waiting.'

'As you're not really waiting anyway, I suppose.' Rachel laughed. 'I mean, with your trips south.'

In the shadows of the car, Jennie blushed.

All Edinburgh had come to the Mound, or so it seemed, but that was the way of the city. Created long ago when excavations were made for the New Town, the Mound was not just an artificial hill. It was a focal point for whatever was going on. Meetings, marches, victory parades, coronation celebrations, people liked to meet on the Mound. Line the pavements, spill over on to the grassy slopes below the Assembly Hall, look up at the Castle that graciously looked down.

Now, police and TV cameras had joined the crowds waiting for the appearance of Car 217 on its farewell journey. But things were running so late, there were rumours that the TV crew might have to pack up and go. What a shame, eh? Where was the procession, then? Held up all along the route, by revellers clinging on to the tram and the old horse bus brought out of retirement for the occasion. Och, couldna blame folk, could you? Wanting to say goodbye to the past?

Somewhere in the crowd was Abby, who had come over from Logie's with Lindsay, now working part-time in Accounts, and Hamish from Tailoring, where he was a junior cutter. Young Nina Muir was there, too, all on her own, as Donnie had had another attack and Sally was looking after him, worried sick over Nina alone in all the crowds. And with her interview at Logie's next day too!

'You be careful,' she had called, as Nina went joyously out for one of the new buses. 'You come straight home, soon as you've seen the tram away!'

Jessie Rossie, like Madge, had said she would no' be going to the Mound. What a piece of nonsense, eh? But Ken had been persuaded to go by Kate, who told him it was high time he went somewhere other than the pub, his only solace since Ivy died in March. Just another attack of bronchitis, they'd all thought, but one night Ken had gone up to bed and found her dead, her eyes open and staring, her cigarette, luckily in its ashtray, still curling smoke across her face.

'I'll niver get over it,' wailed Ken. 'I just want her back, Kate, I just want her back!'

'We all want her back,' Kate told him. 'But you'll have to face it, she's no' coming. Now, you come on out and see the last tram and try to take your mind off things. I'll be there with Will.'

'He really annoys me,' she murmured to Will at the foot of the Mound where she had told her father to meet her. 'Never took a

111

scrap of notice of ma mother when she was alive. Now she's dead, he canna stop thinking about her.'

'That's the way it goes.' Will turned up the collar of his good dark overcoat against the wind. 'You only appreciate things when you've lost them.'

'Ah, that's not true.' Kate squeezed his arm. 'I appreciate you, Will, and thank God I havena lost you!'

She looked at him in the light of the street lamps. thinking how well he looked, how prosperous. He had done well at the bank since his return from Korea; there seemed no ceiling to his ambition or prospects. Six months before, they had taken the plunge and moved in together, finding a New Town basement flat that suited them both, especially since Kate was now working for an Edinburgh evening paper and no longer had to travel to Glasgow. Will had been a little apprehensive at first about their sharing a flat when they were not married, but the sky had not fallen in, nothing had been said by anyone, they were radiantly happy. Sometimes a little worry crossed Kate's mind that she was perhaps too happy. Things had dropped into her lap with too little effort, and she wasn't used to getting things without effort, hadn't been brought up in Catherine's Land for nothing. But she was a realist. If there was no need to worry, she wouldn't worry.

'Now where is that man?' she asked. 'I told him where to stand.'

'Be lucky to find him in this crush,' said Will. 'He'll be OK, anyway.'

'I'm no' happy about him being on his own, he'll be feeling depressed as it is, and I told him to come.'

'Hi!' cried a voice, but it was Hamish who had reached them, not Ken. 'Look who I've found!' He was holding Nina Muir by the hand.

She smiled shyly at Kate and Will. 'I was trying to climb up on the steps of the gallery, but I got trapped in all the folk. Then Hamish rescued me. Havena seen a thing so far.'

'Nothing seems to be happening anyway,' said Kate. 'And I've lost ma dad. If you see him, tell him I'm here.'

'Sure, but guess what, Nina's got an interview at Logie's tomorrow,' Hamish announced. 'All set to follow in Aunt Abby's footsteps!'

'Oh, dinna say that!' Nina said quickly. 'I'm no' trying to do that.'

'Well, you're going to do well in Accounts, you've got just the head for it.' Hamish grinned. 'Me, all my brains are in my fingers!'

'As long as you're happy,' Will said stiffly, and Nina saw that it was true, he didn't like Hamish being a tailor. She was mystified that anyone should find fault with Hamish, so tall, so handsome, and kindly with it. Anyway, what was wrong with being a tailor? It seemed to her a very superior calling. Maybe not as grand as working in a bank – Nina had never even been inside the banks in George Street or Princes Street, her dad put his takings in the CWS – but grand enough if you made suits in a place like Logie's.

'Look out!' cried Hamish. 'Something's happening! There's the old horse bus at the top of the Mound!'

Down came the horses, snorting and tossing their heads, as young people ran alongside and the policemen kept the crowds back. Through the rising mist, the watchers could make out the star of the show, a lighted tram, following the bus. Car 217 was about to make its final descent of the Mound.

Chapter Twenty-Four

'I suppose you'll think me a fool,' said Jennie, blowing her nose. 'Crying over a tram?'

'Feel a bit weepy myself,' Rachel admitted. 'When you think of all the times we've jumped on those old boneshakers.'

'Why don't you do a painting? Call it Last Tram Down the Mound?'

'Not my sort of thing.'

'You needn't make it look like a real tram.'

'Then you wouldn't like it, would you?'

Rachel glanced at her watch. 'Maybe we should be getting back now. Ma will be wanting to make your cocoa and I'll have to get Malcolm something to eat.'

But Jennie caught her arm.

'Rachel, there's Abby!' she cried. 'Oh, I bet she's had enough, she can't stand crowds.'

Rachel, on seeing that Lindsay was with Abby, looked down her nose. There was something of a cold war between her and the Farrells. Gail, so like Bobby, had become Rachel's darling, yet was regarded as exclusively Farrell property, or so Rachel believed. It was as though she and Bobby were one and the same, and because he took no interest in Gail, Rachel was not expected to take an interest either.

'It's so unfair!' Rachel had once exploded to Abby. 'I know Bobby is at fault, I am not trying to excuse him, but the fact is, the life he leads is just not suitable for a family man. Playing here, playing there – and now he seems to be getting interested in these rock people – rock and rollers, whatever they are. How could he possibly have Lindsay and Gail down in London?'

'He might occasionally come to Edinburgh. Lindsay was saying he hasn't seen Gail for a year or more.'

'She doesn't want him to come, Abby, she's told him so. After all, she's quite happy, isn't she? Working at Logie's, with Monica and some girl looking after Gail. But where do I come in? I have some rights, don't I?'

'I'm sure they don't mind your seeing Gail, Rachel. They're not as bad as you make out.'

'I always feel as though I have to go cap in hand, that's what I don't like.'

'These situations are difficult, always hurt somebody.'

'Yes, but why should it be me?' cried Rachel.

As Abby and Lindsay came up join them, Rachel noted how attractive Lindsay had become, how poised and confident, compared with the nervous girl who had once appeared to worship Bobby. She doesn't need Bobby, Rachel said to herself, perhaps he always knew that, deep down. She knew it wasn't true, but it made her feel better.

'No Malcolm?' asked Abby.

'Had to go to a meeting, I'm afraid.' Rachel's eyes moved to Lindsay. 'Your mother not with you, Lindsay?'

'It's Cora's night off, so Mummy said she'd babysit. I felt a bit guilty, but she's always happy to sit for Gail.' Lindsay smiled. 'Sometimes I think she'd like her to wake up, so that she could play with her.'

'Can't she play with her when you're at work?' asked Rachel caustically.

'I'm only part-time, you know, and Gail's at nursery school three mornings a week.'

'At nursery school? You never told me she was at nursery school!' Rachel's eyes were outraged. 'And she's only three, far too young!'

'I'm sure I did tell you,' Lindsay answered calmly. 'And she's quite old enough, she loves it.'

'Come on, let's go and listen to the speeches,' Abby said hastily. 'And maybe get ourselves on TV, if the chaps haven't packed up.'

'They have,' said Jennie. 'Went some time ago. Everything was running too late.'

115

'And so am I running late,' said Rachel. 'Come on, Jennie, I'll take you home. Abby, it's far too crowded round the bigwigs, you'd better go home too.'

'Maybe you're right.' Abby and Lindsay began to move away. 'But I wouldn't have minded hearing the speeches. Somebody's got to sing the swansong for the dear old trams.'

'Shall we go?' asked Will. 'We've seen all we want to see, haven't we? I want my supper.'

'But I haven't found Dad,' Kate protested. 'I don't like to go without seeing him.'

'He might not have come. We can't hang around all night.'

But Kate's eyes had brightened. 'Will, wait, I think I see him! He's walking away – there's a woman with him.'

Will's gaze followed Kate's pointing finger. In the glare of the street lighting, Ken Rossie's features were clear enough, but the woman with him had turned aside, Will couldn't see her face. She seemed youthful, though, with a slender figure and unfashionably long dark hair.

'Who's he with?' asked Will, feeling a strange unease.

'I've no idea. Quick, let's catch them, before they disappear.' Over her shoulder, Kate called back, 'Dad would never pick anybody up, he must know her, anyway.'

'I hope I don't know her,' thought Will, and wondered why such a thought should have entered his mind.

'Found you at last!' cried Kate, putting her hand on her father's arm. 'What a scrum, eh?'

'Aye, we'd given you up, Kate, we were just away for a drink.' Ken nodded to Will, whose eyes were on the stranger standing to one side, her face still averted. 'Now, who'd you think this is, then? Come on, then, let 'em see your face, Sheena, no' shy, are you? Do you no' remember ma Kate? And Will Gilbride?'

'Oh, God,' whispered Will, as the woman shook back her hair and looked at him. 'Sheena MacLaren!'

He remembered her. Remembered her face, which was lovely still, bending over himself and Hamish. 'Och, they're grand wee boys . . .' And she had packets of sweeties that his mother had said they could have in the morning, but now they must away to their

116

beds, and the woman had tucked them in. A few weeks later, she had left for London with his father.

'Hello, Will,' she was saying softly. 'You'll no remember me, eh?

'You're wrong,' he answered, through shut teeth. 'I do remember you. The people in my family will never forget you. We're not likely to forget a woman who ruined all our lives.'

'Dad!' gritted Kate, 'what the hell do you think you're doing, letting that woman meet Will? Do you no' remember what she did?'

Ken's heavy face was falling, he was like a child who'd been told he'd done wrong when he thought he'd done well.

'Kate, I niver thought – it went out o' ma head – Will, I'm sorry.' He put out a hand to Will that Will ignored. 'But it's a long time ago, eh? Sheena's no' been here for years, and she's on her own, her man's dead, her mother's dead – we just met in the crowd and got to talking – och, there's no harm done — '

'No harm?' Will turned icy blue eyes on Sheena's suddenly nervous face. 'There'd better be no harm done. No more harm, that is. If I catch you anywhere near my mother, Mrs Whatever you call yourself, watch out! You'll not cause mischief this time and that's a promise!'

'I niver,' she began tremulously, but Will snatched at Kate's hand and ran with her from the Mound like a man with the devil after him.

'Don't speak to me!' he cried. 'Don't say a word till I calm down!'

Chapter Twenty-Five

That night, they scarcely slept. Will tossed and turned, Kate tossed with him. At four o'clock, Kate got up and made tea, but Will lay staring into the darkness and said he didn't want any.

'Try not to think about her,' Kate whispered. 'You'll probably never see her again.'

He shook his head. He would not be comforted.

It was a relief when morning came, though it was as black as the night and they had to have breakfast by electric light. The old kitchen of their basement flat was full of shadows. Probably no more cheerful, Will thought, than when maids like his Aunt Abby had worked there long ago. He felt a great depression lying on his heart. And Kate had burnt the toast again.

'I wish you wouldn't always burn the toast,' he said fretfully. 'Every morning I pretty well break my teeth on it. And why can't we ever have bacon and eggs? I don't know when I last had a cooked breakfast.'

'Bacon and eggs?' Kate repeated incredulously. 'I'm no' your mother, Will, it's no' ma job to get your breakfast. Think yourself lucky I make you anything at all.'

He stood up, handsome in his dark business suit and crisp white shirt that he took to the laundry himself. Though Kate ironed very well, there was no guarantee that she would clear the washing basket at any given time. A feature article for the paper – yes, she would meet the deadline. Household tasks had to take their turn. Last night's dishes were still piled in the sink, for instance, and Will's eyes rested moodily on them. They moved to Kate's shoes, lying kicked under the table, a pile of her papers on the kitchen cabinet. Why could she never put anything away? At least, she'd watered the leggy geraniums on the windowsill and looked herself as fresh as paint. Always did. That was the mystery.

Kate's eyes were following his.

'Now what's wrong?' she asked, dangerously calm. 'Comparing ma housekeeping with your mam's?'

'She likes things tidy, Kate.'

'She does not like things tidy. Your mother and your gran have been brainwashed into thinking they like things tidy!'

'It's pretty obvious that no one's brainwashed you, then,' he said shortly.

'What's got into you this morning?' Kate bounded to her feet. 'You ken fine I've got a job to do. I canna be for ever cleaning and tidying. Anyway, I wasna born with a duster in ma hand. You can do housework as well as me.'

'OK, OK.' Will took his briefcase from a chair and began checking some papers. 'Maybe we ought to find a cleaning lady. If you don't find that too undemocratic?'

'I'm no' keen on the idea of servants.'

'From what I've heard, cleaning ladies rule the employer, not the other way round.'

'We'll do the work ourselves.' Kate's tone was final. 'Both of us.'

Will gave an exasperated sigh and snapped his briefcase shut. 'I'm off, we can argue this out later.'

He went to get his coat, but Kate followed him, throwing her arms around him.

'Dinna go like this, Will. You're upset over that woman, but I keep telling you just to put her out of your mind. It's true, you know, it was all a long time ago.'

He stared down at her, his face set and hard. 'You didn't see your dad packing his bag,' he said in a low voice. 'You didn't see him running away from you down the stair. That woman you tell me not to think about ruined our lives.'

'She could never have done it alone, Will. She could never have made your dad leave if he didna want to go.'

Will freed himself from Kate's arms and buttoned on his coat. 'Well, let's see what happens now she's met YOUR dad.'

'What do you mean?'

'Didn't you see the way he was looking at her last night? He was sweet on her when he was young. Jamie Kemp once told me every man in Catherine's Land was sweet on Sheena MacLaren.'

Kate flushed a deep red. 'Ma mother's only been in her grave six months, Will. Dad's no' looking at any woman the way you mean.'

'I hope you're right.' Will kissed her cheek. 'See you tonight.'

After he had swung himself out of the door, Kate ran to watch him mount the area steps to the street. They had had a spat. So what? It meant nothing. They often had disagreements that blew up, then blew away and only made them keener to make love. Today though there had been a critical look in Will's eye that Kate didn't remember seeing before. The wretched Sheena must have soured his outlook so that even Kate herself was at fault to him.

'Damn Sheena MacLaren!' thought Kate, and began to clear the breakfast dishes to add to the pile in the sink. She supposed she ought to wash them, but knew she was cutting things fine already. Never mind, she would tidy up as soon as she got home, wouldn't make a thing about Will's helping this time, just sweeten him up a bit to get him through this bad patch. But as she went on her way to her newspaper, Kate couldn't help feeling she needed a little sweetening herself. It was all very well, being tolerant. She was prepared to be that, prepared to remember that there must be give and take in a relationship. Just as long as the giving didn't have to come only from her.

By the time Will arrived at the grand portals of the Scottish and General Bank in George Street, he was feeling more cheerful. This was the place where he always felt at home. This was his sanctum, his church, devoted not so much to the making of money as the power of money. And here money ruled and the rest of the world bowed down, including Sheena MacLaren, whose own power was meaningless, as he now saw. Why had he allowed himself to feel such fear at her return? Kate had been surprised, he had been surprised himself, by how deeeply the old wounds had penetrated, how easily they had been reopened. But it was his mother's hurt that mattered. Whatever happened, she must not meet Sheena MacLaren again. It was all a long time ago, Kate had said. But not too long ago to be forgotten.

Since joining the bank, Will was aware that he had rapidly fulfilled the promise he had shown on appointment. It gave him confidence, that his superiors should think so highly of him. He felt himself poised easily on the rungs of the ladder to the top and saw no reason why he shouldn't reach that top one day. As he unlocked his desk in the office he shared with his boss, George Buchanan, investments manager, and a colleague, Alex Seton, he felt proud to be part of the expanding postwar world, proud and lucky. He and Kate were part of the new generation of lucky people, the world their oyster. He felt sorry now that he had criticised her. Especially as there was no point. Kate was not going to change for any man.

Mr Buchanan came in, a solemn-faced man in an Anthony Eden hat and a long black overcoat which he carefully hung up in his personal oak cupboard. There was a small mirror on the inside door at which he smoothed his grey hair and ran a little finger over each eyebrow. Polite good mornings were exchanged, then Mr Buchanan looked at the clock.

'Mr Seton not in yet?'

'Not yet, sir.'

Alex was often late, always had an excuse. When he arrived a few minutes later, his face flushed with hurrying, his brown eyes sparkling, it was apparently the new 23 bus that had been at fault.

'Always knew where you were with the trams, but these buses' – he shook his head – 'can't get used to them somehow.'

'I am sure the buses will prove to be just as efficient as the trams, Mr Seton,' Mr Buchanan told him, 'Perhaps more so.' He turned his gaze on Will. 'Mr Gilbride, I have a message for you. Mr Kerr would like to see you this morning. At your earliest convenience.'

Will stared. Mr Charles Kerr was the assistant bank manager, an eminence only slightly less grand than the manager himself, Mr Theodore Porteous.

'Mr Kerr wants to see me now?'

'If you please, Mr Gilbride.'

Will glanced at Alex, who was quietly grinning.

'Promotion, Will? Or, the sack?'

'Mr Seton!' Mr Buchanan was frowning. 'Better go along now, Mr Gilbride.'

'Yes.' Will stood up, straightening his tie. 'I – I don't suppose it's anything important.'

'I'm sure I couldn't say,' Mr Buchanan replied.

Chapter Twenty-Six

The assistant manager's office was vast, with long Georgian windows facing the street and a sea of polished wood block flooring. The walls were panelled and hung with portraits of former worthies of the bank; the chairs were large and upholstered in leather. When his secretary ushered in Will, Mr Kerr rose from his desk with a welcoming smile.

He was handsome, with a head of strong blond hair and cool grey eyes. Very sure of himself, very aware of his advantages, that included a New Town flat, a house in the Borders, an attractive wife and two children at boarding school. The sort of man Will would like to be, could in fact see himself becoming, if his luck held. At the moment, he was not too sure about his luck.

He took the chair Mr Kerr indicated, trying to look confident and at ease. In fact, he was worried sick. He could think of no reason why he should have been summoned in this way. Alex had joked about the sack or promotion. Will was sure he was due for neither. If he had made some terrible error, he would have known about it by now, and it would have been Mr Buchanan who would have shown him the door. He was not due for promotion, having only recently been given his present post in Investments. Which left –

Kate.

No, it couldn't be that. They didn't know he was living with Kate, and if they did, was it likely Mr Kerr himself would raise the matter? Was it likely anyone would raise it? Will's mouth was dry, his palms wet. As he raised his eyes to the assistant manager's, he could only pray he'd got this whole thing wrong.

'Cigarette, Will?' asked Mr Kerr, passing a handsome box.

'No, thank you, sir, I've given up smoking.'

Was it good or bad, Will was wondering, that Mr Kerr had used his first name? That was not common practice. It must mean something.

'Very wise, you're an example to me.' Mr Kerr flicked a silver cigarette lighter to his own cigarette. 'Now to business. Something a little awkward, I'm afraid. I hope you won't mind if I speak freely on a rather delicate matter?'

Not Kate, groaned Will, please, not Kate.

'Of course not, sir,' he answered easily.

Mr Kerr hesitated. 'I understand you are at present renting a flat in the New Town?'

'That's correct, sir.'

'And sharing it with a young lady?'

Will looked down at his hands clasped on his knees. It had come, then. Sometimes you were afraid when you'd no need to be. Other times, it was like this. Your worst fears realised.

'Yes,' he answered quietly. 'I'm sharing with a Miss Kate Rossie.'

'An unconventional arrangement, Will.'

'I know, sir.'

'Any particular reason for that?'

'I – it's the way Miss Rossie wants it.'

'Is there a relationship involved? A serious relationship?'

'Yes, there is. We love each other.'

'The usual practice in that case is to get engaged and then marry.' Mr Kerr smiled. 'Suits most of us.'

Will took out his handkerchief and wiped his dry lips. 'The thing is, Kate – Miss Rossie – is a journalist. She's very keen on her career.'

'In the modern way, of course. And why not? I'm all for women having jobs until they settle down.' Mr Kerr suddenly leaned forward. 'Why can't you marry her, Will?'

'She won't have me, sir. She doesn't approve of marriage.'

For once, Charles Kerr's poise faltered. He stared at Will in astonishment, his cigarette half way to his lips.

'Doesn't approve of marriage? I don't believe it! Every woman wants marriage. For God's sake, what's she got against it?'

'She thinks people should be able to make a commitment without it. She thinks women are better off remaining independent.'

'And do you agree with that?'

'No, I don't. I want to marry her. But there's nothing I can do.'

Mr Kerr shook his head. 'I hope that's not true, Will.'

Will raised his head. He felt suddenly cold, as though an icy wind were blowing though the centrally heated office.

'What do you mean, sir?'

'I mean, this could affect your career. At least, with the Scottish and General.'

As Will sat quite still, Mr Kerr said persuasively, 'Look, the last thing we want to do is to encroach on the private lives of our staff, but you must see the situation as it is. We live in a conventional world, we live by rules. Rules that keep society together. It may be all right for some to live without rules – it's a free country, unless crime is involved – but you work for a bank, Will, particularly you work for the S and G.'

'I understand you, sir.'

'Do you?' Mr Kerr shook his head. 'Have you really taken on our identity? It goes without saying, all bankers have to guard their reputations for probity. At the S and G, we also consider the views of our clients. Perhaps you think them an old-fashioned lot, too bound up with the kirk and that sort of thing.' Mr Kerr grinned and shrugged. 'But most of them are just ordinary conventional people who live by the rules I've been talking about. The point I'm making to you, Will, is that we must live by those rules too. It's expected of us. It's right.'

'Shall I—' Will cleared his throat. 'Shall I be asked to resign?'

'No. We all think very highly of you. That's why I'm talking to you like this now. You have a very fine career ahead of you, which we don't want you to jeopardise.'

'What am I to do?' Will asked huskily.

'For your own sake, consider your position. Are you prepared to do that?'

'Yes, sir, I am.'

Mr Kerr immediately stood up. He came round his desk and as Will struggled to his feet, put his hand on his shoulder.

'I knew you'd see sense,' he said genially. 'Whatever happens in this life, Will, it's not worth throwing away one's bread and butter, not to mention jam. Now you have a word with your young lady and explain the situation. Before you know it, you'll be

124

walking down the aisle and we'll be presenting you with a silver salver. That's our usual wedding gift, you know.'

'Is it?' asked Will. Somehow, he was dazedly getting himself out of the door.

Walking back to his office, past the clerks at their ledgers, he felt hollow, robbed of all that had given meaning to his life. A little while before, he might have been pondering, as he so often did, how the bank might be dragged into the twentieth century, what sort of methods could be implemented, how far this new automation on the horizon would affect them. Now, all that was in his mind was his own situation. And who had revealed it to his superiors.

Kate liked to invite friends from the paper round for a drink and an improvised meal. Will had occasionally included people from the bank. One or two of these very clerks, for instance. Alex Seton. They would have seen the set-up. The obvious fact that he and Kate were living together. Beautiful Kate without a wedding ring. Hell, what a fool he'd been.

At his own desk, he busied himself with papers, not caring to meet Mr Buchanan's cold eye, or Alex's smile. Alex was probably the one, he thought. Always behind him on the ladder. Willing enough to push him off.

'No sack?' asked Alex, coming close and cheerfully whispering.

'No sack. Mr Kerr just wanted me to do something.'

'What sort of thing?'

'Nothing to interest you.'

'Not to do with work, then?'

'I said it wouldn't interest you.'

Will would have liked to punch him, or anybody. He leaped to his feet.

'Will you excuse me, Mr Buchanan?' he cried. 'I have to make a phone call.'

It was his lunch hour and he was standing outside the door of a small café at the east end of Princes Street, waiting for Kate. He thanked God he had been able to contact her, he couldn't have borne waiting to talk until he got home.

Two people walked past. Hamish and Nina Muir. Oh, God.

'Will!' cried Hamish. 'Didn't see you there at first. Nina, here's Will. Tell him the good news!'

'Good news?' asked Will, his hands tight fists in his trouser pockets.

'Nina's got the job! At Logie's! Just had her interview.'

'Congratulations, that's wonderful.'

Please God, may they go, thought Will.

'I'm taking her to the George for a celebration. Want to join us?'

'Out of my league.' Will managed to grin. Lunch at the George? Was Hamish in love, or what? 'I'm waiting for Kate.'

'See you, then.'

They were long swallowed up in the lunchtime crowds before Kate's voice said at Will's side, 'This had better be good. I've had to leave a story half written. What's up, Will?'

Chapter Twenty-Seven

Sitting opposite her across a table as he had done so many many times before, Will felt his heart leap at Kate's beauty. What did it matter if she burnt the toast and never put anything away? What did it matter if she didn't want to be married? That was her choice. Why shouldn't she make it? She was worth a thousand banks – be damned to the S and G! He'd tell her now that she needn't worry, he was not going to give her up or make her do something she didn't want to do. But what he heard himself saying was, 'Kate, will you marry me?'

Her great dark eyes stared.

'Is this what you've dragged me across town for? I believe we have discussed it before.'

'Please answer me, Kate. It's very important.'

She buttered a bread roll.

'Feeling guilty because you were mad at me this morning? Why do you still think an engagement ring is going to make me feel good? You know ma views, they havena changed.'

The waitress brought their cheese omelettes. They picked up their knives and forks.

'Something's cropped up,' Will said with an effort at calmness. 'Mr Kerr spoke to me this morning.'

Kate gave him a sharp look. 'About me?'

'About us. He – well, he sort of said —'

'What? Sort of said what?'

'Oh, Kate – this is so bloody painful.' Will lowered his eyes. 'It was a mistake coming here, we can't talk with all these people around us.'

'They're no' listening. Just tell me what that fellow said.'
Kate's eyes were pebble hard.

'He said we should get married.'

'And what the hell has it got to do with him, may I ask?'

'A lot. He's senior management. He holds my job in his hand.'

'He's threatened to dismiss you?' cried Kate.

'No, but he made it pretty plain that my career is going nowhere if I don't obey the rules.'

'What rules? Who says bank employees have to be married?'

'You know what rules I'm talking about. The rules of society. Don't pretend they don't exist.'

'They shouldna!' Kate began to eat fast, as though she were making some kind of point. No bank was going to stop her having her lunch. No bank was going to give her orders.

'I hope you told this guy what he could do,' she said, biting her roll with good strong teeth. 'He has his nerve!' She looked hard at Will. 'You did tell him, eh? You told him what you thought of his damned S and G?'

She had only said what he himself had been feeling, but suddenly Will was angry with her. It came to him with unpleasant force that she had made no effort to see the situation from his point of view. OK, the S and G was stuffy and conventional, but by those same tokens it was rock solid. Respected. Important. With its own place in the Edinburgh hierarchy and a damned good place too. He had been given a chance to climb its ladder and here was Kate shaking that ladder, for the sake of principles he didn't even accept. Why couldn't she for once give in?

Kate had stopped eating. 'You are going to tell him?' For the first time she seemed a little uncertain. 'You're going to tell him you're prepared to resign?'

Will stared down at his omelette growing cold. 'I'm not sure yet what I'm going to do.'

'You're willing to let the bank interfere in your private life? Tell you what to do because they pay your wages!'

'All they're saying is that if I want to do well with them, I have to obey the conventions. It's not unreasonable, they have to think of their clients.'

'Give me strength!' cried Kate. 'We have to get married, because of their clients?'

'I want to marry you because I love you. We'd be married now, if it weren't for you and your damned principles!'

Kate's eyes blazed. 'All you want is for me to do what you say, is that it? As though we were living in the Middle Ages?'

'You know that's not true,' he said wearily. 'All I'm asking is that you give a thought to my career. Is that too much?'

'You've got rights,' she said eagerly. 'Every worker's got rights, that's what the party's always fought for.'

'I'm not a striking miner, Kate. I'm just a chap who likes his job and wants to do well.'

'No matter what?' The fire had died from Kate's gaze. 'Will, shall we go?'

'Yes.' He pushed away his plate. 'Let's get out of here.'

But in the street, it was worse. So many people. Just the two of them. They felt against the world.

At the foot of the Princes Street monument to Sir Walter Scott, they stared into each other's eyes.

'I'll tell you something,' Kate murmured. 'This has shown me how you really feel.'

'I love you, Kate, that's how I feel.'

'No' enough to say to hell with the bank.'

'They only want me to marry you and I want to do that anyway.'

'And if I ask you to choose? Me, or the bank?'

He grew white. 'I shouldn't have to choose, Kate. It's not necessary – oh, please, don't look at me like that!'

'Will, it's what I always said. You and me, we're too different. We want different things.' Kate moved her head and for some time watched the people passing by. 'I think it'd be easier all round, if I moved out.'

'No!' Will grasped her hands. 'You can't say that, Kate, you can't make a decision like that, here' – he looked wildly around – 'in the street, for God's sake!'

'It'd no' be different anywhere else, Will.'

'You know I can't let you go. I won't – I won't let you go.'

Kate freed her hands from his and laughed. 'Try and stop me.'

'Wait, wait! Oh, look – oh, God – how can you do this?'

'How can I? You ask me that? Goodbye, Will.'

'You don't give a damn,' he said slowly. 'Do you? You don't give a damn.'

'Think that, if it makes you feel any better,' she said over her shoulder, and began to walk away. He stood and watched her. He felt his life blood draining away, as he saw her hatless tawny head getting further and further away from him, but he made no move now to call her back. He knew there was nothing he could do, except the one thing she wanted him to do. And he couldn't do that.

When he reached the bank, he hesitated for some time before going in. He felt strange. As though he were there in body but not in mind. As though his mind were elsewhere, floating he didn't know where. All he knew was that he wasn't going to be able to work that afternoon. In fact, he couldn't imagine ever working again, ever being himself, bringing his mind back into his body that would never again know Kate's.

But he found himself going up the steps, moving the heavy swing doors, walking through the vaulted entrance hall and looking at clients as though they existed for him, when all they were were pieces of cardboard he felt he could have blown away. A fair-haired girl turning from one of the counters seemed to know him. Took a step towards him, ready to speak, but he walked straight past her with heavy flat sleepwalker's steps. It was only when he was back in his office that he realised the girl had been Sara Farrell. It didn't mean a thing.

'You're a little late, Mr Gilbride,' said Mr Buchanan. 'Not going to blame the new buses, I hope?'

Alex Seton gave a rueful grin, but Will made no reply.

'Well, we'd better get on. Have a lot to do.'

Mr Buchanan placed a file on Will's desk. 'Like to cast your eye over this for me, Mr Gilbride?'

'Certainly, Mr Buchanan,' said Will.

Chapter Twenty-Eight

'You're a fool, you are,' Biddy told Kate. 'As daft as they come. Why'd you have to give up Will Gilbride? A grand catch like him?' She laughed, throwing back her thick permed hair. 'I ken what I'd have done, if he'd offered me a ring!'

Kate, sitting at the uncleared table in her sister's living room, did not raise her eyes. All that past week she'd spent with Biddy, she'd had to endure Biddy's advice. If she didn't find a place of her own soon, she would go crazy. She knew that what she had done was right for her, but continually being told she'd made a mistake was not helping her at all. A flicker of spirit rose and burned and she looked up at Biddy with a bright hard stare.

'Thing is, you're not me,' she said levelly. 'You canna tell what I want. What's wrong with your Ewan, anyway?'

'What's right, you mean? He's no Will Gilbride, that's for sure. He hasna the looks, he hasna the manners.'

'You're being a bit unfair, Biddy.'

'Aye, well, if he didna drink half our money away before I see it, mebbe I'd be fairer. He's no' the fella I thought I was marrying, I ken that.'

'My point, Biddy. Things change when you sign yourself away. I've seen it all ma life, and I'm no' getting maself involved.'

'Too late,' retorted Biddy. 'Things've changed for you, anyway. You changed 'em yourself. Want some more tea?'

'No, thanks. I'm away to see Dad and Gran. I've a party meeting tomorrow night, so I'll no' be able to go then.'

'You and your meetings.' Biddy yawned. 'I couldna be bothered. Suppose I'd better get on.'

But she made no move and nor did Kate. Biddy's children were

131

in bed, Ewan was away to the pub. The two sisters were alone, surrounded by drying washing, scattered toys, the remains of a meal; each contemplating the collapse of their different dreams. Finally, Kate stood up and found her coat beneath half a dozen others hanging on the back of the door.

'Better go, Biddy. I'll do that ironing for you when I get back, so leave it for me, eh?'

'I'll no' need telling twice.' Biddy stirred herself to see Kate to the top of the stair. 'Listen a minute, Kate – I'm serious, you ken. You should take that Will Gilbride when you've got the chance. He'll no' stay single long.'

'Biddy, he made his choice and it wasna me. Is that plain enough for you?'

'You said he wanted to marry you.'

'He wants to do well at the bank. Look, I'll see you later.'

'Bring us back some boilings for the kids!' Biddy shouted down the stair as Kate went hurrying away. 'Dad always lets us have a few sweeties!'

'OK,' called Kate.

Her sister's dissatisfaction weighed on Kate's spirits almost as much as her own misery. Things had gone sour for Biddy, as they had gone sour for their mother. And pretty well every other woman who tied the knot, reflected Kate, waiting at the bus stop in driving rain. But for herself and Will, it could have been different. They would have kept the magic alive by staying lovers, not struggling with the ball and chain of marriage. Only Will couldn't see that. He wanted what the bank wanted, he wanted to be Mr Conventional, doing what the clients expected. Well, let him please the clients, if he didn't want to please her. She would lead her own life and it would not include Will Gilbride, however handsome he was, however much money he brought home.

Tears mingled with the rain on her cheeks, but she brushed them aside and by the time the bus came was almost composed, ready to greet her dad and meet her gran's sharp eye.

The window of the little shop in the Haymarket seemed rather forlorn when she stopped to look in. It had always been her mother's task to do the Christmas display. Now it was left to Dad to twine a few paper chains in and out of the faded dummy boxes

132

of chocolates and packets of Craven A and Woodbines. A piece of tinsel had been stuck over the 'For Sale' and 'Wanted' board at the side of the door, obscuring some of the handwritten postcards, but as far as Kate could see there were no offers of accommodation. Not that she'd particularly want this area, anyway, but staying on with Biddy was not an option. She was really willing to consider anything.

The shop bell jangled as she let herself in and her father, leaning over the evening paper on his counter, looked up. So did the woman standing so close to him, her cheek was almost touching his. When she saw Kate, she showed no reaction, but Ken at once moved his face from hers.

'Kate! What a treat to see you, then.' He grinned self-consciously. 'Er – Sheena's giving me a hand.'

'Nice to see you,' said Sheena.

Kate nodded without speaking.

By the harsh shop lighting, she could see that Sheena did not look so young as in the shadows of the Mound, but she was still an attractive and charming woman. Her clothes were timeless, long drifting garments you didn't really notice, and her hair, too, was unfashionably long, framing a face free of make-up. How confident she is, thought Kate, how sure that there would always be a man around somewhere to take her in tow. She would be like that even if she lived to be old, getting some ancient buffer to fetch her shawl in the nursing home. Oh, she had been wrong about Will's father, Kate decided. This one could have made him do anything she had a mind to ask him.

'Live round here?' Kate asked, taking off her wet raincoat.

'I've a wee room Newington way.'

'No' exactly near.'

'It's nae bother to come over.'

'All her own idea,' Ken put in proudly, but his gaze on Kate was defensive.

I bet it was, thought Kate.

'Gran in?' she asked aloud.

'Gone to the pictures with Madge Gilbride. *Carousel*. It's a musical.'

'Lucky Gran. But I was hoping to see her. I'll mebbe run up and leave her a note, eh?'

'Want Sheena to make you a cup o'tea?'

'No, thanks. But Biddy said she'd like a few sweeties for the kids.'

'Biddy?'

'I'm staying with her. Just for a few days.'

Ken looked blank. 'You're no' with Will?'

Kate hesitated. She glanced at Sheena, who was making a great show of tidying some magazines. It's nothing to do with me if Kate's lost her boyfriend, she seemed to be saying. I'm no' listening, am I?

'I'm no' with Will,' Kate answered.

She didn't stay long. As soon as she'd scribbled a note for Jessie to give her her dreary news, she was on her way, kissing her father's cheek, sliding her eyes from Sheena's limpid gaze. Every moment she spent in the shop, she fancied she could smell her mother's cigarette, feel her thin unhappy presence, and wondered that her father didn't feel it, too, as Sheena wound herself into his life. Will had warned her of what might happen, and here it was, happening before her eyes. She couldn't wait to get away.

Though the rain had stopped, the night was damp and chill, but Sally Muir was outside the door of the grocery shop turning the Open notice to Closed.

'Why, hello, Kate!' she cried with pleasure. 'Been to see your dad?'

Scarcely waiting for an answer, she rattled on, saying she was waiting for Nina, who had already begun working at Logie's. Had Kate heard she'd got the job in Accounts?

'Yes, I was delighted, Mrs Muir. She's done really well.'

'Aye, we're proud enough, Donnie and me.' Sally smiled. 'He's no' so bad at the moment. Will you no' come in for a cup of tea, Kate?'

'Thanks, but I must get back. Give my best to Mr Muir, eh?'

Kate was about to walk on when Sally said, with another proud smile, 'And guess who's taking Nina out these days, Kate? Hamish Gilbride!'

'Hamish?'

'Aye, did Will no' tell you? I think Hamish is really sweet on her. Not that we want her to start getting serious when she's just got her job, but he's such a nice lad, eh? Och, Jennie did a good job wi' those two boys, Hamish and your Will.'

My Will. The sudden pain in Kate's heart was intense. It was all she could do to get away from Sally without breaking down, but when she was on the bus taking her back to Biddy's, she couldn't stop the tears falling again. If only he had come a little way to meet her! Even just said he would consider resigning, so that she could be sure he really loved her. Well, it was all too late now and she was left with empty weeks and months stretching ahead, while she waited for time to do its work. If it ever did.

It came to her that while she was in Edinburgh, her city but Will's too, she might never come to terms with her pain. There were too many things to remind her of what she'd had and what had been taken away. A fresh start in a new place might be the only answer. Maybe she should look for a job somewhere else. Not Glasgow, for that was too close. Maybe not in Scotland at all. Don't go to London, Will had once written, don't go to Fleet Street, and she had laughed at the very idea. Now, though, it didn't seem to be anything to laugh at. On the contrary, it made good sense. And there was something else – London was the centre of British politics. She couldn't be in a better place to make a start in her true career.

Before she went into Biddy's flat, Kate dried her tears and blew her nose. She wouldn't fool Biddy, of course, and wasn't even trying to fool herself. It would be a long long time before she got over Will, but at least she had a new hope to comfort her.

'Hi, Biddy!' she called. 'Here's your sweeties. But guess who I saw at Dad's? That awful Sheena MacLaren!'

'I'll be round there tomorrow,' cried Biddy.

Chapter Twenty-Nine

After work on the following Saturday, Hamish and Nina also went to see *Carousel*, sitting happily in the two and threepennies, holding hands and eating toffees from Donnie's shop, letting the Rodgers and Hammerstein music flow over them.

'Och, was that no' lovely?' Nina breathed, as they came out. She hummed a little of 'You'll Never Walk Alone', and took Hamish's arm. 'Do you no' think that's a beautiful song?'

He laughed. 'If you say so. I'm not musical.'

'The words, though, Hamish. It's the words I was thinking of.' She looked up into his face. 'Make me think of walking with you.'

He hugged her arm close. 'Suits me,' he whispered. 'You know how I feel.'

They had to wait some time for a bus and when it came had to stand in the aisle, smiling at each other, as the driver's cornering jerked them together.

'Wish I had a car,' mouthed Hamish.

'One day,' Nina mouthed back.

Outside the door of the locked shop, they kissed goodnight long and lingeringly.

'I'd better not stay too long,' Nina sighed. 'Dad has to let me in.'

'And I suppose they'll be waiting up?'

'Oh, yes! Never go to bed till I'm in.'

They kissed again, then Nina said softly, 'You ken you're the only thing that's got me through ma first week, Hamish? Och, Logie's – it just terrifies me.'

'Come on, everybody feels like that in a new job.'

'Did you? In Tailoring?'

136

'You bet. Should have seen me when I first tried to do cutting! Fingers were like jelly.'

'Yes, but it's different for you. You're right for your job and I'm not.'

'What do you mean? You can do figures – book-keeping – you're perfect for your job.'

'No. I can do the work, I'm no' saying that, but I'm no' right for Logie's. I'm niver going to end up like your Aunt Abby, running the place.'

'Nobody expects that!' He shook her gently.

'My mam does. Och, the sky's the limit for me, Hamish. She sees me up there at the big desk, all the partners coming to me for my decisions.' Nina laughed drearily. 'And all I want to do is help her. Dad's getting worse, he'll no' be able to work much longer, but Mam'll no' admit she needs me. I have to have ma career.'

'Try not to worry, sweetheart. You've got me.'

'That's what I say, I couldna manage without you. Oh, Hamish—'

They were locked in each other's arms again, when there was the sound of bolts being drawn on the door behind them and they sprang apart.

'Is that you, Nina?' came Sally's voice, and Sally's head in curlers came round the door.

'Yes, Mam, just coming.'

'Is Hamish with you?'

'Just going, Mrs Muir.'

Goodnights were called, last hugs made, then Nina was inside and Hamish was making his lonely way home.

Thinking of Hamish, Nina was enchanted by her own good fortune. She couldn't believe that anyone so wonderful should be even interested in her who was so quiet, so ordinary, never mind in love. Yet, the unbelievable had happened. He cared for her, he wanted to look after her, and so far he had. It was true what she had told him. Without the thought of Hamish downstairs in Tailoring, she'd never have got through.

The terror of her first day still clung to her like the memory of a bad dream. The arrival at the famous store, the huge doorman looking down his nose and pointing a finger. The trembling walk through the Cosmetics Department where all the assistants looked like film stars, the gliding up in the staff lift with people who didn't speak to her, the knocking on the door marked Accounts. Even to relive it made Nina's mouth seem dry.

Yet, Mr MacDonell, who ran the department, and Mrs Gilbride, senior accounts clerk, had been very kind, and the work had not been too difficult. Nina did have a talent for figures, her success in the book-keeping classes had proved that, but what frightened her was that to work at at Logie's meant more than just being able to do your job. It meant being a part of a great organisation run for the kind of people Nina had only seen from afar. It meant being able to mix with folk like Mrs Gilbride who'd been to university. It meant following in the footsteps of Abby Baxter, who'd shot up the ladder like a rocket on a stick. Of course, there were ordinary people on the staff, too. Counter assistants who were probably not as bright as Nina herself. But they could cope with Logie's because they wanted to work at Logie's. And she didn't. There was the truth of it, hidden from her mother and Mrs Baxter like a secret burden. If it hadn't been for Hamish, she could never have borne the weight.

On Monday morning, while Nina was making her effort to face Logie's again, Abby Baxter was asking Lindsay about her progress.

'Oh, she's settling down gradually,' Lindsay answered cautiously. 'She's bright enough. It's only her nerves she can't handle.'

'I suppose we have to remember it's always a bit daunting in one's first job.'

'Can't believe you were ever daunted,' Lindsay said with a grin.

'No, I'll have to admit, as soon as I set foot in this place, I knew it was for me. I was lucky, I suppose, to get what I wanted.'

'Very lucky.' A shadow crossed Lindsay's face. 'Thought I knew what I wanted once, but seems I was wrong.' She put on a smile. 'Well, I'd better get back to work, unless there was something else?'

'No, just keep an eye on young Nina and let me know how she gets on. I feel a little responsible for her, you understand?'

'Of course. I'll see she's OK.'

As Lindsay turned to go, Abby said quietly, 'On a personal note, have you heard that Will and Kate have split up?'

'Yes, I'm really sorry. They seemed so happy.'

'Happy, but perhaps not suited.'

'So Sara thinks, and she's not shedding any tears. She's been waiting for this for years.'

But Sara was clever enough to wait a while longer before making her move. While Edinburgh watched its Christmas trees going up and coming down again, battled through the sales, accepted Harold Macmillan as Prime Minister in place of Anthony Eden, Sara kept watch. She worked hard at the Festival Office as plans went ahead for the 1957 Festival, and went out as usual to dances and parties, roaring away with everyone else the Bill Haley hit: 'One, Two, Three o'clock, Four o'clock Rock! Five, Six, Seven o'clock, Eight o'clock, Rock!'

But she never lost her touch with the bush telegraph of the city that told her what was happening. When she heard that Kate Rossie had gone to work at the London office of the *Glasgow Herald*, she judged her time had come.

Surprise, surprise, one blustery day in February, she just happened to be cashing a cheque at the Scottish and General, when Will Gilbride, immaculate in business suit and well-laundered shirt, crossed the marble floor of the vestibule.

To his destiny, thought Sara. And it's me.

'Will, hello!'

'Hello, Sara.'

'I haven't seen you in ages.'

He stared down at her without a smile.

'How are you, then?'

'Very well. And you?'

He shrugged. 'I work hard.'

'You know what they say about that?' She put her hand on his arm. 'All work and no play — '

'Makes Will a dull boy?' He did not detach her hand, but she felt he might as well have done so. 'I'm that, all right. So what?'

'So, I take you to lunch.'

'I don't bother with lunch these days, thanks all the same.'

'All right, we'll go for a drink. Suits me.'

'Usually, I just walk.'

'I'll walk with you, then. There's nothing I like better than walking in the wind, ruining my hair-do, but what the hell!'

'Mustn't risk ruining your hair-do, must we?' Still unsmiling, he took her hand and this time held it. 'Come on, I'll take you for a drink.'

It was all working out just like one of the plays she booked for the Festival, except that when Sara was facing Will over a table in the George Hotel's cocktail bar, she suddenly felt less sure of herself.

It's the way he's looking, she told herself uneasily. Worn. Defeated. As though he had been through a very bad experience, which, of course, he had. Was it over? That was the point. Sara nibbled a crisp and could think of nothing to say. Which was so unusual, Will broke the silence himself.

'What happened to that guy you were once engaged to?' he asked flatly.

'You mean, Nick Ainslie?'

'Have there been others?'

'No, no others.' She laughed nervously. 'He's OK. Quite friendly with my sister, as a matter of fact.'

'I suppose you know Kate's gone to London?'

'I'd heard. I'm sure she'll do very well.'

'Wants to be an MP eventually.'

'Really?'

Will set down his glass, his eyes on Sara suddenly bleak.

'Look, can we stop this idiotic small talk? Just what is it you want, Sara?'

'Want?'

'You and me to pick up something we never even started? If you're looking for a relationship, I'm not. At the moment, I just want to be left alone to get on with my job.'

'Do you always talk like this to somebody who just wanted to give you lunch?' cried Sara. 'What makes you think I want a relationship?'

A dusky flush rose to Will's cheekbones. He lowered his eyes. 'Sorry – I suppose that sounded pretty rude.'

'Rude and uncalled for.'

'You'll have to forgive me, I'm out of practice at polite conversation.' He gave a weak smile. 'Never was one of your smoothies.'

140

Sara kept her face expressionless.

'You do understand, Sara?'

'You needn't have accepted my offer of a drink.'

'I suppose I wanted to.'

'So you could slap me down?' She stood up and pulled on her coat. 'Well, I have to go. You're not the only one who works, you know.'

He followed her into the street, his face darkly set.

'Look, maybe I could ring you sometime? Are you still at your mother's?'

'Oh, God, no. I have my own flat. Gail is adorable, but Mummy's fussing round her is just too much.' Sara was being very cool, very composed. 'If you really want my number, I'll give it to you. If you're trying to be polite, forget it.'

'I want it.'

They both remembered she had given him her number once before. She guessed he had thrown it away. He knew he had. This time, he put her scrap of card carefully into his wallet while she watched.

'Goodbye, Will.'

'Goodbye, Sara. I'll be in touch.'

She made no reply, walking smoothly away from him, taking her time. After a sticky start, things had gone well for her. Better than she'd expected. Now the ball was in his court and she was pretty sure he'd return it. Then what? She knew what she wanted. Herself in white, floating down the Cathedral aisle on Will Gilbride's arm. A dream ending to her long patient wait. It did not occur to her, as she made her way back to her office, that that would in fact be only a beginning.

Chapter Thirty

In the late summer of 1957, the announcement of Miss Nina Muir's engagement to Mr Hamish Gilbride appeared in *The Scotsman*. On the same day, Miss Sara Farrell's engagement to Mr William Gilbride was announced in *The Scotsman*, *The Times*, *Daily Telegraph*, and *Glasgow Herald*. This last notice was seen in London by Kate Rossie, who set her mouth in painful lines, but made no comment.

'Oh, poor Kate,' moaned Biddy, reading *The Scotsman* in her flat.

'That's it, then,' snapped Ken Rossie, in his shop. 'Our Kate's lost Will.'

'Good riddance,' Sheena retorted. 'She's better off without that stuck-up piece o' nothing. Look at the way he spoke to me on the Mound that time, the cheeky devil!'

'Aye, well, he was only thinking of his ma, Sheena, canna blame him for that.'

'His ma!' Sheena tossed her head contemptuously. 'Jennie used to be ma friend, but she just couldna take it that Rory wanted me and no' her. Your Kate's well out o' that family, toffee-nosed show-offs.'

'Will'd have done well by Kate,' Ken said doggedly. 'And I want to see her wed.'

Sheena glanced round the shop which was empty for the moment, and moved closer to Ken. 'Is there no one else you'd like to see wed?' she whispered, with her lips against his face.

'Och, Sheena!' He twisted round and held her fast. 'You ken I'd marry you tomorrow, if it wasna for ma mother.'

'So now it's your ma we have to worry about!' cried Sheena,

pulling herself away. 'You run round after her like you were still two years old, Ken. She's had her life, remember, why can she no' let you have yours?'

'She just thinks of Ivy,' Ken muttered, staring down at his fingers blackened from newsprint.

'Well, Ivy's gone, she'll no' come back, so where does that leave you? Are you planning to live like a monk the rest of your life? You're still young, Ken, you've got years ahead of you.' Sheena took his hand. 'And your shop's doing well, everything's fine. Or would be, if it wasna for your ma putting her spoke in.'

'She'd niver stand for you living here, Sheena. I'd no' waste ma breath asking her.'

'Let her move somewhere else, then.'

'She's nowhere to go, this is her home. I canna just show her the door.'

'Well, it's up to you what you do.' Sheena took her hand from his and threw back her long dark hair. 'But I canna promise to stick around here waiting on you. I've been thinking, I'll get maself a job in Glasgow. Plenty going on there and it's no' so dear as here.'

'Sheena, you'll no' do that!' He snatched her to him, frantically fondling her hands, staring into her eyes. 'You'll no' leave me? You're the only thing's made ma life worth living, kept ma wits in ma head. If I dinna have you, I'll no' be able to keep going, I'm telling you. Och, you'll no' go, eh? Promise me!'

'If you promise me a wedding ring.' Sheena again slipped from his embrace and fixed him with her clear, light gaze. 'That's the deal, Ken. It's me or your mother, you'll have to choose.'

The shop bell rang, a customer came in.

'Twenty Senior Service, please,' he said, glancing at Sheena, who had turned aside to pile up a small display of Mars Bars and chocolate flakes. She gave the man a sideways smile that made him blink a little, while Ken, his broad face blank with misery, reached for the cigarettes.

Nina, engaged to her dear Hamish and with her little ring to prove it, was, of course, blissfully happy. Yet she still felt beset by problems. Her father's health was no better, her mother was over-working, trying to cover for two, but often behind with orders and slow in service. People were drifting away, takings were down, there seemed nothing Nina could do.

'I'd leave Logie's tomorrow, if she'd let me help,' Nina told Hamish, 'but she still keeps talking about ma career, even though I'm engaged. Thinks what your Aunt Abby could do, I can do, be married and still get to the top of the tree.'

'At least, she's not stopping us getting married,' Hamish pointed out. 'I was afraid she'd give me the order of the boot.'

'Come on, she thinks you're wonderful! No, she wants us to be married, all right, but that's another thing. She wants me to have a perfect wedding, because when she married Dad, they couldna afford a proper wedding at all, so I've got to have all the works and we canna afford it either. Hamish, I dinna ken where to turn!'

'To me!' He folded her in his arms and kissed her gently. 'I'll let you into a secret – I don't want a grand wedding, I'd settle for a register office any day. And no reception, just a honeymoon.'

'I wouldn'a mind a nice dress,' Nina said thoughtfully. 'Do you think your mother would make me one?'

'Sure she would. I bet she's looking at patterns already.'

'It's a shame she hasn'a been able to marry again herself. That Mac's a lovely man, eh?'

'He's OK,' Hamish said shortly. 'I wasn't so keen at one time, but – well, it's her life. And I've got used to the idea now.'

'Maybe they'll be able to work something out one day.'

'In the meantime, I'm thinking about us, not them.' Hamish kissed Nina. 'Just as long as you fix us up with something, I don't care what sort of wedding we have.'

'It canna be in a register office, Hamish, it'll have to be in the kirk, or it'll no' count.'

'The kirk it is, then,' said Hamish. 'Only make it soon.'

Monica had already booked the Cathedral in the West End for Sara's wedding in October, and her plans were well in hand when she gave a little dinner party in August, to which Hamish and Nina were invited. In spite of her graciousness and the easy manners of her daughters, Nina was terrified, and even Hamish was subdued. Will, who had been doing duty as host, offered to drive Nina home at the end of the evening, but Hamish said, no, they'd walk, needed the exercise, after all the wine, etcetera.

'Needed the air,' he told Nina, as they strolled through the

144

streets crowded with Festival visitors. 'Phew! I felt suffocated in there! Rather Will than me to take on that lot.'

'They were all very nice, Hamish.'

'True, but I kept thinking I ought to call Mrs Farrell Your Majesty and go out backwards, don't know about you.'

'Oh, Hamish!' Nina was laughing, beginning to feel better. 'I suppose she's just been used to money all her life and having everything just so. Did you see that silver? And the flowers and starched napkins? Is that the sort of life Will wants, d'you think?'

'It's what he's always wanted, since he was a kid.'

'He wouldna have got it with Kate.'

'No.' Hamish gave a long sigh. 'But does he want it with Sara?'

Nina was silent. She was thinking of how her mother's eyes would shine when she told her of all she had seen at the house in Selkirk Street, of how she would like it for her, for Nina. Well, why should she no' want it?

Maybe I want it, too, thought Nina. But then she looked up into Hamish's handsome, benevolent face, and her love for him put all the Farrells' silver and flowers and starched table napkins out of her mind.

Chapter Thirty-One

It was some days later, on her way to her teabreak, that Nina met Mrs Farrell and Sara passing through one of Logie's long carpeted corridors. She would have preferred just to smile and hurry on, but Sara made her stop.

'Nina, how nice to see you! Mummy, here's Nina.'

Mrs Farrell inclined her head. 'Good morning, Nina.'

How splendid they looked, how beautifully dressed and secure! Whatever happened to them, Nina thought, they would always have that easy self-assurance that would never be hers, however hard she worked, however well she did. She came from Catherine's Land and there was no self-assurance there. Only a very special person such as Mrs Baxter could forget that, or someone like her own good-natured Hamish. But Will Gilbride remembered. That must be why he was marrying Sara.

'We're on our way to the Bridal Department,' Sara confided. 'I'm having a try-on of my dress. Like to come and see?'

The Bridal Department! That place of hushed luxury and attendant goddesses! Nina had only seen it once, and then only from the door.

'Oh, I couldn't,' she answered hastily. 'Thanks ever so much, but I'm at work, you see, it wouldna do.'

'You have a coffee break, don't you?' Sara hooked Nina's arm into hers. 'Come on, we'll take the lift.'

Wishing she could just quietly disappear, Nina was transported to the hallowed ground of the Bridal Department, where Mrs Farrell took a little gilt chair and indicated that one should also be placed for Nina. With a lift of her pencilled brow Miss Audrey Brown, one of the hovering goddesses, placed the chair, but when Mrs Farrell ordered coffee, Miss Brown could not restrain herself.

'And for Miss Muir?' she asked, and Nina, her eyes cast down, knew just what she was thinking. Coffee in the Bridal Department for that little junior from Accounts? What next?

'If you please,' Mrs Farrell said coolly, and Miss Brown withdrew. Who was she to argue with a lady who was not only a valued customer, but also the widow of Mr Gerald Farrell, once chief executive? While Sara retired to a fitting-room, an elegant tray was brought to Mrs Farrell and Nina, and Miss Brown, stiff as a poker, poured their coffee from a silver-plated pot.

'I take it you will also be having your wedding dress made here?' Mrs Farrell asked, as Nina crumbled a shortbread.

'Me? Oh, no, Mrs Farrell, I couldna afford to buy ma dress here.'

'But surely you will be entitled to staff discount?'

'Yes, but it'd still be too much. Hamish's mother is going to make ma dress for me.'

'Ah, yes. I believe Mrs Gilbride is a very talented dressmaker.' Mrs Farrell smiled kindly. 'My dear, I'm sure it will be lovely.'

Lovely, maybe, but not like Sara's. As the curtains of the fitting-room parted and Sara appeared in her wedding gown, walking slowly, her blonde head bent, her mouth curved in a little self-mocking smile, Nina caught her breath.

'Oh, it's beautiful, beautiful!' she cried, and Mrs Farrell gave a soft sigh of agreement.

'Perfect, Sara, perfect! Turn round, let us see the back.'

'I'm all pins,' said Sara, as the two black-dressed needle-women gathered up her train and turned her round. 'Ouch!' She put her hands to her slender waist. 'Oh, there's something sticking in here.'

'Sorry, Miss Farrell.' One of the women made to remove the pin, but Sara laughed and said it didn't matter, she'd suffer to be beautiful. And she knew she was beautiful, like a fairy-tale princess in her long trailing satin with bell sleeves and a neckline cut low to show her delicate throat.

'Could we try the veil?' asked Mrs Farrell. 'Just to get the idea.'

To Nina she added, 'I wore that veil myself, you know, at my own wedding. Oh, goodness – what an age ago!'

An apprentice was despatched to fetch the veil and the two

fitters reverentially placed it over Sara's head, setting in place the small tiara, pulling forward the folds of tulle, so that Sara became for a moment remote, mysterious, not only a princess but a stranger. Mrs Farrell gave a little sniff and took out her handkerchief.

'Oh, dear, this is how I'm going to be on the day, disgracing myself, you'll see. Why do people always cry at weddings?'

'Mothers, you mean.' Sara flung back her veil, appearing herself again, but still beautiful, still a princess.

As she made her slow progress back to the fitting-room, Nina watched in silence. Something was beginning to hurt, something she didn't at first recognise. She had grown used to accepting her life as it was, so that when anything good happened it was a bonus. Hamish's love was such a bonus, her own wedding was another, she was so grateful for both, she really didn't hanker after all the splendid Farrell possessions. Yet now, seeing Sara in her exquisite dress, seeing her look so much more beautiful than she really was, knowing how much she had and could look forward to, a great scorching envy suddenly filled Nina's soul. She wanted, with a fierceness she had never experienced before, to be like Sara. To have what she had, to look like she did. To be a princess. And why not? They were marrying brothers, they had something in common. All that was different was that Sara had money and Nina had not. It was the old unfairness at work again, the inequality that kept the poor in their place and always would.

It'd take so little, thought Nina, moving back in a daze to the Accounts Department. The sort of money that'd never be missed. No' a fortune, nothing like that. Just enough for a really beautiful wedding dress, to make her mother happy, to make Hamish proud.

'You're late back, Nina,' Lindsay remarked, surprised, for she knew Nina was usually too nervous to be late.

'I met your mother, Mrs Gilbride, and Sara. They asked me to got to the Bridal Department, to see the wedding dress.'

'Did they indeed? Well, that's all that's occupied them for the past six weeks, so I suppose they're dying to show it off. Was it gorgeous?'

'Gorgeous. Made Sara look – out of this world.'

'A miracle.' Lindsay laughed. 'There's never been anyone more a part of this world than Sara. Well, now you're back, you'll find a stack of invoices on your desk. See they get paid, will you?'

'Yes, Mrs Gilbride.'

Nina sat at her desk, trying to adjust from the enchantment of the Bridal Department to the reality of the work before her. Gradually, the details of the invoices sorted themselves out, the names of the firms, the sums to be paid. Not large sums, really quite small amounts ... Nina picked up her pen, her eyes thoughtful, her brain suddenly, wonderfully, alert.

Chapter Thirty-Two

Replies to the wedding invitations were beginning to come in. To Lindsay's chagrin, Bobby had accepted.

'Oh, why did you invite him?' she groaned to her mother.

'He was on Will's list, what else could I do? Besides, Rachel would have been upset if we'd missed him out.'

'I can't think why he wants to come.'

'Perhaps his conscience is troubling him?' Monica suggested. 'It's a long time since he saw his parents. Or Gail.'

'You know he isn't interested in Gail,' Lindsay snapped.

To Jennie's quiet pleasure, Mac had also said he would be attending Will's wedding.

'He'll be staying with Abby and Frankie, of course,' Jennie told Madge, as they worked together on their wedding outfits, Madge's a powder-blue suit, Jennie's a raspberry-red dress and jacket.

Madge gave a wry smile. 'You know he might as well stay here, Jennie. I don't mind.'

Jennie looked embarrassed. 'No, it's all right, Ma. He likes to see Frankie, talk about the war and that.'

'Well, I'm not going to say again that I think it's time you two got married.'

'Sounds like you are saying it.'

'Hamish has come to terms with it, we'd all be very happy for you.'

'Mac and I are happy as we are. After all, you took your time marrying Jim, Ma, didn't you?'

'And regretted it.' Madge was frowning over the jacket lining she was hand-stitching. 'The thing is to be sure, when it comes to marrying. Do you think Will is sure?'

Jennie looked taken aback. 'He'd never have got this far if he wasn't.'

'I don't know, sometimes things snowball. Does he really love Sara?'

'He seems to. And I think she'll be right for him.'

'For the wrong reasons, mebbe. Will's always been impressed by people like the Farrells.'

'He's not mercenary, Ma, or he'd never have taken up with Kate.'

Madge took off her glasses and put down her sewing. 'I think I'll have to get you to finish this for me, Jennie. My eyes aren't what they were.' She stood up and stretched a little. 'You know, I sometimes think Will hasn't got over Kate.'

'Of course he has, Ma, it was just a boy and girl affair.'

When they were living together? Madge did not ask the question. It was better not to worry Jennie. Anyway, she might be wrong, perhaps Will and Kate had forgotten each other. Jessie said Kate was doing well on the London paper and making her mark with the local Labour Party. Didn't sound as though she was broken-hearted. Whatever the truth of things, there was nothing Madge could do. Folk just had to work things out for themselves and you had to let them do it. Especially when you were old.

'It's good that Bobby's coming up, isn't it?' Jennie said, hoping to distract her mother's interest from Will. 'You'll be glad to see him again, won't you?'

Madge's eyes brightened. Poor Bobby . . . always in disgrace. Well, his gran for one didn't think he was as black as he was painted.

'This could be a turning point,' she told Jennie. 'He might have had a change of heart, want to be with Lindsay and Gail again.'

'Shouldn't bank on it,' said Jennie.

A week before the wedding, Bobby arrived at the Farrells' front door.

'What are you doing here? Lindsay asked coldly. 'You're too early.'

'Thanks for the welcome.' Bobby gave a crooked smile. 'I'm here on holiday, as a matter of fact, at Mum's request.'

'And you're doing what she wants? That's a change.'

'Aren't you going to invite me in? I've got a present for Gail.'

'We're all very busy, we haven't got time to entertain you.'

'You'd like me to see Gail, wouldn't you? You're always saying I never take any notice of her.'

'I am not "always saying" anything at all about you, Bobby, but I suppose now you're here, you'd better come in.' Lindsay grudgingly showed him into the hall. 'But Gail's not long back from nursery school, she's upstairs having a rest.'

'I can surely say hello?'

'Who is it, Lindsay?' called Sara, appearing from the study with a bundle of thank-you letters for the post. 'Oh, it's you, Bobby. What are you doing here? You're too early.'

'So nice that everybody's pleased to see me.' Bobby pecked Sara on the cheek. 'You're looking well, Sara, being a bride suits you.'

'You're looking thinner.'

'I always look thinner. Never have time to eat.'

'Are you coming up to see Gail, or not?' Lindsay asked from the staircase.

'Coming!'

'What have you brought her?' Lindsay asked in a whisper, on the landing. 'She may have it already. Mummy's just about bought up Logie's toy department for her.'

'Where is dear Mummy?'

'Gone out to try on more hats, she can't make up her mind what kind she wants.' Lindsay looked in the paper bag Bobby handed to her. 'Oh, Lord, Bobby, what's this?'

'It's a ball. It's pink. I thought she'd like pink.'

'It's a BABY'S ball! It's made of wool.'

'You mean it's no good?'

'I mean, she's four years old, she stopped playing with this kind of ball ages ago.'

'Four?' Bobby looked penitent. 'I keep thinking of her as such a little thing.'

'She was two when you last saw her. This ball wouldn't have been right even then. You just don't think, do you?' Lindsay shook her head. 'But come on, then, if you want to see her.'

She opened a door, putting her finger to her lips, and they both looked in at a child lying quietly on a pretty flounced bed in a room filled with toys. Dolls, teddybears, a rocking horse, a doll's house, a blackboard with chalks, an enormous hamper bursting with cuddly animals.

'You're right,' Bobby whispered. 'This could double as Logie's, or Hamley's come to that.'

'Not my fault. I told you, it's Mummy. She can't resist giving Gail everything in sight. To make up.'

'To make up for what?'

'You should know.' Lindsay approached the dark-haired child on the bed, who slowly opened her eyes. 'Gail, darling, are you awake? Here's someone to see you.'

'Who?'

'Daddy,' said Bobby, giving a self-conscious smile.

The little girl pulled herself into a sitting position and fixed Bobby with a steady gaze from large dark eyes. My eyes, he thought. Ritchie eyes.

'My daddy's in London,' Gail said clearly.

'I've come from London specially to see you.'

Liar, thought Lindsay.

But Bobby was staring at his daughter.

She wasn't really pretty, not as pretty as his mother had been in her early photographs. But she was bright. Anybody could see that. Bright and quick. Another Gramma Ritchie, from what he'd heard of his great-grandmother. Another Aunt Abby. And his. His daughter. He felt rather odd, saying that word in his mind. Felt something crossing between himself and her. His daughter. He said the word again, just to himself, aware that Lindsay was beginning to look at him curiously and that he didn't care. This was what she'd wanted, wasn't it? When she'd first given him the baby that was Gail to hold. Only, it hadn't happened then, it had happened now.

He sat cautiously on the end of the bed, while Lindsay and Gail watched.

'I've got a present for you,' he whispered. 'It's only a ball. Your Mum says it's a baby's ball. You might not want it.'

'Let me see it.'

'Please,' Lindsay said mechanically.

'Please,' Gail repeated.

He put the soft pink ball into her chubby hands and she turned it over, studying it.

153

'Do you like it?' asked Bobby. 'Will it do?'

'I like it. I like baby things.' She looked into his face. 'Thank you.'

He wished she'd called him daddy, but knew he mustn't expect too much. He stood up and looked at Lindsay.

'Couldn't I take her out for a walk or something? She doesn't seem at all sleepy.'

'I don't think she knows you well enough to go out with you, and I haven't the time.'

'If I took her out, she'd get to know me.'

'I'm sorry,' Lindsay said firmly. 'You do understand, don't you?'

'No, I don't.'

Bobby went to Gail and kissed her lightly on the brow. 'I'll see you soon, darling, I'll come and take you for a walk. Would you like that?'

'When will you come?'

'I'm not sure. Maybe tomorrow. I'm just going to talk to Mummy.'

Bobby took Lindsay's arm and moved with her out on to the landing.

'Why are you being so difficult? Why can't I take her out?'

'I'm simply saying that you can't expect a child to feel at ease with somebody who turns up out of the blue. She hasn't seen you for two years, she can't remember you.'

'I am her father, Lindsay.'

'Who didn't want anything to do with her! What's different, Bobby?' Lindsay's eyes were angry. 'You were her father two years ago, didn't make you want to take her out then.'

'She was in a push-chair, she was crying — '

'Oh, of course! A crying little two-year-old is not the same as a nice easy four-year-old, is that it? Bobby, will you just go?'

'I want to spend time with Gail, I want to get to know her.'

'Well, it's just not possible!'

'Mummy,' came Gail's voice. 'Where are you? I want to show Daddy my new dress. I want to tell him I'm a flower-girl!'

'Not just now, darling.' Lindsay turned back to Bobby. 'Look, you wanted to see Gail and you've seen her, so will you please leave?'

'May I come back tomorrow?'

'Oh, what is this?' Lindsay put a distracted hand to her brow. 'What are you playing at? If it's the doting father, you're a bit late in the day.'

'I know it sounds crazy, but just then when I saw her, I felt so strange, different from any way I've ever felt before. I thought, my God, that child is a part of me, she's mine!' Bobby's great Ritchie eyes on Lindsay were shining. 'You can understand that, can't you? Didn't it happen to you?'

'Four years ago, when she was born,' Lindsay answered, through shut teeth. 'But how would you know? You weren't around.'

'I'm here now, and all I want is to be with her, watch her grow, watch her learn.'

'Now she's out of nappies.' Lindsay smiled grimly. 'I'm afraid this is just what I'd have expected of you, Bobby. The big theatrical gesture, when all the work's been done. But as I told you, you're too late.' She turned him towards the stairs. 'Better go now, before you run into Mummy with her new hat.'

'All right, I'll go.' Bobby began to move slowly away. 'But I promise you, I'm coming back tomorrow. I think I have the right.'

'As far as I'm concerned,' Lindsay shouted down the stairs after him, 'you have no rights!'

When she heard the front door bang on him, she stood for some time, her hand to her heart, then she turned and went back into Gail's room.

Chapter Thirty-Three

When Bobby arrived at the Selkirk Street house the following day, he was carrying a large sheaf of pink roses and a box of chocolate teddy bears. A bony young woman with carrot-red hair opened the door to him and seemed uncertain whether to let him in or not, but Monica came sweeping up as soon as she heard his voice.

'Cora, leave this to me,' she told the nanny. 'You go back to Gail.' With her haughtiest manner, she turned to Bobby. 'And what are you doing here today? The wedding is not until next week.'

Swallowing his irritation and putting on a charming smile, Bobby asked if he could see Lindsay, since he would like to arrange to take Gail out for a walk.

'Lindsay has had to look in at Logie's and Gail is watching television.'

'Television?' Bobby raised his eyebrows. 'I'm sure a walk would do her more good.'

'Lindsay always lets her see *Watch With Mother*, and she left strict instructions that you were not to take Gail out. I'm sorry.'

As Monica made to close the door, Bobby inserted himself into the hall.

'At least, take my flowers, Mrs Farrell. I brought them for you.'

'Flowers?' She looked at the roses doubtfully.

'And the sweets are for Gail, of course. Oh, please, do let me see her. I know up to now I haven't done well as a father —'

Monica's eyes bulged with outrage.

'Haven't done well?' she repeated. 'I should say you haven't done well. How dare you come here wanting to see Gail just when

156

it suits you? After you've neglected her ever since she was born and left Lindsay to do everything!'

'I know, I know, I'm sorry, I really am. It's all true what you say.' Bobby's smile was rueful. 'But anyone can change, Mrs Farrell, and I've changed. I want Gail to know she has a father who cares for her. Is that too much to ask?'

Monica hesitated. She looked again at Bobby's roses.

'It's not for me to say,' she said stiffly. 'It was Lindsay's decision that you shouldn't see Gail, and I can see her point.'

'I know I don't deserve any consideration,' Bobby said softly. 'But we have to think of Gail, don't we? A child needs two parents. I see that now, and I want to make it up to Gail and Lindsay, for the way I've behaved in the past.'

'Well . . .' Monica stood, knitting her brow. 'All right,' she said at last. 'I don't think it would do any harm if you were just to say hello. Gail's in the study.'

'Hello, Daddy!' cried Gail, swinging round from her seat next to Cora in front of the television set. 'Look, it's Andy Pandy! That's Teddy – he has a spotted bow, just like my teddy – and that's Looby Loo – oh, she's so funny!'

'She adores *Watch with Mother*,' Monica said indulgently.

'If I watch it, will it be called *Watch with Father*?' Bobby whispered, sitting on the floor beside his daughter.

'Daddies don't watch this,' Gail answered, not taking her eyes from the screen. 'But you can, if you like.'

'Thank you, Gail,' he said humbly.

When Lindsay returned from work at five o'clock, it was to find Bobby and Gail in the kitchen, eating buttered toast and laughing together, while Cora and Mrs Robson, the housekeeper, smilingly looked on.

'Oh, no,' groaned Lindsay. 'What's been happening? I left strict instructions —'

Bobby leaped to his feet. 'Lindsay, don't be angry. I persuaded your mum to let me in, just to say hello.'

'And where is my mother?'

'Er – gone shopping, I believe.'

'Didn't want to face me.' Lindsay set down her bag and kissed Gail. 'Well, you seem to be enjoying yourselves, anyway.'

'We've played lots of games, Mummy,' Gail told her. 'Mostly,

I won and Cora came second. Daddy always lost, didn't you, Daddy? He's not used to games.'

'How about a cup of tea, Mrs Gilbride?' Mrs Robson asked. 'You look tired.'

'I feel tired,' Lindsay murmured, sinking into a chair.

'Well, this evening, you can relax,' said Bobby. 'I'm taking you out to dinner. It's all arranged. Please, don't say no.'

'May I have one of my chocolate teddy bears?' asked Gail. 'When you're out?'

Bobby had chosen an expensive French restaurant for their dinner, which made Lindsay raise her eyebrows. Looking round at the restrained decor, the shaded lamps, the obviously well-heeled diners, she gave a little laugh.

'Pushing the boat out, aren't you? Must be doing well in London.'

'Better than I was.'

'Even with all this rock and roll? I mean, that's not your scene, is it?'

Bobby shrugged. 'I'm getting by. But I didn't ask you to dinner to talk about my career.'

'No.' Lindsay sipped her aperitif and looked down at her menu. 'Let's at least order before we start arguing.'

'Lindsay.' Bobby leaned forward. 'The last thing I want to do is to get into a slanging match over Gail. Haven't you understood yet? I really have changed.'

'The wine waiter's hovering, Bobby. Better make a decision.'

To Bobby's intense annoyance, Lindsay kept him at bay until the coffee stage was reached, when she lit a cigarette, sat back in her chair and said, 'OK, let's get on with it. What is it you want?'

'I'll tell you.' Bobby had ordered himself brandy, which Lindsay had refused, and he drank some now, as though giving himself courage. 'I want you and Gail to come down to London. I want us to live as a family.' He paused for her to make some move, perhaps cry out, but she said nothing. He stared at her. 'You don't seem surprised. Have you been thinking about something like this?'

'I've been expecting it. Seemed to be the obvious next step for you.'

'I know it's come late, I don't blame you for being angry with me, but I've needed time, that's all, to find out my real feelings.'

'And what are your feelings?' she asked studying her cigarette.

'Well, that I love Gail.'

'And me, of course?'

'Don't say it bitterly like that, Lindsay. I do love you. I always have, in my way.'

She met his gaze with a long clear look. 'No, Bobby, that's not true. You don't love me. I don't think it's possible for you to love anyone.'

'I tell you, I do love you,' he whispered. 'And I love Gail.'

'No. Only as an extension of yourself. That's the way a lot of people love their children. Maybe it's the way your mother loves you. I don't know. But I want more than that for Gail.'

'You won't come to London?'

'There'd be no point. Besides,' she faltered a little, 'there may be someone else. I mean, someone else here. For me.'

Bobby went very pale. 'Another man? You didn't tell me.'

'We haven't exactly been in touch lately, have we?'

'Who is it? Do I know him?'

'It's Nick Ainslie. He was once engaged to Sara.'

'And now he's taken up with you?' Bobby laughed. 'How very convenient. So much for your love for me, Lindsay!'

Lindsay flushed. She stubbed out her cigarette. 'What I feel for Nick isn't the same as I feel for you. He's just a very kind, very easy person, who's my good friend. I don't know if it will be more than that. It might be.'

'You're going to ask me for a divorce?'

'Oh, no. Well, not yet. I told you, we're not at that stage.'

'But for the sake of this very good friend, you won't come to me in London? You won't let us be a family, let Gail have two parents instead of one? And you talk to me about what you want for Gail!' Bobby's pallor had faded and there were spots of colour on his cheekbones. He drank off the brandy in his glass and stood up. 'I'll get the bill. I think we can say this evening is at an end.'

'You haven't been listening to a word I've said, have you?' Lindsay cried, outside the restaurant. 'It's not because of Nick I won't come to you in London. I explained why I wouldn't come, but as usual, you've refused to listen.'

'I've listened, all right, and I heard you say I didn't love Gail, which shows you don't understand me at all.' Bobby's eyes were glittering in the lamplight. 'But I'm Gail's father and nothing you can say can take that away from me. I'm going to see her whenever I want to, and you are not going to stop me!'

Lindsay gave a long shuddering sigh and turned aside. 'Let's go,' she said in a low voice.

'You needn't give me a lift,' Bobby muttered. 'I'll take a taxi home.'

'Oh, don't be absurd. Let's try to behave like civilised beings, for God's sake!'

They made their way to the car park through streets that were still busy, even though it was late, even though October was the city's quiet time when the Festival was over and the winter festivities were yet to begin. Neither spoke and though they were together, it seemed to Lindsay that they might have been in different worlds. But that was so often the way it had been for herself and Bobby. As she drove him home to Morningside, she could feel his resentment simmering and knew he was brooding on what he saw as wrongs done to him, just as his mother liked to do. In spite of her own sense of grievance against him, she couldn't help feeling sorry for him.

'Look, I don't want to seem unreasonable,' she told him, as she drew up at the gate of his parents' house. 'If you really want to see Gail from time to time, I'll make no objections. I mean, keep in touch.'

'See Gail from time to time?' he repeated. 'That's your offer, is it?'

'It's as good as you're going to get.'

'We might be divorced now,' he commented bitterly. 'I'm allowed access, but you have custody.'

'Bobby,' Lindsay said quietly, 'you gave me custody.'

160

Chapter Thirty-Four

Taking advantage of Lindsay's permission, Bobby took Gail out every afternoon of that last week before the wedding. They went to the park, the zoo, the seaside at North Berwick, the toy department at Logie's (for yet another doll), the cinema to see cartoons – but everywhere they went, Cora went too.

Bobby had nothing against her, she was a pleasant, helpful girl, but he still asked Lindsay why they always had to have her tagging along.

'Well, she is Gail's nanny,' Lindsay replied. 'And there are times when a little girl needs a woman around. Supposing Gail wants to go to the loo?'

'Fathers can organise that, surely?' Bobby drew his brows together. 'You don't trust me, is that it?'

'Of course I trust you! Why must you always be so extreme, Bobby?'

'You think I won't look after Gail properly, need Cora along to check up on me?'

Lindsay shook her head in exasperation. 'It's not that at all. Anyway, Cora won't be coming with you tomorrow, it's her day off, but there's a wedding rehearsal at the Cathedral at three o'clock, so Gail must be back in time for that.'

'Three o'clock? That gives us no time at all! Do you realise it's my last chance to see Gail? I have to go back to London on Sunday.'

'I'm sorry, but you must have Gail home by a quarter to three. A quarter to three, without fail.'

He gave a reluctant nod. 'OK, we'll take the bus to the Botanics, feed the ducks and come straight back.'

'You'll be all right on the bus? I'd run you there but you know what it's like, I've a thousand things to do.'

'We'll be fine. Gail loves going on the bus.'

The following afternoon, Bobby collected Gail as usual and Lindsay waved them off, watching with a smile as Gail danced along, holding Bobby's hand and chattering about her flower-girl's dress and how she would not be wearing it today because today wasn't the proper wedding, only pretend.

'Bobby!' Lindsay suddenly cried.

He turned and looked back. 'What is it?'

'Remember, a quarter to three without fail.'

He made no answer, but walked on, Gail still prattling. For no reason that she could define, Lindsay watched them until they were out of sight.

The bus stop was at the end of the street but Bobby, holding Gail's hand, walked straight past it.

'Daddy, stop!' cried Gail. 'This is where we get the bus!'

'We're not catching the bus, we're taking a taxi. Know what a taxi is, Gail?'

'Yes, it's a car. Why are we taking a taxi, Daddy? Where are we going?'

'To the station,' he said hoarsely.

He had had no plan, it had just come to him as they neared the bus stop, what he might do. You couldn't call it kidnapping. A father couldn't kidnap his own daughter. There must be some other word that meant taking your child when you had a right to take her. He couldn't think what it was, but there must be one, because he knew he wasn't doing anything wrong. Lindsay had refused to let them be a family, refused in effect to let him be a part of Gail's life, for what were visits from time to time? Her 'good friend' would be seeing Gail all the time, whereas he had been told to 'keep in touch'. Well, it wasn't enough, and Lindsay would understand it wasn't enough, once she knew he had taken Gail to London.

For, of course, he was going to tell her. He was going to explain that all he wanted was to have some time with Gail, so that she would learn to know and trust him, to love him for what he was, and not for the sort of villain her mother and grandmother might

162

make him out to be. There would be no question of Lindsay's having to go through what his father had gone through, that time he himself had been taken to London by Rachel. She had snatched him from his nursery school and run off with him to a friend's, because his father had thrown her out of the house. He'd been so small at the time he had understood nothing, but later he'd realised that his mother must have had an affair and his father had found out. Probably he had told her she would never see her son again and her response had been to snatch him. As he supposed he was snatching Gail now. But all had ended happily for his parents and it would end happily for himself and Lindsay, too. She would see sense. She would have to.

'Why are we going to the station?' asked Gail, when they had found a taxi. 'I wanted to see the squirrels. I wanted to feed the ducks. Look, I've got the bread.'

'We'll see the ducks and squirrels another day.' Bobby smiled fondly. 'I thought today you might like to see the trains.'

Gail's dark eyes were puzzled. 'I have to go to the pretend wedding today, Daddy. That's not where the trains are.'

'Well, you just wait and see what we find when we get there.'

'You mean the pretend wedding will be at the station?'

He wet his dry lips. 'No, but there'll be lots of nice things there. Nice things to eat. Trains to ride in. You'd like to ride in a train, wouldn't you, darling?'

'I have to go to the pretend wedding,' she said again, and echoing her mother added anxiously, 'without fail.'

When they reached Waverley, Gail jumped out of the taxi and stood looking round at the dark, cavernous place, where people were rushing by and trains at distant platforms were letting out frightening shrieks and roars. While Bobby paid the driver, she stood very still, her eyes very large in her small worried face, her lower lip trembling. She was still tightly holding the paper bag with bread for the ducks.

'Is this the station?' she asked, as Bobby swung her up into his arms.

'Haven't you ever been here? Haven't you ever been on a train?'

'I can't 'member, I don't know.' Her lower lip was still trembling and he was horrified to see tears welling in her eyes.

163

'Daddy, I don't like it here. I want to go to the church, I want to go to the pretend wedding.'

'Darling, listen. Daddy has to go away, back to London, and he thought you'd like to go too. See his house and all his things.' He held her close. 'We're going to buy you some new clothes, pretty dresses and shoes, lots of new toys, but first we're going to buy you a ticket. Would you like to come with me and buy a ticket?'

'No!' she screamed, struggling so violently in his arms he had to set her down. 'I don't want a ticket! I want Mummy, I want Mummy! I don't want to go to London!'

People were beginning to turn round, to stare, their faces hostile. Bobby could see them thinking, What was that man doing to that little girl? The sweat began to pour down his face as Gail screamed and screamed, and would not let him pick her up, would not let him comfort her. His mind seemed to have switched off, he could not think what to do next; it was as though he were trapped in a nightmare that would never end.

'Bobby?' A man was beside him. Two men. One he knew. Curly greying hair. Anxious blue eyes. Uncle Frankie.

'Bobby, what the hell is going on?'

'Oh, God, Frankie!' He could have fallen into his uncle's arms. 'It's Gail – she's so upset – I don't know what to do with her – I thought she'd like to see the trains.'

'Gail!' Frankie bent down and swooped her up, while the man with him, stockily built with sea-green eyes, looked on in wonderment, and Bobby stood, poleaxed.

'Gail, you remember me, darling? Uncle Frankie?' Frankie held her gently in his arms, crooning and swaying until her screams gradually subsided and she lay against him, her small body racked by long shuddering sobs. 'Remember me? Remember I was the one who brought you the big teddy? The one with the spotted bow?'

'Spotted bow,' she repeated, the tears gathering again. 'Oh, Uncle Frankie, I want to go home.'

They took a taxi to Selkirk Street. While Bobby sat slumped in despair, Frankie tried to scrub Gail's face with his handkerchief, and the man who had been introduced as Mac kept an embarrassed silence.

'Bobby, what the devil was going on back there?' asked Frankie. 'Gail's in a terrible state.'

'I told you – I was going to show her the trains.'

'He said he was going to buy me a ticket,' Gail said clearly. 'He said we were going to London and he was going to buy me new clothes and lots of toys.'

'This it?' asked the taxi driver, as his passengers sat in stunned silence.

'Look, Frankie, I think I'd better take this taxi on,' Mac muttered. 'Mebbe I'll go to Jennie's and come to your place later, eh?'

'Good idea.' Frankie carried Gail out of the taxi, and Bobby dazedly followed. Mac handed out Frankie's case, said he'd settle the fare, and was borne away in the taxi, sighing with relief. On the pavement outside Monica's handsome front door, Frankie and Bobby exchanged glances over Gail's dark head.

'You're going to have to face the music, Bobby,' Frankie said quietly. 'There's nothing I can do. You have a witness.'

'Oh, God,' whispered Bobby.

The time was two o'clock. He couldn't believe it. The whole nightmare had taken little more than an hour. But as soon as Lindsay saw Gail's tear-stained face, there was no doubt that there was going to be music playing, loud and clear.

'Now, don't worry,' Frankie tried to tell the women, Lindsay, Monica, and Sara, milling round Gail. 'She's fine, she's OK, just needs her face washed – and her mum.'

Lindsay, shooting a blazing look at Bobby, snatched Gail to her and hurried up the stairs, while Monica followed, clucking with horror at the idea that Gail should have been in the slightest way upset.

'What's happened?' cried Sara. 'Bobby, what did you do?'

Frankie took her arm. 'How about us making some tea?' he asked. 'I'm parched.'

Bobby said nothing. He went into the drawing room and shut the door. He knew he wouldn't have long to wait.

'All right.' Lindsay was with him, advancing like an avenging angel. 'Just tell me what happened.'

'How – how's Gail?' he asked shakily.

'She says she wants to go to the rehearsal. Mum's getting her ready.'

'What has she told you?'

'I haven't asked her to tell me anything. I'm asking you.'

Bobby ran a hand over his face. 'I know it's no good saying I'm sorry —'

'Sorry?'

'I don't know what came over me. It was like a bad dream. One minute I was taking Gail to feed the ducks in the Botanics, the next I was in a taxi, taking her to the station.'

Lindsay went white. 'The station . . . Oh, God, Bobby, what were you trying to do?'

'I don't know. I was crazy, I think. I mean, I had nothing for her – no clothes, no toothbrush, nothing. I suppose I thought, when I got her to London, I could find a nanny – and then I was going to take time off, stay with her – so that she got to know me.'

'London!' shrieked Lindsay. 'What are you talking about, Bobby? You couldn't have been trying to take Gail to London! Why? Why would you do that?'

Bobby sank into a chair. 'Like I said, I wanted Gail to get to know me, to learn to love me. I never meant to keep her, I knew I couldn't do that.' He raised dead dark eyes to Lindsay's face. 'In fact, when it came to it, I don't think I'd ever have got on the train. I think I'd have realised then, how crazy it all was. Lindsay, please believe me, I wouldn't have carried it through!'

'Believe you?' Her eyes were black pits in the whiteness of her face. 'Bobby, I don't think I'll ever believe you again. I never want to see you again and I'll never let you see Gail, never! It's all over, do you understand? Over!'

As he sat with his head in his hands, Monica's voice came from the hall.

'Hurry up, Lindsay, it's time to go. Gail is ready and we don't want to keep Will waiting at the Cathedral.'

Keeping her eyes on Bobby, as though she didn't trust him not to try to touch her, Lindsay retreated from him.

'Goodbye,' she said flatly. 'Don't be here when I get back. Don't come here ever again.'

Then she opened the door and left him.

Chapter Thirty-Five

The October weather was kind to Sara on her wedding day. Though it was not warm, there was no biting wind, and as she arrived at the Cathedral on the arm of the family lawyer, she was greeted by sunshine. When she made her way up the aisle, attended by her pretty flower-girl and grown-up bridesmaids, gasps of admiration followed, and Nina's heart swelled with pride. Such admiration was going to be hers, too, Everything was working out according to plan, and by next spring she would have enough for all she needed, her mother wouldn't have to worry about a thing. Though Sally was worried enough that afternoon, thinking of Donnie lying at home, gasping like a landed fish.

'I should niver have left him,' she whispered to Nina. 'I'll no' stay for the reception.'

Nina, gazing at Hamish, who was Will's best man, was only half listening. 'Mam, he's OK, he wants you to enjoy yourself. Will you look at Hamish, then, in that morning suit? Is he no' handsome? He's going to wear morning dress for our wedding, too.'

'Niver,' murmured Sally, but now it was she who was not listening.

Monica, as she had foreseen, spent most of the ceremony in tears, partly for Sara, partly for Gerald, whose elegant presence she so acutely missed. But she looked quite lovely in the hat she had finally found to match her dress, even though she had spent a sleepless night worrying over Gail's terrible experience with Bobby.

'We must just forget it for today,' she had told Lindsay at

167

breakfast, while Gail was still asleep and Sara had not yet arrived from her flat. 'Luckily, Gail is with us, safe and sound, there's no need to worry.'

'Isn't there?' asked Lindsay, who was looking so pale and strained, she seemed to have aged years overnight. 'I shall never have another moment's peace, I can tell you that.'

'My dear, Bobby's gone back to London today and out of your life. I don't believe he will dare show his face here again, after what he tried to do.'

'We can't be sure of that. I know Bobby – when he wants a thing, he wants it, and that's all there is to it. I don't trust him.'

But from the way Bobby had looked when he'd left them, Monica privately thought that he would not try to come back. Poor Rachel and Malcolm. How one's heart went out to them!

Rachel and Malcolm, sitting close to each other for comfort, felt like pariahs.

'I'm sure everyone is looking at us,' Rachel whispered, as the bride and groom left the altar to sign the register. 'They know about Bobby, of course. They all know.'

'The damned fool,' groaned Malcolm. 'What possessed him, to try a trick like that?'

'He wanted his child, Malcolm. He wanted his rights, and I don't blame him. If Lindsay had agreed to go back to London with him, he wouldn't have felt driven to take Gail.'

'As you felt driven to take Bobby?'

'Oh, Malcolm!' Tears sprang to Rachel's eyes. 'How can you drag up all that old history now? Are you blaming me for what Bobby did?'

'All I'm saying is, children have long memories.'

'Oh, dear,' thought Abby, 'Rachel's crying. This business with Bobby must be opening old wounds.'

No one in the family would ever forget that terrible time when Rachel had had a silly affair with the painter, Tim Harley, and ended up taking Bobby to London. Thank God she and Malcolm had seen sense, they'd put Bobby first and stayed together. So, what had gone wrong for Bobby after that?

Abby sighed and wished, as Monica had wished, that Gerald had been there to see his daughter's marriage. How handsome he would have looked, how distinguished! How he would have revelled in an occasion such as this! Abby took pride in the fact that her own nephew, now marrying into Gerald's family, looked handsome and distinguished too. A credit to Jennie, and all the Gilbrides. Yet, Abby couldn't help feeling a nagging little reservation at the back of her mind. Wasn't Will just a shade too composed for someone on his wedding day? Shouldn't he have been nervous up there at the altar with Sara? Muffing his lines, fumbling for the ring? He had just stood there, looking fine and upstanding but not, to Abby's mind, a man in love. As the bride and groom returned from the vestry, she pressed Frankie's arm. Maybe she was wrong, maybe Kate Rossie was far away from Will's mind that day.

'Don't they make a beautiful couple?' she whispered, determined to believe what was being presented to her.

'Aye,' agreed Frankie, thinking of Bobby, rattling back to London, crazy devil, his own worst enemy. What were Rachel and Malcolm feeling now, bravely outstaring the curious glances coming their way? Wishing they could start again, maybe? Have Bobby back the little boy who had listened to Frankie playing the 'Teddy Bears' Picnic'? Trouble was, you didn't get second chances in this life. One bite at the cherry was all you could expect, and even that sometimes turned out bitter.

Out pealed the organ in the 'Wedding March'. Down the aisle went the bride and groom, out into the autumn sunshine, Monica following, sniffing behind her lace handkerchief, Gail dancing round the bridesmaids, waving to her mother standing with Mr Ainslie.

'Oh, Will, I'm so happy,' Sara told him as they posed for photographs. 'Aren't you?'

'Of course I'm happy.' He smiled into the camera. 'I've got everything I ever wanted.'

'You mean me?' Sara laughed up at him, as her veil wafted around her, and the photographer in rapture cried, 'That's good, that's lovely! Hold it, please, hold it, if you can!'

'I can hold it for ever,' Sara answered, and knew the picture would be wonderful.

Standing in the crowd of guests watching the bridal party depart for the reception, the Gilbrides' old friends from Catherine's Land

169

stayed together, thrilled to be going on to the Caledonian themselves, delighted to have been part of Will's wedding.

'I'll say this for Madge and Jennie, they dinna forget you,'
Peggie Kemp declared, brushing confetti from her coat. 'Aye,
they're no' ones for putting their noses in the air, eh?'

'That's no' what you said when Madge got her bungalow,'
Jessie said smartly.

'Water under the bridge, Jessie, water under the bridge. I think
she's done well for us, and that's a fact.'

'Even asked the Finnegans,' Betty Kemp put in. 'But Marty's
no' well and Nancy hasna come. Sent a present, mind – a tablecloth, Madge said, hand crocheted!'

'Canna imagine that lot at the Cally!' grinned Jamie.

'Canna imagine us, come to that,' Peggie said with a laugh.
'But we're going! Jessie, where's your Ken?'

'Had to mind the shop,' Jessie answered grimly, thinking he
might not be alone in doing that. 'Didna want to come, anyway.'

'On account of Kate, eh?'

'Kate's all right,' Jessie snapped. 'She's doing fine in London.'

Aye, they said, they could believe that.

'Let's away for the champagne!' cried Peggie.

But something was happening. A policeman had dismounted from
a motorcycle and was asking questions of guests leaving for the
reception. Someone pointed out Jennie.

'Need to speak to a Mrs Muir,' he told her. 'Is she here?'

'Why, yes, somewhere – I'll find her.' Jennie, under the brim of
her wedding hat, had turned pale. 'But what's wrong?'

'Need to speak to Mrs Muir,' he repeated, and Jennie, turning,
saw Sally hurrying towards her, with Nina following and the
wedding guests standing aside to let them pass.

'Is it Donnie?' cried Sally. 'Oh, God, is it Donnie?'

It was Donnie. He was in the Royal Infirmary.

'I'm afraid the hospital want you to go at once, madam,' said
the policeman. 'Have you got transport?'

Chapter Thirty-Six

Donnie was in a side ward, with a nurse by his bed. There was an oxygen mask over his face and his eyes were closed, but his breathing, usually so laboured in a severe attack, was oddly quiet. As soon as she saw him, Sally burst into tears. She tore off her hat and pulled the flower from her coat.

'He's going, Nina,' she whispered. 'This time, he's going, I can tell.'

'No, no, he's been like this before and he's pulled through!' cried Nina. 'He'll pull through again!'

'Not this time,' said Sally.

She was right. A few minutes later, the oxygen mask over Donnie's face fluttered and lay still, and the watching nurse sprang to his side. She listened to his heart, then rang a bell and as Sally and Nina clung to each other, a doctor came running. For some time he and the nurse bent over Donnie, then Sally and Nina were asked to wait outside. Their wait was not long.

'I'm sorry,' the doctor said gently. 'There was nothing we could do. His heart just couldn't take any more.'

'Would you like to go in now?' the nurse asked sympathetically. 'We'll leave you for a few minutes.'

While her mother laid her cheek against her father's face, Nina sat motionless. Suddenly she couldn't cry any more. She thought of all that she had planned and of how it didn't seem to matter, how nothing mattered any more.

'Come and kiss your dad,' Sally said brokenly, and Nina obediently pressed her lips to Donnie's brow, then silently withdrew, leaving her parents alone. Outside the door, a fair-haired man in morning dress was waiting. He came forward and took her in his arms.

'Oh, Hamish.' She leaned against him, aware that her tears were flowing again. 'How did you get away? Were you no' wanted at the wedding?'

'Think I could stay there now? I gave my speech to Nick Ainslie, he's going to read it for me.'

'Would you like – to see Dad?'

'Later. Let your mum have as long as she can.' Hamish ran his finger around his white collar. 'Wish I wasn't wearing this lot,' he muttered. 'Had to come just as I was.'

'Dinna worry, we're all wearing the wrong things.'

And Hamish wouldn't be wearing morning dress for their wedding now, Nina reflected. In fact, she couldn't picture them even getting wed.

When Hamish telephoned Jennie at the Caledonian with the news that Donnie was dead, the Gilbrides reluctantly agreed that they must stay on at the reception. But those others who had known him were undecided what to do. Should they stay, or go? As the rest of the guests talked and laughed and the champagne flowed, it seemed to the people who had once known Donnie in Catherine's Land that they perhaps should just go home. But where was home? They were all scattered now. They no longer had homes they could share, they could no longer feel united in the presence of sorrow, as in the old days. In all the press of well-dressed people around them, they felt alone.

Madge was particularly affected. Donnie had always been a favourite of hers, such a sweet-natured boy, always so ready to oblige. Look how he had helped her on that dreadful day when Jim's wife had died in the blitz on Clydebank! Drove her in his van to the hospital where she had searched for Jim and Bella, bought her a sandwich, made her eat it. Tears ran down Madge's face as she remembered these things and Jessie pressed her hand.

'Aye, he was a grand laddie, but he was always sickly, Madge. He niver expected to make old bones.'

'Poor Sally.' Madge blew her nose. 'Donnie's sufferings are over, but she has to live on.'

'And we ken what that's like,' Jessie muttered. 'At least, she's got Nina, eh? Niver a bit o' trouble, that girl, she'll be a comfort to her ma.'

'Are you all right, Gran?' asked a sombre-faced Will, coming up with Sara. 'I know Donnie was special to you.'

'We're all wondering if we should just go home,' Madge answered.

'Oh, please, don't do that!' cried Sara. 'Please, don't anyone go home. We're so very sorry about Mr Muir, but we do so want you to stay.' She stooped to kiss Madge's cheek. 'Do stay, Gran,' she whispered. 'May I call you Gran?'

Madge smiled. 'I'd like you to.' She patted Sara's hand. 'And maybe we should remember that this is your day, Sara. I know Donnie wouldn't have wanted it spoiled.'

There was a murmur of agreement and Donnie's old friends stayed on for the speeches, the cutting of the cake and the drinking of the toasts. Only when the dancing began did they make their regrets to Monica, who was so very kind and understanding, Madge felt a twinge of conscience that she had ever thought her distant. Abby and Rachel felt they should stay with Jennie and Mac until the bride and groom left for their honeymoon, but Frankie offered to run Madge home.

'Unless you'd like to go to our place?' he suggested. 'We'll all be going back there.'

'I think I'd just like to go home, thanks all the same,' Madge replied. 'I don't mind being alone, I'll probably go to bed early.'

And think about the old days in Catherine's Land, when Donnie had been a boy running down the stair past her door, and Jim had come striding up with his cap on his thick hair, and the gas jets had flickered as they had stood together, laughing. All gone. Jim. Donnie. Even the Catherine's Land they had known. But Donnie was at peace and she would pray for him.

173

Chapter Thirty-Seven

Kate had spent Will's wedding day interviewing a Glasgow Labour MP for a profile for her newspaper. They had got on very well. Adam Lock was her sort of person. Keen, bright-eyed, intelligent, desperate to get the Labour Party back into power to work for true social justice. There was no doubt that he had wonderfully helped to occupy her mind, even though he couldn't altogether stop her occasional visions of Will in morning dress leading Sara, the stunning bride, down the aisle of the Cathedral. It was like seeing a little television picture that switched itself on when her guard was down and in spite of all her efforts, that guard kept slipping. Why should she care, that Will had given Sara something she herself had turned down? She could have been the one in white, drifting on his arm to blissful married life. Only that was something she had never wanted. Love, she had wanted, and believed was hers, but Will had betrayed her love for a job at the bank. She was more than ever determined, on his wedding day, that she would forget him.

Adam Lock did not trouble to conceal that he was attracted to her. When the interview was over and the photographer had departed, there came the moment when his eyes said so much, he scarcely needed to put his dinner invitation into words. Afterwards, she couldn't think why she had turned him down. Interest from a man like him, a shadow cabinet minister, tipped for great things, undoubtedly appealed. She wanted great things, too, and he could point her in the right direction. Apart from that, he was very attractive. And unattached. What a fool she'd been, then, to say no, she was sorry she couldn't make it. It wasn't because she wanted to sit at home and think about Will. No, damn him, it wasn't! It was true, all she wanted was to forget him. Yet somehow that evening she didn't feel like having dinner with another man.

'Well, I must confess I didn't think I'd much hope,' Adam said with a smile. 'How about a telephone number?'

She gave it to him and he said he'd ring. She was sure he would.

'Great to hear a Scottish voice in this benighted capital,' he told her, escorting her to the lift of his apartment block. 'Even if it does come from Edinburgh.'

'But not from Morningside,' she said with a laugh. 'I was born in a tenement.'

'As you know, so was I. That's one thing we have in common, but my guess is we'll find we've more. Goodbye, Miss Rossie.'

'My name's Kate!' she called, stepping into the cage of the lift.

'Kate,' he repeated, watching as the lift moved off.

She felt again she'd been a fool to turn down his invitation.

Her flat was two rooms, with kitchen and bathroom, on the ground floor of a shabby Victorian house in Streatham. There was a narrow untended garden to which she had access, and a shared entrance hall with original tiled floor and a table for tenants' letters. Although it wasn't really like it, the place reminded her of Catherine's Land. There was the same warmth about it, of people together, the same inheritance of long-lost gentility, of things being run-down and the forlorn hope that they would one day be repaired.

A letter was waiting for her when she arrived home, or, rather, a note. It was from Moray Chalmers, who had recently been appointed to a post on a London Labour daily.

'Coming round this evening,' it read. 'Bringing dinner. Love, Moray.'

'Oh, no,' thought Kate, and knew Moray had written rather than telephoned because he'd guessed she would refuse him. He too knew what day it was.

'*Fait accompli*!' he cried, arriving with bottle of wine and a bag of groceries. He kissed Kate on the cheek and emptied the bag on her kitchen table. 'See, I've got crusty bread, spaghetti, cream, streaky bacon, and Parmesan. Now, don't say you've no eggs!'

'Of course I've got eggs,' she said loftily, thanking her lucky stars she had done some rare shopping the day before; stocking her refrigerator was not one of Kate's priorities. Moray, however, prided himself on his gifts as chef, and when he had poured them both a glass of wine, flung back his black hair, and tied a teatowel round his waist (Kate, of course, had no aprons), he set to work on his spaghetti alla carbonara.

'Which will be out of this world,' he promised Kate. 'I know this Italian guy and he let me into the secret. You need plenty of fat. Yes, don't frown. Fat is the thing for flavour, so I don't derind the bacon completely, I cook it and chuck it in when it's all nice and shiny. If everything comes out a bit greasy, what the hell? Italians don't bother about their waist lines!'

'You're working very hard,' Kate said dryly, as she drank some wine. 'But it's really not necessary. I'm not crying my eyes out because Will's got married. I knew what I was doing when I split with him.'

He gave her one of his dark astute glances. 'There is a difference, though, even today, between a chap that's married and one that isn't.' He threw handfuls of spaghetti into the water he had brought to a boil. 'I mean, it draws a line. Marriage, I mean.'

'I drew the line,' Kate said coldly. 'What he does now is of no interest.'

'No changing your mind now, that's the point. Unless, of course, he changes his and they divorce.'

'I'm glad I'm not hoping for that on their wedding day.' Kate laughed briefly and set out plates. 'When will that be ready?'

'Smells good, eh? Won't be long. You hungry?'

'Hungrier than I thought.'

The spaghetti was very good. Kate and Moray mopped their plates with the crusty bread, then sliced more bread and ate it with cheese. Moray poured the last of the wine and Kate, feeling pleasantly full and a little hazy, made coffee.

'See,' said Moray, when they were sitting with the coffee in front of her ancient popping gas fire, 'This was better than being on your own, wasn't it?'

'Yes. Yes, it was. I'm grateful, Moray.'

'Though if I know you, you could have been out with half a dozen guys if you'd wanted to.'

'I did have a dinner invitation,' she told him, with a smile. 'Adam Lock asked me, after I'd finished ma profile.'

176

'Adam Lock?' Moray's tone was cool. 'Surprised you didn't go. He's a high flyer who could take you up, too.'

'I didna want to go.'

'Bet he asked for your phone number.'

'Should have been a detective, Moray.'

'I'm a journalist, that's even better. Did you give it to him?'

'Moray, do I have to tell you everything?'

'You did give it to him.' He lit a cigarette. 'Why don't I just stop hoping I'll ever get anywhere with you?'

Kate opened her eyes at him. 'You want that?'

'Why d'you think I moved south? Not for the sake of a new job that doesn't pay much more than my old one.'

'Oh, Moray.' She looked uneasy. 'I'd no idea.'

'Oh, come on, you'd an idea. All women know when a man's interested.'

'I always used to think you were teasing.'

His face darkened. 'As a matter of fact, I was always deadly serious. But you could never see anyone but Will.'

'That's changed.'

'Has it? Why did you want to be here on your own tonight?'

She shrugged and sprang to her feet. 'Let's tidy this lot away, shall we?'

She picked up their coffee cups and carried them to the kitchen, but Moray followed.

'Since when have you been keen on tidying?' he asked gently, and spun her round into his arms. 'Kate, I know this isn't the time, but we've been friends for so long and I'm sick of being friends.' He kissed her slowly. 'I want something more. Why the hell not?'

For a moment, she allowed herself to take pleasure in his kiss, in being in his arms. It was so nearly the right thing. But she was already drawing away, when her telephone rang. Moray swore richly, but Kate shook her head and answered it.

'Is that you, Kate?' she heard her father's voice. 'Just ringing from the shop.'

'Anything wrong?' she asked quickly.

'Aye. Donnie Muir's gone.'

'Gone?'

'I mean, dead. Died today. While Sally was at the wedding.'

'Oh, no . . .'

Kate listened, as her father filled in details, but her thoughts

177

were back in Catherine's Land. Buying liquorice bootlaces and 'soor ploom' sweeties from Donnie Muir's shop. Herself in plaits, Biddy wearing lipstick she'd have to rub off if Dad saw it, dear sweet Mr Muir finding cigarettes for Mam and a few eggs, eh? She'd always remembered his cough and his wheeze, but never heard him complain. Oh, poor Sally, poor little Nina. What a thing to happen on Will's wedding day!

'Thanks, Dad,' she said. 'I'll be in touch.'

'Bad news?' Moray asked sympathetically.

'A friend has died. He used to have one of the shops at Catherine's Land. Died of asthma, while his wife was at Will's wedding.'

'That's a shame.'

'Yes, Will would have been upset.' Her eyes flashed a little. 'He's not completely cold, you know!'

'I know.' Moray held her close for a moment. 'I said this wasn't the time, didn't I? Just forget what happened, eh? At least for now.'

She kissed his cheek and thought it best to say nothing.

Moray insisted on tidying up the kitchen for her, rapidly and efficiently restoring order, while Kate thought of Donnie, and then of Ivy.

'I wish I was home,' she murmured, as Moray said goodnight. 'I wish we were all back in Catherine's Land.'

'Have to move on, Kate. You know that. Everyone leaves the past behind.'

She wasn't old enough to have many links with the past, but Donnie was part of what she had, and when you lost part of your past, as she was beginning to learn, something inside you died. When she was in bed, listening to the London traffic, it came to her with surprise that for some time she had stopped thinking of Will, even though this was his wedding night. Then she did think of him.

Chapter Thirty-Eight

After the funeral, Sally said she would be keeping on the shop. Why, what else could she do? It was her only way of making a living and Donnie had not been able to leave her anything, they'd never had a chance to save.

'It's too much for you, Mam,' Nina said earnestly. 'You canna run it alone.'

'I've been running it on ma own for months, Nina.'

'Aye, and it's gone down, you ken that well. You're just going to have to let me help you.'

'You've no' got the time, pet. Your job at Logie's has to come first.'

Nina hesitated. 'I'm thinking of leaving Logie's.'

Sally caught her breath. 'Leaving Logie's? What are you thinking of? You canna talk of giving up your career!'

'I am engaged, Mam. I'll no' be at Logie's for ever, anyway.'

'Aye, but married women can work now, and even if you've a family, you'll be able to go back when the kiddies are older. It'd niver do to give up Logie's!'

Nina looked away. 'Why can you no' just let me help you, Mam? It'd be the best thing, honestly.'

'Listen, if you want to please me, you'll stay where you are. It's what your dad would've wanted too. And I can manage, in the shop, I dinna need you, and that's the truth.'

'All right, then.' Nina sighed. 'I'll stay on at Logie's.'

Sally pressed her hand. 'There's a good girl. And when we're – feeling better' – her voice faltered – 'we'll think about your wedding, eh? We'll make it really nice, for your dad's sake.'

'I'm no' interested in the wedding just now, Mam. Hamish and me, we're prepared to wait.'

'Give it time, pet, see you how you feel.'

'Yes, I'll do that,' Nina agreed.

Another Christmas came and went. Early in February, Will and Sara moved into a West End flat with large rooms that Monica helped to furnish, and Sara enjoyed herself, choosing fabrics and working out colour schemes. On the oak chest in the hallway, Will placed his silver salver from the bank. Every time he passed it, he felt a dart of pain, remembering his interview with Mr Kerr. He wished he could have put it somewhere else, but Sara said the hall was the obvious place and didn't he want people to see it? He left it where it was and tried not to look at it.

On Christmas Eve, Mac had given Jennie a pretty little old-fashioned ring that had been his mother's. He had applied for a shore job and though no date was set, it seemed as though they were finally moving towards marriage, though Jennie still said she couldn't see how she would ever leave Madge.

'You might still beat me to the altar,' Hamish said, pleasantly. 'The way things are going.'

'Well, poor Nina has to wait for a proper time of mourning, Hamish. Sally won't be wanting to think of a wedding just yet.'

'It's Nina who doesn't seem to want to think of it,' Hamish muttered. 'One minute it was all me getting morning dress and I don't know what, now – nothing.'

'But things are still all right between you and her?' Jennie asked anxiously.

'Oh, yes. No problem there. I just feel there's something going on I don't understand.'

'It's not long since her dad died, remember. You must give her time to get over that.'

'Think that's it?'

'I'm sure it is.'

Hamish's brow lightened. 'No point in worrying, then, eh?'

'The day you start worrying, I'll really have something to worry about myself,' Jennie said with a relieved smile.

On a stiffly blowing day in March, Nina was sitting at her desk in

Accounts, staring at the work that had to be done. She was feeling a dull throbbing ache of grief for her father mixed with a familiar anxiety, an anxiety that was fast developing into fear. Something made her look up to find Mr MacDonell's eyes fixed on her, but as soon as he met her gaze, he looked away. A cold hand seemed to squeeze Nina's heart.

'He knows,' she thought. 'Mr MacDonell knows. Oh, God, what's going to happen to me?'

She half rose, thinking she would go to Mrs Baxter, tell her everything, take whatever was coming to her. But she couldn't do it, she hadn't the courage. As Mr MacDonell steadfastly kept his face averted, she sat down again and tried to write, but her hand was shaking too much for her to hold the pen. In a way, it was a relief when Lindsay Gilbride appeared at her desk and whispered, so that no one else could hear,

'Nina, Mrs Baxter would like to see you.'

Abby Baxter's office was always awe-inspiring. The big desk, the portrait of Logie's founder, the atmosphere of solid work, solid values, everything that was correct and conventional. It seemed to embody all that terrified Nina about Logie's. Within its panelled walls, it held the pinnacle that everyone was supposed to want to reach, the very thought of which made Nina want to run for her life.

But Mrs Baxter herself was always kind, always fair.

Why didn't I come to her? Nina asked herself, sitting without hope opposite Mrs Baxter's desk. Now she'll never know I wanted to come, she'll never know how bad I feel.

'Good morning, Nina.' Abby's voice was brisk. 'I think you know why I've sent for you, don't you?'

Nina nodded dumbly.

'Would you like to tell me about it?'

Nina shook her head. 'I canna, Mrs Baxter.'

'Well, then, I'll tell you. Discrepancies have come to light in the Accounts Department. Invoices from some of our suppliers appear to represent goods we have never ordered or received. Those bills have been settled, but not credited to the firms' accounts. Do you know anything about that, Nina?'

Unable to speak, Nina stared into Mrs Baxter's eyes like a rabbit facing a stoat.

'Come on, Nina.' Lindsay, sitting near her, put a hand on her arm. 'It'll be better if you talk about it.'

'It will,' Abby agreed. 'It's time, Nina. It's time to tell the truth.'

'I want to—' Nina got out, and stopped, putting a hand to her eyes, as though to shield them from Mrs Baxter's gaze. 'But I canna,' she said again, 'I canna say the words.'

'Oh, Nina, —' Abby sighed. 'Why did you ever think you could get away with it? You didn't even try to alter your handwriting, or your figures. Mr MacDonell and Mrs Gilbride know our suppliers, they know what we order and when the firms supply. Did it never occur to you that they'd soon spot what was going on?'

'I niver thought,' Nina whispered. 'I niver used ma head at all. I was just looking at the invoices one day and it seemed—' she gave a great gasp and began to sob, 'so easy.'

'Yes, too easy.' Abby nodded. 'It's always been easy for people who work with money to steal it. You're not the first to be tempted, you won't be the last. But I have to tell you, Nina, I never expected it of you.'

Sobs continued to shake Nina. She could not look up.

'Will you tell me why you did it?' Abby's voice was suddenly gentle. 'Was it for your dad? Was it to help him, or your mother, in some way?'

'No.' Nina swallowed her tears and sat up straight. 'It wasna for anybody but maself. I stole the money to buy a grand wedding dress. I wanted to look like Sara.'

'Wanted to look like Sara?' Lindsay repeated faintly. 'Oh, Nina!'

'And I wanted to pay for the reception,' Nina struggled on. 'I wanted to tell ma mother she didna have a thing to worry about, I'd pay for everything.' At last Nina was able to meet Abby's eyes. 'That's why I took the money, Mrs Baxter, I'm no' going to pretend different. But I can pay it all back, it's in the post office, I've niver spent a penny. Didna want to. After ma dad died.'

Abby hesitated. 'I'm glad you can repay the money, but I'm afraid it won't alter the fact that what you did was wrong.'

'I ken that,' Nina muttered.

'Morally wrong and legally wrong.' Abby's dark eyes were stern. 'A criminal offence. I wonder if you know what that means?'

'Prison?' Nina turned white. 'I'll be sent to prison?'

'It's a first offence,' Lindsay said quickly.

'I appreciate that.' Abby paused. 'In fact, I've already decided not to take the matter to my board. There will be no prosecution.'

'Oh, Mrs Baxter.' Nina was trembling.

'I believe you are genuinely sorry for what you did, and have learned a bitter lesson.' Again Abby paused. 'You must realise, however, that I've no choice but to dismiss you.'

Nina, so pale she seemed bloodless, was motionless.

'I'm sorry, there's no other course. We operate on trust at Logie's, it's all we can do. You have forfeited that trust.'

'Forfeited your trust!' Nina started up wildly. 'Aye, it's true, it's true! I'm no' to be trusted! I've thrown everything away, everything I worked for, everything ma folks wanted!'

Abby came round her desk and put her arm round Nina's heaving shoulders. 'Nina, my dear, calm down. You mustn't let this spoil your life. You've made a bad mistake and you have to take the consequences, but what you must do is build on what you've learned. Put this behind you, never fall from trust again.'

'But what'll I do now, Mrs Baxter? What 'll happen to me now?'

'You'll work out your notice and quietly leave. No one in the office need know the reason.'

'But ma mother, Mrs Baxter, what can I tell her? She's that proud of me – if she finds out, it'll break her heart!'

'She won't find out. No one here will tell her. Just say you want to leave to be married, or to help her, something like that. The last thing we want is for her to be hurt.' Abby returned to her desk. 'Now, you'd better go back to Accounts, Nina, and try to do some work. Don't worry about Mr MacDonell. He knows the situation, but he'll say nothing.'

'Mrs Baxter, thank you for being so kind to me. I dinna deserve it.'

'Remember what I told you, Nina. Understand what you did, but don't let it ruin your life. Build on it.'

'Yes, Mrs Baxter.'

'And though all this must be kept from your mother, I'd tell Hamish if I were you. There shouldn't be secrets between you and him, and it would be too hard for you to keep this one.'

'I've already decided to tell Hamish,' Nina said bravely.

* * *

183

In spite of the gritty wind, they took their sandwiches to Princes Street Gardens and sat on a bench together. Nina had powdered her face and put on lipstick, but Hamish was not deceived.

'Been crying, haven't you?' he asked quietly. 'Better tell me what's wrong.'

'I've done something terrible, Hamish.'

'Terrible?' He tried to grin. 'What's that, then? Answered back to Mr MacDonell? Got your sums wrong?'

'I've stolen some money.'

His grin died. 'How? How could you have stolen money?'

'I work in Accounts, remember. Mrs Baxter says it's always easy for folk who work with money to steal it.'

'I don't believe it.' Hamish took a long breath. 'I mean, why would you? There must be some mistake.'

'There's no mistake.' She looked at him steadily. 'I wanted to have a wedding dress as good as Sara's, I wanted a nice reception. So I made up some invoices and I paid them. I paid the money to maself.'

'Nina!'

'Oh, Hamish!' She threw her sandwiches to the ground and flung herself into his arms. People were looking, but she didn't care, she was oblivious of everything except herself and Hamish and the burden she was unloading on to him. 'Och, I'm so ashamed, I canna tell you! I feel so bad, I wish I was dead.'

He held her close, he stroked her hair. 'Don't talk like that, Nina, never talk like that. Tell me what happened. They found out, I suppose?'

'Yes, I was so stupid, I didna even hide what I was doing. I was like someone crazy, I thought the money was there and they'd niver miss it.'

'Are they going to prosecute?' he asked, gently wiping the tears from her face.

'No, Mrs Baxter said she wouldna take it to the board.'

'Thank God for that.'

'But she's given me the sack, Hamish. She said she'd no choice. I'd – I'd forfeited their trust. And it's true, Hamish, it's all true. I did, I let them down, I let everybody down!'

'Ssh, ssh, calm down. No need to get excited. When do you have to leave?'

'They're letting me work out ma notice, they're no' telling the folk at the office.' Nina was resting more quietly in the circle of Hamish's arms. 'And Mrs Baxter said ma mother needn't know, that's what was worrying me more than anything. If Mam had found out, I dinna ken what I'd have done.'

'Well, she's not going to find out, so things aren't as bad as they might have been.' Hamish looked into Nina's drenched eyes. 'And you've still got me, you know.'

'Have I?'

'I'm not the sort to change. I love you, Nina.'

'How can you, Hamish? When I've ruined everything?'

'You haven't ruined everything. You've done something wrong, something daft, but it's not the end of the world. You just lost your head and made a mistake. Plenty of people do that when temptation's put in their way.'

'You wouldn't, Hamish.'

'I might. I don't know.'

'No, you're good.' She ran her fingers down his face. 'You're too good for me, Hamish. I canna marry you.'

'Yes, you can, and you will. We'll put this behind us, we won't think of it ever again.'

'I'll think of it every day of ma life!' she cried. 'Every time I go past Logie's, every time I remember Accounts!'

'Maybe you won't have to go past Logie's.'

'What do you mean?'

'I wish you hadn't thrown your sandwiches away,' he murmured. 'I'm still hungry. Let's go to the pub and get something else to eat.'

'Hamish, what did you mean, I needn't go past Logie's?'

'I'm thinking, I'm working it out.'

Over a large soft roll filled with bacon and tomatoes, he told her what he thought they ought to do.

Chapter Thirty-Nine

'Australia!' Jennie's eyes were huge with disbelief. 'What are you talking about, Hamish? You can't go to Australia!'

It was a Sunday afternoon. Madge and Jennie, with Hamish and Nina, were in the drawing room of Will's flat, having afternoon tea served by Sara with all the stops out. The Farrell silver teapot, the wedding-present china, plates of thinly cut sandwiches, sultana scones, a fruit cake from Logie's. But it was Hamish who had invited himself and his family. He felt he'd be more confident with Will's support in breaking his news. In hurling his bombshell.

Will was playing his part well. 'Seems to me it's not a bad idea. Australia's an up and coming place and they're keen on Scots. Hamish can probably get an assisted passage.'

'I don't care about all that!' cried Jennie. 'I just want to know why Hamish wants to go to the other end of the world!'

'Yes, why?' asked Madge. 'Why would you want to leave your home and family, Hamish? Everything you know?'

'Won't anyone have something else to eat?' Sara asked desperately, as Hamish made no reply. 'Another scone? More cake?'

When everyone shook their heads with polite murmurings, she leaped up and bore away the tea things, firmly turning down Nina's offer to help, eager to get away to the kitchen. If there was anything she hated, it was family ding-dongs like this, and her weekends with Will were so precious, wasting a Sunday afternoon was just too maddening. She decided not to return to the fray for a while, but washed up the china instead, then studied again her designs for modernising the kitchen. Now that was something she really enjoyed doing.

Hamish, under his mother's angry eye, had finally been driven to making some sort of explanation.

'I know it's hard to understand, but a lot of Scots are emigrating to Australia and New Zealand. They feel they might do better away from this country. I mean, it's still a place for the haves, isn't it? Nina and me just want to be accepted for what we are, not who our fathers were, how much we've got.'

'This is something new, isn't?' exclaimed Jennie. 'How come you've suddenly started to talk like Kate Rossie, Hamish? She hesitated. 'Or your dad.'

'There's a lot of truth in what Hamish says,' Will said into the awkward silence. 'When you work in an Edinburgh bank, you get to know the attitudes.'

'Hasn't stopped you getting on, Will,' Madge observed mildly. 'Or Abby, or Malcolm and Rachel.'

'They've got special talents, Gran,' Hamish said quickly. 'I'm a tailor. I'm not going to run Logie's, or get pictures in the galleries. Will doesn't even think I'm a professional man, do you, Will?'

Will shifted uneasily. 'You've done very well, I've never said any other.'

'Well, I reckon I can do even better in Australia. I love my job, but I don't see why I should be fixed at a certain point in the scale because of what I do. In Australia, they're only interested in people as people.'

'I'm still not convinced, Hamish,' Jennie said quietly. 'Let's forget the class system. Just give us the truth.'

Nina raised her fair head. She looked at Jennie.

'Mrs Gilbride, I think it's right you should know the truth.'

'Nina!' groaned Hamish in warning, but he knew he was too late.

'Ma mother doesna know this, and I hope she never will, but it's my fault Hamish wants to emigrate. He thinks we should make a fresh start.'

'Why?' asked Jennie blankly.

'Well – the truth is – I've been asked to leave Logie's.' Nina's voice was so low, her listeners were straining to hear her. 'I – I took some money.'

There was an appalled silence. Nina's head was drooping, as

though she could no longer hold it up, but they could see the scarlet colour rising to her brow.

'Nina, why did you do that?' Jennie asked, exchanging glances with Madge. 'Was it for your dad?'

'Everybody thinks it was for ma dad, but it was just for me. I wanted —' Nina stopped, looking round to see if Sara had reappeared, but she was still in the kitchen. 'I wanted a grand wedding, I wanted to pay for it all maself. So I made up false invoices and Logie's found out.'

'But they're not going to prosecute?' asked Will.

'No, Mrs Baxter was very kind.'

'It was a first offence,' Hamish put in quickly. 'And Nina hadn't spent the money, she could pay it all back.'

'When ma dad died, I didna want it,' Nina said drearily. 'I couldna understand why I'd taken it, it was all a nightmare.'

'You poor girl,' Madge said softly. 'What a time you've had!'

'It was ma own fault, I brought it on maself.'

'That makes it worse.' Madge leaned forward and took Nina's hand. 'But you've been punished, Nina, and you've learned your lesson. There's no need for you to go to Australia.'

'I should say not,' said Will. 'We don't exactly have transportation these days. For goodness' sake, Nina hasn't even been prosecuted.'

'You sound as though you think she should have been,' Hamish said fiercely. 'I thought you were backing me up in this?'

'You didn't tell me why you were going to Australia, I only got half the story.'

'I suppose we can't expect a fellow who works in a bank to be sympathetic! And of course, you've never been tempted yourself, have you?'

'No, I haven't. I've seen what happens to people with sticky fingers. If you ask me, Nina's been damn lucky.'

As Nina's head drooped further on her breast, Hamish leaped from his chair, his normally calm blue eyes flashing.

'Just don't say another word, Will,' he shouted. 'I always knew you were a cold fish, but I never thought you'd be so bloody insensitive to somebody who's never had half the advantages of your wife!'

'Hamish, sit down!' cried Jennie. 'Things are bad enough without you two fighting!'

188

'And swearing,' said Madge. 'On a Sunday, Hamish!'

'Sorry, Gran,' he muttered. He put his arm around Nina's shoulders. 'Maybe we'd better go.'

'No, no.' Will cleared his throat. 'I'm sorry too, Hamish. I shouldn't have said that about Nina. I didn't mean it.'

'That's all right, then,' Hamish conceded. 'I still think we should go.'

'Wait,' Jennie said desperately. 'We haven't really talked this through. Will's right, Hamish, there's no need for Nina to run off to Australia, as though she'd murdered somebody. And there's Sally to consider, isn't there? Surely you're not planning to leave poor Sally with no one?'

'She's coming with us, she wants to.'

'Sally? I don't believe it! She'd never leave Scotland, never leave Edinburgh!'

'She says there's nothing for her here now, Mrs Gilbride,' Nina said quietly. 'Now that Dad's gone.'

'And she agrees with me.' Hamish stood up. 'There are more opportunities for us in a new country, we could have a better life. Nina wasn't altogether right when she said we were emigrating because of her. I genuinely want to go.'

'There's nothing more to say, then,' said Jennie. 'You'll go, you'll make your new life, and that'll be it for Ma and me, won't it? We'll never see you, never see the grandchildren.'

'Mum, Australia isn't the moon!' cried Hamish. 'Oh, I know it seems hard, but we'll come back to see you, and you can come out to see us. It won't be as bad as you think, honest it won't.'

He put his arms around her, and then around Madge.

'Gran, we won't be saying goodbye. We'll still see each other, and if we do have any children, you'll see them too!'

'Yes, I know, Hamish.' Madge kissed him. 'You have to do what you think is right. Young people can't do just what the old folk want all the time.'

'Will, where's Sara?' Jennie asked bleakly. 'We have to be going now.'

'Would anyone like a sherry?' asked Sara, entering on cue with a silver tray of bottles and glasses. 'Oh, Nina, don't rush away, we've hardly had time to talk!'

Chapter Forty

Will drove Madge and Jennie home. No one spoke, until Jennie burst out,

'It's all Nina's fault. I don't care what Will says, if it hadn't been for her being so stupid, he'd never have thought of emigrating.'

'Whatever the reason, he's going,' said Will.

Jennie put her hand on Madge's shoulder. 'So how can I leave you, Ma? With Will gone and me gone, you'll have no one to call on. Hamish has always been so good —'

'I can look out for Gran,' Will snapped. 'I'm not going anywhere.'

'You know you have no time. You're like Abby and Rachel, no time, no time, never any time.' Jennie set her chin firmly. 'The way I see it, Ma, you need me more than ever and I'm not going to let you down.'

'Let's talk about it later,' Madge said wearily. 'My head's aching, I could do with some more tea.'

'Looks like you'll have to make some anyway,' Will remarked, turning into the bungalow's small driveway. 'You've got a visitor.'

'Why, it's Jessie!' Madge exclaimed. 'Whatever is she doing here?'

'Oh, Lord,' Jennie muttered. 'I don't feel like seeing anyone at this moment, even Jessie. Thanks for the lift, Will.'

'Mum, I'm sorry about Hamish, I know what it's going to mean to you.'

She pressed his hand. 'Still got you, anyway.'

They walked up the path and greeted Jessie, who rose from her seat on the front door step. She was very pale, the shadows under her eyes like dark bruises.

'Hello, Mrs Rossie, how are you?' asked Will. He was never at ease with Kate's grandmother who blamed him, he was sure, for the split with Kate.

Jessie gave him a wavering smile. 'Just thought I'd come and see your gran. Everything all right with you and Sara?'

'Fine, thanks, we're both fine.' Will was moving hastily back to his car. 'Well, I'd better be getting back.'

They waved him off, sensing his relief at leaving them, three women ready to talk, three women seeking consolation.

Anyone could see, thought Madge, putting her key in the door, that Jessie was bursting to tell them her bad news, and when she'd told them, they would be able to tell her theirs.

'So, what's happened, then?' she asked and Jessie sank into an armchair with a long dramatic sigh.

'Just what I was afraid of, Madge. Ken's gone and married Sheena MacLaren. Niver said a word. Went off and got wed at the register office last week and didna tell me till today. Can you believe it?'

Madge shook her head sympathetically, while Jennie lit the gas under the kettle.

'You'd like a cup of tea, Mrs Rossie?'

'Aye, I would. I couldna eat ma dinner, when he come out with the news. There we were at the table, I'd just dished up, and he says, "Ma, I've something to tell you." I says, "I hope it's no' what I think it is," and he says, "well, if you think I've married Sheena, I have." I sat there and couldna say a word. I mean, the great fool! What's he think he's playing at?'

'What did you do, then?' asked Madge, looking in a tin for the remains of a Dundee cake.

'Well, I just ups and puts ma coat and hat on, and out I walked. I thought I'd go to Biddy's, but then I remembered it was Sunday and Ewan'd be at home. Couldna face listening to them two scrapping their heads off, so I took the bus and come to you, Madge, niver thought you'd be out.'

'We went round to Will's for tea.'

'Very nice, eh?' Jessie blew her nose. 'Och, I just sat on your step and waited. Couldna think of anything else to do.'

'But if you don't stay with Ken, Jessie, where will you go?' asked Madge.

'No idea, and that's the truth. I always tellt Ken, that if he

191

brought that baggage home in Ivy's place, I'd no stay, and I meant it. I says, I'd rather sleep in the street, than have Sheena queening it over me in ma own home.'

'So you'll look for another place?' asked Jennie.

'Aye, but search me where I'll find one. Or pay for it, come to that.' Jessie picked a nut from her piece of Dundee cake and crunched it in her large false teeth. 'I've only ma pension.'

'It's a shame there's no one else in the family to help,' said Madge. 'If things'd been different with Biddy —'

'Och, she's sick of everything – sick of Ewan, sick of the kids – I'd be daft to go there. No, this time I want to be on ma own.'

'You mean that, Jessie?'

'I do. I've had enough of ma family, I've had enough of young people.'

'How about old people?'

'If you're meaning a retirement home, Madge, forget it. I've no' got to that stage yet, and I hope I niver do. Sitting around all day, staring at the wallpaper, waiting to die!'

'I wasn't meaning a retirement home, I was meaning my home. I was wondering if you'd like to share with me.'

'Share with you, Madge?' Jessie asked incredulously. 'How d'you mean? How could I?'

Jennie's eyes were fixed on her mother's face. 'I know,' she said quietly. 'I know what Ma's thinking.'

'All right, what am I thinking?' asked Madge, smiling.

'You're thinking that if Jessie comes to stay with you, I'll be free to go to Southampton. Is that it?'

'Well, haven't you kept that poor Mac waiting long enough?'

'I haven't exactly done that, Ma.'

'You know what I mean. All this going up and down to Southampton, it's not the same. Wasn't even the same when Jim just lived across the landing from me, we weren't really together.' Madge gave Jennie a long steady look. 'I don't want you to miss out on that, Jennie. Being together.'

'I know, Ma.'

Two pairs of blue eyes turned on Jessie, who appeared so dazed, she couldn't finish her tea.

'What do you say, Jessie?' asked Madge. 'Would it suit?'

'Suit? Madge, it'd be an answer to a prayer! But what'd the family think? Your Will, you ken, and Hamish?'

'Hamish isn't going to be here to think anything,' said Jennie flatly. 'He's going to Australia.'

'Niver!' shrieked Jessie. 'Australia? Why? Why'd he want to go there?'

Madge shrugged. 'He thinks he'll do better there than here. Nina agrees.'

'They're marrying and emigrating? I canna believe it. What about poor Sally, then?'

'She's going, too.'

'Sally Muir? Going to Australia? Och, this world's no' the one I used to know, Madge. Folk from Catherine's Land going to Australia? It doesna make sense.'

'Makes sense to them,' Jennie replied. 'Anyway, they're not from Catherine's Land, are they? We're none of us from Catherine's Land now.'

'I've niver been the same since I left,' Jessie muttered. She raised her eyes to Madge. 'You ken, Madge, I'm no' the same as family. It'd no' be the same, having me sharing your house.'

'You're a friend, Jessie, and a good friend. We'd get on, wouldn't we?'

'Aye, anybody could get on with you, Madge. But it's a big step for you. I mean, are you sure?'

'I'm sure. It would solve a problem for you, and it would relieve Jennie's mind about me.'

Jessie gave a long sigh. 'Canna believe it,' she said with a little laugh. 'Me, living here . . . apple tree and garden and all . . . Wait till I tell Peggie!'

They were discussing practical details – how much Jessie would contribute to bills, which room she would have, when she would move in – when the doorbell rang. Instantly, Jessie was alert.

'Ken,' she whispered. 'I bet you, it's Ken. He's no' a bad lad, eh? He'll have been worrying about me.'

Ken stood in the doorway, his heavy face wearing a mixture of relief and irritation, like a parent who has found a lost child.

'Ma,' he groaned. 'Why did you no' tell me where you were going? I've been all the way to Biddy's.'

'I dinna need to tell you ma business,' Jessie answered, with a toss of her head. 'Like you dinna tell me yours.'

'I was that worried – you went off in such a state.'

193

'Why should I no' go off? You went off and got married without a word to me. I'm supposed to take that and lump it, am I?'

'Ma—' Ken glanced woefully at Madge and Jennie, who tactfully said they'd things to do in the kitchen, but Jessie lumbered to her feet.

'Dinna go,' she ordered. 'Might as well tell Ken what we've decided.'

'What? What've you decided?'

'Madge wants me to come here, to live with her.' Jessie's dark-stained eyes were full of unshed tears. 'And I've said I would. That'll be all right with you, eh,? You'll be glad to have me out of your hair, when you bring that woman home?'

'Sit down, Ken,' Madge said hastily. 'I'm sorry to spring something like this on you, but it would seem to be a good idea for us all.'

'Aye – aye.' He put his hand to his brow. 'But I niver wanted Ma to go, we neither of us wanted that.'

'Dinna tell me what Sheena wants!' cried his mother. 'I ken fine what she wants, and so do you!'

For some time, mother and son went on batting words at each other, until it was agreed that Jessie should make her move when Jennie left to get married, but until then would put up with Sheena and Sheena would put up with her. At which Ken gave her a hug and she gave him a kiss, and they both said they would go home.

'I've got Donnie Muir's old van outside, borrowed it from Sally,' Ken told them. 'So come on, Ma, get your hat on, and we'll go back.'

'Is Sheena there now?' Jessie asked suspiciously.

'No, she's moving in tomorrow, but you remember what you said, Ma, you're going to get on, eh?'

'Well, if I ken it's no' for ever, I suppose I can manage.' Jessie flung her arms around Madge. 'Och, hen, I canna tell you what you've done for me, I canna put what I feel into words, but—'

'Go on, Jessie, there's no need to say anything.' Madge gave her a little push towards the waiting van. 'This is a two-way thing, we're helping each other, isn't that right?'

'If you say so.' Jessie hugged Jennie and climbed into the seat next to Ken's. 'Seems to me I'm getting the most out of it. Och, will you look at poor Donnie's old van, then? Remember him going out with the messages, Madge, in the old days?'

'I remember everything!' cried Madge,

She and Jennie watched the rear lights of the van until they disappeared round the corner of the road, then they turned back into the house. Now that they were alone, there was no need for masks. Jennie's face showed a mixture of relief and sorrow, Madge's calmness had turned to resignation.

'You're sure this is what you want, Ma?' Jennie asked, warily.

'I'm sure. I told Jessie that and it's the truth.'

'Well, I know you get on well with her and she's a good, genuine person.' Jennie sighed. 'But having her around all the time, what's that going to be like?'

'It's as I say, we're helping each other.'

'You're only doing it for me.'

'No, for Jessie, too. She'd never stand sharing a place with Sheena.'

'But there's nothing in it for you, Ma.'

'There's plenty in it for me. I'll have company, I'll be able to stay on in my own home, and I'll know you're happy. That's more than enough, I'd say.'

Jennie's lip was trembling, she looked suddenly young and very vulnerable. 'All right, so I can go away without worrying, that doesn't mean I'm not going to miss you, Ma.'

'Jennie, it's the way things are. You have to think of Mac, after all.'

'Yes. And look on the bright side, I suppose.' Jennie's voice was thick with emotion. 'At least I'm not going to Australia.'

Chapter Forty-One

Three months later, in separate and quite ceremonies, Jennie married Mac and Hamish married Nina. Madge's sense of loss was tempered by the news that Sara was to have a baby in December, to be Madge's great-grandchild, maybe a little girl! But nothing comforted Jennie when the time came to say goodbye to Hamish, on the deck of a ship about to sail from Southampton.

'We'll get back when we can, and you'll come and visit us,' he said desperately. 'Won't you?'

'You know we can't afford to do that. Perhaps once in a lifetime.'

'Oh, Mum —'

At the anguish in her son's eyes, Jennie steeled herself to smile, say, well maybe they'd try to do better than that. Even save up and come by air.

'Do the pools,' put in Mac, with a grin. 'Och, it's true what Hamish says, Jennie, he's going away, but no' to war, no' to the moon. There's life as we know it in Australia, eh?'

'Jennie, I ken how you're feeling,' Sally said, fiercely hugging her. 'There's no' much I can say, but Hamish is a good lad, he'll keep in touch, and you'll be with us out there in our thoughts, I promise you!'

'That's true,' a woebegone Nina said eagerly, clasping Jennie's hand. 'We'll be thinking of you all the time, thinking of Scotland, thinking of home.'

'You'll be making a new home for yourselves,' Jennie said gently. 'That's the way it goes. Look at me – I'm making a new home, even at my age!' She glanced at Mac, who put his arm around her. 'But I'm keeping my old home in my head, you'll do the same.'

'It's already there,' said Hamish. 'Edinburgh, Catherine's Land, the lot.'

'Catherine's Land,' sighed Sally. 'Och, it's another world, eh? Go and see it for us, Jennie, what's left of it, think of the old days.'

They clung together, kissing, hugging, making their last farewells. In spite of the noise around them, klaxons blowing, a band playing, all the sounds of a great ship making ready to sail, they and those around them saying goodbye were locked in their own worlds of heartbreak. The orders were sounding for those not sailing to go ashore, but still they clung and kissed and would make no move.

Mac touched Jennie's arm.

'I know, I know,' she murmured. 'I'm coming.'

These were the worst moments, the last moments. While Hamish, with Nina and Sally hanging on his arms, stood frozen, Jennie finally walked down the gangway and off the ship. As she turned for one last wave, Mac held her tight.

'When will we see them again?' she whispered, aware now that the liner was moving. With all its flags flying and its passengers waving, the band playing, 'Will Ye No Come Back Again?', the great ship was on its way. It had happened. Hamish had gone.

'I don't know when it'll be, but you will see them again, that's for sure,' said Mac. 'Come on, love, let's go back. I've a surprise for you.'

'A surprise?' she asked drearily, wanting to see the last, the very last, of the ship.

'Look.' Mac took an envelope from his pocket. 'Train tickets. I got a few days' leave, thought you'd like a trip home.'

'To Edinburgh? Oh, Mac!'

The next day found them in their railway carriage, looking out at flying scenery. To The North, said a painted sign. While Hamish, Nina and Sally sailed onwards to the Antipodes, Jennie and Mac travelled home.

Part Three

1962–1964

Chapter Forty-Two

Pink? Grey? Caramel?

On a September evening in 1962, Kate, in her flat in London, was deciding what to wear. Now an MP – she had won an Edinburgh by-election the year before – she was about to appear on television, discussing the problems of women in the workforce. Dressed in what? She had four possibles, all suits. A bright pink she had bought in a fit of madness; two dark grey that she wore for the House; and a Jackie Kennedy boxy outfit in caramel bouclé. Which of these would make her look good for the coming ordeal? Which of these would stop her feeling scared stiff?

Appearing in public usually held no terrors for her. Addressing meetings, canvassing, speaking in the House, all of these she could handle. But TV was different. The audiences were huge and faceless. She knew she wouldn't feel in control and would be at the mercy of the interviewer, whose aim would be to catch her out if at all possible. All she could do was keep her head, remember her homework and try to look terrific. But why was it only women who were expected to look terrific?

She studied her possibles again. As she would be seen in black and white, the colours didn't matter, but she didn't like herself in the pink and felt she should have a change from the grey. That left the Jackie Kennedy number. Could anyone imagine Jackie Kennedy discussing women's problems in the workplace? 'How I cope with the White House', for example? What a waste of time it was, worrying about clothes, when there were so many real problems to tackle, problems she had been elected to help to solve. At the back of her mind there was also the nagging fear that even those problems might not matter. If the rumours going around were true, Russia was planting missile sites on Cuba, ready to target America and start a third world war. She could wear whatever she liked then.

Her doorbell rang and she knew it would be Adam Lock, come round to give her moral support. Adam was an old hand at television appearances. With his confidence and quickness of mind, he came over well. Kate envied his professionalism, knew it could only be hers with practice, practice that would take its toll.

She threw on the caramel suit, added a chunky necklace, ran a comb through her hair, and answered the door.

'Hi.' Adam kissed her lingeringly, then held her at arm's length. 'You're looking good, Kate. That suit's fine.'

'How about make-up? The studio do that, don't they? Or should I put some on, anyway?'

'Even you will need something for the lights, but leave it to them.' Adam moved to to Kate's small drinks table. 'Shall we have a whisky?'

'Not for me. I need a clear head tonight.' She was checking her handbag for tissues, comb, mirror, anything she could think of.'Adam, do you think they'll understand my accent?'

'Sure they will, they understand mine.'

'You've lost yours, though.'

Adam poured himself a whisky and grinned. 'Kate, dear, so have you.'

'I have not! I don't sound English!'

'No, but a couple of years ago you'd have said "havena" and "dinna". See what I mean?'

She looked a little chagrined. 'It's mixing with all this lot at Westminster, what's a Scot to do?'

'One of these days we'll have our own parliament. For now, you stop worrying. Why all the nerves?'

'It's just the box. I'm not used to it.'

Adam drank his whisky. 'Have to get used to it, Kate. It's the key to success. Kennedy's proved that. And why do you think Macmillan's got the edge over Gaitskell?'

Hugh Gaitskell, the Labour leader, public school-educated and thought of as a bit of a toff, had done badly at the 1959 election, trailing Macmillan by nearly a hundred seats.

'Macmillan's a showman,' answered Kate. 'Gaitskell isn't. Are you saying we've all got to be exhibitionists?'

202

'Sweetheart, if you would do the dance of the seven veils at the next election, we'd be home and dry!'

'Adam, be serious!'

He laughed and kissed her again. 'We're going to win next time whatever happens. You remember that tonight, eh?'

She made a face. 'Just wish it was over. If I've got to be a TV star, maybe I'll be having second thoughts about being a politician.'

'Not you. It's your life's blood. That's why you keep all us guys at bay, right?'

'Haven't exactly kept you at bay, Adam.'

'No.' His eyes on her were watchful. 'But you won't marry me.'

'I don't want to marry anyone.'

'Because of that guy in Edinburgh?'

'Let's not talk about him.'

'He's married, isn't he?'

'And has children.' Kate took out her keys. 'Look, this is not the time to be talking about my past history.'

'As long as he is history.'

'Shall we go?' asked Kate.

Chapter Forty-Three

Earlier that day, Will Gilbride had been having his usual scratch lunch in an Edinburgh city pub. Unless he was entertaining a client, he rarely had time for more than a sandwich and a gin and tonic. As head of the S and G Investment Portfolio, he had been busy enough, but since he'd taken on responsibility for future computerisation, he seemed to have been eating, sleeping and living at the bank. No wonder Sara complained she never saw him. Sometimes he wondered if he would recognise himself.

John Frobisher, from Mortgages, deep in financial pages, asked absently,

'Like another?'

'Better not,' Will answered. 'Got work to do.'

A hand fell on his shoulder. He looked up to meet the jaunty face of Alex Seton, still with Investments, still two rungs below Will on the ladder.

'Hi, Will! Seen *The Scotsman* today?'

'No. Should I have done?'

'Got a picture of your old flame. On the box tonight for your entertainment, the lovely MP for Edinburgh Toll!' Alex threw out his arms expressively. 'The one and only Miss Kate Rossie!'

Will went an angry red. 'What the hell are you talking about, Alex?'

'I'm telling you. Your Kate's on the telly tonight. Some boring talk programme with women MPs. Though if I remember Kate, she'll not be boring, eh?'

'Do you mind not talking to me like that?' Will asked icily. 'Kate Rossie is not my Kate, she's nothing to do with me. I haven't seen her for six years.'

'Yes, cut it out,' John Frobisher snapped. 'Can't you see you're embarrassing Will?'

Alex grinned. 'Sorry, old man. Just wanted to tell you about the programme in case you missed it. Seven o'clock, BBC.'

As he began to weave his way through small tables to the exit, Will called after him,

'I shan't be watching, anyway!'

'Take no notice of Alex,' John advised. 'You know what he's like, he's just trying to take a rise.'

'I know.' Will dabbed at his brow with his handkerchief. 'Hot in here, isn't it? Look, John, I think I'll get back now.'

'Me too.'

John laid his copy of *The Scotsman* on the table. His eyes slid to Will.

'I've finished with this. Don't want it, do you?'

'No, I don't want it,' snapped Will. 'Thanks, anyway.'

Walking back to the bank, he was glad to have John Frobisher with him to keep his mind occupied with work. Yet floating over their work talk was the memory of Kate.

It was true he hadn't seen her for six years, except once or twice in the distance at civic functions, never to talk to, and he could also truthfully say that his old feeling for her had faded. It had been the strongest love of his life, but it was a boy's love and it was over. His love for Sara was quite different. A married man's love for his wife, made up of familiarity, shared experiences, shared responsibilites. They had two children now, James, nearly four, and Stephanie, nearly two. They also had a large house on the South side, an au pair for the children, and a cleaning lady three times a week. Their holidays were spent abroad, and when Will could manage it they went to concerts, the theatre, and restaurants. All in all, it was a very pleasant existence, as far removed from tenement life as you could get, if you thought about it. But Will didn't often think about it, any more than he thought about Kate Rossie. He'd moved on. But now, damn his eyes, Alex Seton had turned him back.

There was always a selection of newspapers in the main hall of the bank, certainly always a *Scotsman*, but Will didn't pause on his way to his office to look for one. The last thing he wanted was for Alex to find him hunting through the paper for a picture of

Kate. Especially when he was not interested. He had no intention of watching her programme.

Yet he went home early.

Sara greeted him with surprise.

'Darling, how come you're back so soon?'

He kissed her cheek, thinking she looked well in her cream shirt and fawn slacks. She hadn't changed in the five years they'd been married, except that she was perhaps a little less bubbly. He didn't know if that was his fault. Probably his mother-in-law thought it was. Monica was always saying he didn't spend enough time with Sara, which of course was true. As soon as he got this computerisation project off the ground, he'd do something about it. And that was a promise.

He glanced at his watch. 'I suppose I am rather early. Just felt a bit weary, thought I'd take a break.'

'Well, the casserole won't be ready for a while. Come and have a drink in the kitchen.'

Herta, the German au pair, was giving the two beautiful blond children their supper at the long scrubbed table. As soon as they saw him – and he felt guilty that they weren't used to seeing him before bedtime – they ran to him, screaming a welcome and he gathered them up into his arms.

'Now, look what's happened,' cried Sara, laughing. 'You've got milk all over your suit!'

'I get a cloth,' cried Herta, who was thin, with bleached fair hair and eyes so pale they seemed colourless, but were in fact green. 'See, I sponge – is clean. Now, you children, please to come back to eat!'

'I think I'll change anyway,' said Will, accepting a drink from Sara. 'Have my shower and get rid of the bank for the night.'

'Amen to that,' Sara said with feeling. 'Why can't you feel weary more often?'

Carrying his drink through the comfortable spaciousness of his Edwardian house, Will was deliberately keeping his mind blank. He had felt weary, he had felt like a break, but that was nothing new. Par for the course, in fact, and all he did usually was have a cup of coffee and keep going. Tonight, though, his eyes had been on the clock.

Seven o'clock, BBC.

He finished his drink and ran the shower he'd had installed at great expense; stripped, soaped, scrubbed, found casual clothes to wear, crooned cheerfully an Elvis Presley number, 'Love Me Tender.'

Seven o'clock, BBC.

Wouldn't do any harm, just to tune in, see what Kate was up to these days, would it? My God, she'd come a long way from Catherine's Land too. Only for her, being a Labour MP, coming from Catherine's Land was a part of her appeal, something to be proud of. She didn't have to try to suppress it, as he did, hating to see in the eyes of colleagues that tiny flash of surprise when they realised he was not quite one of them.

The children were on their way to bed by the time he had changed, and he helped Herta tuck them up, James in his small bed, Stephanie in her cot, both so beautifully cosseted, yet somehow so vulnerable.

'Now, I'll read you a story, shall I?' said Will. 'What would you like?'

'I don't want a story,' James declared. 'I want to watch telly with you, Daddy.'

Will, balancing himself on a tiny chair, felt somewhat taken aback.

'Who says I'm going to watch television?'

But James was already drifting into sleep, his thumb in his mouth, and Stephanie's eyes were closed. After a few minutes, Will tiptoed away.

Seven o'clock. BBC.

There she was. Sitting in a BBC studio with three other women, looking just the same. No, she was thinner. And her hair was longer. But still so beautiful. She stood out from those other women as though she were a film star and they were extras. Why, no one in their right minds would give those other poor souls a look!

'Lovely, isn't she?' came Sara's voice, and Will did a double-take.

He'd been so mesmerised by seeing Kate on the television screen, it hadn't occurred to him that the set was already switched on in the study and that he hadn't switched it on himself. His eyes moved to Sara, who was sitting on the sofa, eyeing him in return.

'Did you know Kate was going to be on TV?' she asked coolly.

'Do I ever know what's on TV?'

It wasn't quite a lie, he told himself, and crossed his fingers in his pockets.

Sara's gaze returned to Kate. 'I must admit she's done very well,' she said grudgingly.

'Yes,' Will agreed.

He felt raw with embarrassment, looking in on Kate, sitting next to his wife. He wished he could turn the television off, but Sara would have found it strange. Anyway, she appeared to be listening.

'Miss Rossie,' the sharp-nosed interviewer was saying, 'as a Labour MP, how do you see your party helping women in the workplace? I mean, if you were to come to power?'

'WHEN we come to power,' Kate replied easily, 'you can be sure we shall have the interests of women very much at heart. Our women's sections have campaigned for equal rights with men for many years, and the Labour Party will continue to give them every support. It will take time, but equal pay will have to come, along with fairer taxation and better child care provision. At the moment, we have a full programme of social reform, but we shall be considering —

'Oh, God,' sighed Sara. 'She may look better than other politicians, but she sounds just the same.'

'Not so Scottish,' Will pointed out. 'And not so belligerent. At least, on the surface.'

'I'll bet she's ready for battle, just the same as she always was,' snapped Sara.

'Doesn't need to fight with this fellow though, does she? He's eating out of her hand.'

'Like all men.' Sara stood up. 'Well, I think the casserole will be ready now. Have you had enough of this?'

'Yes, quite enough.'

And Will pushed the switch and watched Kate dwindle to a tiny spot of light, then vanish.

Chapter Forty-Four

They had supper with Herta at the long kitchen table, covered now with a checked cloth and decorated with red candles in pottery holders. Herta ate very well, but said she was worried about the Russians. Germans were always worried about the Russians. They liked Americans. It was the Americans who had saved them from the Russians. She did hope that the Russians would not fire missiles at the Americans from Cuba.

'I'm sure you don't need to worry about that, Herta,' Sara said, who was not sure at all, but liked to keep Herta happy.

Herta opened her pale eyes wide. 'Oh, yes, Mrs Gilbride, we must worry! Everyone is saying that the missiles are already in position. That man Castro does everything the Russians want. He does not like the Americans.'

'Not surprising, seeing as they tried to kill him,' Will remarked. 'Remember the Bay of Pigs invasion last year? Complete fiasco.'

'So now he lets the Russians attack America?' Herta shuddered, but continued to eat heartily. 'Mr Gilbride, will this mean a third world war?'

'I've no idea. The best thing is not to think about it. As there's nothing we can do.'

'Don't worry, it may never happen, is what they used to say in the war,' said Sara, taking a blackberry tart from the oven. 'So I'm told, I was only a child myself.'

'I was not born till nineteen forty-four,' Herta reminded them with glum pride. 'But I know about the Russians. I know what they do.'

'Let's have some pudding,' said Will.

* * *

After supper, Sara asked Herta if she would make a start on the packing.

'Packing?' Will repeated.

'Have you forgotten I'm going to Elie tomorrow? With Mummy?'

'Oh, yes, Elie.'

Will had forgotten, but now he remembered. This was another of the little holidays Monica was always dreaming up for Sara and the children, evidently believing their family holidays in France and Spain were not enough. The Farrells had friends who frequently loaned them their holiday house in Elie, a quiet seaside village in the East Neuk of Fife. It was a wonderful place to go to relax, but Will hardly ever got there. When he did, he usually took the opportunity to call in on Jennie and Mac, who lived in a fishing village further down the coast, where Mac, having retired from the merchant navy, helped his brother run a garage.

'You remember, we timed it for that course of yours in London?'

'Computer Applications, yes, but I'm not going till Monday. What do I do for the weekend?'

'Come over and join us, for once,' Sara said sharply. 'At least for the Sunday.'

'I'll do that,' said Will, glad that he could please her.

It seemed he hadn't succeeded. When they went to bed that night, she was very much the ice maiden, still resentful about something. He had a painful feeling he knew what it was and tried to take her in his arms, hoping he was wrong, but she jerked herself away.

'Come on, Sara —'

Lying rigidly beside him, she only said coldly,

'You haven't forgotten her, have you?'

'Who?'

'Oh, don't be ridiculous. You know I'm talking about Kate Rossie.'

'I haven't forgotten I once had an affair with her, if that's what you mean. But I don't think about her. I haven't seen her in years.'

'Saw her tonight.'

'A shadow on the television? You think that counts?'

Sara was silent for a while. She moved a little nearer to him and again he put his arms around her and drew her close.

'The thing is, Will,' she said in a whisper, 'I'm getting a bit tired of being the one who loves.'

'What do you mean?'

'Well, they say that in a relationship, there's always one who loves and one who's loved. I'm the one who loves.'

'Sara, that's a terrible thing to say! A relationship's a partnership, people are equal. You know I love you.'

'I think you're happy with me.'

'Well, there you are, then!'

'But is that the same as being in love?'

'Listen, I think you're talking too much.' Will's hand crept round her breast. 'Nights aren't for talking, analysing, all that stuff. You know what nights are for.'

They made love and it was good. As Sara lay sleeping quietly beside him, Will was sure he'd convinced her of his love for her. It was not romantic passion, but then what couple who'd been married a few years, with a house and bills and children, could aspire to that? He felt he was no worse than most other husbands.

But as he turned over to seek sleep himself, two things came into his mind. One was Kate Rossie's face. The other was the memory of his lie to Sara.

Kate and Adam were not asleep, though Adam kept groaning and asking couldn't Kate settle down?

'I'm too wound up,' she murmured. 'Still reliving the programme. It's not easy, coming down to earth.'

'Why not get up and make tea, or something?' sighed Adam. 'Just as long as I get my sleep.'

'You really think I made sense tonight?'

'Darling, I've told you a hundred times, you were perfect. Gaitskell will have you marked down for the next junior cabinet job going, I promise you.'

'On the strength of one TV appearance? I don't know whether to be pleased or not.'

'I told you, politics and television go hand in hand now. Keep a high profile on the box and you'll end up in Downing Street.'

Kate laughed and swung herself out of bed. 'I think I will make some tea. Want some?'

'No, just want some sleep. I have to leave early in the morning, remember. Don't want reporters seeing me sneaking out of your flat.'

'Adam, I'm not famous enough to have reporters on my doorstep.'

'Hope not, but you never know.'

Waiting for her kettle to boil, Kate looked out of her kitchen window. Beneath a lamp in the street below, a poster flapped on a newsboard.

'Soviets Admit Sending Arms To Cuba' read the headline.

As Kate turned away to make her tea, her little triumph on the TV programme seemed of very small account.

'Hi,' muttered Adam, appearing in his dressing-gown. 'I might as well have some of that tea. Can't get to sleep myself, now. Or, should I have a whisky?'

'Tea,' Kate said, pouring it. 'Listen, Adam, what do you make of this Cuban thing? Think the Russians mean anything?'

'Who knows?' Adam hunched over the kitchen table, his hands round his mug of tea.

'They say the arms they've sent are only for defence.' Kate shivered. 'Doesn't seem likely, somehow.'

'Not at all likely.'

'But why would Khrushchev want to start another war? He knows it would mean destruction all round this time.'

'He doesn't want to start another war, he's just arm-wrestling with Kennedy. Wants to show the world that the president is just a little kid who doesn't know how to stand up to top dog Russia.'

'What if Kennedy does stand up to Russia?'

'We pray.' Adam gave a great tearing yawn. 'Och, it'll never happen, Kate. Kennedy knows the score. Better to lose face than lose the world. Let's go to bed.'

The following morning, Adam left early, but not before he and Kate had read the first papers, which were full of the Russian action, but also found space for a review of last night's discussion programme, particularly Kate's contribution.

'Told you,' said Adam, 'you've been noticed, you're on your way.'

Kate wouldn't admit it, but felt a pleasant warmth inside when she viewed her chances of future success. She was not vain; all

212

she wanted was the opportunity to do her best for the people. For that, you needed power, and to gain power you had at some time to be noticed. So, television had its point, after all.

Parliament was not in session, and Adam was returning to his Glasgow constituency that day, but Kate said she'd work to do at the House of Commons and would not go back to Scotland until the end of the week. They arranged to meet for dinner in Edinburgh.

In Edinburgh itself, Will was waving goodbye to Sara, who was driving the estate car packed with luggage and children, buckets and spades, teddies, boxes of groceries, and Herta, still darkly worrying over the world situation.

'Have a good time, drive carefully,' called Will. ''Bye, James, take care of Mummy. 'Bye, Stephanie, 'bye Herta!'

'See you for lunch on Sunday,' said Sara. 'Don't forget.'

'Of course I won't forget. Afterwards, I'll look in on Mum.'

'Better give her a ring first.'

'I'll do that.'

The long car slid away, James's hand waving, and Will turned back into the house. Everything was very quiet. Too quiet. Will didn't like it. He made the phone call to his mother, his briefcase under his arm, then thankfully locked up and went to the bank.

Chapter Forty-Five

Apart from missing Hamish, Jennie was idyllically happy. She hadn't felt so happy since before Rory had left her, but she didn't think of that time, or any time but now. She and Mac semed to have settled without a ripple into the little Fife village where Nairn McKendrick had his garage. Mac got on well with his brother and turned his hand to anything that was needed, from fixing cars to doing the accounts, while Nairn, who was a widower and a calm solid man, not unlike Mac himself, was relieved and happy to have his company and Jennie's.

All the family came over regularly to visit the little colour-washed cottage Jennie and Mac had bought, to sit watching the sea, forgetting the city for a while, sometimes staying a night or two. Madge and Jessie were enchanted, particularly Jessie, who had had so little experience of the sea.

'Och, it's paradise!' she exclaimed, sitting one evening looking over the bay, turning a seashell in her worn fingers. 'Jennie, are you no' the lucky one, eh?'

'I am, I know it,' said Jennie.

'I know you think of Hamish,' Madge said quietly, 'but he's doing so well, maybe we shouldn't wish him back.'

Hamish had not wasted his tailoring skills. He and Nina had settled in Sydney, which Hamish had judged to be the most likely place to sell custom-made suits, and within a year or two his business was booming. Nina kept the books, Sally looked after the children, Fiona and little Madge; they built a fine large house, with a quarter-acre section, they couldn't have been happier.

Except of course that they missed the family back home, as they admitted on their first trip back.

'But what can we do?' asked Hamish, who was larger and more bronzed than when he'd left. 'We can't have everything. It's true we miss Edinburgh and all of you, that goes without saying, but we had to make a choice and we've made it. I reckon it was the right one. Sometimes we feel quite Australian now.'

'Good on you,' Will had said, with a laugh, but Hamish hadn't smiled.

'No point in emigrating if you want to stay the same. Isn't that right, Nina?'

'Oh, that's right,' Nina had agreed. 'You have to integrate. That's what they call it, that's what we're doing. Mam as well.'

Where Nina, like Hamish, appeared to have grown larger, with a plumpness that made her serene, Sally had grown smaller. She'd always had a worried look and it had not left her, in spite of her daughter's happiness, her son-in-law's prosperity. Madge said it was her opinion that Sally was still grieving for Donnie and for Edinburgh, and Jessie agreed.

'Aye, you canna teach an old dog new tricks, hen. Sally's no' young, like Hamish and Nina. She'll niver make an Australian.'

'Never make old bones,' thought Madge, but did not say so. Instead she spent a lot of time with Sally and the dear little girls, both the image of Hamish.

'Some compensation,' she said softly on one occasion, and recognition had sparked in Sally's eyes. She clasped Madge's hands in hers.

'Aye,' she agreed. 'Keep me going, eh? At least, I'm needed.'

'That's the thing,' said Madge. 'We all have to feel that.'

Saying goodbye to Hamish and his family the second time had been worse than the first, because this time there were the children to miss as well, Fiona not yet three, young Madge still a baby.

'How old will they be, when we see them again?' asked Jennie.

'Not much older, because you'll be coming out,' Hamish told her. 'Mac says the garage is doing well, you should be able to afford a trip.'

'And the planes are so quick,' put in Nina. 'Compared with that sea trip, eh? Promise you'll come soon?'

It was something to look forward to, something to ease the pain of parting, and Mac said he'd always wanted to see Australia. So much space, so much that was new and exciting.

'If we liked it, and if your ma wasn't with us, mebbe you'd like

215

to settle out there, too?' he asked Jennie idly, but Jennie was horrified.

'Me? Oh, I couldn't, Mac. I could never leave this country. Besides, I've got Will.'

And here was Will, coming over from Elie to have a cup of coffee after Sunday dinner. He'd telephoned earlier, so they were expecting him; but Nairn, who always spent Sunday with them, was already snoozing in his chair. Jennie put her finger to her lips and carried the tray of cups into the sun room Mac had built at the back of the cottage.

'Coffee for you and me, Will, tea for Mac. Want anything to eat?'

'No, thanks, had a big lunch.' Will laughed. 'It'll have to last me till I get to London tomorrow. I never cook when Sara's away.'

They sat looking out across the bay towards North Berwick. The September day was fine, there were late holidaymakers picking their way across the sands, and a few boats in the water. No fishing boats. This village had never had much of a fishing trade and now its little harbour was given over to tourists, who came for the season, then laid their boats up.

Maybe I'll get a boat, thought Will, taking in the peace around him. Get right away from the bank and Edinburgh and London.

'Going on another course?' asked Mac. 'Computers again?'

'Sort of seminar. Business applications.'

'What are computers?' asked Jennie.

'Machines to do your work for you. Routine work.'

'Won't they cause unemployment?'

'No. Well, I hope not. The unions are keeping watch.'

'They could get out of hand,' said Mac. 'Science fiction stuff. End up taking over the world.'

'That is science fiction stuff.' Will grinned. 'It'll be a long time before the S and G lets our clerks stop using pen and ink.'

'Changing the subject,' said Jennie, 'Sara's asked us over to Elie next week. She rang up this morning.'

'That's nice.'

'Is she all right, Will?'

'Why shouldn't she be all right?'

'I don't know. She seemed sort of quiet.'

'Quietened down a lot lately,' said Mac.

'Well, people do, don't they?' Will drank more coffee. 'She's got children, responsibilities – can't be a young thing all her life.'

'That's true,' Jennie agreed. 'Listen, did you see Kate on the telly the other night? She's done well, hasn't she?'

'Very well.' Will stood up. 'Hope you won't mind if I make tracks? I've a stack of work to get through before I go away.'

'Oh, Will, you've only just got here!'

'I know, I'm sorry. I'll come for a proper talk next time.'

Nairn was just struggling up from his sleep when Will passed his chair.

'Will! Nice to see you!'

They shook hands, Will made his apologies, promised to come again soon, then made his way to his car. Mac opened the door for him.

'What do you make of this Cuban business?' he asked quietly. 'Not another war?'

'Don't say that!' cried Jennie. 'Will, I couldn't bear it if you had to go to war again!'

'I wouldn't be doing that, Mum. Not this time.' He shook his head. 'I think it won't come to anything. The Russians are just playing games.'

'From what I know of the Russians,' Mac said grimly, 'they don't play many games.'

Chapter Forty-Six

Will was lying on his hotel bed, smoking a cigarette. The first day of the seminar – Computer Applications in Business and Banking – had gone well. Jeff Guthrie, the American running it, certainly knew his stuff. Had laid it on the line to all those dinosaurs who still couldn't grasp why they should computerise and computerise fast.

'Think Stone Age and twentieth century,' Guthrie had told them. 'Think that kind of difference. You'd better believe it, these babies are going to change the world as we know it.'

'If Khrushchev doesn't do it first,' someone had muttered.

Guthrie held up his hand. 'If you don't mind, we won't go into that right now. That's negative and we're positive. We have to operate on the principle that we are going to survive. Otherwise, what the hell are we all doing here, anyway?'

Good question, thought Will. No, seriously, he'd enjoyed the day's talk and the dinner afterwards. Later, he'd join the guys in the bar, but first he'd ring Sara.

She was fine, the children were fine, her mother was fine.

'And the weather?'

That was fine, too.

'Missing me?

'Of course. How's the computer thing going?'

'Would you believe – fine?'

She laughed, but he thought she seemed cool. To hell with it, he was beginning to get tired of placating her. Telling her he would call her when he got back, he rang off. And then his eye fell on the Post Office London Telephone Directory beside his bed.

Kate wouldn't be in it, of course. All MPs would be ex-directory, otherwise, they'd be pestered by calls day and night. On the other hand – no harm in looking. His cigarette hanging from his lip, Will opened the book.

Rossie, K.

He stared at the name and the Finchley address, until he remembered his cigarette and hastily stubbed it out.

Rossie, K.

Well, it probably wasn't her. The odds were loaded against it. All the same —

He picked up the telephone and asked for an outside line, asking himself, was he crazy? Maybe, but what harm would it do to say he'd seen her programme and give her a word of congratulation? What they'd had was so long over, she'd understand that this was just a call from an old friend that meant nothing at all. So why was he making it?

If a stranger answered, he decided, he would just say, 'wrong number' and put the phone down. If Kate answered, he might still put the phone down.

The number rang and rang. She's out, he was beginning to think, and thanked God for making his decision for him. Then Kate's voice said, 'Hello.'

'Is that — ' He cleared his throat. 'Is that Kate Rossie?'

'Speaking. Who is this?'

'Kate, it's Will. Will Gilbride.' He tried to laugh. 'A voice from the past.'

'What are you doing in London?' she asked, without expression.

'Oh, business. A computer seminar for the bank.'

'For the bank. Of course.'

That was a mistake. Why had he mentioned the bank?

'And why are you ringing me?'

'Well, I thought – you know – I'd just see how you were. Never thought you'd be in the book.'

'I don't make myself inaccessible.'

'Yes, well, I'm glad you don't.'

'Really? It's six years since we met. Why the sudden interest?'

'I suppose it was seeing you on the television the other night.'

'That's honest, anyway.' She laughed, and it was Kate's old laugh he remembered so well. 'It's crazy, you know. I make a hundred speeches and no one takes a blind bit of notice. I do one telly interview and I'm a celebrity.'

219

'Might have to go ex-directory, after all. But you were very good. That's what I wanted to tell you.'

'Thank you.' Her tone changed. 'How's Sara?'

'Very well. We have two children now, a boy and a girl.'

'That's wonderful.'

There was silence between them. Will felt his control slipping away.

'Couldn't we meet for a drink?' he asked hoarsely.

'I don't think that that would be a good idea.'

'Look, I'm in London, you're in London. Why shouldn't we meet, just as old friends?'

'Because we were more than friends once.'

'We're civilised people. Just a drink and a talk, what's wrong with that?'

'There's a pub near my flat,' she said, hesitantly. 'It's called the Falcon. How far away are you?'

'That doesn't matter. I'll take a taxi. When shall I come?'

'Say, half an hour?'

'I'm on my way.'

The Falcon was dimly lit and crowded, which suited Will. He had become very nervous about meeting Kate again face to face. People around were a kind of camouflage. He sat near the door, wondering if she would come.

She came, and in a plain dark dress looked even lovelier than on the television screen. It made him feel better to see that she too was nervous. As she accepted a gin and tonic, her ringless hands were shaking.

'I told you this wasn't a good idea,' she said, fixing him with her Renoir eyes. 'What have we got to talk about, after all this time?'

'I could tell you all my news. If you don't know it already.'

'I do know it. I spend half my time in Edinburgh and always see Biddy. Need I say more?'

'Well, then you could tell me your news. For instance, is there anyone – special?'

'I don't think that's really any of your business, Will.'

'Sorry.' He looked steadily into her face. 'It's just that I still care about you, Kate. I'd like to think you were happy and fulfilled.'

220

'I have everything I want. Just like you.'

'Yes, it's true, I have everything I want.'

Their hands were still shaking, their eyes on each other were large and tragic. They had one more drink, then Kate said, 'Shall we go? I don't want to be too late, I've paperwork to do.'

They walked through the streets without speaking. Will was on fire. He knew Kate was the same. But at her door, she said quite composedly, 'Goodnight, Will. Thanks for the drink. It was nice seeing you.'

'Aren't you going to ask me in?'

'No. I told you. I've work to do.'

'Kate —'

'Goodnight, Will.'

She already had her key in the door when he grasped her wrist with a dry, hard hand.

'I don't go back until Thursday. Could I give you dinner tomorrow night? Please don't say it wouldn't be a good idea. It'd just be a one-off. Then I'll be out of your hair, I promise you, no trouble to you at all.'

She was fighting to say no, he could almost see hear the battle raging in her mind. But she was losing it, and he was winning. He made no attempt to kiss her, or to say anything more to persuade her, simply stood waiting for her to concede.

'If it's just dinner,' she said, at last. 'I'm – pretty busy.'

'Me, too. Shall we meet here? About seven?'

'About seven.'

He watched the door close on her and waited to see her light go on. Just like old times. Standing outside her flat, watching, waiting. Like old times, but so different. He began to walk away, wondering if she was watching from behind her curtain. He had the feeling she was not. She'd given in too far, she would now be regretting it. But they would still be meeting tomorrow night at seven o'clock.

Chapter Forty-Seven

He kept on walking, going he didn't know where. Not back to his hotel, anyway. He couldn't face those guys whose only problems were computers. If somebody would just program me, he thought, to stop me feeling the way I do. A cruising taxi caught his eye, but he couldn't take it, he had nowhere to go. He saw a pub and wandered in, his head so light he might have been drunk, but he wasn't drunk, and he could do with another drink. Something strong.

A tall thin young man with long sandy hair was next to him at the bar, ordering beers. They looked at each other.

'Will!' cried the long-haired man.

'Bobby,' said Will. 'What the hell are you doing here?'

'I live here, this is my local. How about you?'

'Just down for a course.' Will ordered a whisky. 'Can I get you anything?'

'No, thanks. I'm with my group, you want to come over?'

'Your group?' Will looked beyond Bobby to where a little knot of young men with matching fringed hair cuts were sitting together. 'What group?'

'The group I'm managing. They're called the Fireboys. They're good, really good.'

'I thought you were a jazz pianist. What's all this about managing?'

'Look, don't you want to meet the guys?'

'No.' Will shook his head dazedly. 'I've been over indulging – just want a quiet drink – if you don't mind.'

'OK, I'll take the boys these beers, then sit with you for a minute. Catch up on the news, right?'

* * *

'You do look a bit under the weather,' Bobby said consideringly. 'Been out with the fellows from the course?'

'Something like that. We're looking into computers.'

'Coming thing, eh? You still with the bank?'

'Oh, yes. Still with the bank.'

'And got two kids, I hear. Lucky devil.'

Will stared. 'Never thought I'd hear you say that, Bobby.'

'No.' Bobby's face darkened. 'Well, I blew it, didn't I? Let's not talk about it, do you mind?'

'Tell me about this managing. What happened to the piano?'

'Rock and roll happened.' Bobby shrugged. 'Oh, people are always going to want to listen to jazz, but these days it has to be the best and I'm not it. Took me a long hard time to find that out.'

'I'm sorry.'

'No, it's OK.' Bobby drank his beer and smiled. 'It's damn' funny, Will, but you know how my dad was always wanting me to be an accountant like him? Well, I suddenly discovered that the money thing is what I can do. For other people. I can make the deals, I can work out the contracts.' Bobby laughed. 'I couldn't get my own career off the ground, but I can succeed for other guys. Crazy, eh?'

'No, makes sense,' said Will.

'Yeah, well as long as I get my cut, I don't mind if I don't get the glory. All started with a guy who thought he could sing like Elvis Presley. He couldn't, but for a while I got him work. When he faded, I met the boys I'm with now. The rest, as they say, is history.'

'Are they really good?' asked Will.

'I told you, didn't I? They're up and coming, like the Beatles. Due for a big hit soon. Another whisky?'

'My turn.'

Will, his head still spinning, set up fresh drinks and the cousins sat eyeing each other in strange harmony.

'Ever see Lindsay?' Bobby asked casually.

'Oh, yes. She and Sara are very close. We see Lindsay a lot.'

'With Gail?'

'Yes, she's a lovely girl. Very like your mother. Surely they let you see her?'

'I never ask.' Bobby set his lips in a narrow hard line. 'In fact, I don't get up to Edinburgh these days. My folks came down once

– wasn't a success. I think they got the message – best to leave me alone.' He hesitated. 'How about that fellow of Lindsay's? She still sees him?'

'I believe she does.'

'And he'll see Gail, right?' Bobby pushed his beer away. 'When her own father never gets a look in. Maybe you'll say for good reason. Maybe you're right. That's why I never wanted to be a father, Will. You can do so much bloody damage.'

Will felt a sudden cold feeling round his heart. He said nothing.

'I mean, look at me, look what happened to me. Taken away by my mother, never thought I'd see my dad again. Look at you and Hamish.' Bobby shook his head. 'Boy, did your father mess up YOUR lives!'

'I didn't understand what happened at the time. I suppose I see it better now.'

'You do? I'd never have forgiven him. Just like I've never forgiven myself. Oh, better stop this, Will, must be getting maudlin.' Bobby stood up. 'I'll get back to the boys.'

They shook hands.

'It's been good to see you,' said Will. 'Shall I tell your folks we've met?'

'If you like.' Bobby flung back his sandy locks. 'No need to say too much, OK? And don't mention my hair.'

'OK,' said Will, laughing.

They went to the door of the pub and stood looking out at the endless traffic.

'What do you make of this missile crisis?' asked Will, for something to say that would stop him feeling the hollow sensation inside his chest.

'What missile crisis?' asked Bobby.

Will returned to his hotel, feeling quite sober. It was as though a fever had gone, leaving him only pain. In his room he sat on the edge of his bed and looked at the snapshot he always carried of Sara and the children. It had been taken in the garden. James was laughing at the camera, but Stephanie was sleeping in Sara's arms and Sara was looking down at her, smiling. It was one of his favourites.

He put it back in his wallet and sat with his head bent low. He

224

was thinking of his mother standing in the door of her room in Catherine's Land, watching his father throw things into a suitcase. He remembered how he'd been so surprised at the way she looked. How he'd wondered what had happened to her. And what had happened to his dad.

'Boy, did your father mess up YOUR lives . . .'

Will covered his eyes with his hand.

A long time later, he picked up the telephone.

'Kate? It's Will.'

'Yes?' Her voice sounded high and rather afraid.

'I've been thinking – maybe we shouldn't meet tomorrow.'

'Oh? Had a change of heart?'

'That's not how I'd put it.'

'Well, I'm sure you're right.' She was silent for a moment. 'It was just a fancy, wasn't it, seeing me again? Because you saw me on television?'

'You think it was only that?' He remembered the way she had looked at him in the pub. He knew she didn't think that.

'You've a right to think badly of me, messing you about,' he went on, his voice shaking. 'The truth is, seeing you again on that programme did stir something. Something I thought was dead. While I thought it was dead, I was OK. Was it like that for you?'

'There's no point in talking like this, Will. We both know what we had is over.'

'I thought it was over,' he admitted. 'I was happy enough. Seems if I see you, though, it can all come back.' He hesitated. 'Then I could be hooked again.'

She was silent. He wished he could see her face, guess what she was thinking.

'You can't afford to get hooked, Will,' she said finally. 'You have a wife and children.'

He felt the knife turn in his heart.

'That's why I called you.'

'And I said you were right.'

The minutes ticked by. The receiver in his hand was heavy and slippery with his sweat.

'Kate? Are you there?'

'I'm here.'

'I'll say goodbye. Thank you for seeing me.'

225

'You must have guessed, I wanted to. Goodbye, Will, and good luck.'

Before he could respond, she had rung off.

He felt a great sick bitterness rising in him, as he lay on his bed and smoked more cigarettes. He had made a sacrifice and he should have felt good about it, but he didn't. He felt resentful. Yet it was true, he loved his family. He hadn't wanted to hurt them. When he'd looked at what he wanted, he'd drawn back from taking it, because of two little children and a woman who'd grown quiet. But not taking it hadn't stopped him wanting it.

'Oh, Kate,' he groaned and, stubbing out his cigarette, lay in misery.

Kate was angry. Not only with Will, but with herself. Happy and fulfilled, Will had said he wanted her to be, and she had been just that. Until he'd come back into her life, stirring up what had been dead and should have been left buried. The worst was that she had let him do it. Agreed to talk, to meet for a drink, to meet for dinner. Hadn't been able to say no. She, supposed to be so strong.

Hunched in her chair, she stared grimly at the late television news. More evidence of Russian soldiers and technicians landing on Cuba. Should have worried her. Would worry her when she remembered it, only just then she couldn't take it in. What had happened to her, she asked herself, when she had heard Will's voice again? Some sort of madness? She knew it was madness on his part, a madness that had taken them to the edge of the abyss. But it was he who had regained his sanity, he who had pulled them both back, not she. That was what hurt. Next time, she resolved, she would be the one to pull back. But there would not be a next time.

She switched off the television and put a call through to Glasgow.

'Adam? Kate here. Look, I'm coming up to Edinburgh tomorrow. Can we meet in the evening?'

'Sure, it's what we said,' he answered sleepily. 'Is there anything wrong?'

'No. Why do you ask?'

'You sound a bit low.'

'I suppose I've finally come down to earth.'

'Don't say that. Everybody up here is buzzing about you. The word is, you've done yourself no harm with your broadcast. Stand by for Gaitskell's call.'

'Oh, Adam!' She made herself laugh.

'No, I'm serious. It may not come tomorrow, but I'll be seeing you in the Cabinet Room one of these days.'

'We'll have to win the next election first.'

'And we will. Hell, I miss you Kate.'

'And I miss you. See you tomorrow, Adam.'

'You bet. Goodnight, Kate.'

'Goodnight, Adam.'

Now she was alone. She took off her dressing gown and slipped into bed. Late night traffic noise filled her room. She didn't hear it. Deliberately, she was thinking of Adam. 'I'll be seeing you in the Cabinet Room,' he had said. She tried to see herself arriving at Number Ten, the policeman acknowledging her, the PM greeting her. There she was, at that great oval table. A great joy should be filling her heart at even the possibility of dreams realised. And gradually the joy did come. When she finally fell asleep, Will Gilbride's face had faded again from her mind.

Chapter Forty-Eight

The eyes of the world were on the small island of Cuba, but there was still no hard evidence that the Russian missiles were in position.

Frankie, now home for good from London, told Abby that he didn't believe they were. It was all part of Khrushchev's great bluff, his game of cat and mouse with the West.

Abby looked at him sombrely.

'If the missiles are in position and if they're armed with nuclear warheads, they could do thirty times as much damage as the Hiroshima bomb. So the papers say.'

'I'm sure it's true, but why would the Russians want to blow up the world? They'd go with it, right?' Frankie cheerfully began to sing the Tom Lehrer song, 'We'll all Go Together when we go.'

'Stop that!' Abby ordered sharply. 'Oh, I feel so sick inside, Frankie. Here we are, planning our retirement —'

'You've still got a year to go.'

'Yes, and I may not even be here! If the Americans retaliate, we'll all become involved, there could be a nuclear holocaust.'

'Honey, don't write us off before the missiles are even in position.'

'You don't know that they're not,' said Abby.

Madge and Jessie weren't worrying about the Cuba crisis. There was no point, said Jessie. What could they do about it, anyway?

'It's the old story,' said Madge. 'Anything for a sensation. There's not much happening, so they find something like this.'

'Only thing is, that President Kennedy looks so young. I canna feel he's old enough to ken what to do.'

'He's got advisers, he doesn't do things on his own.'

'Aye, but they say it'll be him that could start the next war, eh? Our Mr Macmillan's old enough to be his dad, he ought to tell him a thing or two.'

'So is Khrushchev old enough to be his dad. Will says that's the trouble. He wants to put the president in his place.'

'He's no' old enough to be my dad, I'd learn him a thing or two!' Jessie laughed sourly, then lowered her voice. 'Listen, I didna tell you, Biddy says Sheena's been seen in pubs with a whole lot o' different young men. What do you think o' that?'

'I hope it's not true!' cried Madge.

'So do I. It'll kill our Ken. He dotes on that little tart like she was a princess. And she's no chicken, how's she get young men trailing after her?'

'That sort attracts young men till they're taking their pension.' Madge gave a reminiscent smile. 'Her mother was just the same.'

Ken, at his counter, was looking over the top of his glasses at Sheena. She was supposed to be marking off the ordered evening papers, but had said she'd like to step out for a breath of air, she wouldna be gone long.

'I could do with a hand,' Ken said hesitantly. He thought Sheena was looking very pretty that evening, pretty and excited, her cheeks flushed, her clear eyes alight. She didn't look to him as though she needed a breath of fresh air.

'I'll only be a minute.' Sheena kissed his cheek and he smelled the new scent she had treated herself to, from Boots.

'There'll be the usual rush, though.'

'Aye, well you can manage for a few minutes, eh?' She smoothed back his greying hair. 'Then when I come in, I'll feel more like working. Always does me good, to get a bit of fresh air.'

'But where'll you go, Sheena?'

'Och, round the block. No' far.' She gave him her lovely smile, put on a jacket and went out, clanging the shop door behind her. He looked after her, his face deliberately blank. He wasn't going to let himself wonder where she might be going, because he didn't want to know. Before they were married, she'd never gone out for these little breaths of air, now she was always missing. Six years they'd been married. She'd said the other day that that was a long time. His heart missed a beat as he remembered, and his hands on the evening papers trembled. If he was to wake up one morning and find her gone —

' 'Evening, Mr Rossie,' a customer said. 'Bad news, eh?'

'What news?'

'Have you no' read the headlines?' The man laughed. 'Got the paper right there under your fist. "US planes reveal launching sites in Cuba". The missiles are in place. It's official.'

'It's official,' Will told Sara. 'The Russian missiles are in position. American U2 aircraft have seen them.'

Sara, who had returned that day from Fife, stopped unpacking.

'Have they got – what are they – warheads?'

'Dunno. But the Russians have already admitted sending arms to Cuba. I guess they could arm the missiles any time.'

'Worrying.' Sara finished emptying a suitcase.

'You can say that again.'

'I thought you seemed a bit down.'

'Me?' Will shook his head. 'I'm not down. Well, obviously, I'm not happy about all this Cuba business. I mean, if any missile hits the States, it's not just going to be the Americans in trouble. Anyone'd feel down over that.'

'And that's all it is?'

'Why all this interrogation?' Will turned her to him and held her close. 'I'm just the same as I always am. And glad to have you back.'

She released herself and began piling clothes into a laundry basket.

'You haven't told me about the course,' she said lightly. 'Did you learn anything?'

'Not a lot, but it was useful, all the same. I discussed my plans for implementation with the American in charge of the seminar and he's given me the names of some possibles for doing the work. Obviously, we're going to need an expert programmer — '

'Did you see Kate Rossie?' asked Sara.

Will froze. It was as though she had quietly kicked him in the stomach. For a moment he couldn't get his breath.

'Kate Rossie?' he stammered. 'No, why should I?'

'You did see her, didn't you?' Sara's eyes were flinty. 'Please don't lie to me, Will. Anything's better than that.'

He collapsed into a bedroom chair. He kept his eyes down.

230

'All right, I had a drink with her. That's all, Sara, I swear. That's absolutely all.'

'You expect me to believe that?'

'If you want the truth, that's it.'

'Why did you get in touch with her? After all these years?'

'I don't know – old times' sake, maybe?' He ran his hand over his eyes. 'I suppose it was just seeing her again, on the TV that time.' He looked up into Sara's unyielding face. 'Sara, it was just a silly whim, it meant nothing. We both agreed, you know, it was nice to talk — '

'Nice to talk! Will, how stupid do you think I am?'

He stood up. 'But we made no plans ever to meet again. Please believe that. Kate's a beautiful woman, but we've nothing in common, never have had, really. She's wrapped up in her politics.'

'And what are you wrapped up in? Your wife and family?' Sara leaned forward and struck Will across the face. 'How dare you try to pretend to me that there's nothing between you and Kate Rossie? You're in love with her and you always have been, you should never have married me. Well, one thing's for sure, we don't have to stay married.'

'Sara!' roared Will, but she was already throwing his pyjamas and dressing gown at him.

'You can sleep in the spare room tonight,' she told him icily. 'And tomorrow we can work out what to do.'

'Sara!' He held her arms fast. 'For God's sake, think of the children. Are you prepared to ruin their lives, for the sake of one drink with Kate Rossie?'

'You know it's not for one drink,' she whispered, her eyes filling with tears. 'You're asking me to share my marriage.'

'No, no! How can you say that?'

'Because it's true. You're asking me to share my marriage with your thoughts of her. It's too much, it's not possible.' As he dropped his hold on her, she turned away. 'I can't do it, Will, even for the children.'

It was ironic, he thought later, lying on the spare-room bed, that his sacrifice had been for nothing. Bloody funny, really. There he'd been, agonising over cheating on Sara and the children, so he hadn't cheated, he'd given up Kate, and he'd been treated as though he'd cheated anyway. Sara had demanded the truth, but

231

she hadn't accepted the truth that he had chosen her and the children. And now she was going to punish him. She was going to destroy what they had, what he'd fought with himself to hold, she was going to break up the family, just as surely as his dad had broken up his family, running down the stair to Sheena MacLaren.

No! He sat up, staring red-eyed in the darkness. He would not let her do that. He would not let her put his children through what he'd been through himself. Whatever it cost him and Sara to stay together, stay together they would. No court would give her a divorce on the strength of what she imagined his thoughts of another woman to be, and if she walked out on him, she might lose custody of the children herself. He lay back against his pillows slightly comforted by these thoughts, but did not, of course, sleep.

Chapter Forty-Nine

Now the eyes of the world were not on Cuba, but on President Kennedy in the United States. What would he do, now that he knew for sure that Russian missiles were pointing at his country? Everyone had ideas. He was the only one with the power.

'If he makes a first strike, he could kill too many civilians,' John Frobisher said to Will. 'He won't want to put himself in the wrong.'

'And he won't want to try another invasion,' Will answered. 'Not after Fidel Castro won hands down when they tried that before.'

'Those U2 photos show that the missiles could make a hit anywhere at all in the States,' a junior cashier put in. 'Makes you freeze to think of it, doesn't it? Will we be next?'

'Kennedy wants action of some sort,' said John. 'They say his best bet is to try for a blockade. Stop Russian ships with weapons reaching Cuba.'

'Supposing they have enough weapons in Cuba already?'

'The theory is that they haven't. Of course, the West can't be sure, but let's not think the worst.'

President Kennedy in a statement to his country said that the United States and the world were passing through one of their most critical periods. Obviously, he wanted his country to survive, without, he finished sombrely, beginning the third and probably the world's last global war.

If there were those who had thought the crisis the result of media hysteria, Kennedy's final words convinced them that it was for real. They could be on the brink of a different war from any the world had known before. A war to end all wars, not with peace, but with annihilation. And everything rested on the shoulders of a boyish fellow in the White House, who would have everyone's advice, but who carried the ultimate responsibility for bringing about Armageddon. He was said to be in a state of shock.

Who wouldn't be? asked the world.

As the October days went by, there was no lessening in the feeling of crisis. President Kennedy went on American television and radio again, calling on Khrushchev to end his threat to world peace. It became known that a letter had been delivered to Khrushchev, making it plain that if any missiles hit the United States, the American government would not hesitate to retaliate. And it was a known fact that the United States had more missiles than Russia.

No reply was received.

'It's all too much like nineteen thirty-nine,' Frankie commented glumly. 'Remember waiting for the Germans to answer our ultimatum? If they didn't withdraw their troops from Poland, we'd declare war?'

'And we all know what happened then,' said Abby.

The one hope everyone clung to was that this time things were so different from any previous time, the outcome would have to be different too. But news arrived that an American blockade had been put in place and that Russian ships and submarines were sailing towards it. Khrushchev was reported to have said that if the United States stopped his ships, he would order his submarines to sink American ships. The world held its breath.

Sitting together in stony silence Will and Sara followed the situation on the television. They had reached an understanding of sorts, after Will had laid his arguments on the line and Sara had reluctantly accepted them. Without evidence against him, it would not be easy to obtain a divorce. To leave him would put her in a very difficult position. In any case, the children would suffer.

'Very well,' she told him, 'I'll stay. But don't expect things to be as they were.'

'After what's happened lately, I don't expect anything,' Will replied.

But standing on the edge of another abyss and not of his making, Will suddenly stretched out his hand to his wife.

'For God's sake, Sara, have a heart! We may be watching the beginning of our own destruction. Are you going to hate me till the end?'

She did not take his hand. She looked at him coldly.

'Don't try to use the crisis to make me accept things, Will. Our marriage is a sham. Whatever happens today, nothing can change that.'

It was 10 a.m. on 24 October. Two Russian ships, with others behind, were approaching the barrier. Sixty-three American ships were standing by. The world was balanced on a tightrope.

The minutes went by. The Russian ships continued on their course. Watches showed 10.25. The Russian ships stopped. Hearts seemed to stop. Then the Russian ships turned back, and, with the others that had been following, steamed away.

The Americans had won.

Hearts began to beat again. The world was back on its axis. But the crisis was not over. The missiles pointing at the United States were still in position in Cuba. More sites were still being constructed. Khrushchev had lost face once, he was not likely to do it again. The boy wonder in the White House was going to have to come up with something that would give him a way out. What Kennedy came up with was a promise never to invade Cuba again. In return, the Russians would have to be prepared to dismantle the missiles and allow the United Nations to inspect the sites.

There was more suspense, more holding of breath, until on 28 October, Khrushchev finally agreed to dismantle the missiles. The world had peace again, perhaps only by the skin of Kennedy's teeth, but what did the margin of victory matter? He was a hero, he had kept his nerve, his reputation was secure.

'Khrushchev won't call him a boy again,' Frankie said to Mac.

'Dinna suppose he feels like one,' Mac replied with feeling. 'I think I've aged ten years maself.'

There was a general feeling of celebration in the air, as though a war had been won. The crisis had been a war of nerves, rather than a war as such, but people felt that its ending promised well for peace. It would be a long time before the Russians dared to take on the Americans again, perhaps after this they never would. Of course, there was the Berlin Wall, there was no peace between the divided Germanys, eastern Europe could not be described as free, but for the time being people in the West wanted to put the cold war out of their minds and celebrate.

'I think we should give a party,' said Abby. 'Everybody come round to our place and bring something to eat!'

'And a bottle,' added Frankie.

Chapter Fifty

Everyone agreed that this was a great idea, and on a frosty evening in early November, Abby's flat was packed with Gilbrides and Farrells, colleagues and friends. While Frankie played the piano, hotting up the atmosphere, the bottles went into the kitchen, and the huge buffet began to mount up in the dining room. Chicken dishes, beef dishes, jacket potatoes and salads, savoury rice, cheeses, trifles, syllabubs, and, in pride of place, a massive Black Forest gateau, the latest craze in puddings, courtesy of Logie's Bakery Department.

'Oh, isn't it lovely, not to have to worry about rationing any more!' cried Jennie. 'I used to think it would never go.'

'Aye, a spread like this would have knocked us for six,' Mac agreed. 'Couldna even have imagined it.'

'Everyone's done so well,' Madge murmured to Jessie. 'And looks so happy. Except for Sara.'

'And Will,' said Jessie. 'What's up? Have they had a row or what?'

'I don't know the details, but Jennie did say she thought they weren't getting on.'

'Och, they'll no' be the first couple to run on the rocks, Madge. Dinna worry, they'll sort it out.' Jessie scraped the last speck of cream from her trifle dish and shook her head. 'Biddy says even Ken and Sheena are no' doing too badly at the moment.'

'How lovely Biddy looks tonight,' Madge commented. 'So like Kate. Any news of Kate, Jessie?'

'Seems she's keeping company with another MP, a fella from Glasgow.'

237

Wonder if Will knows that? thought Madge. Should he care, anyway?

'Feels like VE Day all over again,' Nick was remarking. 'Only, no flags.'

'Except for the Americans,' said Malcolm. 'I'll bet they've got the Stars and Stripes up everywhere.'

'I don't blame them,' said Lindsay. 'They deserve to fly their flag, they've saved the rest of us.'

'Aye, you have to give credit where credit is due,' put in Mac. 'Young Kennedy's got what it takes, after all.'

'Now he'll go from strength to strength,' said Nick. 'They say the sky's the limit for him, now.'

'And that gorgeous wife of his,' added Monica.

No one raised the spectre of what would have happened if young Kennedy had not won his arm-wrestling with Khrushchev. No one now even allowed that thought to enter their minds.

After supper, the carpet was rolled back in the drawing room, the furniture pushed to one side, and everyone got up to dance to Frankie's record collection. He had everything from wartime favourites to the latest releases.

'So, if you don't like the twist, you can wait for a foxtrot!' he announced, to which Malcolm muttered that he certainly would wait for a foxtrot, or a quickstep, or anything that was proper dancing and not the sort of thing you did if you were having a fit.

'Come on, Malcolm, you ought to move with the times,' Frankie told him. 'Like your Bobby.' He scrabbled among his records. 'See, here's one of his group's singles.'

'His what?' asked Malcolm, frowning.

'Hasn't he told you he's managing a group now? They're called the Fireboys.'

Rachel looked blank. 'We don't know a thing about this. We thought he was still playing the piano.'

'Sorry if I've spoken out of turn,' said Frankie. 'Didn't know it was a secret. Anyway, here's their latest, it's called "Wait For Me". Not too bad. And there's a picture of Bobby on the back, with the group.'

'Where? Let me see!' cried Rachel.

'Good God!' whistled Malcolm. 'Will you look at his hair? It's worse than ever. You'd better not let your ma see this, Rachel.'

'She wouldn't mind, she doesn't mind what Bobby does. But lots of young men wear their hair like that, Malcolm, he's only following the fashion.'

Malcolm grunted and called across to Will, who was sitting alone. 'Hey, Will, when you saw Bobby in London, did he tell you about this managing a group idea?'

'Oh – yes – I'm sorry – he did,' Will answered. 'He said he'd found he was quite good at it, the financial side, too.'

'Financial side! Since when has he been interested in money?' Malcolm snorted. 'I didn't know he could add two and two.'

'Why, he got Maths Higher!' Rachel said indignantly. 'Why can you never give him credit for anything these days?'

'Because I used to give him too much.'

As Malcolm took himself off for another drink, Rachel told Jennie that she actually felt rather proud of Bobby.

'I mean, it's enterprising, isn't it, to switch to something else and do well? But why couldn't he tell us about it? He's always so secretive. It's as though he wants to keep his life quite separate from us.'

'Young people are like that,' Jennie observed, watching Will, who had found Sara and appeared to be asking her to dance. Thank goodness she was accepting. From the look on her face, she might have refused.

'We can't go on like this,' Will was saying, as he and Sara moved slowly through a foxtrot. 'We've agreed to stay together, so we must try to get on.'

'You know how I feel,' Sara replied.

'Yes, but you needn't feel the way you do. I'm here with you. Doesn't that mean anything?'

'We're together because of the children, that's all there is to it.'

'No, no, it's not.' Will glanced desperately at the people dancing near them. 'Look, we can't talk now, let's talk again when we get home. Please, Sara?'

'All right,' she agreed listlessly. 'Actually, I wouldn't mind going home now.'

'OK, let's say goodnight.'

At least, thought Will, there was somebody who was happy at

239

home, and that was Herta. Since the news of the Russian climb-down, she had been honey itself, always smiling, finding nothing too much trouble. Please God, he and Sara could get back too, if not to happiness, to something that wasn't out and out enmity.

'They've gone,' Jennie said.

'Who?' asked Rachel.

'Will and Sara. I'm worried about them. They don't seem happy.'

'Oh, people always have their ups and down.' Rachel drank some wine and shook back her still dark, glossy hair. 'Know what I've been thinking, Jennie? I might start a new canvas. A big one. With all my work at the College, my own work's really getting neglected these days. It's time I did something new.'

'What'll this one be?'

'Something very topical. I've worked it all out. There'll be sea and ships —'

'If we can recognise them!'

Jennie was not alone in finding Rachel's subjects difficult to identify. Her blocks of colour required to be viewed at great distance, and even then didn't always emerge from the canvas as anything recognisable. Only her war scenes and Rory's portrait had been painted in conventional style, and Jennie pondered now as she often did these days what she should do with that portrait of Rory. At present, it was in her spare bedroom, but it didn't seem right somehow to have a painting of her former husband in the house she shared with her second. Still, Mac never complained, and where else was the portrait to go?

'And missiles,' Rachel was continuing. 'I see the missiles as something very sinister – menacing – perhaps like sharks – oh, yes, it will be very frightening.' She shuddered a little. 'I'm quite frightened myself, as a matter of fact, thinking of it.'

Jennie shuddered, too. She felt a sudden panic seize her, an unreasoning fear that made her stretch out her hand to her sister.

'Don't frighten us too much,' she whispered. 'Maybe the missile crisis isn't suitable for you to paint.'

'Since when have I painted suitable subjects?' asked Rachel. 'In fact, that's what I'm going to call it.'

'What?

'Crisis,' Rachel replied. 'It's perfect for what I have in mind.'

240

Chapter Fifty-One

Rachel decided to begin her picture on the following Saturday, when she could work at it all day until the light failed. That was the trouble with November, you had to snatch the light when you could. She had rather a headache and hoped she wasn't getting the flu that was going around, but it would take more than flu to keep her from her work once she'd made a start. Two aspirins and a cup of tea would do the trick and she needn't bother about lunch; Malcolm was playing golf.

'You getting down to it?' he'd asked, zipping himself into his jacket. 'Should have a nice clear run without me to bother you.'

'I just hope you'll get your game in.' Rachel looked out at the clouds scudding across the grey loaded skies. 'Looks to me as though it's going to rain, if not snow.'

'If I can't see the ball, I'll retire to the nineteenth hole.' Malcolm gave Rachel a perfunctory kiss and departed, while Rachel with satisfaction closed the door on him and hurried upstairs. She already had her huge canvas in position in her top-floor studio, two of her students having helped the evening before to place it on its double easel. Now she put on her paint-spattered overall and tied a scarf over her hair, experiencing as she always did the wonderful exhilaration that came when she was about to embark on a new painting. When her pictures were finished, she rarely took any interest in them, but when she was working on a canvas and it was going well, there was nothing more exciting in the world.

Not even sex, she thought, smiling to herself, knowing some of her students might not have agreed with her. But they wouldn't be the best students. Work came first for artists.

She steadied her stepladder and mounted to begin the priming of the canvas. Her headache was really bad, the aspirins hadn't done any good at all. Maybe, when she'd finished the priming, she'd have a cup of coffee and see what else there was in the medicine cupboard. This vast canvas was certainly going to be taxing, but the size was right, exactly what she wanted. In her opinion, you could never paint a small picture of the sea. The sublime called for space, that was one of her absolute rules.

By the time she had made herself coffee, she was shivering and her head felt as though a brass band were playing inside it, complete with drums. She could find no other pain-killers and swallowed some more aspirin, then wearily returned to the studio where she mixed a pale blue paint and began her first blocking in of shapes. Later she would be using a palette knife to apply her colours, but for now she preferred one of her large brushes. If only she felt better . . . It wasn't doing her headache any good to stretch from the top of the stepladder to the corners of the canvas, but she was determined not to give up. These daylight hours were so precious and she was so keen now to put some body to her vision, she must just keep going and hope that the aspirins worked soon.

All that morning she worked on, while the dull November light streamed in over her canvas. Several times she had to descend the ladder and take steps backwards to check at distance that she was getting what she wanted, then it was up the ladder again, for more stretching, more effort. At lunchtime, she began to feel quite dizzy and decided she would have to have something to eat, after all. Her throat was sore, but she felt she could manage some soup. Yes, soup would be soothing and do her good, give her the energy she needed. She turned to apply a last bit of paint, pleased with the sinister shapes that were to be her missiles, and the threat of something undefined in the darkness of her sea that would be the ships.

'Good,' she said aloud, 'it's coming.'

And leaned across from the top of her ladder to the top of the canvas, where there was to be the palest suggestion of a cloud —

'Oh, God!' she shrieked, as her brush slipped from her hand and hit the wet canvas. Oh, see the paint dribbling down the picture, she would have to do something about that, but now her head was spinning, and she was sliding, sliding down the steps, falling, falling, passing the missiles that were sharks, entering the deep water that was closing over her head, only it wasn't water, it was paint-stained floorboards that were rising to meet her.

'Help!' she cried. 'Help me! Oh, God, please help me!'

But only her canvas looked down where she had fallen, her neck at a strange angle, her head no longer spinning.

Malcolm came back in mid-afternoon, feeling frozen and ready for some tea. What a damn silly idea it had been to play golf on such a terrible day! He hadn't played well, there'd been nobody of interest in the clubhouse, he wished he hadn't bothered going.

'Rachel!' he called, taking off his wet jacket and cap and shaking them. 'I'm home!'

There was no answer. She must be still up in her studio, where she wouldn't hear him anyway. He hurried into the welcome warmth of the kitchen, where the kettle was singing on the solid fuel stove, and set about making tea himself. No doubt Rachel could do with a cup, too, and perhaps something to eat; she probably hadn't bothered about lunch, knowing her when she had a picture on the go.

He found some scones and heavy-handedly tried to spread them with butter that was hard as a brick. Never mind, they'd taste all right and the tea was good and hot. He set a tray, singing under his breath, 'Let's twist again!', which he detested, but couldn't get out of his brain. What a world they were living in, eh, where young fellows could make a fortune, singing songs like that? Was Bobby making money too, from his ridiculous group, the Fireboys? Never in a million years. If only he'd get his hair cut, though. It was just as well he never came to Edinburgh. What would folk think of him?

Making the long ascent up to Rachel's studio, he called out that he had brought her some tea.

There was no reply.

She might at least answer, he thought, she might at least open the door.

But when he had set down his tray and opened the door himself, he knew at once that Rachel was never again going to open a door for him, Rachel was never again going to answer anything he said.

Chapter Fifty-Two

Abby took charge of everything. It was she who rang Jennie and Will and sent a cable to Hamish. It was she who broke the news to Bobby in London. It was she who broke the news to Madge.

'Oh, poor Ma,' sobbed Jennie, who with Mac had come at once to her mother's bungalow. 'Oh, I can't take it in. Rachel – my sister! How will Ma bear it? Rachel was the baby, Rachel shouldn't have gone first!'

'We'll have to try to be strong, for Ma's sake,' Abby said desolately. 'Just – do what we can.'

'But how did Rachel come to fall, Abby? She must have used that ladder hundreds of times and never had an accident.'

'They found an aspirin packet in the kitchen. The doctor thinks she may have had a temperature from flu and that could have made her dizzy.' Abby rubbed her eyes. 'Then, it was just bad luck, she could have broken her leg or an arm, but the way she fell, she broke her neck. I'm afraid there'll have to be a post mortem.'

'Oh, poor Rachel!' moaned Jennie. 'Oh, I can't believe it, I can't believe I'll never see her again!'

'Come on, love, come and sit down,' Mac said gently. 'Let the tears flow, that's the only thing to do.'

'Jennie's gone to pieces,' Frankie said to Abby in a low voice. 'It's up to us to look after your ma.'

But the person who best looked after Madge was Jessie. That was because she knew what it was to lose a child, which was all so wrong and upside down, because a child should not go before a parent.

'I niver thought I'd go on living after ma Billy went,' she told

Madge, 'but you go on, you ken. You get to feel grateful in the end, for what you had.'

'Grateful for what you had,' repeated Madge. Her face, always so sweet in expression, was just the same, yet at the same time mysteriously changed out of all recognition. Jessie couldn't say why, but it just wasn't Madge looking out of those eyes, it wasn't Madge talking in that strange flat voice.

'She was the youngest,' Madge was murmuring. 'And the prettiest, though I never let on I thought that, you know. But she wasn't easy, poor Rachel, never easy. Always expected something better than what was there.'

'Aye, she wasna easy, but she was clever, Madge, eh? Really talented. Pictures in the galleries and lecturing and all that. You can be proud of her.'

'Yes, I am proud, very proud.' Madge's voice faltered. 'Abby says there'll be a memorial service. Folk will come from all over to pay their respects.'

'Is that no' wonderful?' Jessie stood up slowly. 'Madge, here's Malcolm coming,' she whispered. 'Och, the poor man!'

Like Madge, Malcolm looked the same, yet a stranger. He knelt by her chair and took her hand.

'Ma,' he asked, 'have you been able to cry?'

'No, I haven't cried.'

'Nor me.' He took her in his arms. 'I think I might cry now.'

'And I will,' sobbed Madge.

'Aye, they'll be better now,' Jessie told Abby coming in with a tray of tea. 'The two of 'em's greeting like bairns. Dinna bother with that tea. Just let them have their cry out, then.'

'Did you get on to Bobby?' Jennie asked wanly. 'Is he coming?'

'Of course he's coming,' Abby replied. 'He's taking the sleeper, he'll be here first thing tomorrow morning. I hope he'll be some comfort to Malcolm.'

'Shouldn't hope for too much,' said Jennie.

Abby and Frankie had wanted Malcolm to come to them, just for a few days, but he was adamant that he would stay in his own home. What was the point of moving out? He would only have to come back. This house had been Rachel's home too, he didn't want to leave it, even for a night. Besides, Bobby was coming, Bobby would expect to find him there.

'At least let us stay with you tonight,' urged Abby. 'You shouldn't be on your own, Malcolm.'

He raised his faded eyes. 'I'd rather, Abby, if you don't mind.'

She touched his hand briefly. 'All right, Malcolm. I understand.'

It was early next morning and still dark when Malcolm heard a taxi pull up outside the house. He was up and dressed and had been waiting for some time. Now he opened the front door.

'Is that you Bobby?'

'Just coming, Dad.'

Bobby paid off the driver and swung up his one bag. He stood looking at the figure of his father, silhouetted against the light of the hall, then he dropped his bag and ran to take his father in his arms.

Inside the house, Malcolm ran his eyes wonderingly over his son. He was wearing a conventional grey jacket and black tie, which was strange enough, but there was something else.

'You've cut your hair!' he exclaimed.

'Yes. Had it done at the station.'

He's done that for Rachel, thought Malcolm. He's done it for me. And his face crumpled. It cut him to the heart, that gesture of Bobby's. It brought it home to him what had happened, it seemed a symbol of the tragedy that had struck his life and changed it for ever.

'Come on in the kitchen,' he muttered, taking Bobby's arm. 'I'll make you some breakfast.'

'I'm not hungry, Dad.'

'Some coffee, then?'

'I just want to talk.'

It was warm in the kitchen, where they sat at the table, the sense of Rachel's absence piercing them like a sword.

'Oh, Dad, I feel so bad,' Bobby stammered.

'Don't say it, Bobby, don't talk about it now.'

'I have to, I have to. I can't grieve, because I feel so guilty. I feel – I don't know – eaten up inside.' Bobby put his hand to his brow. 'All those years when I had the chance, I never came, never wrote, and now, when I want to see her — ' He stopped and looked at Malcolm. 'Where is she, Dad? Is she upstairs?'

'No, no, they've taken her away. There'll – have to be a post mortem.'

'She just fell from her ladder?'

'They think she got dizzy, maybe had the flu.'

'I want to see her. When can I see her?'

'They'll tell us. They'll tell us when we can have the funeral.'

Malcolm made them coffee. Drinking it gave them something to do.

'I've been talking about myself,' Bobby said quietly. 'But how are you?'

Malcolm shook his head. 'I don't know. Feel – numb.'

'You'd been together so long.'

'Aye.' Malcolm stirred his coffee. 'She wasn't easy, nobody could say that, but I think she did love me. In the end, I think we were happy. We worked it out, made a life that suited us.' He fixed his eyes on Bobby's face. 'And I certainly loved her, you know. Right from the time she was a schoolgirl in ringlets. Never knew then she was going to become a famous artist. Rachel Ritchie . . . She was very well thought of, Bobby. There'll be a good show at the memorial service.'

'I never let on, but I was proud of her,' Bobby said, after a pause. 'Proud and envious. I wanted to do as well. Never did.'

'She loved you, Bobby, that's what you have to remember. I know you never wanted us to love you – no, don't speak.' Malcolm held up his hand. 'I know you found it a burden. You were the only one, you carried it all, but you'll understand now, won't you? How it was? Parents have to love their children.'

Bobby cleared his throat. 'I've already learned that,' he said quietly.

They went up to Bobby's old room, where Malcolm said he would leave Bobby to unpack.

'I've put some towels out. Tell me if you need anything.'

'I'm fine, Dad, thanks.'

Malcolm shivered. 'I've put the radiator on, but it still feels cold in here.'

Because no one's been in it for so long, thought Bobby.

When he was alone, he hung his dark suit in the wardrobe and put the rest of the few clothes he had brought into the chest of

247

drawers. The house seemed very quiet and it occurred to him that this was the first time in his life he had been in it without his mother. He sat in a chair by the window, filled now with grey winter light, and let his memories fill his being. Mum in her painting clothes, placing colours with her knife, standing back, checking the canvas, narrowing her beautiful Ritchie eyes. Mum as a very young woman, himself a little boy, content to be in her arms. He hadn't minded her love then, it had been all he wanted, love from his mother and father and to be the only one.

Ah, how things had changed. Soured. How often he had heard his mother say, you were so sweet when you were a little boy. But he hadn't stayed a little boy, he hadn't stayed sweet. He had changed and maybe his parents had changed, too, wanting always more than he could give, so that there had been constant tugging from one side to the other and no one winning.

Don't think of it, he told himself, rising from his chair and pacing the room, still so cold the chill seemed to be entering his bones, but was of no importance. Don't think of what went wrong, think of the happy times. But what right had he to think of the happy times? His guilt rose and suffocated. If only he'd come up more, if only he'd written. But he'd thought his parents would last for ever, he'd thought he had all the time in the world. Suddenly, time had run out.

'Dad!' He ran downstairs. 'Dad, can we go and see Gran?'

Chapter Fifty-Three

Abby and Frankie arrived, as Malcolm and Bobby were about to leave. Though they made no comment, Bobby could tell they were surprised by his appearance.

'It's wonderful to see you,' Abby told him, as Malcolm went for his car. 'You'll be a great help to your dad. There'll be a lot of phone calls and press interest, you know. Maybe you could help to shield him from that?'

'Of course, but first I want to see Gran.'

Abby's face was pinched, her eyes red-rimmed. 'Yes, she needs you, Bobby. You were always one of her favourites.'

'Always forgave me everything, I know.'

'And this is a time for forgiving, Bobby.'

'I don't know if I can forgive myself, that's the trouble.'

'Think about your father. What you can do for him. Oh, he's so glad you came, Bobby!'

Am I some kind of monster, Bobby asked himself, that they think I wouldn't come to my own mother's funeral?

He spent a long time with his grandmother, whose eyes had brightened when she saw him. For some time they said nothing, just sat holding each other's hands.

'Hamish is coming,' Madge said at last.

'Is he? That's good to know.'

'And it's good to see you, Bobby.'

'You knew I'd come, didn't you? You didn't doubt me?'

'Of course I knew you'd come.' A smile crossed Madge's strange features. 'I know you better than any of them.'

'You do. And you always brought out the best in me.'

'Well, it was there to bring out, dear. Remember that.'

Abby had been right about the telephone, also the doorbell. All day, people kept contacting the house, expressing sympathy, requesting information about the funeral, delivering sympathy cards and flowers, wanting to know if there was anything they could do. As Malcolm wandered from room to room, the scent of winter flowers filled the air.

Bobby, dealing with all the activity with a competence he could scarcely believe, was glad to have so much to do. He knew he should make some calls of his own, to the group, to contacts in London, but he didn't know what he wanted to say. London seemed so shadowy, he had the curious feeling that he couldn't even remember it, yet only yesterday it had been the centre of his universe.

In the middle of the afternoon, the doorbell rang again. It was Lindsay, standing with a tall, dark-haired girl in school uniform, who was holding a bunch of long-stemmed carnations.

'Oh, Bobby, how are you?' Lindsay burst out. 'Please, may we come in?'

He showed them into the kitchen and with shaking hands took down a vase to fill with water for the flowers.

'Dad's resting at the moment,' he said hoarsely. 'But I know he'll want to see you. I'll make some tea first.'

'Bobby, I don't know what to say to you.'

'Lindsay, don't say anything.'

Bobby's eyes moved to his daughter's face. She was so like his mother, it hurt. It also hurt that she was looking at him warily, as though she didn't trust him, though of course he wasn't surprised. Young though she'd been at the time, she probably still remembered that he had tried to take her away. He couldn't imagine now why he'd done that. More shadows filled his mind. Nothing of those old days seemed real.

'Hello, Gail,' he said, forcing himself to smile. 'Would you like a biscuit?'

She shook her head and Lindsay said sharply, 'Answer your father, Gail!'

'No, thank you,' Gail said politely.

'Let me make the tea.' Lindsay loosened her coat and filled the kettle. 'Though we don't really need any.'

250

'We find it gives us something to do,' Bobby said.

'I'm sure you've been kept busy anyway. It's so wonderful that you're here, for your father's sake.'

'You didn't think I wouldn't be here?' he asked quickly.

'No! No, of course I didn't.'

Lindsay's tone was so vehement, Bobby was sure she'd thought exactly that. He watched her make the tea, feeling sick at heart. This mirror everyone was holding up to him, he didn't want to look in it.

Malcolm held Lindsay and Gail close when they took in his tea.

'If there's anything we can do, you will let us know, won't you?' Lindsay asked. 'My mother's very anxious about your meals. Can we make you something? You won't want to be cooking for yourselves.'

'Abby's doing supper tonight.' Malcolm looked vaguely at Bobby. 'And I think other people have offered, haven't they?'

'Yes, everyone's being very kind.'

'Very kind,' Malcolm agreed. 'Very kind.'

The days passed. Hamish arrived by air, and he and Bobby fell almost at once into the friendship they'd shared at Heriot's so many years before. Bobby had always got on well with Hamish and Will, but these days it was clear Will was going through a bad patch. Abby said he and Sara would sort things out, they only needed time. Bobby wasn't so sure. For now, it was Hamish who gave him support. And support was needed.

Everyone said that Bobby and his father would feel better after the funeral, but that couldn't take place until the results of the post mortem were known. These revealed that Rachel had indeed been suffering from a viral infection at the time of her fatal fall, which made the family feel a little better: at least, there was an explanation and explanations helped. Rachel's body was released to the undertaker's and a date set for the funeral, but first Malcolm and Bobby went to see her for the last time.

'She won't look like herself,' Malcolm muttered. 'They make them up, you know, they look different.'

'We should see her, though, Dad,' said Bobby. 'Everyone says it's something you have to do, so that you can come to terms with what's happened.'

'Come to terms!' Malcolm groaned. 'I'll never do that.'

Rachel looked very beautiful, very peaceful. The morticians had not overdone the make-up, though it was true she did look different, Rachel, yet not Rachel. They were glad they had seen her, were loath to leave her, yet at the same time relieved when they gave way to other members of the family. Madge had not come. She would not change her memories of Rachel in life, she declared. She didn't need to see her in death to know that she had gone.

The funeral, on a bitterly cold day, was private. Rachel had asked in her will to be cremated, which upset Madge a little, she wasn't used to it, and it did seem a little frightening. When it was over, everyone went to Abby's and sat quietly together, just the family, and Abby and Jennie served things to eat that nobody wanted but ate all the same.

Jennie announced that she had decided to give Rachel's portrait of Rory to the Gallery of Modern Art. It was the only portrait Rachel had ever painted and would be important for the gallery's collection of her works. It wouldn't be lost to the family, they could go along and see it whenever they wanted. Both Will and Hamish approved of the idea, and Madge said Jim would have been so proud to see his son's portrait on display.

Rachel's will brought no surprises. Her few pieces of jewellery went to her mother and her sisters, with a cameo brooch for Lindsay, while the capital she had amassed from the sale of her paintings went mainly to Malcolm, Bobby and Gail, with smaller legacies to Will and Hamish. Several paintings were also left to the family and Bobby's choice was an abstract called 'Harlequin'. As a child he had liked to study it and try to pick out the Chinese lanterns Rachel said were there. It was a little game they used to play, sometimes he could see them, sometimes he couldn't. On the day he put the picture up in his bedroom, he could see them quite clearly.

'You're very welcome to come and see Gail whenever you want,' Lindsay told him. 'I'm at work full time now, but Gail goes to Mum after school. If you liked, you could collect her sometimes and take her there.'

'I'd like that, if Gail wouldn't mind.'

'No, she's happy about it.' Lindsay hesitated. 'I suppose you'll be going back to London soon, won't you?'

'I haven't made any plans.'

'You'll be coming back anyway for the memorial service?'

'Oh, sure I will.'

'Well, let me know when you want to pick up Gail.'

'I'll do that. Thank you, Lindsay.'

More days went by. One evening, Malcolm and Bobby were alone, having supper cooked by Bobby. Pork chops and apple sauce. He told Malcolm he'd become quite a dab hand at cooking. It was surprising what you could do when you tried.

'When do you think you'll be going back?' asked Malcolm after several false starts at getting the words out.

Bobby stacked their dishes. 'I've been thinking about that.'

'Won't want to leave your group too long, I suppose?'

Bobby turned his dark gaze on his father's face. 'I might be leaving them altogether.'

Malcolm cleared his throat. 'Trying something new?'

'Yes, but not in London. Dad, I don't know how you'll see this, but I've been thinking I might stay on in Edinburgh.'

'Stay on?'

'With you.'

Malcolm sat back in his kitchen chair. His hand on his pipe was trembling. 'I – don't understand. How could you do that? There's nothing you're used to here. I mean – what would you do?'

'I might take an accountancy course. I might try for the Scottish Office. I haven't decided.'

'Bobby.' Malcolm tried to laugh. 'I can't believe this! After all these years, you're thinking of — '

'Reverting to type? Turning into a conventional Edinburgh middle-class gent?' Bobby shrugged. 'I can't explain it myself. Something's just seemed to wither inside me. All that I wanted, I don't want any more. It's fallen away from me, like a shell.'

'You're not doing this out of pity for me?' Malcolm asked sharply. 'I wouldn't want you to do that. I'm low at the moment, but I'll recover, I'll be able to get on with my life, you know.'

'It's not out of pity. It's something I want to do myself. Because I've changed. Maybe I might have changed anyway, but what's happened has just knocked my old life on its head.'

Bobby sat down at the table and looked earnestly at Malcolm. 'After all, Dad, what would my future have been down there in

London? A not very talented chap managing younger chaps and getting older and older, maybe succeeding, maybe not? I was always rebelling against something, I guess, but that's all over now. I want to stay here, make a life with you, if you want me, earn a living, get by. Dad, what do you say?'

'Oh, Bobby, you know what I say.' Malcolm felt for his son's hand. 'If you're sure, only if you're sure, it'd be an answer to a prayer to have you here.'

'I'm sure, all right, so that's settled then.'

Bobby rose and began to run hot water into the washing up bowl. Malcolm took up a teatowel.

'We won't have to do this all the time, you know,' he told Bobby. 'We can get a housekeeper.'

'Yes, when we've sorted ourselves out.'

'You haven't thought any more about Lindsay?'

'Lindsay? No. If she's any sense she should get a divorce from me and marry that faithful fellow she's got in tow. He's a nice chap, he'd be good for her.'

'If you're really going to stay on in Edinburgh, perhaps you ought to tell her that.'

'Perhaps I will.' Bobby hung up the dish mop, 'But now I have some calls to make.'

'To London?' Malcolm heaved a great sigh. 'Bobby, I wish I could tell you —'

'You don't need to tell me anything, Dad. I'm the one who owes you, not the other way round.' Bobby dried his hands. 'When I've finished my calls, shall we go and see Gran again? Give her my news?'

They both knew they would have given the world to be able to give his news to Rachel.

254

Chapter Fifty-Four

The winter of 1962–1963 was severe. It seemed to those who were mourning Rachel that the long dark snow-gripped days matched their feelings. There seemed to be no end to winter or their grief. When Hugh Gaitskell, the leader of the Labour Party, died suddenly in January, 1963, it was yet another reminder of the transitory nature of life.

Kate Rossie, though stunned by the death of her leader, took courage from the announcement that his successor was to be Harold Wilson. If the truth were faced, Gaitskell had always seemed to her too much of a gentleman to defeat the gentlemen Tories. Wilson was a very different character, one who combined a first-class mind with the strength and ruthlessness required to win. If anyone could return the Labour Party to power, it would be he.

'You'll do well with Wilson,' Moray told Kate. 'You're clever and not afraid to speak your mind. Of course, what's in his mind, he keeps to himself.'

'Thing is, has he seen me on television?' she asked jokingly. 'I'll never make the shadow cabinet if I don't get known on the box!'

'With Wilson in charge, you should be thinking about the real thing, not shadows,' Moray replied. He looked at her consideringly. 'I bet your boyfriend's thinking along those lines.'

'Are you talking about Adam Lock?'

'How many boyfriends have you got?'

'Moray!'

'Oh, I know, it's none of my business. I was never in with a chance, was I? Well, I wish you luck. He's going places and so are you, you'll make a good team.'

'We are not a team,' Kate said coldly. 'We have a relationship, but it's not important.'

Moray laughed shortly. 'Does he know that?'

'I'm very grateful to Adam for all that he's done for me, I like being with him, he likes being with me. Can we leave it at that, please?'

'Whatever you say.'

'We have an election to win, that's what matters to me.'

'And me, but there are other things in life.'

'I know,' said Kate.

She was pleased that she had succeeded so well in putting Will out of her mind. The death of his aunt had brought him back for a while; she'd even thought of writing to him. In the end she'd thought it better to write only to Malcolm. Although the funeral was for family only, it soothed her heart to send flowers, for her grief over Rachel's life cut short was genuine. Will's aunt had been a difficult woman but a talented artist. It made Kate shiver to think that one should have to go before one's work was done.

Whenever she went up to visit her constituency, Kate called in on her father, enduring the company of Sheena, who was still around.

'I keep wondering if she's going to do a bunk,' Kate told Biddy. 'But maybe she's decided she's better off being Dad's darling than some young fellow's slave.'

'Canna see Sheena being anybody's slave,' Biddy retorted. 'And I think she might still go. Then what'll happen to Dad? It'll be the death of him.'

'Oh, I don't think so. Folk don't usually die from broken hearts.'

'And you should know?' asked Biddy.

'Thank you very much, my heart's in one piece,' snapped Kate.

Gradually, the long winter faded. The snow and ice melted, the first spring flowers appeared, and Rachel's family began to learn to live with their loss. Which was not to say that life was good again, only easier to bear. The memorial service, attended by so many eminent artists, gave them consolation. At least Rachel had been appreciated, at least the work she had left would endure.

Bobby, after much deliberation, had decided to try for the

256

Scottish Office and took a simple pleasure in being accepted. For the first time since he was a little boy, he found his actions being approved by his family. It was a strange sensation. Even Mrs Farrell smiled on him again and sometimes he felt that Lindsay too had softened towards him, but he made no effort to make sure. Though he was making his way slowly towards normal life, his guilt was a dark burden he felt he would never lose. Fighting his corner for Lindsay was something he couldn't face. In fact, he couldn't even bring himself to find out if she wanted a divorce. Better to put off thinking about that until she told him, he decided.

One bright spot in his life was getting to know Gail. Until he began work at the Scottish Office, he had taken to collecting Gail from school, as Lindsay had suggested, and it had been a great relief to him that Gail didn't mind, even seemed to enjoy chattering about her life on the walk to her grandmother's house. Yes, she enjoyed school, but was no good at drawing, she was never going to be a famous artist like Grandma Gilbride. What she liked was learning French and German. If she got to university, she would study modern languages.

'Useful, if we get into this Common Market,' commented Bobby.

'Oh, but I shan't work in Europe,' Gail told him. 'Mum wants me to join Logie's.'

'Well, that would be a good idea, too. It was your father's family firm, and you know how well Aunt Abby did there.'

'Yes, it's such a shame she has to retire this year, isn't it? Mum says she's going to be absolutely LOST!'

Abby did retire in the summer. For one who had served Logie's so long and so well and held its greatest office, the occasion obviously had to be marked in splendid style. There was detailed press coverage, interviews on local TV, a portrait commissioned for the boardroom, and not one but three farewell parties arranged: a partners' dinner, a lunch for suppliers and reps, and a grand buffet and dance for all the staff. All kinds of people Abby had once worked with came back to be remembered. Miss Inver, who had once been her boss in Accounts, now very old and frail; Clare Naylor, Bernard Maddox and Ian Fox, colleagues who had held the fort with her during the war; long-retired doormen, sales assistants, waitresses, board members – everyone wanted to say goodbye.

257

Through it all, Abby bore up gallantly, as though it were the most natural thing in the world to say goodbye to her whole life, as though she were not facing the future with ashes in her mouth and a complete absence of ideas as to what she might do. She laughed and chatted, she accepted her handsome silver leaving presents, she even made a point of making her successor feel welcome, though this was a brash, hard-nosed forty-year-old, who said he had a 'million ideas' for changing Logie's and made Abby wish with all her heart that it had been Lindsay who was taking on her mantle.

'Oh, Abby, you know I'm not ready!' Lindsay cried.

'You're already a junior partner, you're on your way,' Abby told her. 'One day I know I'll see you following in your father's footsteps.'

'Not in yours, Abby, not in yours, I could never follow you.' Lindsay shook her head in despair. 'What on earth are we going to do without you? This place'll never be the same.'

'Everyone can be done without,' Abby said sturdily, and felt a pang because she knew that it was true.

Still, there were plenty who agreed with Lindsay that Logie's would never be the same without Mrs Baxter, who had been Miss Ritchie, who had started as a junior in Accounts and ended up at the top of the tree. On her last day they were queueing up to shake her hand, some with tears in their eyes. There were cries of Will You No' Come Back Again, and Abby, holding flowers, promised with tears in her own eyes, that of course she'd be back, she wasn't leaving Edinburgh, she'd often be looking in.

But she knew it wasn't true. She wouldn't be looking in. It wasn't the thing to do, to go back, this was the end for her. She must face her new life in retirement with dear Frankie at her side, and that was that. For the last time, she walked through the swing doors into the sunshine of Princes Street and stood with Frankie, watching all the people passing by who didn't know she'd just left Logie's. Usually, she collected her car from the rear of the store, but today she had decided that she would like to walk for a little while in the gardens. Just get her bearings, as it were.

'Get you, with all those flowers,' Frankie remarked. 'You look like the Queen.'

'Lucky Queen,' Abby replied. 'She can go on for ever. There's

258

nothing like work, Frankie, it's better than all the leisure in the world.'

'Only you would say that, Abby.' Frankie grinned. 'I'm quite enjoying being retired myself.'

'Because you're not. Why, you're still playing whenever you can get a booking!' Abby took his arm. 'There's the difference, you see. I can't run Logie's in my retirement, but you can still play your piano.'

'Honey, I promise you, in a week or two, you'll be wondering how you ever found the time to go to work.'

'Doing what?'

'Well, seeing to your ma—'

'And?'

He shrugged. 'I don't know. You'll find something.'

They crossed Princes Street and looked back at Logie's basking under its awnings, its flags flying overhead in the clear blue sky.

'Ah, I can't believe it,' Abby whispered. 'It seems only the other day that I was creeping in there for my interview and you wouldn't come in with me because you were afraid of the doorman!'

'Sure I was. He was just the type to throw out a guy like me, trained to see at a glance I didn't have a penny to my name!'

'Well, I didn't get thrown out.' Abby gave a faint smile and shaded her eyes to look up at the Castle. 'But where've they gone? All those years?'

'That's what everybody wants to know,' said Frankie.

'I remember standing here watching the hunger marchers in nineteen thirty-three. The poor devils had had to sleep on the pavement and they were all making tea and washing in the fountain. Everybody in Logie's was so shocked!'

'Would be, knowing them.'

'And then when the war started,' Abby went on, not listening, 'there was those planes having a dog-fight over the city, we were all outside, watching. Gerald made us go in, there was shrapnel everywhere.'

Tears welled in Abby's dark eyes again. 'It's hard to think of Gerald, Frankie. What would he have made of me retiring? I was always the young one!'

'You made chief executive, don't forget that,' Frankie said softly. 'He'd have been proud of you.'

259

'But, oh God, Frankie what am I going to do now? I don't feel any different, I don't feel ready to retire!'

He took her arm. 'Let's not walk in the gardens, let's go get the car and go home. We're having dinner with the family tonight, remember.'

'All I've done lately is eat,' sighed Abby, wiping away her tears. 'Is that how folk spend their retirement?'

Chapter Fifty-Five

Among the messages to Abby on her retirement had been one from Kate. She had always admired Will's clever aunt, recognising that she and Abby were two of a kind. Strong, principled characters, willing to make sacrifices, not just for their careers, but for the things they believed in. Abby had climbed as high as it was possible for her to go, while Kate was young and still had her way to make, but that way was mapped out, clear and certain. As Moray had predicted, Harold Wilson had spotted her potential and appointed her shadow junior minister for the Home Office.

'Now the sky's the limit,' Adam told her, opening champagne. And it seemed to Kate that he was right.

Back in Edinburgh, the news was not so good. Sheena had finally left Ken.

He had almost forgotten his fears that she might leave him. Throughout the summer of 1963, she had seemed so much more settled, had given up her little outings for breaths of air, was content to stay at home with him. Then one black November morning, the blow had fallen. He had woken to find her gone.

At first he'd thought she'd just slipped out somewhere, but where would she go? Sheena was notoriously unwilling to leave her bed, always waiting till the last minute to get up and face the day. Ken, his heart beating alarm signals, ran into the living room and switched on the light. Dust, crumbs, unwashed cups, but no Sheena. He ran downstairs to the shop, switching on lights everywhere, calling her name, but the shop was empty. Then he saw the note on the cash register and the sweat broke on his brow.

'Dear Ken,' Sheena had written in her sprawling hand,

'I want to say I still love you. Sorry I can't stay but that's me, always on the move. We've had some good times, I'll no' forget them. Mebbe I'll come back one day, here's to you,

all my love Sheena.'

'The bitch, the bitch!' cried Ken, collapsing into a chair. 'How could she do this to me? All I ever did was love her! Where's she gone, then? Who with? She's no' gone on her own, she's been planning this for months, sweetening me up, making me think she wanted me.'

He leaped up and scrabbled in the cash drawer of the till. How much had she taken? All seemed to be in order. Maybe she hadna taken anything, only herself . . . only herself. Tears forced themselves down Ken's wrinkled cheeks. Sheena, Sheena, he keened, rocking himself. Och, what a fool he'd been to marry her, but if she were to walk in now, wouldn't he just take her in his arms, smooth back her lovely hair, kiss and forgive. She was never going to walk in, she was never coming back to him. It was all over, he had to face it, he was alone. Tears still blurring his eyes, he reached for the telephone and rang Biddy.

She came straight round, her beautiful eyes alight with excitement, and put the kettle on.

'Dinna you worry, Dad, you just stay calm and I'll make you some breakfast.'

'I couldna eat anything, Biddy, just a cuppa tea'll do. And ma heart's that bad, I canna open the shop today, you'll ha' to put a notice on the door.' Ken drank his tea, holding the cup with shaking fingers. 'Och, I'm on ma way out, I'll no' survive, I'm telling you.'

'Yes, you will survive, you're upset, but you ken very well, Sheena's no' worth dying over. And I'll open the shop for you.' Biddy's eyes were straying over the cigarettes and sweets, the piles of papers waiting to be sorted. 'You just tell me what to do.'

Kate telephoned Biddy, asking how Dad was coping. Should she come up? Och, he'd weather it, her sister told her, there was no need for Kate to come up. She, Biddy, would handle it. In fact, she'd had an idea, one that would solve all Dad's problems.

Having cooked her father an excellent tea that he'd managed to eat, Biddy sat down with him to outline her plan.

'The thing is, Dad, ma kids are growing up now and I'm looking for something to do. I've got a little cleaning job but I'm no' keen on it. Why do I no' come here and help you run the shop?'

Ken wiped his mouth and studied his elder daughter. She was looking very lovely, flushed and animated. He hadn't seen her look so well in a long time.

'I could do with a hand,' he answered cautiously. 'It's no' an easy job, you ken. No' much rest. Every day, the damned papers, except for Christmas Day and Hogmanay. You'd ha' to get round here good and early.'

'Aye, well, what I was thinking was that Ewan and me and the kids could come and stay.'

'Stay!' cried Ken, appalled. 'All of you?'

'We could fit in, we'd be no trouble. Then I'd be on the spot and you could have your lie-in, Dad. First time in years!'

'I dinna ken, Biddy, I'm no' in practice with young folk, I like ma peace and quiet.'

'But the kids'll be away to school and Ewan'll be away to work, there'll only be me, Dad, and you need me.' Biddy bent a stern gaze on him, which he failed to meet. 'You ken fine, you do, Dad. You're no' up to doing everything yourself. And then I've been thinking —'

'Oh, Lord, no more thinking!' groaned Ken.

'There's that store room at the back. We could make that into a living room for Ewan and me, then we wouldna be in your hair. And I was thinking as well that we could expand the business a bit. I could do carry-out rolls and sandwiches.' Biddy's eyes were shining. 'All the folk going to the station'd be keen to pick up stuff, you ken. I could get a deal for the rolls from Mackenzie's, do ma own fillings and make a good profit. Och, Dad, what do you say?'

'Supposing Sheena comes back?' he said slowly. 'We're still married, you ken.'

'You show her the door.' Biddy's lip curled. 'Or I will. She's no good to you, Dad, you should niver have taken up with her, specially after what she did to the Gilbrides. Did that no' tell you what she was like?'

'She had a way with her,' Ken muttered. 'Always such a way. Like her mother.'

'I'll show her a way! Right out of our lives!' Biddy poured her father another cup of tea. 'I'll tell Ewan, shall I? That we're shifting?'

'All right,' sighed Ken, who knew defeat when he saw it. 'Tell Ewan.'

'It's no' a bad idea,' commented Jessie, sitting knitting with Madge. 'Biddy's keen to have a job and working in a shop and seeing folk all day'll be right up her street. Then Ken'll be able to have a bit of a rest and take care of hisself.'

'As long as Sheena doesn't come back,' said Madge.

'Biddy'll sort Sheena out, nothing she'd like better!'

'But Ken did love her, Jessie.'

'He'll get over it.' Jessie finished a row and fiercely stuck her needles into her ball of wool. 'Great soft thing. He's past the age for all that love nonsense.'

'Some folk think you're never past the age.'

'Aye, men. Anything for a bit o' skirt.' Jessie glanced at Madge, who had stopped knitting and was sitting staring into space. 'Och, Madge, I'm sorry, chattering away. You're thinking o' Rachel. It's next week, eh?'

'The first anniversary, yes.' Madge stood up. 'That's always a bad day.'

Some days before that bad day came another. One for the whole world.

264

Chapter Fifty-Six

The date was 22 November. President Kennedy and his wife, Jacqueline, were visiting Dallas, Texas. The day was sunny, the crowds were out in force, cheering the motorcade. Suddenly, from a building on the route, a gun was fired. In the rear seat of the presidential car, President Kennedy slumped. His frantic wife leaned over him, but already his blood was staining her poor little suit that must have seemed so elegant only a few minutes before. A short time later, in a statement from a Dallas hospital, the President was declared dead. His Vice-President, Lyndon Johnson, was sworn in as President, watched by Jackie Kennedy in her blood-stained suit, and the rest of the world.

'Oh, it's too horrible!' cried Sara, watching with Will the terrible events unfolding on television. 'I never knew such things could happen. A president shot in the street in broad daylight!'

'Only last year after the Cuban crisis we were saying he would go from strength to strength,' reflected Will. 'And now this. It doesn't seem possible.'

They watched the arrival of the President's body in Washington, the gathering of his family, stony-faced in grief, the new President and his wife being greeted at the White House. They knew, of course, that whatever happened, life had to go on, even if it could never be quite the same. Even if for a long long time people were going to feel their world shaken and unsure, because of events in Dallas.

They were not made more secure by the news that Lee Harvey Oswald, the arrested suspect, had himself been shot while in custody by a man named Jack Ruby. To the tragedy of the

President's death were now added suspicion and mystery, suggestions of plots and cover-ups. As Will said to Sara, it was all becoming like some kind of thriller you could never believe. Except it was for real.

'That poor woman,' wailed Giannetta, the Italian au pair who had replaced Herta, now at university back in Germany. 'That poor Jack-ee!'

'Can't bear to think of her,' said Will, carving portions of chicken. 'Such a beautiful woman, too.'

'They were such a 'andsome couple, sighed Giannetta, her dark eyes melting into tears. 'Everyone say, what a perfect marriage!'

'Don't know about that, there've been a few rumours. Kennedy was a terrific guy, but maybe no saint.'

'Who knows what anyone's marriage is like?' asked Sara. As she set a dish of vegetables on the table, her eyes met Will's in a long cold stare.

They had coffee in the study while Giannetta, still shedding tears for the beautiful President, worked upstairs on her English and the children slept.

'What did you mean by that remark about Mr Kennedy?' Sara asked. 'I haven't heard any rumours.'

'All kept under wraps, but I've met Americans – bankers, reputable fellows – who say he played the field.'

Sara nodded. 'So his marriage was as much of a sham as ours?'

He stared at her, his face darkening with emotion, and it seemed to him that this had all happened before. He and Sara sitting together, locked in hostility; fearsome events happening off stage; even the same word spoken by his wife echoing in his brain. Sham, sham, sham. They had made no progress, no progress at all. He had thought she was feeling better, accepting things, but here it was again. Sham, sham, sham.

He pushed his coffee cup away and lit a cigarette, drawing on it with desperation.

'Sara,' he said quietly, 'what do you want me to do?'

She was silent, her face set in the hard lines he had come to dread.

'I can't take much more of this, I'm telling you.'

'What do you think it's like for me?' she flashed. 'Every day

Mummy rings up and asks if we've sorted things out, as she puts it. Every day, she says she wishes I'd married dear kind Nick.'

'And sometimes I wish that too!' cried Will.

Sara leaped to her feet. 'Well, if that's the way you feel —'

'No, no!' He grasped her arm. 'Look, we made an agreement to stay together and try to get on and I thought we were doing that. We've made love and you haven't objected. Why do you have to keep putting us back to square one?'

'Sometimes, it just comes over me, Will, how much I thought I had, and how none of it was true.'

'Ah, Sara!' Will put his arms around her. 'You make yourself so unhappy, talking like this. Can't you understand, I do love you? As my wife. Surely that's all that matters?'

'I suppose so.'

He was relieved to see that her expression had softened, though she would not raise her eyes to his.

'Shall we try again?' he asked gently, still holding her close.

'Looks like we'll have to.' She pulled herself free and picked up the coffee tray. 'I'll just take this away, then I think I'll have an early night. I'm desperately tired.'

And probably have a headache, he thought wryly. There would be no making love that night, then, but he hadn't expected it. He still thought he had won a small victory. At least, Sara had agreed to try again, that was something. At least, she had not threatened to walk out with the children, which was his greatest nightmare. He switched on the television and watched for a while the nightmare that was the American people's, as the endless speculation over Dallas went on and on. Then he too went to bed.

267

Chapter Fifty-Seven

Sometimes Will thought he should get out to the Bruntsfield Club where he had a subscription he never used, and knock hell out of the golf balls. Maybe that would relieve his feelings. But he never had the time.

Malcolm, on the other hand, had too much time and was glad to take up his golf again. After Rachel's death he had resigned from the office and done nothing. Now he was out on the course most days, had lunch at the clubhouse, was beginning slowly to feel himself making a life again. He still missed Rachel. Her beauty and spirit, her vivid personality, even her moods that could descend like lightning from a summer sky. She'd been difficult, yes, but so alive. And now was dead. He had to fill the void somehow. The golf helped, but so did Bobby. In fact, without Bobby, Malcolm didn't think he could have survived at all.

He marvelled often over his strangely changed son. Might almost have called him born-again, except that there was no religion involved. There was no doubt that it had been Rachel's death that had changed him; why, Malcolm didn't seek to understand. All he knew was that his son was a companion again and he thanked God for it. Only wished Bobby himself could find some sort of fulfilment. Seemed happy enough at the Scottish Office, yet sometimes when Malcolm heard him playing the piano in the evenings, he would feel a kind of guilt of his own.

'Seems such a waste,' he once remarked. 'I mean, your musical talent. You never use it now.'

'My musical talent?' Bobby laughed. 'Come on, you know it doesn't amount to much. You said so yourself.'

'No, no, I never said that.'

'Didn't you tell me I should get a proper job and only play for a hobby?'

'Well, now I think you could do more than that. Abby tells me Frankie still plays at hotels and functions. Maybe you could do that?'

'I do have a full-time job, Dad.'

'I know, but you seem to have so few outside interests. You should be getting all you can out of life, a young fellow like you. There's nothing for you to worry about here, now we have Mrs Shepherd the whole place runs like clockwork. So, why not take something up?' Malcolm brightened. 'Golf, maybe? I could pull a few strings, try to get you into my club —'

Bobby laughed again and held up his hand. 'Oh, please, Dad, I might have changed, but not that much!'

'Why, a lot of young chaps play golf,' Malcolm retorted, rather nettled. 'It's not just for old buffers like me.'

'I know, I know.' Bobby put his hand on his father's shoulder. 'But you really needn't worry about me. I'm happy as I am.'

Malcolm hesitated. 'Still haven't considered sorting things out with Lindsay?'

'No,' said Bobby shortly. After a moment, he added, 'We just keep going with the status quo.'

'If she is thinking of marrying Nick, it seems funny she's never asked you for a divorce.'

'He's still around. I don't interfere.'

Lindsay, in those early days of 1964, was a little depressed. She was still with Logie's, still grateful for her seat on the board, but not enjoying working with Neal Crawford, Abby's successor. He was hard and took pleasure in being hard. He had a temper. He liked to think that if people were not afraid of him they would not work well. Lindsay was not afraid of him and was therefore not one of his favourites. Also, she knew he resented her being a Farrell and believed she had become a partner only because of Abby's connection with the family.

'It seems we have an Old Girls' network here,' he sneered pointedly. 'Me, I came up the hard way through merit.'

'He came up by kicking everyone else down,' Hector MacDonell in Accounts murmured. 'Logie's would never have appointed a fellow like him in the old days. But times are changing, gentlemen are no longer required.'

269

'Well, I'm no lady when it comes to standing up for myself,' Lindsay said bravely. 'I'll keep going, whatever it takes.'

It was consoling to tell her troubles to Abby, who was sympathetic, anxious in case the new broom might be sweeping too much away from the store that had been her life. Strangely, though, Logie's had begun to recede from the foreground of her mind. As Frankie had predicted, other interests had presented themselves and the endless time that had yawned ahead was filling up fast. Committees, charities, welfare groups. 'You name it,' she would say, 'I'm in it.' Recently, she had begun working with a group of young drug addicts and it was the drug problem, she told Lindsay, that worried her most of all. Unemployment had risen and if there should ever come a time when young people believed they had no future, she could see them turning to drugs in a big way.

'Part of the trouble is the housing,' she explained. 'It's true, conditions in the old days were appalling, they had to be improved, but what's replaced the old slums hasn't been the right answer. I mean, have you seen some of the local housing? Have you seen those multi-storey flats at Gorgie and Muirhouse?'

'Soulless,' declared Lindsay. 'Where have we gone wrong?'

'Hard to say. The intentions were good, but they haven't worked out. Of course, it always comes down to money in the end. No council's got a bottomless purse. But did there have to be so much concrete? So few trees?'

'Looks like there's work here for Kate Rossie,' suggested Lindsay. 'She's an MP, she could do something.'

'And Labour might get in next time.'

'Now that Macmillan's gone, they've a good chance. Who's going to vote for Alec Douglas-Home?'

The fourteenth Earl Home had resigned his peerage to become leader of the Tory party, but bets for success in the next election were going on the fourteenth Mr Wilson, as he had dubbed himself. And with success for Harold Wilson would come success for Kate.

'Lucky girl,' commented Abby. 'I fill my life with this and that, but she's like you, Lindsay, she has real work.'

When she had switched to full-time work, Lindsay had decided the time had come to be independent and had bought a small flat for herself and Gail in the Murrayfield area of the city. Monica

270

had been desolate, but had bravely said she 'quite understood' and anyway Murrayfield was not so far away from Selkirk Street, they would be able to keep wonderfully in touch. And, of course, she would be free to babysit at any time!

'I don't need a babysitter!' Gail complained, but Lindsay said she wouldn't have a moment's peace leaving Gail on her own, and in any case, Grandma loved to come. Not that Lindsay went out so often; usually only on Saturday for a meal with Nick. It was their little institution, looked forward to by both.

One Saturday evening in April, Monica came round as usual, and while Lindsay finished getting ready, said, quietly, 'Why don't you do something about Nick, Lindsay? I'm sure Bobby would give you a divorce and then you could make sense of your life. It's quite ridiculous, living the way you do.'

'Mum, Nick and I have no plans to marry,' Lindsay told her. 'We're just good friends.'

'Oh, where have I heard that before?' cried Monica. 'Men and women can never be just friends.'

'Well, we are and we're happy that way.'

'But how long can the situation go on? You're not getting any younger, you know.'

'I wonder why people think they have to tell other people that?' Lindsay asked coldly. 'It's never necessary.'

That evening, she and Nick went to an Austrian restaurant, one of their favourites. To begin with, Nick was his usual calm self, but as the meal progressed, he became more and more fidgety, until Lindsay began to worry that he might suddenly be going to change their pleasant relationship and propose. She did hope not, because that would mean she'd have to turn him down and she didn't want to hurt him, dear kind Nick who had been so badly hurt already.

'Everything all right?' she asked him, over the good strong Viennese coffee.

'Fine.' He nodded eagerly. 'Fine. But there is something I'd like to' – he cleared his throat – 'say to you.'

Here it comes, thought Lindsay.

'Yes?' she said cautiously.

'Well, the thing is.' Nick ran a finger round his collar. 'There's a new lawyer come to join our firm.'

271

'Oh?' Lindsay looked baffled.

'She's a very nice girl, not long qualified, but very keen and efficient. We think she's going to do well.'

'Is she pretty?'

'Very.' Nick smiled. 'As a matter of fact, she's not unlike Sara. Fair-haired, blue eyes, outgoing. Reminded me of Sara straight away.'

'Would I know her? What's her name?'

'Annette Ferrier. I don't think you'd know her. She's very young.'

'Oh, well, of course I wouldn't know anyone young,' snapped Lindsay.

Nick flushed beetroot red. 'Sorry, Lindsay, I didn't mean – look, you know I didn't mean —'

'Oh, never mind, Nick. Just get out what you want to say. You're engaged, is that it?'

'I am,' cried Nick with relief. 'She's taken me on! I can't believe it. I mean, nobody else has ever wanted to. What can she see in me?'

She can see a senior partner in a successful law firm, Lindsay thought, and felt ashamed of her own spite.

'You might have given me a hint,' she said, after a pause. 'I'd have thought you'd tell a friend you were getting serious about someone.'

'It all happened so quickly, Lindsay, or I would have done. Of course, I would have done!' Nick mopped his perspiring face. 'I mean, we only seemed to go out a couple of times and that was it.' He laughed. 'To tell you the truth, I don't know whether I'm on my head or my heels!'

'Well, I'm very pleased for you,' Lindsay said with sudden warmth. 'You've always deserved to have someone love you and now you've found her. I hope you'll be very happy.'

'Oh, Lindsay, you don't know how much I wish the same for you.' Nick stretched his hand across the table to touch hers. 'Is there no chance that you and Bobby might get together again?'

'I don't think so. I care for him, I always will, and it's wonderful that he's changed so much.' Lindsay looked down at her hand in Nick's. 'But I think he's still in some way – damaged.'

'I don't agree. I think he's just matured. Taken longer than most, that's all.'

'A late developer? I wonder.' Lindsay half rose. 'Nick, I think we ought to be going.'

'Lindsay, wait a moment. I just want to say, my getting engaged, it won't affect our friendship, will it? You've been so good to me, helped me so much, and I'm so fond of you and Gail, I shouldn't like to think —'

'Of course it won't affect our friendship,' Lindsay replied, wondering how he could be so naïve. She hadn't met Annette Ferrier, but there would be no prizes for guessing that the first thing she'd do, now that the ring was on her finger, would be to cut Lindsay and Gail right out of Nick's life. Who could blame her? She was a lawyer, she would be the last to take chances with her marriage and probably agreed with Monica, that men and women could not be just good friends.

When Lindsay let herself into her flat after she'd said goodnight to Nick, Monica looked up from her sewing in surprise.

'Nick not coming in for a nightcap?'

'No.' Lindsay sat down and lit a cigarette.

'Oh, I do wish you'd give those things up, dear. I'm sure they're bad for you.'

'Everybody smokes.' Lindsay shrugged. 'As a matter of fact, I don't think we'll be seeing much more of dear old Nick.'

'Why ever not?'

'He's just got himself engaged. To a very young and pretty lawyer in his firm.'

'Well!' Monica put down her sewing and snatched off her reading glasses. Her eyes were outraged. 'What a cheek! After all this time going out with you, to go and get engaged to someone else!'

'I never wanted to marry him, he knew that. And now I'm very pleased for him, I really am. He deserves his happiness.'

'H'm.' Monica put her glasses into their case and folded up her sewing. 'That's all very well, but it leaves you high and dry.'

'I don't need anyone, Mum. I have Gail, I have my career.'

'And what about Bobby?'

'Everybody asks me about Bobby.' Lindsay drew irritably on her cigarette. 'He doesn't come into it.'

'He's improved a great deal recently,' Monica said hopefully. 'Works at the Scottish Office, looks like everyone else.'

'You mean looks like the people you know.' Lindsay laughed. 'Thanks for sitting, Mum. Maybe I won't be needing you much more.'

'Oh, what nonsense! Look, why don't you tell Bobby about Nick? He may be thinking — '

'I am not telling Bobby anything,' Lindsay said with finality.

Chapter Fifty-Eight

It was his father who told Bobby. Mrs Shepherd, the new treasure of a housekeeper, had just served the breakfast porridge, when Malcolm opened his *Scotsman*. His eyes widened.

'Hey, Bobby, look at this!'

'Look at what?'

Malcolm passed Bobby the paper. 'Engagements column. Second one down.'

Bobby's eyes flickered over the page.

'Well, well,' he said quietly. 'You think it's the Nick we know?'

'Of course it is!' Malcolm was excited. 'Nicholas John Ainslie. That's the one. Lindsay's admirer. Engaged to a girl from Gullane. Probably her father's a golfer. Lovely golf round that part of the world. But what a strange thing, eh? I thought Nick was all set to marry Lindsay?'

'Seems not.' Bobby began calmly to eat his porridge.

'Aren't you interested?' asked Malcolm, after watching him for a moment or two.

'Sure, I'm interested, but I don't know that it will affect me. Come on, Dad, don't let your porridge get cold.'

Malcolm picked up his spoon.

'Nick's a nice fellow,' he said slowly. 'I'm very pleased for him.'

'So am I,' said Bobby.

That evening, the telephone rang in Lindsay's flat. She had been sitting with Gail, who was supposed to be doing maths homework, but had been brooding over the announcement of Nick's engagement.

'Why did he want to marry someone else, Mummy?' she pressed. 'Why not you?'

'I'm still married to Daddy, Gail, you know that.'

'But lots of people get divorced and I thought you and Daddy would get divorced and then you'd marry Uncle Nick.'

'I didn't know you wanted me to divorce Daddy, Gail.'

'I don't, I just want you to be properly married to somebody, and if you're not going to be with Daddy, I thought it would be nice for you to have Uncle Nick instead.'

'Well, Uncle Nick and I never did want to get married, you see, we were just friends.' Lindsay tapped Gail's exercise book. 'Come on, what about this homework? Talking isn't going to get it done, is it?'

'Are you still going to be friends with Uncle Nick, then? Even though he's going to marry Annette Marion Ferrier?'

Gail's really been studying that announcement, Lindsay thought, with an inward smile. 'Of course,' she said aloud. 'I'll probably be a friend of hers, too.'

It was at this point that the telephone rang. Lindsay took the call in her bedroom, so as not to divert Gail.

'Hello?'

'Lindsay? It's Bobby.'

'Oh, yes?'

'I suppose this is a bit obvious — '

'Obvious?'

'Never mind. I was wondering, would you like to have dinner some time?'

'Sounds nice.' Lindsay's tone was casual. 'When?'

'Tomorrow any good?'

'Fine.'

'I'll call for you about half-past seven, shall I? I've heard there's a very good Austrian restaurant.'

'I think I'd prefer Scottish. If you don't mind.'

'Oh, right. Scottish it shall be. See you tomorrow, evening then?'

'Tomorrow evening. And thank you, Bobby.'

'Who was that on the phone?' called Gail.

'Daddy, but never you mind. Just get on with your homework.'

'But what did he want? Is he coming round?'

'No, we're going out for a meal tomorrow evening. I'm just going to ring Grandma, see if she can sit for you.'

'You're going out with Daddy?' cried Gail. 'Why, I didn't think you'd ever have dinner with him again!'

'It's a long time since we had a meal together, I must admit.'

Gail twirled her pencil and studied her mother. 'Know what I think? He's seen Uncle Nick's engagement too.'

When was the last time we sat together in a restaurant? Lindsay wondered, as she faced Bobby across their table. Was it the awful time they'd had that blazing row over Gail? Better not think of that, then. Better just think of now.

She had taken particular care over her appearance and Bobby too had dressed well for this upmarket restaurant he had chosen. How he had changed since those long-ago days in London! How they had both changed.

'Let's order,' said Bobby, and the waiter brought their menus.

'Salmon soufflé for a starter, I think,' Lindsay murmured, 'then maybe the gigot lamb?'

She looked up to find Bobby's dark eyes fixed on her, not on his menu. They both immediately looked away.

As the meal progressed, they talked of general things. Bobby's work, Lindsay's work, Gail's education. It was the coffee stage before they said what was in their minds.

'You said you were being obvious.' Lindsay kept her gaze down. 'Were you thinking of Nick's engagement?'

'You know I was.'

'There was never anything between Nick and me.'

'You gave me a different impression once.'

'Did I? That was a long time ago. I must have been – you know – trying to put you off.'

'Succeeded.'

There was a silence between them.

'Well, he's engaged now and I'm very happy for him,' Lindsay said, at last. 'I can assure you, I never wanted to marry him myself.'

'As a matter of fact, you're still married to me.'

'I know that,' Lindsay said quietly.

When they left the restaurant, the April twilight seemed inviting.

'Lovely evening,' Bobby observed. 'Why don't we drive up to Calton Hill and look at the view?'

'Yes, why not? Haven't been up there in ages.' Lindsay felt absurdly nervous, as though she were on one of her early dates with Bobby, when they had both been so young.

'Nice that you have a car now,' she remarked, as they drove high above the city to the vantage point that was Calton Hill. 'I didn't even know you could drive.'

'Good God, of course I can drive, I learned in the army!' exclaimed Bobby. 'Why does everyone think me completely useless?'

'Sorry, I didn't mean that at all.'

'I know.' He grinned. 'I suppose I'm hypersensitive. Comes from having a bad reputation.'

'That's all over now.'

Bobby made no reply. He stopped the car and they sat looking out at the famous buildings and the famous panoramic view. Near at hand were the City observatory, the Nelson monument, and the copy of the Parthenon, a Napoleonic War memorial, usually known at 'Edinburgh's disgrace' because the city never found the funds to finish it. All of these were familiar to Lindsay and Bobby since childhood and it was comforting, somehow, to see them again, together. Their hands met, their shoulders touched, they felt at ease.

'My favourite view,' Bobby murmured, as they watched the lights of the city coming on, tiny golden dots in the dark blue haze. 'Missed this in London.'

'Yet you hardly ever came up here, did you?'

'Knew it was there, though. Nice solid memory stored away to take out when I felt like it.'

'You're glad you came back to Auld Reekie?'

He laughed. 'Auld Reekie is right. Look at that smoke down there, you can see why we need a Clean Air Act. Yes, I'm glad I came back.'

'Don't even miss your group?'

He shook his head. 'I had to try too hard. Now I don't have to try at all.'

How shall I ever fathom Bobby? Lindsay asked herself. Was it because of his mother he had tried so desperately to fit into a mould that wasn't his? Rachel would never have wanted that. Yet it was only since she'd gone that he had seemed to be free.

Bobby slowly turned his head to look at her.

278

'What are you thinking?' he whispered.

'Just that it's nice to be here with you.'

'And you really don't care about Nick?'

'Oh, Bobby, how many times do I have to tell you?'

'He never asked you to marry him, did you say?'

'He never did.'

'I'd like to ask you to marry me.' He laughed. 'Damn silly thing is, we're married already.'

'You could still ask me.'

'All right. Lindsay, will you marry me?'

'Oughtn't you to go down on bended knee?'

'Bit difficult in a car. Come on, what do you say?'

'I'm not sure.'

'Not sure?' In the dusk of the car, his face was pale. 'You wanted me to ask you, I thought that meant you'd say yes.'

'I need to know if you love me.' Lindsay twisted his hands in hers. 'You used not to want anybody's love.'

'You know I've changed. Now I want all the love I can get.'

'From me?'

'From you.'

They moved easily into each other's arms, remembering all their old passion, and after their long kisses and caresses, Bobby took Lindsay's hand and touched her wedding ring.

'I'm going to get you a better one,' he said breathing hard. 'Didn't you say this was the cheapest ring you could find?'

'I'm used to it, Bobby, I shouldn't feel the same with a new one.'

'An engagement ring, then. You ought to have an engagement ring.'

'Oh, it's so crazy!' Lindsay burst out laughing. 'We do everything back to front. You propose after we're married, you want to give me an engagement ring when I've already got a wedding ring, and we fall in love after we've been separated for years!'

'I wish we could make love!' Bobby said urgently. 'Isn't there anywhere we can go?'

'Your dad's at your home, my mum's at my home.' Lindsay ran her fingers gently down Bobby's cheek. 'We'll just have to be patient.'

'There's the back of the car,' he said hopefully. 'No good, eh?'

'Bobby! I like to think I'm young, but not that young. And I don't know if you've noticed, but there are other cars here.'

'You're right, I hadn't noticed.' Bobby sighed deeply. 'Oh, well, better get you home, I suppose. Break the news to your mother.'

'Don't say it like that. She'll be pleased, she wants us to get back together.'

Bobby hesitated. 'Will Gail be pleased?' he asked quietly.

'She will. She told me she wanted me to be properly married to somebody.'

'Nick Ainslie, no doubt.'

'She'd rather it was you, Bobby. You're her father.'

'Gail's the one I really want to tell.' Bobby started the car. 'She's the one who matters most.'

Chapter Fifty-Nine

As Lindsay had predicted, Gail was delighted that her parents were together again. Everyone in the family was pleased, but Gail said she was specially thrilled, because now she was the same as the other girls at school. She had a mother and a father.

'Why, there must be other girls whose parents are divorced or separated,' Lindsay commented. 'You can't have been the only one without a father.'

'But you and Dad were different, weren't you? You never lived together at all.'

Lindsay hesitated. It was tacitly agreed that Bobby's attempt to take Gail away was never to be mentioned. Nor was Gail ever to know that there had been a time when he hadn't wanted her.

'We get on better now than in the early days,' she said at last.

The explanation sounded weak, but Gail seemed to accept it.

'So where are we going to live now? she demanded. 'Can't all live in our little flat, can we?'

'No, we've decided to share your grandfather's house. You won't mind that, will you?'

Gail wrinkled her nose. 'It's awfully gloomy there. Couldn't we live with Grandma instead?'

'Well, your grandfather's very lonely in that big old place and we think we can make it happy again. Especially if you bring your friends in and there are young people around.'

'But isn't Grandma lonely, too?'

'Oh, God, thought Lindsay, why does Gail have to make me feel so guilty?

'I've discussed it with Grandma and she's quite happy about it,' she said firmly. 'We can't live with everyone and we think just at the moment Grandfather needs us. OK? End of discussion.'

In fact, Malcolm had tried to dissuade Bobby and Lindsay from sharing his house. Older people shouldn't live with younger people, was his contention. Everyone had to have their independence. It was true that the Morningside house was too big for him now, but he could always move out and take a little flat somewhere.

'You know you don't want that, Dad!' Bobby had cried. 'You don't want to leave your home, and if you're worrying about your independence, we can be the ones to find a place of our own. We just thought you might want us with you.'

'Bobby, there's nothing I'd like better,' Malcolm groaned. 'But, it's as I say, you should have your independence. I don't want Lindsay thinking she has to look after me.'

'Dad, you're the whizz kid on the golf course, you don't need looking after. But you do need some company. That's all we're offering.'

'I'll take it,' said Malcolm suddenly, and grasped Bobby's hand.

Lindsay, who had been keeping quiet, now came forward and kissed Malcolm's cheek. He put his arm around her.

'Can't wait to have Gail here,' he said shakily. 'But you know there's a lot to do in this house, don't you? Poor Rachel's studio, it's just as she left it. Never seemed to be able to face clearing it somehow.'

'We'll get round to it, when you're ready.'

'Took me months to part with her clothes. In fact, I kept quite a lot. All her favourite dresses. Sometimes I go and look at them and remember her wearing them.'

'Mum does the same with Dad's jackets,' Lindsay said softly. 'Why not? People should be remembered.'

To celebrate their new relationship, Lindsay and Bobby gave a summer lunch party in Monica's garden.

'Our wedding reception,' said Bobby. 'All of twelve years late.'

'But better late than never!' cried Monica, in her element, organising a party again.

282

Lindsay wore a yellow suit and a large hat, and Sara squeezed herself into a small pink outfit, complaining that she'd put on weight.

'It's all this comfort food,' she grumbled. 'Now I shall have to diet. As though I'm not miserable enough.'

'Oh, Sara, are things no better?' Lindsay asked sympathetically.

'We're still together, that's about all you can say.'

'I'm sure Will does love you, you know. Couldn't you forget about Kate?'

'Couldn't I forget about Kate? I'm not the one who remembers her, am I?' Sara turned impatiently away. 'Look, to hell with my diet, where's all Mummy's lovely food?'

'Sara's not looking happy,' Madge observed to Jessie. 'I do worry about her and Will.' She brightened. 'But Bobby is settled with Lindsay and that's more than I ever hoped for.'

'Aye, they're a grand sight, the pair of them,' Jessie agreed, gasping in the warm June weather. 'Must be kicking theirselves, eh? Wasting all them years?'

'Seems to be a family failing,' sighed Madge. 'We can never see that what we're looking for is right under our noses.'

'Sara's put on weight,' Jennie remarked to Abby. 'Not having another baby, is she?'

'Definitely not. Bet Ma thinks that would solve all her problems, but I'm sure it's the last thing Sara's considering.'

'You don't think she'll really leave Will?' Jennie's face was pale with remembered pain. 'Oh, I do hope not, Abby!'

'They seem to be sticking together for the moment, but if you ask me, they're pretty near the rocks.'

'They ought to remember the children!' cried Jennie.

'They are remembering the children. That's why they're still together.'

'I'd really like to have a word with Sara,' Jennie began, but Abby put her hand on her arm.

'Better not, we shouldn't interfere. Anyway, an old flame's just moved in.'

'Who?'

'Nick Ainslie.' Abby steered Jennie away towards Frankie and

Mac who were sampling Monica's curry puffs, and Frankie, seeing their empty glasses, brought them more champagne.

'May I get you another drink, Sara?' Nick was asking. 'Champagne, or something soft?'

'Oh, champagne, please. Need alcohol, don't we, to drown our sorrows?'

'What sorrows?' His eyes, behind his glasses, were sparkling. 'Have you forgotten I've just got engaged?'

'Oh, yes.' Sara's mouth twisted a little. 'Where is she, then, your fiancée?'

'Couldn't come, unfortunately, though Lindsay kindly invited her. Quite a lot on at the office and she's very conscientious.'

'Pity, I should like to have seen her.'

'She's very pretty.' Nick hesitated. 'Rather like you, in my opinion.'

A waitress proffered her tray and Sara, taking a glass, studied Nick's rather overheated face with some interest.

'So you didn't pick someone like Lindsay? I really thought you two were going to make it, you know. Did she say no?'

'I never asked her,' he said stiffly. 'We were always just good friends.'

'Sounds like something out of the newspapers.' Sara raised her glass. 'Well, I wish you and Annette all the very best, Nick. I hope you'll be very happy.'

Nick's gaze wandered round the garden until it found Will, in conversation with Bobby. Unlike Sara, Will appeared to have lost weight. His handsome face looked drawn. Even from a distance there was something dispirited in the way he held himself.

Nick turned back to Sara.

'You're happy with Will, aren't you? he asked anxiously. 'I always thought you'd got just what you wanted.'

'Now isn't there some Japanese proverb that says you should never get that?' Sara smiled and for a moment he saw the old effervescent Sara. 'Oh, I'm all right, Nick, don't worry about me. I really have a lot to be grateful for.'

He heaved a sigh of relief. 'I'm glad. I couldn't bear to think of things not being right for you.'

'You're at the stage of feeling so good you want everyone else to feel the same.' She waved her hand. 'Well, better mingle, I suppose. Keep in touch.'

If Miss Ferrier will let you, she thought wryly and moved to join her mother, who was supervising the arrival of the celebratory cake.

'Not a wedding cake, of course,' she said, dabbing her brow with a lavender-scented handkerchief. 'But Lindsay and Bobby didn't have a cake at all before, so I thought they should have one now.'

'It's beautiful,' Sara murmured, looking down at the names, Lindsay and Bobby, traced in blue icing across the surface of the cake. She felt a surge of envy and a shameful resentment that Lindsay should be so much happier than she was, when until now it was she who had been the happy one. As she had told Nick, it was true she had a great deal to be grateful for, but no matter how often she reminded herself of that, it never seemed to count.

'Well, Bobby, what now?' asked Will. 'A second honeymoon?'

'Never had a first,' Bobby answered with a grin. 'But we are having a few days in Venice. Can't get more conventional than that, can you, and conventional is my middle name these days.'

'Suits you.' Will gave a weary smile. 'And then you're moving in with your dad? Didn't think of starting up somewhere new?'

'He wants to stay where he is and we want to be with him.' Bobby hesitated. 'I think we can make it a happy house again. It's what my mother would have wanted.'

As Gail came running up, to tell her father it was cake-cutting time, Will clapped Bobby on the shoulder.

'It's good to have you back,' he said quietly, and Bobby knew he wasn't referring to his return from London.

Chapter Sixty

The date for the 1964 General Election was set for 15 October. Travelling up to Edinburgh to begin her campaign, Kate felt as thrilled as though she were going to meet a lover. This was what she had been waiting for, what all Labour supporters had been waiting for. A real chance of success, a real hope of forming the next government. For her, of course, it would mean personal advancement, the opening of the door to the inner sanctum of power. The thought was intoxicating.

Of course, everything depended now on how well Wilson could come over to the voters compared with Alec Douglas-Home. To Kate, there was no contest. Sir Alec was undoubtedly a nice man and of noble birth, which might appeal to some, but the acid test these days for a politician was how he or she performed on television and Sir Alec didn't perform at all. It was not his fault, but he always came over as stiff and ill at ease, whereas Wilson was a natural, fielding every question with aplomb, sitting there with his great head stuffed full of brains as though he were born to lead. The Liberals presented no challenge; it could be truthfully said that this was a two horse race, so surely, surely, this time Labour would win.

Kate found Edinburgh buzzing with excitement over an election that could prove a watershed, and at once threw herself into work. Her agent, an unflappable Scot named Chris Henderson, had already organised meetings and canvassing and was quietly confident.

'You got in at the by-election, Kate, you'll walk it this time, with Harold running the show.'

'I'm not taking any chances, Chris, I'm going to go for this all

286

out. But how's my opposition doing? I mean that sweet young Tory.'

'Hugh? Och, the poor guy, you have to feel sorry for him. He hasna the chance of a snowball in hell. Only cutting his teeth, of course.'

Kate reflected on the young Alexander, a businessman's son, fighting his first election.

'Doesn't do to be complacent, Chris. Have you fixed me a debate with him?'

'Sure have. You'll wipe the floor with him.' Chris grinned. 'Am I allowed to say that?'

'When it's over,' said Kate.

Malcolm, a true-blue Tory, announced that he would be addressing envelopes for the local ward's committee, had to feel he was contributing something.

'Mum's taken on delivering,' said Lindsay. 'You should see her! Has her specs on the end of her nose and knocks on all the doors as though she were paying calls. Only works her own area, of course, no going downmarket for her!'

'How about you, Bobby?' asked Malcolm. 'Are you willing to give us some time? Have to keep Wilson out, you know.'

'I'm a civil servant, I don't get involved in politics.'

'Come on, you've a vote, you have to use it.'

'Well, it might not be for the Tories.'

Malcolm eyes grew round with horror. 'What are you saying? You know what'll happen if the socialists get in! There'll be rampant inflation, handouts everywhere, comprehensive education – my God, we can't let it happen!'

'It always puzzles me, Dad, that you came from Catherine's Land, yet you don't want to support the underdog.'

'I do want to support the underdog, Bobby! But in a sensible manner. What has to be understood is that it's the business world that makes the money to fund everything the government does. Money makes the world go round, and taxing capitalism out of existence and giving away what you haven't got is a recipe for disaster!'

'Heavens, Dad, you ought to be out on the campaign trail!' laughed Lindsay. 'Why not go for the compromise like me? I'm voting Liberal.'

'You've just fallen for Jo Grimond,' Bobby told her.

'He's certainly good on television.'

'No politician should ever appear on television,' Malcolm said firmly. 'People should read the party manifestos and make reasoned choices. What's it matter what folk look like?'

'Ask Richard Nixon that, Dad. Remember what they said about him, after he'd been on the box? Would you buy a used car from this man?'

'I'd buy a used car from the fourteenth Earl Home,' snapped Malcolm.

'Think I'll go for the fourteenth MISTER Wilson.'

'Och, this whole thing is descending into farce!' cried Malcolm.

Aware that Kate would be campaigning in Edinburgh, Sara had been trawling the local papers for news of her meetings. She shrank from the idea of seeing her again, but felt a compulsion to seek her out, assess her, find out just what she was up against. When she saw that Kate was to appear in debate with her opposing Tory candidate, she decided that that would be the meeting to attend. Will came home so late from the bank these days, they rarely had supper together; it would be simple enough to leave a message with Giannetta to say she had gone to see a friend. He probably wouldn't even ask where she was, anyway.

The debate was to be held in a primary school in Kate's constituency, a Labour stronghold. Sara arrived early and sat at the back of the hall, which was decorated with children's drawings and cardboard models. There was a typical 'school' smell, made up of gym shoes, plasticine and small bodies, and Sara, trying not to breathe in too deeply, sprayed herself with pocket scent. She looked covertly around, noting that there was a solid block of obvious Tory supporters gathering at the front of the hall, but for the most part the audience looked Labour and proud of it. The red rosettes were certainly outnumbering the blue, but there appeared to be no Liberal or Scottish Nationalist presence at all. Perhaps they had decided to give this one a miss, knowing they hadn't much chance of it anyway.

At seven thirty precisely, the chairman of the meeting, an Edinburgh councillor, escorted Kate and Hugh Alexander on to the platform to the accompaniment of prolonged applause. Sara's chest tightened; for a moment or two she felt she wasn't going to be able to breathe. Then the spasm passed and she was able to raise her eyes to study Kate.

She looked as good as ever. Worse, she looked as young. Perhaps if I were closer, thought Sara, I'd see the little lines around her eyes, by her mouth; after all, she's in her thirties. Oh, but whether she had little lines or not, there was no doubt that Kate, in striking black suit and huge scarlet rosette, had lost none of her beauty, none of her power to attract. On the platform that evening, contrasted with the slight figure of the young Alexander, already looking as though he wished himself miles away, she was indeed like a magnet, drawing everyone's eyes. Were there already sighs of defeat wavering though the Tory ranks?

If they're not defeated, I am, thought Sara dully.

Yet it was true that Will had told her over and over again that he and Kate had nothing in common, and it was plain enough that she was no homebody, would never want to give up her career to bring up children, or indeed for anything else. Sara knew she should perhaps take comfort in this knowledge of Kate, but she was past taking comfort. In the old days, she had had her own attractions, her own strong, bubbling personality. Why should she settle for the label of wife and mother, while Kate Rossie, as beauty and career woman, could still draw Will's love? Because in spite of all he said, in spite of the years that had gone by, he did love Kate. That was the feeling in Sara's heart, and no amount of comfort or gratitude for what she had was going to take it away.

The chairman started the ball rolling by asking Hugh Alexander if he could define the differences between his party's promises and Labour's. Oh, yes, he could, he answered eagerly, evidently having done his homework. His party would be concentrating on the need for an independent nuclear deterrent, they would be taking a world view of what should be done, in contrast to the Labour Party who would merely be thinking along parochial lines —

'Such as repealing the Rent Act?' Kate asked sweetly, knowing that her audience regarded the Tory Rent Act of 1957 as a 'landlords' charter', designed to grind the faces of poor tenants. The Labour supporters roared approval and a voice behind Sara whispered, 'First blood to us!'

'Perhaps Miss Rossie would take us through her party's

proposals?' the chairman suggested as young Alexander floundered into silence, and Kate gladly leaped to her feet.

Oh, she's not just a pretty face, is she? Sara thought bitterly, as Kate launched into Labour's programme: tax reforms; comprehensive education; a ministry for new technology; but she took no interest in Kate's words, or her succeeding one-sided battle with Alexander. She had seen what she had come to see and longed to go, but to leave before the end would make her conspicuous and she couldn't risk Kate's noticing her. She would just have to stick it out.

All around her was murmured admiration for Kate's handling of the debate, of the way she slipped from Alexander's grasp every time he tried to catch her on a point, then was ready with her own next needle thrust which always went home.

'Poor lad,' someone said. 'It's cruel, eh? He's no' got the experience.'

'This'll teach him, to come up against our Kate.'

'Be lucky if he doesna lose his deposit.'

Oh, God, thought Sara, if I could only get out of here!

Time passed. At long last, the debate came to an end, with Kate the obvious winner on points. Hugh Alexander shook her hand, the red rosettes cheered, the blue rosettes looked defiant, photographers from the local papers took pictures. Sara leaped up to make her getaway. And saw Will.

He was standing by the door at the back of the hall, his face strained and pale, his gaze fixed on the people now moving down from the platform. On Kate.

Sara could not move. She was so consumed by anger, she felt on fire. A pulse was beating in her brow, her eyes seemed filled with dust. Will, here. Will, at the first opportunity, come to see Kate Rossie. How dare he try to pretend that she meant nothing to him? If Sara had ever wavered in her belief that her marriage was a sham, Will's action tonight was proof that she was right. With a strange eagerness, she seized on it, straightened her shoulders, took a step towards her husband, who still had no eyes for her.

'Hello, Sara!' cried Kate. 'How good of you to come to my meeting! Is Will here?'

* * *

290

Speechless, Sara stood looking into Kate's face. Yes, there were little lines at her lovely eyes and generous mouth, now Sara could see them clearly. But what did they matter? Kate had won more than her debate that night, she had won a battle she didn't even know she was fighting. She had won, so Sara had lost.

Fighting for composure, she said, huskily, 'Of course he's here, but I must dash. Will you excuse me, please?'

She turned and ran, pushing her way through the groups of people waiting to speak to Kate until she reached the street and her car. Back in the school hall, no doubt Kate would already have moved on to speak to someone else and no doubt Will would be watching, waiting his chance to speak to her too. Or, maybe with all her supporters around her, he would just make eye contact, let her know he would be in touch, even if now he had to find his car and follow his wife home. Home! Sara felt she no longer had a home. Tomorrow, she would leave the house that had become a shell. That was for sure.

When Will came back, he found Sara in the kitchen making coffee. She was alone and disconcertingly calm.

'Giannetta's in bed,' she told him. 'You can talk, if you like. Tell me how much you love me and want to stay with me.'

'Oh, Sara . . .' He sat down at the kitchen table and bent his head. 'You were at the meeting?'

'I was.' Sara drank her coffee, watching him over the rim of the cup. 'And there's nothing to say, is there? Tonight proves that.'

'Anyone would think you'd found me in bed with Kate,' he groaned. 'All I did was go to her meeting, and you went there yourself.'

'For different reasons from you.'

'You don't know my reasons.'

'Don't I?'

'I went there to see the woman you blame for breaking up our marriage. Sara, nothing could be further from her mind. Can't you understand that?'

She shook her head. 'Will, I don't blame Kate for breaking up our marriage, I blame you.'

'That's not fair. You don't know how unfair that is.'

She shrugged. 'I'm not going to talk any more. I need a rest. We both do. From each other.'

291

'You're leaving me?' His voice was empty of emotion, as though he had given up his struggle. 'Maybe it's for the best.'

'You think so?' she asked sharply.

'Well, it's obvious we can't go on like this, tearing each other to pieces. A temporary break will let us put things into perspective.'

'You're saying a temporary break?'

'Aren't you? For God's sake, Sara, give yourself time to think!'

Sara rinsed her coffee cup and set it on the draining board. 'All right,' she said in a low voice. 'We'll say it's temporary. See what happens. I'll take the children and go to Selkirk Street.'

'No.' Will stood up. 'There's no need for you to disrupt the children's routine. I'll move out, find a flat. You can stay here.'

'I suppose it would be easier,' she said reluctantly.

'You'd rather be the one to walk out? Make the grand gesture?'

Her eyes blazed, her lips trembled. For a moment he thought she would strike him, as she had done once before.

'Do you think I care about grand gestures?' she cried.

Will lowered his eyes. 'Sorry. That was uncalled for.' He gave a short laugh. 'But it's ironic, isn't it? Here have I been trying like hell not to seem like my dad, not to seem to my kids to be walking out on them. And now I'm going anyway. I can't believe it's happening.'

'You're blaming me? Will, I've done my best. I've tried to keep us together, but it's too much.' Sara's voice shook. 'I can't do it.'

'All right, you can't do it. Just tell me when I get to see my kids and what you're going to tell them.'

'I'll tell them — ' She shrugged. 'I'll tell them you have work to do elsewhere. They'll believe it, you're always working late anyway.'

'And I see them when?'

'I don't mind. Whenever you like.'

'Thank you.' Will put his hand to his head, which was throbbing with pain. 'That means a lot to me, Sara.'

'I know, and I don't want the children to be deprived of a father. That wouldn't help either of us.'

Sara moved to the door with slow dragging steps. 'By the way,' she called back casually, 'what will the bank think? About our splitting up?'

'Not a damn thing. Times are changing. They don't expect

292

people to live like saints these days.' Will switched off the kitchen lights. 'Anyway, we're not splitting up.'

'You're moving out and I want you to move out.' Sara's light laugh sounded from the foot of the stairs. 'If that's not splitting up, I don't know what else you'd call it.'

'A temporary break,' Will said doggedly. 'You agreed, that's what it would be.'

'Oh, yes, I agreed, that's what we'd call it. Goodnight, Will.'

'Goodnight, Sara.'

They made their way to their separate beds, hers in their double room, his in the spare room which was becoming more and more familiar to him. It seemed a waste of time to go to bed, they certainly would not sleep. Yet, both were so exhausted, sleep did come. Troubled, nightmarish sleep, that left them unrefreshed; glad, in a way, when it was time to get up and begin the new phase of their lives. Their temporary break.

Chapter Sixty-One

Election Night was on its way. Everyone was predicting a landslide victory for Wilson; there were red rosette parties planned all over the country, Edinburgh included, but the Tories were undaunted, they were organising parties too. Wake or victory, the champagne would be flowing either way.

The Gilbrides and the Farrells were planning nothing. The news about Will and Sara had been too shattering. Monica had retired to bed with a lavender compress on her brow. Jennie, who saw the separation as a rerun of her own torment, clung to Mac and said she wouldn't be able to face anyone, even family, for some time. It was the children she worried about, poor little James and Stephanie, so well provided for, so deprived, now that their father had moved out. Madge and Jessie worried too.

'Of course, folk are all blaming our Kate,' wheezed Jessie, 'but how can it be her fault? She hasna seen Will for years.'

'Sometimes these things are nobody's fault,' said Madge. 'But they could all be sorted out with a bit of give and take. It's always the children who suffer in the end.'

'Aye, the poor bairns, eh? Rich or poor, they need their mam and dad.'

'Of course, it's all Sara's fault,' Malcolm told Abby. 'Will says she's got this bee in her bonnet about Kate and just won't accept that he wants to stay with her.'

'Does he, though?' asked Abby.

'Of course he does! He knows Kate was never right for him.'

'It may be that he still thinks about her, even though he doesn't want to break up his home. Maybe that's what Sara minds.'

294

'Young people!' growled Malcolm. 'Won't put up with anything, that's the trouble. The slightest thing that doesn't suit and they're off to the divorce courts!'

'God forbid!' cried Abby. 'Will says this is only a temporary break.'

'Let's hope he's right, then.'

Abby sighed. 'Wouldn't like to come over and have a drink on election night, would you? See the results?'

'No, thanks all the same. I'll be watching with Bobby and Lindsay. Lindsay doesn't feel like going out at the moment. Too depressed over Sara and Will.'

'Snap,' said Abby.

As the first results began to come in, it looked as though the predictions of a landslide victory for Labour might be coming true. More and more seats were falling to them, particularly in the London area, and Wilson supporters were counting their man already home and dry. Yet, as the evening wore on, it became apparent that the Tories were not doing as badly as had been thought. Seats they might have lost, they had retained, and in some constituencies there was even a slight swing their way.

'Looks like Harold's not getting it all his own way,' commented Frankie. 'Shouldn't be surprised if this doesn't turn out to be close.'

'Just as long as Labour wins,' said Abby, drinking coffee to keep herself awake.

Frankie, a life-long Labour man, grinned. 'Can't get over you voting Labour, Abby. What would the directors say?'

'I'm not on Logie's board now and I think it's time for a change,' she said calmly.

'If Labour doesn't get in this time, I think they never will.'

'Labour retains Edinburgh Toll' came a flash across the TV screen, and Abby grasped Frankie's arm.

'That's Kate!' she cried.

Will, sitting alone in his West End flat, drank some whisky and stared at the small TV set he had hired.

So Kate was back. Good for her. He didn't give a damn. All the same, he didn't switch off as the cameras moved to the count at her constituency. There was the returning officer, flanked on one side by Hugh Alexander, apologetic in defeat, and on the other by Kate, radiant in victory. In the background, stood a glum-faced Liberal (who had lost his deposit) but no one was taking any notice of him.

'Kate Marjorie Rossie – twenty-two thousand and twenty three,' the returning officer was droning, 'and I duly declare —' but the rest of his words were drowned by the great roar that went up from Kate's supporters.

'Who's that guy with the black hair?' thought Will. 'That journalist she used to knock about with? God, how they hang around, don't they? Bees to the honeypot.'

And was her second name Marjorie? He'd never known that. What else didn't he know?

But then Kate, stepping forward to make the usual speech of thanks, was so beautiful in her triumph, so unconscious of his own and Sara's misery, he had to leap up and turn her picture off.

'I hope to God Sara's not watching this,' he murmured, topping up his glass, and knew she would be, hugging her desolation round her like a suffocating cloak. The way he felt, that cloak was round him too.

Hours later, Malcolm was exploding.

'Thirteen seats!' he cried. 'Wilson's got in by thirteen seats! So much for the Labour landslide. We could have won, we should have won, just a few more votes and we'd have done it.'

'Can he form a government?' asked Bobby. 'Thirteen seats is not much of a majority.'

'You can say that again.' Malcolm turned bloodshot eyes on Lindsay. 'Your precious Jo Grimond only got nine, so what's the betting Wilson will try a pact to stay in office?'

'Poor old Jo,' Bobby whistled, preparing to go up to bed. 'He won't make a pact with Wilson, chalk and cheese, those two. Come on, Lindsay.'

'Wait, they're going over to the Labour headquarters,' said Lindsay, still hovering at the television. 'Let's see everyone looking happy.'

Malcolm said he couldn't stand it, he was off, but Bobby and Lindsay stayed to watch the prime minister-elect beaming into the cameras, saying all the things they expected him to say. Then Lindsay stiffened.

'There's Kate Rossie,' she said. 'How did she get down there?'

'Obviously, by plane. Probably shared it with that guy standing next to her.' Bobby narrowed tired eyes. 'Adam Lock, Glasgow MP, tipped for the Cabinet.'

'I know who he is,' Lindsay said coldly. 'Another of Kate's men.'

'So they say,' Bobby agreed.

Lindsay's brow darkened and she snapped off the television.

'I don't know about you, Bobby, but I've had enough. I'm going to bed.'

'Me, too,' said Bobby.

'Come on, come on, time for bed!' cried Biddy, shaking Ewan and her father awake. 'You've missed everything, you great soft things, did I no' tell you to cut out the drinking?'

'Did we get in?' yawned Ewan.

'Just. Thirteen seats.'

'Och, that's no good, eh? We'll be out again next week.'

'Did our Kate win?' asked Ken, rubbing his hands over his face.

'Aye. Great big majority, same as last time.'

'You shoulda woke me. I wanted to see her.'

'Och, you were unconscious. Come on, away to your bed, Dad. You ken, I've to be up same time in the morning. Folk'll be wanting their papers, even if I've been up all night, and I've the rolls to do and all.'

'So have I to be up,' muttered Ewan, taking a last drink from the dregs of his glass. 'Bloody elections, they're no' worth it. Doesna matter who gets in, things stay the same.'

'Now that is no' exactly the truth,' Ken was beginning, when Biddy gave him a push to the door.

'Goodnight, Dad!'

'Aye, goodnight. Goodnight, pet.'

Away went Ken, followed by Ewan, while Biddy damped down the fire and put up the guard.

'Fancy our Kate being in government,' she exclaimed to herself, quite without envy, for what she and Kate wanted were different things. 'And her from Catherine's Land like me!'

That said something, did it no'? A face from Catherine's Land in power. Ewan was wrong, as usual. Things didna always stay the same. And a good thing too.

'Are you no' coming to bed?' roared Ewan.

'Coming,' called Biddy.

And put the lights out.

Part Four

1969–1970

Chapter Sixty-Two

Until her father's funeral in November, 1969, Will had not seen Kate for five years, precisely the span of time that he and Sara had been separated. On that disastrous night when they'd agreed to go their own ways, he'd felt too spent, too drained, to try to save their marriage. Yet he'd been confident that the split would be only temporary. Sara would cool down, get tired of living alone, would see sense and allow him to return to her.

She never had.

In a way he'd never anticipated, she began to blossom without him. Embarked on new training, found a job as personnel officer with an electronics firm, borrowed money from her mother to buy out his share of the house. And bubbled again, in her old self-confident way. Even the children he'd been so worried about seemed to be happy with the new regime she'd created for them. Mummy during the week, Daddy at weekends, and in the background the steady old-style housekeeper Sara had found to replace the succession of au pairs. What was there left for Will?

Work. It was an anodyne he was used to and found rewarding. In 1968 when Charles Kerr was promoted to Manager on the retirement of Mr Porteous, Will was made Assistant Manager. Poised dizzily on the upper rungs of the ladder he'd always had in his sights, he could hardly believe his own achievement. Or, that he must savour it alone.

Why had he never sought out Kate? If he'd been asked that question he would have said he didn't know. In truth, it was because he was afraid. Afraid of further hurt. He was the burnt child who fears the fire, too nervous to risk playing with matches.

There was something to be said for a life complicated only by work.

Then, on a grey November day he saw Kate again.

Ken Rossie had died very suddenly. He'd been helping Biddy to carry in the evening newspapers, had bent to cut the string around one of the bundles and never straightened again. 'Massive heart attack,' said the doctor at the hospital to which he'd been taken by ambulance. 'I'm sorry.'

After the funeral service held in a church Ken never attended, the small procession made its way to the Comely Bank cemetery where Ken had once said he would like to be buried next to Ivy. Apart from his family, the mourners were mainly old friends from Catherine's Land, those that were left, for a number had already departed.

'Aye, who'll there be to follow ma Ken?' poor Jessie had sighed. 'When you think, Madge, o' them that's gone.'

'I don't like to think,' Madge said faintly, thinking all the same of fierce little Peggie Kemp and Marty Finnegan who had died two years before, and Donnie, of course, and Sally, who had died in Australia in 1967.

'Oh, let's not talk of them now, Jessie, love. It's too sad for you, too sad.'

Jessie's face had seemed to crumble, as she felt for Madge's hand.

'It's just sometimes, I get the feeling I've been left,' she whispered. 'You ken what I mean? Forgotten.'

'I know what you mean,' said Madge. 'I feel that too.'

But Ken's family were there in force to mourn him, his mother and his daughters, his grandchildren, his son from Aberdeen. And all of Madge's family with the exception of Sara attended, even young Gail, who hadn't known Ken, but wanted to please Gran's friend, poor Mrs Rossie. So, if you counted the few old friends left, such as Jamie and Betty Kemp, Marty Finnegan's family, and the Pringles and the Craigs, the turn-out was not too bad. Quite respectable, really, and not too many for Biddy to cope with back in the room over the shop.

Will first saw Kate in the church, helping Jessie into her seat in the front pew. She was wearing a grey coat and a black hat. He

302

couldn't see her face. When the coffin was borne in, he bowed his head and thought of Ken, one of the Rossie boys, as his gran still called him, gone now to join his brother Billy. Only Dougie Rossie in Canada was left to remember with the Kemps those days when they'd racketed up and down the stair at Catherine's Land, driving Abby crazy, as his mother used to tell Will. He looked along the pew to where Jennie was standing now and saw that she was very pale and holding tight to Mac's arm. A particular ordeal for her lay ahead, for Comely Bank Cemetery was where his father lay. On the day of his funeral, Sheena MacLaren had turned up uninvited and stood under distant trees with her mother, watching the burial.

She'd better not turn up today, thought Will grimly. But there was to be no sign of Sheena at the graveside.

It was as he left the church that Will finally met Kate face to face, as she stood with her family, thanking those who had come to mourn her father. She looked the same as he remembered her, just as lovely, almost as young. Not quite as young. She didn't look twenty any more, though the lines at her eyes and mouth were faint and her hair, what he could see of it under the black hat, was as richly tawny as it had always been. Her hand in his was dry and firm and he thought she seemed genuinely pleased to see him. There was no sign of embarrassment in her manner, but then why should there be? She knew nothing of what had passed between himself and Sara.

'Will, how good of you to come,' Kate said warmly. 'We do appreciate it, we know how busy you are.'

'I wanted to come, we all did. All the family.' He gave a faint smile. 'Remember your dad so well, Kate, from the old days.'

'Will you be coming back to the shop? Biddy's laid on tea.'

'Thanks, I'll be there.'

He moved away. It was time to go to the cemetery.

Chapter Sixty-Three

Biddy had worked hard to bring order to the chaos of Ken's upstairs living room. Kate congratulated her.

'It's looking great, I'm only sorry I wasn't here to help.'

'That's OK,' sniffed Biddy, hurrying to set out the plates of ham and tinned salmon, as the mourners began to stream in. 'You've done your whack, paying for all this. Anyway, the girls came over to give me a hand.'

Biddy's daughters, Pat and Valerie, were married now, neither expecting, thank God, said Biddy, and both of them capable and willing, not at all like their father. It was Iain, Biddy's only son, who had inherited Ewan's shiftlessness. He had already had a string of jobs and was at present unemployed. Kate had promised to 'have a word' with him.

Everyone was relaxing now, as people did after funerals, except for Jessie, sitting with Madge on the sofa, who seemed to be in a world of her own.

'Best let them be,' whispered Biddy to Abby, when she had given them tea. 'Poor things, it's all too much, eh?'

'Yes,' Abby agreed worriedly.

Even allowing for the circumstances it seemed to her that Jessie was looking very unwell and she had never seen Madge appear so old and frail. It came to her with a strange hollow feeling that her mother was not immortal. So many deaths over the years, but never Madge's; all the family thought as Abby thought that Madge would go on for ever. But of course that could not be and for the first time Abby realised it.

She was aware of Gail standing next to her, looking with sympathetic eyes at the two old ladies. Now sixteen, Gail was tall and slender, not conventionally pretty as Rachel had been, but still with a likeness to her that could take the family by surprise. Her long dark hair, matched with her dark eyes, gave her a striking air which had already caused interest among the Academy boys who came to her school for dances, but so far she had shown no interest in boyfriends.

'I should damn well think not!' cried Bobby. 'She's only a child!'

At which Lindsay smiled.

'Poor Gran,' Gail whispered now to Abby. 'She looks so tired. What can she find to say to Mrs Rossie? I mean, there's nothing, is there?'

'Not really. It takes time to get over a loss like hers.' Abby shook her head. 'And at her age — '

She didn't finish her sentence, but took Gail's arm.

'Come and have something to eat,' she said gently.

They were trying some of Biddy's cold boiled ham with pickle and salad when Gail said casually, 'Aunt Abby, who's that boy over in the corner? He keeps looking at me, but I'm sure I don't know him.'

Abby turned her head. She studied the handsome Irish face of the boy Gail had pointed out. Glossy black hair, vivid blue eyes. Oh, Marty Finnegan might have passed away, but her looks lived on in her grandchildren and he was one of them.

'That's Sean O'Dwyer,' she told Gail. 'You've met Mrs O'Dwyer who helps out at your gran's?'

'Oh, yes, Nancy, they call her.' Gail looked at Sean with interest. 'So that's her son? He looks the same age as me.'

'Yes, he's about sixteen. Nancy has two other sons and a daughter. Her mother, Marty Finnegan, was a friend of your gran's in Catherine's Land. In fact, your gran helped to bring Nancy into the world.'

'I suppose people didn't go to hospital in those days,' Gail said vaguely. 'Do you think I should go over and talk to Sean? He looks rather lonely.'

'I don't think you'll need to, he's coming over here,' Abby said, with a smile.

'How long have you got?' Will was asking Kate. 'I mean, how long are you here for?'

305

'I feel bad about it, but I have to leave this evening.' Kate gratefully drew on a cigarette. 'Can't be helped. There's a vote tomorrow I mustn't miss.'

'I'm sure Biddy understands,' Will said, feeling annoyed by the pang her words gave him.

'Oh, sure. I'll be back in a couple of weeks anyhow. I can help sort out Dad's stuff, then.' Kate gave a wry smile. 'There won't be any trouble over the will, he didn't have much to leave.'

'Are you flying back to London?'

'Couldn't get a seat, I'm taking the six o'clock train.'

Will glanced at his watch. 'You haven't much time. Can I give you a lift to the station?'

Something sparked for a moment in her steady gaze.

'I'd be grateful. If it's no trouble.'

'It's no trouble.'

They were exchanging cautious smiles when Stewart Rossie, Kate's brother, came wandering across to join them. He had his father's heavy features but none of Ken's good nature, and had visited his parents so rarely from Aberdeen, his sisters had felt like telling him not to bother attending Ken's funeral. Had to keep the peace, though, so they tightened their lips and suffered. At least he hadn't brought his wife, a woman neither Kate nor Biddy could stand.

'Well, well, look who's here,' he said now, grinning broadly from Kate to Will. 'Is this the VIP's corner, then? Famous lady MP – famous Edinburgh banker – must be, I reckon. Got the time to talk to your brother, then, Kate?'

'I might have, if you hadn't been at the port,' she said coldly. 'I suppose Ewan's been filling your glass, has he? You'd think you'd show more respect.'

'I'm no' drunk!' he protested. 'Och, you'd think you'd show a wee bit more affection to a guy who's come all the way down from the North Sea!'

'A pity you didn't come down more often then, when Mam and Dad were alive!' cried Kate, losing her resolve to keep the peace. 'You know what they felt for you, specially Mam, but you couldn't be bothered to show, could you?' She stood up, stubbing out her cigarette. 'If you'll excuse me, I have to help Biddy. Will, I'll see you later, OK?'

'Oh-ho!' cried Stewart, his eyes gleaming. 'Like that, is it?

306

Now did someone no' tell me you two were love-birds once? What happened, then, Will? Did she turn you down? Turns ivery-body down, ma sister, canna find a man good enough, you ken.'

'Just go and put your head under the cold water tap,' Will said tightly. 'Unless you want me to do it for you.'

'Leave him, leave him,' Kate said hurriedly. 'He probably started drinking before he came and he never could hold it. Oh, Will, I'm sorry!'

'Come on, there's nothing for you to be sorry about!' Will touched her hand quickly. 'He'll be regretting this when he wakes up in the morning.'

'Not Stewart,' she said with feeling, but her gaze on Will was warm.

'Love-birds, love-birds,' ran stupidly through his mind, as he returned that warm look, but he stopped his thoughts short. He would not get involved.

'So, Gail Farrell, you go to St Clare's?' asked Sean O'Dwyer, leaning against the door and fixing Gail with a long blue stare. 'Thought you would, somehow.'

'Why, where do you go?' Gail cried, taking his words for no compliment.

'Catholic comprehensive. Dinna tell me you couldna tell that?'

He looks Irish, she thought, but sounds Scottish. Well, of course he would. No doubt he hadn't even seen the country of his forefathers.

'I don't make judgements on how people look,' she said loftily, and Sean grinned.

'First person in the world not to, then. Och, we're the only young people in this room, so let's no' argue.'

'I suppose that's true.' Gail looked round at the mourners, who were lining up to make their farewells to Biddy and Kate. 'We are the only young ones here. Didn't your brothers and sister want to come, then?'

'All at work. I'm the only one at school and I fancied a day off.'

'You came to get the day off? Not for the funeral?'

At Gail's shocked look, Sean laughed.

'Now why would I want to come to Ken Rossie's funeral? I'm no' ma mother. She was keen, she works for old Jessie, thinks she's terrific, but I dinna ken that lot.'

'Your mum works for my great-gran, as well,' said Gail. 'She was a friend of Mrs Rossie's in Catherine's Land. That used to be a tenement in the Lawnmarket.'

'I know that, didna think you would.'

'Why shouldn't I, when my gran and my grandpa used to live there?'

'No reason.' But Sean was whistling through his teeth. 'I'll tell you something interesting, my gran lived there too.'

'Mrs Finnegan,' said Gail smartly. 'See, I already know that.'

'Looks like we've got something in common eh? Grandparents from Catherine's Land.'

Sean's voice was soft. His intensely blue eyes, fringed with thick black lashes, held Gail as though in a hypnotic spell. She felt exhilarated, yet also strung with nerves, so when her father came to tell her they were ready to go, she was annoyed and relieved in a strange childish mixture. How conventional her father looked, in his dark suit and black tie, the perfect civil servant. Would anyone believe he had ever run a pop group? He really had no right to stare so disapprovingly at Sean's long hair.

'This is Sean O'Dwyer, Daddy,' she said quickly. 'Sean, this is my father.'

'Hi,' said Sean.

Bobby nodded and smiled briefly. 'Oh, yes, I know your mother. It was good of you to come to Mr Rossie's funeral.'

Sean lowered his eyes modestly, and Gail blushed.

'Well, we must be going.' Bobby took Gail's arm. 'Nice to meet you, Sean.'

As they left him staring after them, Gail pulled herself free from Bobby's hand. 'There's no need to hold me like that, Daddy,' she said pettishly. 'I'm not going to run away.'

He turned surprised eyes. 'What on earth are you talking about, Gail?'

She shrugged and made no reply. When Lindsay joined them, she looked from one to the other and raised her eyebrows.

'What's wrong?'

'Let's just make our goodbyes,' said Bobby.

'Oh, Biddy, I hate leaving you like this,' Kate said, holding her sister close. 'But I will be back soon – you can expect me – and then we'll sort things out, OK?'

'Dinna worry, I can manage.' Biddy kissed Kate's cheek. 'Better get going, dinna want to miss your train.' She glanced at Will, standing stiffly at the shop door, and smiled. 'Got your lift, anyway. Thanks for coming, Will, it was good of you.'

As he shook Biddy's hand, Kate buttoned her grey coat and stuffed her black hat into her overnight bag.

'Hate hats,' she said with feeling. 'Especially black ones. Biddy, you'll keep in touch till I come back? I'm worried about Gran.'

'Aye, she's no' so good. I'll phone you.'

'And if you see Sheena MacLaren —'

Biddy's lip took on its familiar curl. 'I'd like to see her try coming back here!' she cried. 'I'm in charge now.'

Chapter Sixty-Four

They had a little time to spare. Why not a quick drink, asked Will.

'As long as it is quick,' Kate replied.

But when they had found a place to sit in the crowded station bar, she would only have a tonic. Had to keep a clear head for her paperwork on the train, she explained. Will got himself a whisky.

'So, how are things?' Kate asked. 'You're looking very well.'

'Looking old.' He touched the few grey hairs at his temples. 'See? Silver threads among the gold?'

'Very distinguished. In fact, I can't even see them.'

Will hesitated, then took a jump into the deep end. 'You know Sara and I are still apart?'

'I'm sorry about that.'

'It's not worked out too badly. I see the children, I get on better with Sara than when we were together, don't know why.'

'She's more relaxed, maybe.'

'Maybe.' Will drank his whisky. 'How about you?'

Her face darkened a little. 'I'm all right.'

'Heard you were doing well since you moved to Health.'

'Not as well as all that.'

'No?'

'No.' She laughed shortly. 'I'm a rebel. Maybe you heard that too? Voted against the government on Vietnam, prescription charges and trade union rights. You name it, I'm out of step. So are most of us on the left.'

'You're not happy with Wilson?'

'Understatement of the year. Shall we talk about something else?'

'How about Adam Lock?'

Kate blinked. 'Adam? I didn't know you knew about him.'

'Edinburgh gossip.'

'It's out of date. Adam and I split up some time ago.'

'I'd have thought you had a lot in common.'

'Once, maybe. But Adam met a pretty little researcher who wanted to be married.'

'Ah,' said Will.

'He's also a Wilson man.' Kate glanced at the clock behind the bar. 'And we said we wouldn't talk about Wilson. Come on, Will, I've got to catch that train.'

'How I hate this station,' Will sighed, as they hurried the length of the platform to find Kate's seat on the waiting London train. 'Always reminds me of partings.'

'Sometimes there are meetings.'

'It's the partings I remember.'

'Pessimist. Here we are, this is me.' Kate found her coach and turned to Will. 'Thanks for the lift, Will, and the drink.'

'One tonic!'

'And thanks again for coming to Dad's funeral. Means a lot.'

'Did you say you were coming back in a couple of weeks?' he asked casually. 'May I give you a ring?'

She looked down the platform, at the train curving away and the porters closing doors, the guard standing with his flag.

'I'd better get in,' she said, after a pause.

'You have your own flat here, don't you?' he cried desperately, as she mounted the steps of the train. 'Couldn't I ring you there? Are you in the book?'

'I'm in the book,' she called, and disappeared from his view.

'Kate!' He ran along the side of the train, looking in at the people still finding seats and putting up luggage, but couldn't see her. The train began to move, he felt stupidly frustrated, as though he were a child, deprived. Then he saw her, in her seat, waving and smiling, and he fell back with a sigh of relief. He was certain now he would see her again.

'So, how did the funeral go?' asked Sara.

It was the following day, a Saturday, and Will had arrived at the Newington house to collect James, now almost eleven, and Stephanie, nearly nine. They did not expect outings now to the

311

zoo or the cinema, were happy enough to return with Will to his flat, to cook sausages or burgers, play records, get Dad's help with homework. It was an arrangement that meant all the world to Will.

'Oh, you know what these things are like,' he answered. 'Turn-out wasn't too bad.'

'You don't think I should have gone? I really didn't know Mr Rossie.'

'I'm sure no one expected you to go.' Will looked round for the children, but they were still upstairs. 'I – um – saw Kate.'

'I didn't think she'd miss her father's funeral,' Sara said evenly.

'She had to go straight back to London. I gave her a lift to the station.'

'Why tell me? I'm not interested.'

'OK, OK. Sorry I spoke.'

'As a matter of fact, I've seen an old friend too.' Sara went to the foot of the stairs and called to the children to hurry, their father was waiting. 'Yes – Nick Ainslie.'

'I thought you often saw him.'

'No, it's been ages. Would you believe, he's separated from Annette? Gave her the push himself, said she was far too young for him.'

'Pity he didn't think of that before they married, then.'

'People don't think, do they? Don't think at all.' Sara took a large tin from the dresser. 'Mrs Lomax made this chocolate cake for you to take. Should help out on the catering front.'

'You bet.' Will took a peek. 'Wow, look at that! Please give her my best thanks, Sara.'

James and Stephanie came tumbling into the kitchen, weekend bags packed, eyes pinned on Mrs Lomax's cake tin.

'Is it chocolate or coffee?' asked James, who was like his mother in looks and personality, but Stephanie, his quiet sister, was already investigating.

'Chocolate!' she cried, and Will swept her up and hugged her. She was not his favourite because he had no favourite, but it was true there was an affinity between them; in her serious little character he recognised himself.

'Come on, let's get going,' he ordered, setting her down. 'Say goodbye to Mummy, you two. Sara, have a good weekend.'

312

'Yes.' She suddenly looked a little embarrassed. 'As it happens, I'm having dinner with Nick tonight.'

'Oh?' He felt it was his cue to say, why tell me? I'm not interested, but cheap repartee was not in his line. 'Please give him my regards,' he said politely, and took the children to his car.

Chapter Sixty-Five

On Sunday morning, when Abby and Frankie were having breakfast, still in their dressing gowns, their telephone rang.

'Damn,' said Frankie. 'What the hell time is this to call?'

'It is nearly eleven o'clock, Frankie.' Abby was on her way to the phone.

'Aye, but Sunday.' Frankie yawned and buttered his toast. 'Tell them we're not at home.'

'Ssh, it's Ma!' cried Abby.

Twenty minutes later, they were on their way to the bungalow. Madge was worried about Jessie, couldn't get her to speak.

'You don't think she's – you know—' Frankie, driving fast through quiet Sunday streets, gave Abby a quick glance. 'Dead?'

'Of course not! Ma may be old, but she knows death when she sees it. No, this is something else. Maybe a stroke.'

But Jessie didn't appear to have had a stroke. She was in her bed, lying against her pillows, her eyes open and appearing normal, but when they knelt beside her and said her name, she made no reply.

'You see?' whispered Madge, hovering close. 'She won't say a word. Won't have anything to eat, won't even have a cup of tea.'

'How long has she been like this?' asked Abby, in a low voice.

'Since last night. She's not been herself since the funeral, but she wasn't too bad yesterday until bedtime. Then she went to bed and wouldn't say goodnight to me. I looked in, I said, how are you, Jessie, and she just lay there, looking at me, without speaking. I thought she'd be better this morning, but—' Madge put her hand to her eyes. 'She's just the same.'

'I expect she's tired,' said Frankie. 'Worn out with grief and shock and the funeral. This'll be some kind of reaction to all that.'

'You're probably right, but I think we should let the doctor have a look at her.' Abby led the way downstairs. 'Ma, what's his number?'

Dr Cooper, on call from the practice, was young and enthusiastic. When he had examined Jessie, he came back downstairs to anxious Madge waiting with Abby and Frankie.

'Well, it's a tricky one,' he told them, his narrow grey eyes alight because this case was more interesting than his usual Sunday call-outs. 'Could be what we call aphasia, that's when a problem with the central nervous system affects speech. Or, could be some sort of nervous reaction. Has Mrs Rossie been upset lately?'

'She's just lost her son, who died very suddenly,' said Abby.

'There you are, that could be it, though of course I can't be sure. We shall need to get her into hospital for tests. Is there a phone I can use?'

Hospital. Ambulance. As Frankie showed the doctor the telephone, Madge burst into tears. Abby put her arms around her.

'Ma, don't worry. Jessie's going to be all right. This is just a temporary thing, you'll see.'

'I don't know, I don't know, she seems so strange, Abby.'

'Yes, but the tests will show what's wrong and then she can have treatment. In the meantime, I think you should pack a bag and come back with Frankie and me.'

'No, no, I'm going in the ambulance with Jessie.'

'All right, you do that and we'll follow. When you've seen Jessie settled in, we'll go to our place.'

'I want to come back here,' Madge said obstinately. 'I don't like being away from home, Abby, even to stay with you. I'll be all right, I can look after myself.'

Seeing the set of Madge's mouth, Abby said no more. She telephoned Biddy, who said she would meet them at the hospital, then helped Madge into the ambulance that had just arrived. Jessie lay quite still where the attendants had put her, her face very pale but her eyes still open and alert.

'OK?' cried one of the men. Madge, very pale herself, nodded, and as the doors were closed, reached over and took Jessie's hand.

'Know what?' Abby murmured, as she and Frankie drove to the hospital, 'I see breakers ahead.'

'With Ma, you mean?'

'With Ma. I know Jessie wasn't able to do much, but when there were two of them, they propped each other up. Now Ma's on her own and she won't be able to cope. Who knows how long Jessie's going to be in hospital? We're just going to have to persuade Ma to come to us.'

'Maybe if we got Nancy to do more hours, she could manage?' suggested Frankie.

'But Nancy's not there at night and Ma shouldn't be alone. I suppose we could get someone to sleep in, but Ma wouldn't want a stranger around. No, she's just going to have to listen to reason.'

'Sooner you than me to try to make her change her mind,' said Frankie.

Madge did not change her mind. Even when Jennie came over from Fife to add her arguments, Madge remained adamant. She might be in her eighties, but she was quite capable of looking after herself. What did they think she was going to do? Leave the gas on, fall downstairs, just because Jessie wasn't around? Of late, she'd been doing most of the chores anyway, on the days when Nancy didn't come, because Jessie hadn't been up to doing very much.

'Now, I know you worry about me, but there's no need,' she told her daughters. 'What you have to remember is that I just want to be on my own, until Jessie comes home.'

'But will Jessie come home?' Jennie asked Abby.

The sisters looked at each other darkly. No decisions could be made until the hospital tests were completed, but in their hearts both were certain that Jessie had taken too many steps downhill ever to live at home again. They grieved for her, but their thoughts were also with Madge.

'Ma would so much hate to lose her independence,' Jennie groaned. 'I don't think we can persuade her to give up her home.'

'Everyone has to face this kind of problem if their parents live to be old,' Abby replied. 'Decisions have to be made and we're the ones who'll have to make them.'

'But Ma's still all right in her mind!' cried Jennie. 'What right have we to tell her what to do?'

316

'Let's hope it doesn't come to that.' Abby, who was smoking more than usual, lit another cigarette. 'Maybe Jessie'll come through this and they'll both go on a bit longer.'

'Maybe,' said Jennie, without conviction. She looked at Abby smoking. 'Hey, give me one of those, will you? I could do with some comfort too.'

But it was Madge who needed comfort. The news came in a day or two that Jessie would not be coming home. Though she had not had a stroke and there was no physical reason to account for her lack of speech, she appeared to have moved into a state of neurosis that would require nursing-home care. It was as though, the doctors said, she had just switched off from living, even though her body was not yet ready for dying; there was no way of knowing if she would ever improve. Best not to hope for too much.

'Och, the poor soul!' exclaimed Nancy O'Dwyer, clearing away Madge's breakfast dishes, while Madge still sat staring hopelessly at the table. 'All been too much for her, eh?'

'My poor Jessie.' Madge raised her eyes to Nancy's craggy, worn features. A good generous girl, was Nancy. Quite without her mother's powerful personality, but that was true of all Marty's children; there had never been room in the Finnegan household for more than one Marty.

'I can't stop thinking of Jessie, you know,' Madge went on. 'I keep seeing her eyes following me, even when I'm away, and I keep wondering if she's talking yet and if I should be there.'

'Poor soul,' said Nancy again, shaking back her mass of thick, dark hair.

'The thing is, if Jessie's never coming back, what can I do? Abby and Jennie want me to give up my home.'

'Mrs Gilbride, dinna say it! They're niver wanting you to go into one o' they old people's homes?'

'No. They think I should stay with Abby.'

Nancy frowned in concentration. 'Well, that might no' be so bad, eh? I mean, your Abby, she'd no' boss you around like some daughters.' She laughed hoarsely. 'Or, like my ma!'

'Yes, but there's all my things,' said Madge. 'My furniture, my bits and pieces. If I've to give everything up, Nancy, I'll feel my

317

life's gone.' Madges voice trembled. 'All I want is my independence. Just to lead my own life, till it's time to go.'

'I think iverybody wants that,' Nancy said quietly.

Later, when she brought Madge a cup of tea and a biscuit, Nancy asked what she thought of her Sean and Bobby's Gail going out together?

'What?' cried Madge, shaken from her preoccupation with her future. 'Why, I didn't know they even knew each other!'

'Aye, met at poor Ken's funeral.'

'Sean asked Gail out at the funeral?'

'No, not then. Seemingly, he went to her school and waited for her. Cheek of it, eh, going to St Clare's?' Nancy smiled, showing gaps in her teeth. 'I says to him, I says, Sean, you've got your nerve, asking a St Clare's girl out, and her in her uniform and all!'

'There's no reason why he shouldn't ask Gail out,' Madge said quickly. 'I mean, they're both just young people. Why not?'

Nancy pursed her lips. 'Well, I dinna think it'd be what your Bobby'd want. He'll be thinking of Academy boys for Gail, eh?'

'Oh, I don't think fathers can choose boyfriends for girls these days, Nancy. Sean's a good-looking boy, and clever. There's no reason why Gail shouldn't go out with him. No reason at all.'

'Aye, well, he asked her to go to the pictures and she said she would, and this Saturday they're going to his school disco.' Nancy put a roughened finger to her lips. 'But better no' say anything, Mrs Gilbride. Gail might no' have told her folks yet.'

'I won't say a word.'

In spite of her own views, when she was alone Madge thought of Bobby and Lindsay and Mrs Farrell in the background, and knew that Nancy was right. Sean O'Dwyer, Marty Finnegan's grandson, would not be the choice of Gail's family for her first boyfriend. Class distinctions had blurred since Madge's youth, and a good thing too, she reflected, but they had not disappeared. Who's your father, where did you go to school, were still questions asked in Edinburgh. Well, let Bobby ask Sean those questions! She, Madge, would remind him that his mother and his father came from Catherine's Land and that that was no disgrace. She'd see to it that he didn't ban Sean, just because he was a Finnegan.

318

Madge drank her tea and lay back in her chair. So much thinking and feeling had made her feel quite weary. But now her own worries came rushing back to fill her mind. What should she tell Abby? She closed her eyes. She'd just have a little rest, think about it. When Nancy came in to take her cup, Madge was sleeping peacefully.

Chapter Sixty-Six

Gail had not told her parents about seeing Sean O'Dwyer. All her life they had given her everything she wanted, but she knew very well that if she wanted Sean as a boyfriend, that would be different. He would represent a first, something she was not allowed to have.

The whole thing was beginning to take on the quality of a dream. From that first dizziness when she had seen Sean waiting for her at the school gate, to the unbelievable moment when he had kissed her good night after the film and she had slid into the house with no trouble at all. Luck had been on her side, for her parents were not yet back from a charity dance and only Grandpa was pottering about. He had completely believed her story of going to the cinema with Selina Duncan, her best friend, he had seen nothing amiss with her scarlet face and trembling lips. She had been able to go to her room and re-run the evening over and over again. Holding Sean's hand throughout the James Bond film, eating the choc-ice he'd bought her, laughing as he dabbed melted chocolate from her chin, walking out into the winter night and not feeling cold, feeling on fire as his hand came round her waist.

'Am I really the first guy you've been out with?' he had asked softly. 'I canna believe it. My sister's had boyfriends since she was ten.'

Gail did not ask him if he had had girlfriends since he was ten, somehow the words for that question would not come. She tried to explain her own lack of experience.

'Well, I go to an all-girls school, you see. The Academy boys only come over for Christmas dances and plays.'

'If I'd come over for a Christmas dance, I'd no' have missed you, I'm telling you.'

'One or two did ask me out. I wasn't interested.'

'And you're interested in me?' Even in the darkness of the street, she could see the light in Sean's eyes. 'Why's that, then? What makes me different?'

'I don't know.'

She didn't know what made him different, but he was.

When they reached the road where she lived, she felt its quietness and solidity as stifling as a blanket. When they came to her grandfather's house, she saw it through Sean's eyes. A middle-class home. A place for the privileged. Would he comment? Sneer? She glanced at him apprehensively, saw the fine eyes sweep down from the well-kept roof, past the long upper windows only one of which was lit, to the heavy front door and the neatly clipped and tidied garden.

'A long way from Catherine's Land,' he said quietly. 'For your grandparents, eh?'

'A very long way. My grandpa trained as an accountant, took night classes, worked really hard. My grandma was an artist. Maybe you've heard of her? Her name was Rachel Ritchie.'

'Aye, I know about her. Bought a postcard of one of her pictures at the gallery. "Tenement", it was called.'

'That was really Catherine's Land.'

'Didna forget it, then.'

'I suppose no one really forgets their roots.'

'And these are yours?' Sean jerked his head towards the waiting house.

'Just as real to me,' she said with sudden spirit.

'Sure. I'm no' blaming you. Dinna be so touchy.'

'I'm not touchy!'

'You're all prickles,' he said gently. 'Like a hedgehog.'

That had been when he'd kissed her, so fast, so expertly, there was no need to wonder how many girlfriends he had had, but Gail had no desire to count them. As she gave herself up to the exquisite novelty of his kiss, it came to her that she knew why he was different. He wasn't a boy, he was a man. He had already entered the world of sex that for her and her friends was still the future, and she had sensed that from the beginning. And had been drawn to him because of it? As her new knowledge flooded her, she trembled in Sean's arms.

'First time I've kissed a hedgehog,' said Sean, lightening the moment, but that did not stop her kissing him back, strongly and passionately.

'Will you come out with me again?' he asked, holding her.

'If I can.'

'There's a disco at ma school next Saturday. Eight o'clock till twelve. All very proper, all very supervised, your folks would approve. Like to come?'

'Oh, Sean, I don't know if they'll let me.'

'For God's sake, it's a school disco, Gail, no' an orgy! Come on, you tell 'em straight out you're no' a kid any more.'

'I didn't even tell them I was going to the pictures with you, they'd never have let me come.'

He was silent for a moment, then he looked up at the house again.

'I see. Different roots, eh? Well, if you dinna want to come on Saturday — '

'I do want to come! I will come! I'll find a way, I promise!'

'OK.' He gave her a beautiful smile. 'Best if we meet there, eh? Know where it is? The Good Shepherd School?'

'I know where it is. But you'll be sure to be there, Sean? I won't know anyone, I'll be worried — '

'I'll be there, Gail. You've no need to worry.'

But Gail was worried. How was she to get to a disco when it had been difficult enough just to go to the pictures? Maybe if she were to say that she and Selina were going somewhere together? No, that wouldn't do. Selina would back her up, but Lindsay often saw Mrs Duncan and it might all come out. Then, wherever she said she was going, her parents would want to take her and that would be out of the question. Unless she just told them the truth, as Sean had advised? Put it to them that she was of an age to go out with boys to discos? Her heart sank even at the thought.

It was Friday before she found the courage to speak to her mother. Lindsay was in the kitchen, organising supper. They were to have a casserole and an apple pie prepared by the daily help, Mrs Allan, who had already left, and Lindsay was hurrying to get

322

the vegetables on. She had a pottery class on Friday evenings, was always in a rush.

Whyever did I pick this time? thought Gail.

'Mummy, I was wondering — '

'Would you mind lighting the gas under those potatoes, Gail?' Lindsay interrupted. 'Thanks. What were you saying, dear?'

'Could I go to a disco on Saturday night?' Gail cried squeakily. 'Sean O'Dwyer has asked me.'

Lindsay set down a spoon with a clatter.

'Asked you? Asked you when?'

'He met me out of school one day.'

'What are you saying? You've been seeing this boy and never told us?'

'He just came to St Clare's,' Gail said desperately. 'We were talking at Mr Rossie's funeral, and then he met me and said would I like to go to this disco. It's at his school, it's all organised by the teachers.'

'Which school?'

'One of the Catholic schools. The Good Shepherd, actually. I've heard it's one of the best, gets very good results.'

'I'm sure, but I really don't think we can let you go to a disco there, Gail.' Lindsay picked up the spoon and stirred the casserole before putting it back in the oven. 'It would be different if we knew Sean, but we don't, we don't know anything about him.'

'Mummy, you know his mother. She works for Mrs Rossie and Gran. Gran's known Mrs O'Dwyer all her life, Aunt Abby said she brought her into the world, that was when she lived in Catherine's Land. So you do know a lot about Sean, he's not just anybody.'

Lindsay bit her lip. 'Knowing about his mother doesn't mean we know him, Gail. And you'd be late back, wouldn't you? You'd be wandering round Edinburgh at all hours of the night with a boy we don't know. I'm sorry, Gail, but your father would never agree. You must just tell Sean you can't go.'

'Mummy, I'm sixteen. Lots of girls go to discos and dances at my age. It's ridiculous to say I'm too young, I might be at university next year, if I get my Highers.'

'I didn't say you were too young, Gail.'

'What, then?'

'That it wasn't suitable for you to be going to something so late with a boy we don't know.'

'So it's Sean who's the problem, is it?'

'At the moment, yes.'

'But if his father was an advocate and he'd lived in Moray Place, you wouldn't have minded at all, would you?' Gail's face was red, her eyes were glittering. 'Well, I think you're a hypocrite, Mummy, and I don't care what you say, or what Daddy says either, I'm going to that disco and you're not going to stop me!'

Gail turned and flung herself out of the kitchen, colliding with her father just coming in, but not apologising, not stopping, just staring at him with stormy eyes and rushing away to her room.

'For God's sake, what's happened?' cried Bobby, turning to Lindsay.

'Adolescence has happened,' she answered bluntly. 'That's what.'

For some time, Gail cried on her bed, while her parents and grandfather discussed the situation in the kitchen. Then Lindsay took out the casserole and sent Bobby upstairs to tell Gail to come down.

'I don't want any supper,' Gail shouted through her door.

'Now, come on, let's discuss this like reasonable beings,' Bobby called back. 'If you come down and have supper, we'll sort something out. But be quick, it's Mummy's pottery night.'

'Oh, yes, pottery night, mustn't let her miss that,' gritted Gail, but after a few moments she wiped her eyes and followed Bobby downstairs.

There was the feeling in the dining room as the meal was served and eaten, that some sort of watershed had been reached. Whatever was decided, things would never be the same again for them as a family. Gail had crossed the line that everyone had to cross some time or other. She was not an adult, had no vote, had no power. But she was never again going to be a child, never again going to be their little girl.

Malcolm, watching Lindsay and Bobby, knew what was in their minds. Hadn't he and Rachel been through it all before when they'd seen their sweet Bobby change almost before their eyes?

Please God, that Gail didn't follow Bobby's path, though, please God that Lindsay and Bobby got it right.

'Oh, I don't think I can go to my pottery class tonight,' Lindsay said fretfully. 'I'm too upset. It's not fair to call me a hypocrite, Gail, when all I'm thinking of is your welfare.'

'That's it,' said Bobby. 'We've nothing against Sean.'

'Except who he is!' flared Gail.

'All right, I admit it!' Bobby, flushing, leaned forward to stare angrily into his daughter's face. 'I would rather his father were a professional man and not Col O'Dwyer!'

'My dad was a housepainter, but he taught us how to behave,' Malcolm said quietly. 'You don't have to be a lawyer or a civil servant to have the right values, Bobby.'

'Col O'Dwyer is a very different character from your dad,' Bobby retorted. 'I know about him from Gran, he's a wastrel, a drifter, leaves everything to Nancy. Now what sort of values is he likely to teach his son?'

'All I want is to go to a disco with Sean,' Gail cried. 'Not marry him!'

'Oh, I can't face any more of this!' Lindsay leaped to her feet and began gathering up plates. 'One minute, everything's peaceful and normal, the next we're all miserable and fighting! It's horrible!'

'If you want my opinion, you should let Gail go out with young Sean,' said Malcolm, rising to help Lindsay with the dishes. 'What harm could it do? You're making something out of nothing.'

'I don't agree,' Bobby said coldly. 'This is something, all right, and I'm going to nip it in the bud. Gail, your mother and I are not going to give you permission to go to the disco.'

'I'm going anyway,' Gail said, her voice shaking. 'And that's all there is to it.'

It was eight o'clock on Saturday night. Sean was standing at the gates to the Good Shepherd School, a sixties concrete building squashed into a narrow site in the Old Town. Yellow lights streaming from the windows showed hordes of young people arriving, and there was already the beat of loud music thudding through the wide open doors. Handsome in black jacket and jeans, Sean narrowed his famous eyes at a car slowly drawing up at the

325

gates. There was a girl in the back who was already wrenching open her door and flying towards him. It was Gail.

'Oh, I'm so sorry, Sean! Daddy insisted on bringing me. I feel such a fool, but it was the only way I could come!'

'That's OK, why should he no' bring you?'

Sean was looking over her shoulder at her father, who was closing the passenger door Gail had left hanging and returning to his seat.

'Thanks, Mr Gilbride!' cried Sean.

Gail's father inclined his head, but made no reply. A moment later he drove away.

'It's great you could make it,' Sean whispered to Gail. 'Shall we go in?'

'Wait, it gets worse.' She held his arm, her eyes on his. 'Daddy's coming to pick me up as well, he'll be here at midnight.'

'Good God, are you Cinderella, or something?' Sean laughed, but his look was stern. 'Well, how about that, then? I suppose we should be lucky he didna decide to come to the disco.'

Chapter Sixty-Seven

Kate had flown up to Edinburgh to try to find a suitable home for Jessie.

'I'm not having her dumped in some awful place where she'll be neglected,' she told Biddy. 'I can afford to pay for proper care and that's what Gran's going to have.'

Biddy raised her eyebrows. 'Shouldna have to depend on money, should it? Thought your lot would see that all old folk got the same treatment.'

'That's the ideal. I'm afraid we haven't achieved it yet.' Kate was shame-faced. 'But when it's your own gran that's involved, you try to find it anyway.'

'Aye, well I'm no' criticising. I want the best for Gran, too.'

As Biddy couldn't leave the shop, it was left to Kate to trawl through the 'possibles', and very tired she grew of the same kind of institutional smell, of the same kind of dreary lounge, of the same kind of unfortunates, waiting for the next meal, or death. Eventually, however, the 'best' was found, a small private nursing home on the outskirts of the city, where the staff was fully trained and the atmosphere pleasant, the rooms fresh and clean. Kate made the necessary arrangements to have Jessie moved from hospital within the next day or two, and returned to the shop to give Biddy the news.

'Thank God, that's a good job done, eh?' Biddy commented, leaning her elbows on a pile of evening papers. 'Did you tell them at the home that you were an MP? Might keep 'em on the ball.'

'I told them, yes, but the way things are going I might not be an MP much longer.'

Biddy stared. 'Why, whatever do you mean, Kate?'

Kate shrugged. 'The way we've been losing by-elections, I reckon we could be out at the next general election. Folk have grown tired of Harold's promises backfiring.'

'But you'll no' lose your seat, Kate! It's rock solid Labour, always has been.'

'Well, we'll have to see how things go.' Kate yawned. 'I'd better get back to my place, have an early night. I'm whacked.'

Biddy was urging her to stay and have a bit of supper, when a woman came through the shop door. She was wearing a trailing raincoat and her dark hair hair hung to her shoulders, though she was clearly not young. After a moment's hesitation, she approached the counter. Biddy was the first to recognise her.

'Oh, God, Sheena!' she cried. 'I never thought you'd have the nerve to show up here.'

Sheena MacLaren, paling a little at the sight of two Rossie sisters instead of one, smiled her charming smile.

'Hello Biddy – hello Kate – been a long time, eh?'

'Not long enough,' snapped Biddy. 'Why've you come back? I can tell you now, you shouldna have bothered.'

'What a welcome.' Sheena flung back her mane of long hair, dyed now both sisters observed, and let her clear gaze wander around the shop. 'Why should I no' come back? I was really sorry to hear your poor dad had died, you ken, and I just wish I could've come to the funeral.'

'To find out about the will?' asked Kate. 'There was nothing in the will for you, Sheena.'

'Was there no'? Well, that doesna matter, does it, because under Scottish law, a wife's entitled to a share.' Sheena nodded her head sagely. 'Aye, wives are taken care of, whatever spiteful husbands do, so I'm staking ma claim. Thought you might as well know.'

'Staking your claim!' Biddy burst out laughing. 'Och, you're a card, you really are. Kate, shut the door, will you? It's closing time and I dinna want to embarrass you, Sheena, by letting folk hear how much you're going to get.'

'Dinna tell me no lies,' cried Sheena. 'You ken I can look it up. Your dad always said there'd be something for me if he went, he always said he'd money put by and I was to have it and no' let you girls cheat me out of ma inheritance.'

'And you didna think he'd change his will after you'd left him?' asked Biddy.

Sheena's lips trembled. 'Change his will?' she whispered. 'No, he wouldna do that. He was mad for me, was Ken, he'd always be wanting me back, he'd never change his will!'

'He didn't,' Kate told her coldly. 'He'd so little to leave, there'd have been no point.'

'So little? What do you mean? He told me himself, he'd money put by —'

'He told you that to try to hang on to you, Sheena. There was no money put by. Where would Dad have got it from? He barely made a profit in the whole of his life.'

'He called this shop his gold mine, it canna be true, what you're saying.' Sheena sank into a chair by the counter. 'Everybody knows, little shops like this make a fortune.' She started up, her colour rising. 'You're making it up, you two, you're telling me lies! But it willna wash, I'll get ma own lawyer, I'll contest the will.'

'Contest away,' said Biddy blithely. 'You'll get nothing.'

'I'll get what's due to me, I'll get ma share!'

'Haven't you heard that old saying, a percentage of nothing is nothing?' asked Kate. 'Don't waste your money on lawyers, Sheena. Dad left seventy pounds in the post office, which wasn't even enough to pay for his funeral. Apart from that, there was the lease of this shop which Biddy has taken on, and that's the lot. Not much, is it, for a man who's worked his guts out for the whole of his life?' Tears suddenly filled Kate's eyes and she turned aside. 'Oh, get to hell out of it, Sheena. You're doing no good here.'

For a long moment, Sheena stared from sister to sister, plainly weighing up whether it was worth her while to stand her ground. Then defeat overtook her. Her still-pretty face crumpled, her full mouth drooped, she turned away. At the closed door, she stopped. The sisters saw her thin shoulders rise and straighten beneath the raincoat, and Kate whispered to Biddy, 'She's preparing for the next assault.'

Just for a moment, they couldn't help feeling sorry for her. Whatever she'd done, she was a pathetic figure. But the moment passed. When she opened the door, a man, a customer, tried to come in. At the sight of Sheena, his eyes lit up.

'Mrs Rossie? You're back? Och, it's grand to see you!'

329

'She's just going,' bawled Biddy. 'And we're closed, Mr Ferguson.'

'Aye, I'm just away,' Sheena said softly, and though they couldn't see her face, from the look on the customer's face, the sisters guessed she was fluttering her eyelashes over her water-clear eyes.

'Wait, Mrs Rossie, I'll just get my cigs, then we'll have a bit chat, eh?' Mr Ferguson said eagerly.

'Do you mind?' said Biddy, advancing towards the door. 'We're closed.'

'Nae bother, I'll get some at the pub.' Mr Ferguson turned to Sheena. 'How about a wee dram, Mrs Rossie?'

'Lovely,' answered Sheena, taking the arm he extended. ' 'Bye, girls,' she called over her shoulder. 'Nice seeing you.'

And the shop door closed behind her.

'Well!' As she and Kate exchanged glances, Biddy's face was dark as thunder. 'Talk about cheek!'

'Come on, you have to laugh,' said Kate.

'Do I?' Biddy stamped along to turn the notice on her door to Closed. 'I dinna feel like laughing.'

In her own flat, preparing for bed, Kate didn't feel like laughing, either. In fact, she felt depressed. Not about Sheena, who had already melted from her mind, but the things that depressed everybody if they allowed themselves to look into the future. Old age. Death. The end of one's hopes.

Heavens, she shook herself. This wouldn't do. She poured herself a whisky and found a thriller to read, to take her mind off the black dog lurking. But thoughts of her foolish old dad and her poor sad speechless gran kept coming back to her, and she couldn't help crying. Cold salt tears for those who'd never had much and had lost what they had.

It didn't help that she herself had lost faith, for the time being at least, in her own party, the party that had been the driving force of her life. How simple it had seemed at one time, how wonderful, to work for the one group that held out hope for the poor and disadvantaged. But somewhere along the way the hope had died.

Where had things gone wrong? Lack of money? Everyone said Wilson had made a mess of the economy, and it was true, there'd had to be cutbacks, harsh restraint. But it seemed to Kate that the

330

malaise had gone deeper than cutbacks. Wilson had achieved some good things, but at the heart of the government the real commitment to social justice was missing. So the left of the party believed, and Kate was now passionately of the left. She had been forced to take a stand, to vote against the government, to become a rebel. It had cost her promotion. So what? Her wings had been clipped, she was no high flyer now, but that didn't matter. What did matter was that she was no longer sure of her role. No longer knew where she was going, in a government that seemed to have moved away from so much that she held dear. Wilson had made a fizzing speech at the Labour Party Conference, members had closed ranks and forgiven him all, for they would soon have an election to win. Win or lose, Kate felt she was looking into an uncertain future. At which point, her telephone rang.

It was Will Gilbride.

Chapter Sixty-Eight

Will said Madge had told him Kate was back in Edinburgh.

'Why didn't you ring me?' he asked.

'I believe you said you'd ring me.'

'Well, here I am, ringing. Can we meet? Don't say you're going back on the night train, for God's sake!'

'I'm going back by plane the day after tomorrow.'

Will gave a whistle of relief. 'Look, I can take a half day tomorrow. May I come to collect you? About two? I want to take you for a drive.'

'A drive? In this weather?'

'It's not far. Just Easterwood golf course.'

'Easterwood? I thought you played at Bruntsfield.'

Will smiled. 'I'm not planning to play golf today.'

'Whatever are you up to, Will?'

'Just want to show you something.'

'I can't think what there is to see on a golf course.'

'You'll find out. Till tomorrow, then?'

'I'll look forward to it,' Kate said dubiously.

'Me too!' said Will.

When she put the phone down, Kate picked up her book again. But she didn't read it.

The following day was cold and colourless, but without mist. At least, thought Kate, I'll be able to see whatever it is Will wants me to see. As they drove out of Edinburgh on the Lanark road, she glanced at him covertly. He seemed on top of the world, she couldn't think why, but his cheerfulness was infectious. She began to feel happier herself.

They turned into the leafy village of Balerno, where new houses were rising fast, but Will kept going into open country where the trees gave way to fine views of the Pentland Hills, and a sign read Easterwood Golf Course. Then he stopped the car.

'Like to get out?'

'We're walking?' She shivered, pulling her coat collar around her face.

'Don't need to, we're there.'

'Where?' She looked around her, mystified. 'I can't see anything except that golf course.'

'See the view, can't you? See the hills.'

'We've come out here to look at the view?'

'No, but the view's important.'

'Oh, do stop playing games, Will! You're behaving like a schoolboy!'

'Why are women such spoilsports?' Will took her arm. 'OK, see the land next to the golf course? With the birch trees?'

'I see it.'

'That piece of land is mine.'

Kate stared. 'You've been buying land, Will?'

'Yes, a plot. A building plot. I've been looking for one for months and now I've found one. Right here.' He took her cold fingers in his. 'I'm going to build a house, Kate. My own house on my own land. What do you say?'

She drew in her breath. 'Why, I don't know what to say! I'm speechless.'

'Is it so out of character for me to build something new?'

'No – well, yes. I thought you'd want the trâditional, I suppose.'

'The traditional. Of course. You see, you're as brain-washed as everyone else in this city. If it's not old, it's out.' Will dropped Kate's hand and began to pace his property. 'To tell you the truth, I've had it up to here with Edinburgh's preoccupation with the past. I'm going to build for today.'

'Preoccupation with the past? When half the city's been rebuilt? How can you say that, Will?'

'Oh, I know it's criminal what's been happening. Don't think I'm saying we should be destroying our heritage. But what gets me are these people who can't see anything good in the new. And we are people of today, aren't we? It'll soon be nineteen seventy.

333

What's wrong with that? Why should seventeen seventy be better, or even eighteen seventy? But you ask the culture vultures here and see what answer you get!'

'Why, Will, what are these hidden depths you're revealing?' cried Kate, laughing. 'I had no idea you felt so strongly, or could talk so well! So, how way out is this house of yours going to be, then?'

'Not too way out, it has to fit in with the landscape, but definitely twentieth century. I've found a good architect and the plans are in now. Should be able to start work in the New Year.' Will waved his arms widely. 'There'll be light everywhere, that's priority. No black paint, no grey stone. No mouldings or decoration. Everything contemporary, because I'm a contemporary man. Will you come and see it when it's finished?'

'You bet I will!'

Will hesitated, he seemed to be coming very slowly down to earth. His blue eyes settled on Kate's face. He took her hand again and it held it fast.

'Will you share it with me?' he asked softly.

Kate stopped laughing. She pulled her hand from Will's.

'Is this a joke?'

'It's no joke. I'm very very serious.'

'Will, if I didn't know you better, I'd say you'd been drinking.'

'Is it such a crazy idea?'

'You know it is. We haven't seen each other for years, we've had no sort of relationship, and you're still married to Sara.'

'I don't think you need bring Sara into this. She's made a new life for herself, doesn't worry about you and me any more.'

Kate's gaze sharpened. 'Did she worry about you and me?'

'Why do you think we split up?'

'I'd no idea. Oh, God, why didn't you tell me? I never wanted to come between you!'

'I know you didn't, there was no point in telling you.' Will took Kate's arm and turned her gently in the direction of the car. 'Let's go back. You're getting frozen.'

They drove in silence back to Kate's flat, Will thinking it better not to talk for a while, Kate too stunned.

'May I come in?' Will asked at her door.

'There's nowhere to park.'

'I'll find somewhere.'

334

'I want to go and see Gran. It's my last chance before I fly back to London.'

'OK. We could just have a cup of tea, couldn't we?'

'That's all it will be, then. I've nothing much to eat.'

'Oh, Kate.' Will smiled wryly. 'You haven't changed.'

Her pied-à-terre was as untidy as he'd known it would be, but the way he felt, a few sliding piles of papers, clothes on chairs, odds and ends scattered around, were not going to put him off. When they'd drunk their hastily made tea, he drew Kate towards him.

'Not still thinking of Sara?' he asked in a low voice.

'I have to think of her, Will. And the children.'

'The children don't come into it. I see them anyway Besides' – he smoothed her hair back from her worried brow – 'I'm not asking you to marry me. Just to share my life, as you did once before.'

'A lot's happened since then, Will.'

'We still feel the same, don't we?'

'I don't know. You said Sara had made her own life. I have, too.'

'You needn't give that up. Unless you want to give it up anyway.'

She stirred in his arms. 'I suppose I might at that. The way I feel at the moment I may not even stand at the next election.'

'Kate! What would you do?'

She shrugged. 'Go back to journalism, maybe. Feel free to criticise again. Or, do Harold's Open University degree. That's about the best thing he thought up.'

'It's not for me to tell you what to do, but if you were to live in Edinburgh again, it would be wonderful.'

'You mean live with you in your new house?' She laughed shortly. 'We'd have come full circle, wouldn't we? What would the bank say about that?'

'Nothing. The bank has finally moved into the twentieth century, in more ways than one. And I've helped them do it.'

For a long time Kate studied Will's face. 'I wonder, would it have worked out for us, all those years ago?'

'Does it matter?' he asked urgently. 'It can work out for us now, that's the point.'

'Things are so different, Will.'

'No.' He began to kiss her. 'They're the same.'

She hadn't meant it to happen. Rolling back the years, making love with Will in an untidy flat, pretending they were young again, that there were no commitments, no wife or children or Gran waiting to be visited, no anxieties, no decisions waiting. There they were, on another divan, and the pleasure was just as great as though they had been twenty-one and as free as the breeze. When it was over and they were slowly dressing, eyeing each other self-consciously, Kate felt so strange, so churned in her mind, she couldn't be sure whether she had regrets or not. She guessed Will felt the same. But there was something special between them and always would be. They both knew that.

'Now,' Kate said breathlessly, 'I really have got to go and see Gran.'

Will drove her to the hospital and when she had kissed sad Jessie's cheek and pressed her hand, wanted to take her on to dinner. But she said, no, she must spend the evening with Biddy, they still had things to sort out.

'I'll take you to the shop, then.'

Their lips met lightly as they made their farewells.

'You'll keep in touch?' asked Will.

She nodded. Her lovely eyes looked into his. 'Do things still seem the same to you?'

'No,' he answered. 'Quite different.'

336

Chapter Sixty-Nine

Another Christmas. Another tree on the Mound, another royal broadcast, families round the box. For the Gilbrides, it was special. Hamish and Nina were back and staying in Madge's bungalow, for Madge herself had finally accepted her fate and moved to Abby's.

'Poor Gran,' said Hamish, talking with Jennie one day before Christmas. 'Must have been awful for her, leaving her home.'

'Heartbreaking,' Jennie agreed. 'And it's not the first time, if you remember what it was like leaving Catherine's Land. But she's cheered up a lot, seeing you and the family, especially as you're staying in her house.'

'When we go back, I suppose it'll have to be sold?'

'Well, there's not much point in keeping it on. Ma will never go back to it. Not with poor Jessie in a nursing home.' Jennie shook her head. 'Old age is a terrible thing, Hamish.'

'Mum, don't you get depressed, too.'

Jennie studied her son's broad tanned face, his blond hair bleached by the sun, his eyes that were not quite meeting hers.

'I'm all right,' she said quietly. 'Is Nina?'

Hamish heaved a long sigh. 'Never could hide anything from you, could I? No, ever since her mother died, she's been down.'

'Poor girl, I know she was very close to Sally. But she's got you and the children and a lovely life in Australia.'

'All she wants is to come back to Scotland because that was where her parents lived. Keeps talking about her roots, seeing her dad's grave, seeing Catherine's Land. I tell you, Mum, I don't know what to do.'

337

'Well, you've brought her back, Hamish. Maybe she'll feel better now?'

'Maybe. But we can't stay here for ever, can we? I've got my business, it's doing well. There's no way I could start up again back here.'

'I suppose not,' said Jennie, who had been hoping that he might have done just that. 'What about the girls? Are they happy in Australia?'

'That's the other thing. They love it, they've never known any other home. If they had to live here in the mist and the rain, they'd never survive.'

'It's not always raining, Hamish!'

'You know what I mean. It's very different from Australia, anyway.'

'And of course you want them to be happy.'

'I want everybody to be happy,' said Hamish glumly.

Will, following tradition, spent Christmas Day with Sara and the children at Monica's. He'd been worried in case Kate arrived, because this time with James and Stephanie was special; there was no way he would have sacrificed it. But Kate had telephoned to say she'd be in America over Christmas and Hogmanay, on a trip she'd planned some time before. So that was all right. He couldn't help wondering if she was making the trip alone. Or not.

He and Sara usually exchanged only token presents around Monica's tree, but that year Will had splashed out and bought Sara an expensive bag from Logie's. It wouldn't take a psychologist to see why, he thought wryly, although he didn't really accept that he should feel guilty. He and Sara had been apart so long and it had been her idea to separate in the first place. She could hardly expect him to keep faithful, so to speak. And what was happening between her and Nick Ainslie?

That was her business, as Kate was his.

'Wow,' said Sara, raising her eyebrows over the handbag. 'I'm afraid I've only bought you a tie.'

'That's OK, I always need ties.'

He thought her gaze on him was a little too intelligent, but that might have been his imagination. All the same, he was relieved when Lindsay came up to talk and he could escape to help

338

Malcolm play with James's new Lego, while Stephanie combed her Sindy doll's flowing blonde hair.

'What's up with Gail?' Sara was asking Lindsay. 'She's looking pretty blue. Didn't she get what she wanted for Christmas?'

'Evidently not.' Lindsay drank deeply of Monica's good sherry. 'Seems she wanted Sean O'Dwyer. At least, she wanted to bring him here.'

Sara grinned. 'And Mummy said no?'

'Bobby said no. I did too. I mean, we have nothing against Sean —'

'When people say that it always means they've plenty against whoever it is.'

'All right, all right, he's not the one we'd have chosen for Gail's boyfriend, but that's not the point. Christmas is for family and he's not family.'

'Not yet.'

'Sara, they are both only sixteen!'

Sara shrugged. 'Well, I hope you've told her everything she needs to know.'

Lindsay's look was sour. 'When I tried to bring up the subject, do you know what she said? Don't worry, Mummy, Sean and I are not sleeping together. Can you believe it?'

Sara burst into laughter. 'Oh, Lindsay! Imagine one of us saying that to Mummy!'

'There would have been a thunderbolt hurled from above. Why, I can remember in my early days in London Mum and poor Rachel coming down to see if Bobby and I were sharing a flat. We went to such lengths to put them off the scent!' Lindsay gave a reminiscent smile. 'How things have changed, Sara!'

Sara eyed Gail listlessly joining in with the Lego building. She murmured to herself, I wonder?

'The thing is, Mum, Gail's just not doing any work,' Bobby was complaining to Monica in the kitchen. 'I mean, she's got Highers in the summer and if she doesn't get the grades she won't be able to get into Edinburgh.'

'She's far too young to go to university, anyway,' Monica said, as she bent over her Christmas timetable. 'I've always said the English system is better, where they take two years for A Levels and then they're more mature. Now, if I put the potatoes in at one,

339

that will mean they'll be ready, say, at a quarter to two, or maybe two o'clock, and if the turkey is resting from half past one, I can finish off the stuffing separately. Oh, dear, we're never going to get lunch over before the Queen, are we? Do you think I should put everything back?'

'And I really do want her to get into Edinburgh,' said Bobby, continuing with his own monologue, 'because there's so much student unrest everywhere else, I'd never have a minute's peace, thinking of her marching or sitting-in or whatever the hell they do – sorry, Mum, but it's all so damned worrying.'

'Bobby, do you think you could ask Sara to come in for a minute?' Monica asked, putting her hand to her immaculate hair-do. 'I think perhaps we should try for lunch after the Queen, in which case, Sara had better organise something for the children. They'll never last out.'

'Oh, give 'em some crisps,' Bobby said abstractedly. 'Do you think you could have a word with Gail, Mum? She goes a lot by what you say, you know.'

'Oh, not any more, Bobby.' Monica sighed. 'She's never actually said so, but I'm sure she thinks I'm a fascist. A terrible reactionary, anyway.'

'I really don't want to know what she thinks of me,' said Bobby.

The long day wound on, and Malcolm was beginning to look tired. He, Bobby and Lindsay, with gloomy Gail in tow, made their farewells. They would all be meeting next day, anyway, for Abby's Boxing Day buffet. Hardly time to snatch a bit of rest before the next onslaught of turkey, as Malcolm said in the car going home, though if he knew Abby there would be a lot more than turkey on show.

'I bet Aunt Abby wouldn't have minded if I'd taken Sean,' Gail muttered. 'But I'm not going to her do, anyway.'

'What do you mean, you're not going?' cried Bobby. 'Of course you're going!'

'No, I'm not. Mrs O'Dwyer has invited me to tea and I've accepted. You see, she doesn't mind if I'm not family.'

Bobby, who was driving, went rigid, but Lindsay swung round and said fiercely, 'Gail, you can jolly well go to your Aunt Abby's first. She's gone to a lot of trouble for this lunch and your cousins from Australia will be there, as well as Gran. I don't care what you've told Sean, you're not missing it and that's final.'

'It's a family thing, Gail,' Malcolm said gently. 'You have to be there.'

'Family, family, all I ever hear is family,' snapped Gail.

She sat with her arms folded for the rest of the drive and when they reached home, ran upstairs to her room and banged the door.

'I don't believe I was ever as bad as that,' Bobby said angrily, but Malcolm, hanging up his coat, gave a small smile.

'You were, you know. She'll come through it, Bobby, you'll just have to be patient.'

And hope you don't have to wait as long for Gail as we waited for you, Malcolm added, to himself.

When Will opened the door of his flat on his return from Monica's, he felt a sudden pang of loneliness. It took him by surprise. For some years now he had trained himself not to mind leaving the children, not to mind his solitary state, even on Christmas night. Yet that Christmas night, he did mind, he didn't know why. Perhaps because with his new house on the horizon, his flat seemed even smaller and drearier than usual. Or perhaps because he was feeling guilty at not having told Sara and the children about his plot of land and his plans.

Why hadn't he told them? He took off his tie and his shoes and flung himself on the sofa, his arms folded behind his head. Because it was his secret, something of his own, nothing to do with his family or anyone else. Yet he had told Kate.

He leaped up and poured himself a drink. Perhaps he shouldn't have told Kate. He couldn't think now why he had. Showing off, maybe? Letting her see he wasn't just the typical stuffed-shirt banker? She'd been impressed, anyway, and that must have been what he wanted. But she hadn't said she'd share the house with him. Elusive Kate, you could never catch her, never hold her for long. They had made love, though. That couldn't be denied, even though there were times when that memory seemed elusive too and was as hard to recall as a dream.

He finished the drink, thought about another, decided to go to bed. Tomorrow, at Abby's, he would tell Sara and the children about the house. After all, work would be starting soon. He couldn't keep it a secret for much longer. But he wouldn't mention Kate.

Chapter Seventy

Lindsay, ready to leave for Abby's, was waiting for the others and idly looking out of the drawing-room window. Suddenly her eyes sharpened. Sean was at the front gate.

Hunched against the December wind, he looked cold. The tip of his nose was red and he had buried his hands in his pockets. For the first time, he seemed not only young but vulnerable. Handsome still, but no threat. Her heart smote her.

'Ready?' asked Bobby, appearing in the doorway. 'Dad's just coming.'

'Where's Gail?'

'In her room. I'm going to give her a shout.' Bobby frowned. 'Hope she's not going to start playing up.'

'Bobby, Sean's out there. He looks so pathetic, poor boy. Why don't we take him with us to Abby's? She won't mind, she always has tons of food.'

'Take him to Abby's, after all we've said? Are you joking?' Bobby's face was crimson as he stared out at Sean, now walking up and down like a guardsman on sentry duty. 'Look at him, Lindsay – he's wearing jeans!'

'All young people wear jeans. Oh, come on, Bobby, you know if he'd been a lawyer's son, you wouldn't have minded what he was wearing.' Lindsay hurried into the hall, crying, 'Gail, Gail, Sean's here!'

Gail's door flew open and she hurtled down the stairs, almost into Lindsay's arms.

'Excuse me, Mum, I must go to him!'

'I know, but, Gail, listen, we've changed our minds.'

'We?' shouted Bobby. 'I haven't said anything about changing my mind!'

'If Sean would like to come with us to Aunt Abby's, I think he should,' Lindsay said stoutly, and as Gail gave a delighted shriek and held her close, looked at Bobby with warning in her eyes. Tightening his lips, he took out his car keys and opened the front door.

'I'll get the car,' he said over his shoulder. 'Tell Dad to hurry up.'

Abby said she was delighted to welcome Sean to her party. She knew his mother, she remembered his grandmother. He probably knew most of the Gilbrides; if he didn't, they were all there, Gail would introduce him.

'So that's the famous Abby Baxter,' Sean murmured, as Gail, smiling radiantly, led him away. 'She's quite something, eh?'

'And started in Catherine's Land, that's the amazing thing.'

'What's so amazing?' Sean's blue eyes flashed. 'Dinna need to go to St Clare's to have brains, Gail.'

'I know, I know, come and have some of this lovely buffet,' she said hastily. 'Though maybe we shouldn't eat too much.'

'Hey, why not?' Sean had taken a plate and was helping himself to Abby's splendid food. 'This is great.'

'Why, we're going to your mother's for tea,' cried Gail. 'Have you forgotten?'

Bobby was consoling himself, as he so often did, in talking to his grandmother. Madge, dressed in one of her favourite lace-collared dresses with her amber beads at her neck, was sitting in state at the end of Abby's drawing room. Someone had already brought her a plate of cold chicken and potato salad, but she wasn't eating; nor was she drinking her wine. She looked recognisably herself, but frail and a little strained.

'How are you, Gran?' Bobby asked softly, taking her hand. 'How's the new life?'

'Oh, it's very nice, dear.' Madge roused herself to smile into his concerned dark eyes. 'Abby's made me very comfortable. I've got my own room with telly and all my bits and pieces. I'm very lucky.'

'But you're missing Jessie?'

'Missing Jessie, missing what's gone.' She sighed. 'Abby took me to see Jessie yesterday. No change, but they're hopeful. Kate's found her a lovely place to live, I think they'll be good to her there.'

'I'm sure they will, Gran. You needn't worry about her.'

'No.' Madge studied Bobby for a moment. 'Everything all right with you, dear?'

'Fine.'

'I see Gail's brought young Sean. He's a nice lad, Bobby. You needn't worry either, you know.'

Trust Gran to smoke out what's on my mind, thought Bobby. He gave what he hoped was a convincing smile.

'I'm not worrying, Gran. Now, aren't you going to eat that nice stuff you've got there? Would you like me to get you something else?'

'I think I'd just like a bit of bread and butter, if you could find it, Bobby. I seem to have lost my appetite these days.'

Sara had not lost hers. When Will found her, she was piling up her plate at the buffet, laughing to someone that today at least she could forget her diet. He thought she was looking attractive and young, with her blonde hair worn longer and all her old sparkle returned. When she moved away, he followed her and they sat together, balancing their plates on their knees, keeping an eye on their wine glasses on the floor.

'Kids all right?' asked Will. 'No ill effects from all that stuff they ate yesterday?'

'They're fine. Tucking in today, with Hamish's two. Aren't they sweet? All so fair.'

They watched the four blond children sitting at a distance, drinking lemonade from wine glasses and giggling together.

'Seem to have settled in, don't they, Hamish's girls?' Will commented.

'Yes, but I'm worried about Nina. She's so thin! Remember how plump she was, the last time they came over?'

'Maybe she's dieting.'

'The funny thing is, all the people I know who are dieting never seem to lose any weight.' Sara looked at Will over the rim of her glass. 'What did you want to talk to me about?'

'How did you know I wanted to talk?'

'I know you, Will, that's all.'

'I see. Well, it's just that I wanted to tell you I've bought a plot of land out beyond Balerno. I'm going to build a house.'

Like Kate, Sara seemed astonished.

'Build a house? Out there? But why?'

'Why not? I want a place of my own.'

She looked at him for a long moment, and he felt his mind was as clear to her as glass. A place of his own, he had said he wanted. And would he be living there on his own?

'Why build?' Sara asked, at last. 'There are plenty of good houses to buy. Good old houses with character.'

'I don't want a good old house with built-in character. I want something new, and I'm prepared to add the character myself.'

'That's original, anyway. I expect the children will be thrilled.' Sara's eyes were straying beyond him. 'Will, do you mind? I see Nina's by herself for a moment. I'll just go over and have a word.'

Politely half rising to his feet, Will watched her go. He wondered why these days she could so easily disconcert him. Perhaps because she had stopped being the one who loved. That always gave power, though it might no longer be wanted.

'Hi, Nina!' Sara exclaimed, inserting herself on to the sofa where Nina was sitting. 'How are you? You're looking well. So slim!'

'Thin, you mean.' Nina smiled, but her eyes were shadowed and there were new lines between her brows. It seemed to Sara that she was beginning to take on Sally's look of constant worry. But what had Nina to worry about?

'Everything's all right, isn't it?' Sara asked cautiously. 'In Australia?'

'Oh, yes, everything's fine. Hamish seems to have the touch for business, all right.'

'And you've really settled there for good?'

'I suppose so. Only I'd rather be here.' To Sara's alarm, Nina's eyes filled with tears. 'It's just since ma mother died, I've felt – canna describe it – sort o' lost. Like I dinna belong and should come home.' Nina took out her handkerchief. 'Brought Mam's ashes back, you ken.'

'Did you?' Sara asked uneasily.

'Aye. She'd niver have wanted to be buried out in Australia. Now she's by ma dad, and I've put her name on the stone.'

'That must be a comfort to you.'

'It'd be more of a comfort if I could stay here. This is where I belong, Sara, this is where I should be.'

'Oh, Nina, couldn't you ask Hamish to come back? I mean, he could start up his business here, couldn't he?'

'He doesna want to, thinks he'd no' do so well. But it's the girls, you see.' Nina wiped her eyes drearily. 'They love being out there. Dinna ken anything else. I couldna ask them to live here.'

'But sometimes you have to think of yourself, Nina. What you want matters too, you know!'

'No' when you've a family. You have to put them first, eh?'

Sara drank some wine. 'I suppose everybody's different, but I don't believe women should always sacrifice themselves to their families.'

'If they were no' happy, I couldna be happy.' Nina shook her head. 'No way out, eh? Och, I'll be all right. Might just need more time.'

'And with Hamish doing so well, you'll be able to come home often for visits, won't you?'

Nina brightened, and as young Madge came running up to ask her to pull a cracker, gave Sara a watery smile.

'Nice talking to you, Sara. Can we meet sometime for coffee? I havena heard any o' your news.'

'Oh, I haven't got any news.' Sara smiled brightly. 'But let's meet for coffee anyway.'

'Dinna get me wrong, this has all been terrific,' Sean was whispering to Gail, 'but when can we leave?'

'Now!' She looked up at him lovingly. 'I'll just get my coat, then we can say goodbye.'

They had made their farewells to Abby and Frankie and Gail was hugging Lindsay in the hall and whispering thanks, when Bobby caught up with them.

'I hope you were going to say goodbye to me,' he said sharply.

'Of course we were, Daddy!' Gail exclaimed. Sean stood stiffly at her side, saying nothing.

'The thing is, I was rather wanting to have a word.'

'Oh, not now, darling, they're just off.' Lindsay was clearly not wanting any trouble.

'Won't take a minute. I just wanted to say to you both that Gail

346

will have to be working very hard for her Highers from now on, so you may not be able to see each other as often as you'd like.' Bobby bent a serious gaze on Sean's handsome unconcerned face. 'She wants to try for university, you see, Sean. I hope you'll understand.'

'Understand very well,' Sean replied. 'I'm trying for university maself.'

Bobby's jaw dropped. 'You are? I didn't know that. No one told me.'

'You never asked,' said Gail. 'I could have told you that Sean's doing Highers next year same as me. He's going to be a civil engineer.'

'I see.' Bobby glanced at Lindsay, who was keeping her face expressionless. 'Well, that's excellent, Sean. Then you'll understand how important it is to get down to work, won't you?'

'As you say, Mr Gilbride. We were planning to hit the grindstone after these holidays.' Sean looked down at Gail and grinned. 'No more going out till summer, eh?'

'Except on Saturdays.'

'If that's all right?' Sean raised his eyebrows at Bobby.

'Oh – yes, of course.' Bobby took some pound notes from his wallet. 'Look, Sean, I'd like you to take a taxi to your mother's, there aren't many buses on Boxing Day. Won't mind taking this, will you?'

'Thanks very much, Mr Gilbride.' Sean's hand closed round the money. 'That's very kind of you.'

'Thanks, Daddy.' Gail kissed him, then Lindsay. 'Sean, let's go and ask Aunt Abby if we can use her phone.'

'That round to Sean, I think,' said Lindsay, with a rueful smile when they were alone.

'We weren't exactly fighting,' Bobby snapped.

'Weren't we?' Lindsay took his arm. 'Come on, Bobby, crack that face, you know you're pleased.'

'So he wants to be a civil engineer,' Bobby said musingly. 'Could have been worse.'

'A jazz pianist, for instance? Or, manager of a pop group?'

For the first time in weeks, Bobby laughed.

Chapter Seventy-One

Gail's euphoria was beginning to fade. It had been such a lovely day so far, with first her mother letting Sean go to Abby's lunch, then her father's being so obviously impressed by Sean's career prospects and giving them money for a taxi and everything. But when they had given the taxi-driver the O'Dwyers' address, neither of them had missed the look on his face, and if Sean had not seemed to mind, it had upset Gail. OK, they were going from a grand New Town address to a council flat. So what? Gail felt for Sean's hand and he looked down at her with a quizzical lift to his brows. Poor Sean, she thought, he'd had things to put up with that had never come her way. Why was life so unfair?

'Thinking of voting Labour?' Sean whispered.

'Sean, can you read my mind?'

He shrugged. 'Doesna do any good. They've no' changed things, have they? Who could, come to that?'

'Don't give that man a tip,' Gail said fiercely, but Sean laughed.

'I'll give him a good one. Make his eyes pop out, eh?'

But when they had paid off the taxi and had the satisfaction of receiving the driver's thanks for his tip, Gail's nerves really began to take over. Here was the concrete block Sean had told her about, facing nothing but more concrete blocks and plots of worn-down grass where a few children were playing. At every window there appeared to be a tiny balcony from which washing blew, but beyond the washing there were the lights of Christmas trees. At least they can afford decorations, thought Gail, taking strength from Sean's arm, but her heart was sinking fast.

'We'll have to take the stairs,' said Sean cheerfully. 'Lift's out of order.'

'How far up are you?' asked Gail, choosing not to read what was written on the walls of the staircase.

'No' far. Fourth landing.' Sean glanced at her, as she kept up with his long leaps upwards. 'Nervous?'

'A bit.'

'No need to be, they're all looking forward to meeting you.'

It seemed to Gail that his tone lacked conviction, but perhaps she was just being over sensitive.

'You've told them all about me?'

'Sure, they know about your folks and where you live and that you go to St Clare's.'

'And they know I'm not a Catholic? They don't mind you going out with a Protestant?'

'They don't mind. They're pretty easy going.'

'I hope they don't think I'm toffee-nosed,' Gail muttered. 'Did you tell them that my dad's family lived in Catherine's Land?'

'I told them everything.' He shook her a little. 'Stop worrying.'

'So, who'll be there?' she asked, steeling herself for a battery of O'Dwyer eyes.

'Only Mam and Dad and ma sister, Teresa. Joseph's got a girl-friend, he's at her place today, and Phil works for the electricity company, he didna get the day off.'

Only three, then, that wasn't so bad. Gail stopped to run a comb through her hair.

'Do I look all right?' she asked anxiously.

Sean drew her into his arms. He kissed her gently. 'You ken fine you look lovely,' he whispered.

'I've got the chocolates for your mum. Maybe I should've got something for the others?'

'For God's sake, you're only coming for a cup of tea!'

'But it's Christmas, Sean.'

'So? You've got the sweeties. They all like sweeties and they'll all like you. Come on, let's get it over with, eh?'

The living room of the O'Dwyers' flat was oblong in shape, with a table and chairs at one end and a television and sagging couch at the other. A Christmas tree with coloured lights shone at the window, and an electric fire with imitation logs glowed in the tiled

349

fireplace. There were several framed holy pictures around the walls and a crucifix by the door, but no books or magazines or plants. To Gail, who had been expecting something much worse, it seemed comfortable, yet not homely. There was an atmosphere of strain.

Nancy O'Dwyer, wearing a bright green dress, came hurrying forward to greet her, and a tall girl who looked like Sean stood up but did not speak. Gail, nervously shaking Nancy's hand, presented the chocolates and blushed as Nancy went into raptures. Logie's Talisman Selection! Everybody knew they were the best. Oh, but Gail shouldna have bothered.

'Sean's Dad's just having a lie-down,' Nancy went on to explain. 'He'll no' be long. Did Sean tell you Phil's out and so's Joseph? Is it no' a shame?'

'I told her,' said Sean.

'Teresa, come and meet Gail!' Nancy ordered, and the tall girl drifted across. She had a mass of heavy black hair falling to her shoulders, her eyes were the same bright blue as Sean's, but her mouth was small and ungenerous.

Oh dear, I don't like her, thought Gail, shaking her hard cold hand. Sean's sister! I've got to like her.

'Sean, go and tell your dad to get up, and tell him to put his tie on, we've got company.' Nancy motioned Gail to a seat near the television, which was showing an old film. 'Teresa, come and give me a hand wi' the tea.'

Sean came to sit next to Gail.

'Shall I turn that off?' he asked, nodding towards the television.

'I don't mind,' Gail whispered.

'Yes, turn it off,' Teresa shouted from the doorway. 'I was watching it, but who cares?'

'Teresa!' her mother said warningly. 'You canna watch it if we're having our tea, can you?'

'I dinna ken why not. We watch everything else when we're having our tea.'

'We've got company today, remember.'

Teresa tossed back her hair. 'Och, yes, the girl from St Clare's. Thought she was supposed to be taking us as she finds us.'

'Do you mind not talking about Gail as if she wasn't here?' Sean asked angrily. Gail sat with her eyes cast down.

There were noises off, indicative of someone thudding out of

350

bed. A few moments later, Sean's father made an entrance, knotting his tie as he came, and yawning. He was a big man, with a heavy bold face, greying hair scraped in strands across his skull, truculent eyes and a small mouth like his daughter's. As Gail stood up to be introduced, she could see no sign of Sean in him at all, for which she was relieved.

'So this is the young lady from St Clare's?' he asked, in an accent that was more Irish than Scottish. 'We are not getting many here like you, I am telling you.'

'No, she's the lucky one,' said Teresa, banging a plate of sandwiches on the table. 'Sean, Mam says you've to pull up the chairs.'

Sean obediently set five scuffed wooden chairs around the table which was covered with a handsome white cloth and set with rose-patterned china.

'What pretty cups,' Gail commented, as she took her place. Her heart was already sinking at the amount of food on display. Ham sandwiches and meat pies, buttered scones and Christmas cake. Supposing she couldn't eat it? She hadn't had much lunch, but she felt so nervous she wasn't sure she could even swallow. There was something about this family that made her feel she was crossing a minefield. The slightest mistake and she could go sky-high.

'Aye, I bought them cups wi' ma first wages when I got back to work after the kiddies,' said Nancy proudly. 'Saved up every week till I'd enough.'

'That's wonderful,' said Gail, and meant it. She had already decided that the only person she could warm to here was Sean's mother. Poor hard-working Nancy, who liked pretty things and had so few.

'So, Gail, what are you going to do when you leave school?' Col O'Dwyer asked, taking a sandwich. 'Got a job lined up?'

'Gail's going to university,' Sean said quickly. 'She wants to study modern languages.'

'I could have gone to university!' Teresa cried. 'Everybody said I was clever enough, just as clever as Sean, but he gets to go and I dinna. It's no' fair.'

'Dinna blame me,' her father said shortly. 'You said you were wanting to earn some money.'

'It was you said I'd to earn some money!' shouted Teresa. 'Is that no' right, Mam? Did he no' say I'd to leave school and take

351

that job in the post office? Then when Sean says he wants to do engineering, or whatever, och, that's OK, that's fine, he can stay on, he can do Highers, but I had to leave! Is that no' what happened?'

'I dinna remember,' Nancy muttered, moving plates around. 'What's it matter now, anyway?'

'What do you mean, what's it matter?' Teresa's blue eyes burned dangerously. 'It's ma whole career that's at stake, that's what! Think what sort o' job I could've got, if I'd had a degree! I'd no' be just a clerk, selling stamps, eh?'

'Oh, be quiet now, Teresa!' Col suddenly shouted. 'It's anything for a bit o' trouble with you.'

'I'll no' be quiet, I've a right to speak!'

'Could you not do the Open University?' Gail asked, clearing her throat, and hoping she had not just trodden on one of the mines she dreaded.

Teresa turned her burning gaze on her and went scarlet.

'Open University, is it? I'm supposed to do a hard day's work, then come home and get out ma books and study till God knows what time? That's for me, is it? While you and Sean can go to college full time, with money to spend and everything? And where am I supposed to study in this place, eh, wi' the telly on the whole time, and no' a bit o' peace from the kids till the wee small hours? You tell me that!'

'Well, do I no' have to study as well?' cried Sean, pushing his plate away. His face too had coloured angrily and his eyes burned like his sister's. 'And never mind the kids outside, you're the one who has the telly on whenever you're in, and I have to put up with that, right? Just give it a rest, Teresa, we've had it up to here with your moaning!'

Heavens, how they all scrap, thought Gail, even her Sean, usually so quiet and pleasant. Here in his home, she could tell he would give as good as he got, and who could blame him? It was clear you wouldn't be able to survive in this family if you couldn't fight back or block it out from your consciousness, the way his mother seemed able to do. What on earth was it like when the other brothers were at home? Her head was spinning; all she wanted to do was get away.

'A wee bit meat pie, Gail?' Nancy asked solicitously. 'Come on, it's tasty. Or else, some of ma cake?'

'Perhaps I could have a piece to take home, it looks so nice,' Gail said faintly. 'The thing is, I must be going, I said I wouldn't be late.'

'And it's Boxing Day, eh? Aye, well, we'll no' keep you, pet. It's been grand meeting you. Dad, has it no' been grand, then, meeting Gail?'

'Aye, grand,' Col agreed, pushing back his chair. 'And do not you be minding us chucking the words about. That's family for you, eh?'

'Like I said, she was supposed to be taking us she as finds us,' Teresa said contemptuously. 'And this is the way we are, Gail.'

'There's a call-box on the corner,' Sean said, as they left the flats. 'I'll get you a taxi from there.'

'Get me a taxi?' Gail repeated. 'Aren't you coming with me?'

'Didna suppose you'd want me to.'

Sean's voice was dead. In the bright yellow light of the street lamps, he looked pale and subdued. Flattened, thought Gail.

'Of course I want you to!' she cried. 'Why shouldn't I?'

'I wouldna blame you if you wanted to finish with me,' he went on doggedly. 'Now you've seen how we go on. I mean, ma family. I thought they'd mebbe soft-pedal a bit, seeing as you're no' used to them, but Teresa kept saying she wasna going to put herself out, you'd to take us as you found us.' Sean groaned. 'Though Mam'd made everything look nice, eh? And put on a good tea?'

'Lovely,' said Gail. 'I appreciated it. And she was so kind to me, really made me welcome.'

'Couldna make up for Teresa.'

'I'm not going out with Teresa,' said Gail. 'Actually I feel sorry for her. She should have been allowed to go to university if she wanted to. No wonder she's bitter.'

'Och, she just wants something to complain about.' Sean's eyes were brightening. 'I'll come with you, then, shall I?'

'I wish you would.'

They clung together, kissing, until Sean finally drew away to make the call to the taxi firm.

'Think we'll get the same man?' asked Gail.

'If we do, he'll get another surprise when we want to go to Morningside.'

But it was a different taxi-driver and he was a dour old man who obviously didn't care where they wanted to go as long as he got double fare for Boxing Night and a whacking big tip. They got him to stop some way away from Gail's house, so that they would be out of Bobby's sights as they kissed again and caressed, forgetting in the rapture of each other's nearness the tingling misery of the afternoon.

'Mum keeps trying to tell me the facts of life,' Gail whispered. 'I told her she'd no need to worry. Sometimes I wish she did, though. I mean, have need to worry.'

'Och, Gail, dinna tempt me,' Sean murmured. 'I'm just glad we're no' going to be seeing each other so much.'

'We've still got Saturdays.'

'Aye, but we've to think o' the damned Highers.'

'You're as keen as Teresa on your career, aren't you?'

'I am,' he said seriously. 'Let's no' make life complicated.'

'But you do love me?' she cried, alarmed.

It was not often they talked of love by name. For a moment Gail was sorry she had spoken of it then. But Sean's embrace melted her regrets. She knew he was grateful to her for not holding his family against him, but then her own family had been embarrassing too. Perhaps families were always embarrassing.

But when Sean had left her and she had to go in to face her parents, she couldn't think what to say about the O'Dwyers.

'How did you get on?' Lindsay asked eagerly. 'How did you find them? What was the flat like?'

'Oh, very nice,' Gail answered cagily. 'Mrs O'Dwyer keeps everything tidy. And she'd some lovely china.'

'You liked them, then?' asked Bobby.

'Oh, yes. They made me very welcome.' Gail put her hand to her throbbing head. 'Do you mind if I don't bother with supper tonight, Mum? I've had far too much to eat today and I've still got to eat some of Mrs O'Dwyer's Christmas cake, she gave me a bit to bring home.'

'Oh, just as if you'd been to a children's party!' cried Lindsay, laughing.

'Well, she was very kind.' Gail moved to the door. 'I think I'll just go up and do some work.'

'Excellent,' said Bobby, smiling, but as Gail went out, he turned to Lindsay. 'Where on earth would Nancy O'Dwyer have got lovely china?' he asked wonderingly.

354

Chapter Seventy-Two

The New Year brought in a new decade. 1970. Everyone said it would be funny to write it, but in no time at all the swinging sixties had passed into history. They'd been terrific years. So much had happened. Moon landings, the Beatles, mini-skirts, everybody doing their own thing. Frightening years too, at times. The Cuban crisis, Russia shaking its fist. Now in a multi-racial Britain with its eye on European membership, the glasses were being raised to a peaceful and prosperous future, with or without the Labour government. Preferably without, was the view of many. It was certainly Will Gilbride's. If the Labour government fell, Kate might give up politics. That would be worth more to him than seeing Edward Heath in Number Ten.

It was almost time to say goodbye again to Hamish and Nina. While Jennie took Nina and the children last-minute shopping, Will showed Hamish round the site of his house. Building work had already begun, but was being held up by bad weather; there had been frost and some snow, might well be more. Still, Hamish could get the idea.

'Yes, I can see it's going to be quite a place,' said Hamish, blowing his reddened nose. 'Thing is, who's going to live in it?'

'Well, I am, of course,' Will said sharply.

'On your own?'

Will hesitated. 'Not necessarily.'

'You're going to try to get back with Sara?'

'I don't think so. We're pretty content as we are.'

'The kids as well?'

'Yes, it's worked out better than I thought.'

355

'Know what they told me? That you and Sara were going to be like Gail's mum and dad. Apart for years, then together again.'

'That's ridiculous!' cried Will. 'They've never said anything like that to me!'

'Well, they wouldn't. But that's what they're waiting for.'

Will stood watching the men with hard hats going about the work of building his house. The cold wind that blew his hair and tugged at his coat seemed to be turning him to stone, but then he shook his head and turned to Hamish.

'Kids!' he said with a smile. 'You never know what's going on in their heads. I'll have to have a talk with them. Make it clear that their mother and I have different lives to lead.'

'So, if it's not Sara who is coming here, who is?' asked Hamish. 'Not Kate Rossie, I hope?'

'And why shouldn't it be Kate Rossie?' Will's gaze was icy.

'She's bad news, Will. She's only got one love and it's politics, right? She'll never share your house with you.'

'Well, that's just where you're wrong! For a start, she's not even sure she wants to stay in politics. For another, she's thrilled with the house. She'll be quite happy to come here when she's in Edinburgh.'

'Oh, well, then.' Hamish shivered in the wind. 'Any chance of getting back to the car? And a stop at a pub for a hot toddy?'

'You're on,' said Will.

'Are you sure you're going to be all right, Nina?' Jennie asked, over coffee in Logie's. 'Hamish has to get back to the business, but you could always stay on for a bit, you know. I'd be glad to help.'

Nina shook her head. 'Thanks ever so much, but I'm no' too bad now. I've got Mam's grave fixed up and I've seen Scotland again, I'll be OK.'

While Jennie studied her worriedly, Fiona and young Madge drank their fruit juice and stared at the Edinburgh ladies sugaring their coffee, buttering scones, talking non-stop.

'If you're sure,' Jennie said after a while.

'No need to worry, honestly. Hamish says we can come over more often and that'll keep me going. I want to go back, I want to be with Hamish, that's ma place.'

'He'll look after you, Nina. It's all he wants to do.'

356

'I ken that. I've been lucky, eh?'

'He's been lucky, too.' Jennie sniffed. 'But I'm going to miss you all so much! I hate it when we have to go to the airport. It's taken over from Waverley, you know. We all used to hate going there. To say goodbye.'

But the journey to the airport had to be made, the last kisses exchanged, the tears shed, then those who were left were waving as the London plane took off, climbed and disappeared into the clouds.

'First leg, eh?' Mac murmured, taking Jennie's arm. 'And the shortest.'

'Poor things,' said Abby. 'Is it tomorrow or the next day they get home?'

'Lose track of time when you cross the date-line,' said Frankie. 'Why don't we go and have a coffee?'

'Nina's so much braver than I ever gave her credit for,' Jennie remarked, as they took their trays to a table in the crowded cafeteria. 'She's really suffering going back, you know, but she says her place is with Hamish and the girls.'

'I think she'll rally, once she's there,' Abby told her. 'She's depressed because she's lost her mother, but she'll adjust. You have to, don't you?'

She and Jennie exchanged glances. Their shared thought was clear. Would they ever adjust to losing Madge when the time came? As Abby said, they'd have to.

They were leaving the airport together when Abby knocked Jennie's arm and indicated ahead of them a tall woman in a grey coat pulling her case along on wheels.

'Kate Rossie,' she whispered.

They were about to call her name, when Kate leaped into an airport taxi and was driven smartly away.

'Didn't even see us,' said Abby. 'She'll be up to visit her constituents, I expect, and Jessie.'

'And Will?' thought Jennie, but said nothing. She had her own suspicions concerning Will's split with Sara, but kept them to herself. It didn't do sometimes to put things into words.

Will, troubled by what Hamish had told him, made an unscheduled call on his children that evening. They were both doing homework in his old study, while Sara was upstairs.

'Hi, Dad!' cried James, with relief. 'You can help me with my maths!'

'I don't need any help,' said Stephanie who was colouring in a map of Australia for a project. 'I can work by myself.'

'Wait till you get to algebra,' sneered James. 'If they ever do algebra at St Clare's.'

'Of course we do algebra!' Stephanie glared. 'We do everything!'

'Stop the scrapping,' ordered Will. 'I want to talk to you.'

But when the two faces of his children were turned expectantly towards him, he didn't know how to begin. Was it possible that through all the years he and Sara had been apart, these two had been living on the hope that they would come back together? He felt a hole where his stomach was, thinking of himself in his fool's paradise, so confident that his children had escaped his own trauma. James and Stephanie had not escaped. They had simply put all their feelings on hold until he and Sara came together again, like Bobby and Lindsay. When that didn't happen, how would they take it? Will knew, all too well.

'I just want to explain a bit,' he said hesitantly. 'About—'

He stopped and at the limpid looks fixed on him lowered his own gaze.

'Explain what?' asked James, passing the time by sharpening his pencil on his Pink Panther sharpener.

I can't do it, thought Will, passing a hand across his face. I can't put it into words. If they're happy, why make them unhappy?

'I wanted to talk about our holiday this year,' he said, scraping his throat to get the words out. 'You'll probably be going somewhere with Mummy, but where'd you like to go with me?'

'Australia,' Stephanie said promptly, at which James collapsed in giggles.

'Oh, Steph, you are a twit! We can't go to Australia, it takes for ever! We've only got school holidays.'

'It's not a bad idea,' Will said seriously. 'Uncle Hamish does want us to go out sometime, but I've the new house to think of, so we can't go this year. Any other ideas?'

'Why don't we just come over and stay in the new house?' asked James. 'It'd be great!'

'Mummy could come as well,' said Stephanie. 'She'd like it, because it'll be different. All new, not old like here.'

'What's all this about Mummy?' asked Sara, appearing in the doorway.

'Dad was asking about holidays,' James told her, 'and we said we could all go and stay in the new house.'

Sara looked blank. 'Why would we want to do that? It's practically in Edinburgh.'

'No, it's in the country,' said Stephanie, 'and it's different. Mummy, we want to, we want to!'

'It's all arranged, we're going to Brittany with Grandma. I told you that some time ago.'

'Well, could we go after we come back from Brittany?' cried James. 'It'd be fun!'

'You two can go,' said Sara. 'If Daddy wants you. Now, have you finished that homework? Supper's ready.'

'You don't want to stay and have something to eat?' she asked Will, at the front door, but he said he'd work to do that evening, he'd better get home.

'If you don't mind my asking, why did you come? Just to talk about holidays.'

'Have to book up early these days.'

'Yes, that's why Mummy's already booked Brittany.'

'Sounds good.' Will opened the front door. 'Well, better not keep you from your supper. I'll be round at the weekend, as usual.'

' 'Bye, Will.' Sara's face was impassive as she closed the door.

Will's heart was heavy in his chest as he let himself into his flat. Everything looked dark. Stale. Even the thought of the new house did not cheer him, when he pictured Kate's being there and his children finding out. He was separated from their mother, he had every right to see another woman. But how explain that to them? He had already discovered that evening just how successful he was at explaining. So, he should give up Kate? He'd already done that once and Sara had undermined his sacrifice. He really didn't see why he should do it again.

He sliced some tomatoes and took a steak from the fridge. Why not do what the kids had done and just wait? See what happened? He might never see Kate again, anyway. That would solve all his problems. But as he relieved his feelings battering the steak, he couldn't imagine not seeing Kate again.

His supper was over and he'd had two glasses of wine, was settling down to his paperwork, heart still heavy behind his breast bone, when the telephone rang.

'Hi, Will,' said Kate. 'Want to meet?'

Chapter Seventy-Three

Kate and Biddy went to see Jessie whenever they could; Madge visited religiously every week. Abby would drive her, leave her for an hour or so, then collect her, looking in on Jessie herself to say hello, though of course she never received any reply. A recovery had not been ruled out, but Jessie did not progress. Madge was convinced she knew everything that was going on, but it was hard to say how true that was. All Jessie did was lie in her bed, or sit in the residents' lounge. She might have been enjoying the view of the gardens, she might have been watching the television, there was no way of knowing. She did not communicate.

Over the months, Madge had come to know Garthfield quite well. It was certainly well run, almost like a pleasant, private hotel. Only, of course it wasn't a hotel. It was a half way house between life and death. Those who came there were not yet ready to die, but they had finished with life. Going to work, making decisions, cooking, gardening, entertaining, all the things that made up ordinary life had dwindled for them to putting in time around three meals a day. Joining in the activities if you were able, lying in bed if you were not. Or, maybe, like Jessie, sitting in your chair in a world of your own.

'Oh, please God, may I die at home,' was Madge's prayer when she had visited Garthfield.

On a softly sunny day in May, Madge, arriving for her weekly visit, found Jessie in her room. She was looking pale but well, in a fresh white blouse and navy skirt with a pretty brooch, a present from Biddy, at her neck. After Madge had kissed her cheek and taken a chair, Jessie fixed her with the usual unblinking gaze that Madge, even after so long, still found disconcerting.

'Shall I open the window?' she asked brightly. 'Seems a bit stuffy in here, doesn't it? But it's a lovely day, Jessie. When Abby comes, I might get her to push you out into the garden. The fresh air would do you good.'

Poor Jessie, always looked so pale. But it didn't mean anything; even as a young woman, she'd never had much colour. Madge, limping along to put the grapes she'd brought into a bowl by Jessie's bed, reflected that she was probably the only person left who remembered Jessie as a young woman. And Jessie would be the only one to remember herself. That was a depressing thought, if you liked! At least, they had each other.

The room was very quiet. Outside in the garden, a few residents walked the paths with zimmer frames, not talking, but concentrating on where they had next to put their feet. Madge, back in her chair, was panting with her own exertion, when a strange sound cut the air.

'Madge?'

Madge sat upright and put her hand to her heart.

'Madge?' came the hoarse whisper again, and Madge burst into tears.

'Oh, Jessie, you said my name!'

She caught Jessie's hands and kissed her strange, bewildered face.

'Jessie, you're talking, you're talking! They said it might happen, but I never thought it would! Oh, Jessie!'

They were still clinging together, both in tears, when Abby came in and asked what was happening.

'Oh, Abby, Abby, Jessie said my name! She said, Madge, twice! Can you believe it?'

'Ma, that's wonderful!' Abby knelt by Jessie's chair and Jessie turned her solemn gaze on her.

'Abby,' she whispered, and it was Abby's turn to feel the tears sting her eyes.

'I'll go and tell the nurses,' she said hastily.

When Madge went to bed that night, she was feeling happier than she had felt in a long time. Jessie talking again! Back in the world! Dr Vincent, the young doctor who had been called to see her, had seemed as genuinely pleased as Madge and Abby.

'We knew it might happen, but quite honestly, we hadn't much hope,' she told them after she'd examined Jessie. 'And working here, to have a recovery – well, you can imagine how we feel!'

'What will happen now?' asked Abby. 'You think Mrs Rossie will continue to improve?'

'I think there's a very good chance, but I'm going to make an appointment for her at the hospital so that she can be assessed. At the moment, she's trying to talk all the time, but I'd like her to rest. Good news can be as taxing as bad, sometimes.'

They took the hint and said they'd go, but Madge went back to kiss Jessie's cheek again and press her hand.

'I'll be in to see you tomorrow, Jessie,' she whispered. 'And then we'll discuss plans.'

'Aye, if I could just get home again, Madge. See what you can do, eh?'

'The bungalow's still there, we haven't sold it. Before you know it, we'll be back together again.'

Jessie, who so rarely smiled, smiled now, a wide radiant smile, as Madge left her and gently closed her door.

'I wouldn't bank on getting back to the bungalow, Ma,' Abby said cautiously, on the way home. 'Jessie has a lot of ground to make up, and you're not the fittest person in the world, you know.'

'We could get more help from Nancy, Abby, and one of the nurses was telling me that the Council might help, too.' Madge's face had taken on the stubborn look that Abby knew so well. 'I don't see why we shouldn't go back. In the old days, people didn't go into nursing homes, and if Jessie doesn't need one, I think we should try to manage.'

'All right, let's see how things go. It's just wonderful, anyway, that Jessie is her old self again.'

'Oh, Abby, you don't know what that means to me,' said Madge.

In the night she lay awake a long time, planning her return to independence. It could be done. All it needed was someone to do the heavy work, and maybe a bit of cooking, and she could do the rest. Abby couldn't be kinder and Frankie was a dear good man, but the truth was, this was their home and not Madge's. That said it all.

When she finally moved into sleep, it was to dream of Catherine's Land, as she so often did. This time she was cleaning

363

the stair again, and people kept passing her, minding her bucket, and telling her she was doing a grand job, hen, and they'd take their turn next week. Some of the people she knew: Peggie Kemp, Joanie Muir, Sadie Pringle; others were strangers, she couldn't think what they were doing there, but someone said they were students, they had come to live in Catherine's Land. The time was going by and she hadn't finished her cleaning. She knew she must finish it before dawn, but the more stairs she scrubbed, the more there seemed to be. She was sitting, crying, when Jessie appeared, looking oh so pale, but all dressed up for her work as a waitress at the café near Holyrood.

'Why, Jessie, how smart you look!' cried Madge, rising, but Jessie shook her head. 'I canna talk,' she said, which was so funny, because there she was, talking! 'Goodbye, Madge.' And away she went, running down the stair.

'Jessie! Jessie!' cried Madge, and started up, wide awake.

Her room was filled with sunlight, it was going to be another lovely day, but a stranger was standing in the doorway, so still, so white, for a moment Madge thought she was back in her dream. The stranger was Abby.

'It's all right,' Madge whispered. 'Don't worry. I know what you're going to tell me.'

'Oh, Ma!' cried Abby, throwing herself into Madge's arms. 'I'm so sorry, I'm so sorry!'

'Jessie's dead, isn't she?'

'She died in her sleep. They said the shock of talking again had been too much for her heart, she just slipped quietly away. No pain, Ma, she wouldn't have known anything about it.'

'It's what she would have wanted,' Madge said quietly. 'She told me after Ken died that she felt she'd been left behind. That's me now, isn't it? There's no one left from the old days but me.'

Chapter Seventy-Four

Another funeral. Another church no one knew. Another graveside. The same mourners as before, except that Stewart Rossie hadn't made it from Aberdeen – pressure of work, he said – and the young lovers, Gail and Sean, were involved with exams. The real difference between Jessie's funeral and Ken's was that Ken's had been a winter leave-taking and here they were saying goodbye to Jessie in the spring. Seemed all wrong. Sunlight on new leaves, the sense of sap rising, life's cycle beginning again. May was not a time for dying.

Will, standing next to his mother and Mac, could not help his eyes going to Kate, as she looked down at her grandmother's grave at the end of the committal. She was wearing a dark linen suit but no hat, and the sunlight touching her tawny hair was harsh on the grief in her face. This was where it had started again, he remembered; his relationship with Kate. In this place, at this kind of ceremony. And where would it end? If it ended at all. He felt a guilty relief that Sara was not present; she'd had to attend a conference in Glasgow. Or had she invented that, because she'd known that Kate would be there? He didn't think so. Kate didn't bother Sara now.

As people began to turn away from the graveside, he moved swiftly to catch Kate.

'Kate, you know how sorry I am.'

'Yes. Thanks.' Her great Renoir eyes were dull.

'The thing is, I can't go on to Biddy's, I have a meeting I mustn't miss, shouldn't really be here now. Can I see you tonight?'

'I don't think so, Will. I want to spend some time with Biddy and the family.'

'You're not going back tomorrow?' he asked with dread.

'I have to. Harold's told us, he's calling the election in a month's time. You can imagine what that means.'

'For God's sake!' Will ran a hand across his brow. 'I haven't seen you in weeks, why can you never spare any time? I thought you were giving up on politics?'

'We can't talk now.' Kate began walking towards the cemetery gate and the waiting funeral cars. 'Look, my flight's not till evening. I could see you in the morning, if you liked.'

'The morning? No, I couldn't get away before twelve.'

'Twelve o'clock at the George, then. For a bar lunch?'

'Fine.'

Will fell back, as Kate joined Biddy at the cars. Frankie passed him, walking slowly, Madge's arm in his.

'Oh, Gran,' Will sighed.

'Will.' She gave him a gallant smile.

'I have to get back to work now, Gran, but I'll come and see you this evening, if that's all right?'

'Might want to rest, you know,' Frankie said to Madge.

'No, what's the point of resting? I'd like to see you, Will.'

So, he would be be spending time with his grandmother rather than Kate, after Jessie's funeral. It was better that way. Madge needed him. And Kate didn't? He wasn't sure. He'd find out tomorrow. Maybe.

They both arrived punctually at the George bar next day, and ordered wine and smoked salmon sandwiches. Kate was wearing her dark linen suit again and had made up her face to conceal her past tears. Will, spotting several people he knew, was already wishing they'd chosen to meet somewhere further afield, but time as usual was short. As they began to eat, he tried to keep his face blank. Knew he wouldn't be able to keep it that way.

'So, the election's set for June?' he asked without preamble. 'What happens if you lose?'

'To me? I'll go into opposition, like everybody else.'

He drank some wine, aware that his face was already showing his emotion.

'I thought you said you'd consider leaving politics, if Labour lost the election? I thought you said you might be leaving politics anyway?'

'I did say that.' Kate gave a rueful smile. 'I suppose I was depressed. Thought I'd blown it.'

'Are you saying you haven't?'

'Well – nothing's certain.' She looked down at her plate. 'But it's possible I may be going to get promotion, after all.'

'In Health?' he asked, as though it made a difference where it was.

'No, something new.'

'You're going to get a ministry?'

'Ssh.' She shook her head at him. 'Let's just say that it's been forgive and forget time.'

'It doesn't go against your principles, to take a job from a guy you don't admire?'

'I thought about that for a long time,' she said seriously. 'I decided in the end that it would be right to accept the post if offered, because of what I could make of it. Not for myself, for the people. It's not as though I despise Harold, anyway. He's a brilliant man. I just haven't always seen eye to eye with him in the past.'

'And how are you going to feel if you do end up in opposition? You really want to sit looking at the Tories for the next five years?'

'I think it might make me keener than ever to fight the good fight.' Kate's eyes were luminous on Will's. 'You're looking stunned. What difference does it make, what I do? I'll still be coming up to Edinburgh. Always supposing I win my seat again, of course.'

'You know that's a foregone conclusion,' he said glumly.

'I'm not so sure. I've got a Scottish Nationalist snapping at my heels and they've been giving Harold a few frights lately, as you know.'

'Still coming up to Edinburgh,' he repeated slowly. 'And I see you if you've time?'

'That's's not enough? It's all you asked for, if you remember.'

'I remember.' Will, conscious of eyes, whether there were eyes on him or not, suddenly got to his feet. 'Kate, let's go. We can't talk here.'

'Story of our lives,' she murmured, as they moved out into the sunshine of George Street. 'Trying to find somewhere to talk.'

Will glanced at his watch. He had half an hour.

'Let's walk in the gardens,' he suggested.

Keeping away from the floral clock where the tourists were gathered, they climbed to the grassy slopes beneath the high terrace of Ramsay Gardens. The Castle's dour pile reared to their right. On their left was the dramatic outline of the Assembly Hall above the Mound.

'Essential Edinburgh,' Kate observed. 'Face that launched a thousand boxes of shortbread. I miss it, you know. Westminster's not the same.'

'Westminster's where the power is.'

'Maybe not for ever.'

'You're turning Scot Nat?'

'Never! Has to be more to a party than nationalism.' Kate took Will's arm. 'Will, where are we going?'

He didn't pretend not to understand her.

'I don't know, Kate.' He looked down at her face, still so lovely. 'Maybe nowhere.'

They found a bench and sat down, watching the distant crowds of Princes Street.

'I think you want more than I can give,' Kate said, after a pause. 'You've been used to more, haven't you?'

'How do you mean?'

'Well, with Sara you had a full married relationship. Shared home, interests, children, the lot. With me, you'd never have that.'

'Didn't seem to matter.'

'Didn't?' She raised her eyebrows. 'We're already talking past tense?'

From behind them, the one o'clock gun suddenly boomed out from the Castle, catching them by surprise as it could always catch out tourists and residents alike.

'I shouldn't be here,' cried Will, leaping up, as Kate shuddered, putting her fingers in her ears. 'Oh, hell, this is no way to end a relationship!'

She stood up, squaring her shoulders as though preparing herself for ordeal.

'You want to end it, Will?'

He stood looking at her. 'Want isn't the right word.'

'What about should?'

'Oh, God, I don't know! Will you walk with me to the bank?'

They were silent until they reached the grand portals of the

368

Scottish and General, when Kate said, with a wry smile, 'My rival. How I hated this place in the old days!' She turned to look at Will. 'Nothing's changed, has it? We both put other things before love and we still do. I think you're right. We should end it. Before we get in too deep.'

'There's a chance of that?'

'Who knows? You're very special to me, Will.'

There was a grinding pain in his breast. He couldn't look at her.

'And what do you think you are to me?' he asked.

Later, he sat at his desk, staring sightlessly at papers, as he had sat so long ago, after he and Kate had parted for the first time. He had known then precisely what his feelings were. Now he couldn't be sure. There was pain, and there was sadness, that something bright and shining had left his life. But there was also – he felt ashamed to admit it – a certain relief. Relief that he needn't tell his children about Kate, needn't summon up the effort to become a part of her high-powered style, needn't do anything to change the status quo.

What was the matter with him? Was he growing old? No, he was just at the age when men began looking round for newer models than their wives. But they were trying to live in other people's futures. He'd been trying to go back to his own past. If Kate had said she would marry him all those years ago, if he had said he would give up the bank for her, would they have been happy together? He didn't think so. They were as Kate had always said, too different, they wanted different things. And there was something else. Kate was a wonderful person. Too wonderful, perhaps, to grow used to, to be comfortable with. So much colour and verve and energy had to be harnessed to something more than a mere man.

'Kate's only got one love,' Hamish had said, 'and it's politics. She'll never share your house with you.'

No, looked like he would be living there alone. And until his hurt receded, he would not complain.

A secretary came in with letters to sign. With a superhuman effort he had to conceal, Will moved back into his own world.

Kate, in her plane flying over cloud to London, was saying goodbye. Goodbye Gran. Goodbye Will. There were tears in her eyes for Jessie. And for what she'd had with Will and now had lost.

Let's face it, Kate Rossie, she told herself, you've been dumped.

Not strictly true, of course. If she had chucked politics, if she had come up to Edinburgh, lived with Will in his new house, there would have been no question of saying goodbye. Or would there? A tiny doubt niggled her mind, as she drank her mineral water and chewed drearily on peanuts. Will was not the same Will of her youth. Nor was she the same Kate. Life had not so much changed them, as strengthened their differences. They were too different, it seemed, even for a love affair.

Ah, but they'd had their moments! She dwelt on them, indulging herself in memory just for this flight, until she reached London and took up her life again. All the razzmatazz of an election awaited her and she knew she was looking forward to it. Then what? Victory and a ministry? Or years in the wilderness? Whichever, she would be in there, fighting, doing her job. Tomorrow she had a lunch engagement with Moray Chalmers, planned some time ago to put out feelers for a job back on a paper. He'd said she was crazy even to think of leaving politics, and she saw now that that was true. Everyone had to follow their destiny. As the plane landed and she breathed in the London air, it seemed to her that she could already smell election fever. Will had not completely left her heart, he never would, but as she hailed a taxi Kate's mind had already moved forward, to her real life, her own world. She still put on dark glasses, though, to hide her tears.

Chapter Seventy-Five

Harold Wilson lost the June election. The economy was improving, local election results had shown a swing to Labour, he'd been confident of victory. But it was Edward Heath who moved into Number Ten. Labour was once again in the wilderness.

Though her majority was dented by her Scottish Nationalist opponent, Kate retained her seat and was given the ministry she had been promised, much to the delight of the media. She was certainly the best-looking member of a shadow government anyone could remember, and as she sometimes tartly reminded her interviewers could do the job too. It became more and more difficult for Will to avoid seeing her photograph, or hearing her on TV or radio, but he managed it, and even when he actually saw her – at the opening of the Commonwealth Games at Meadowbank Stadium – he only smiled and nodded. The greatest help to him at this time was that his house was finally completed and that his children were able to stay with him during the summer holidays. After they'd returned from Brittany, of course. It pleased him that they seemed to enjoy themselves as much at Balerno as abroad; not that he wanted to compete with Sara in any way.

Edinburgh had been delighted to play host to the Commonwealth Games, known as the 'Friendly Games', because, amazingly, everyone involved got on so well. A splendid new pool had been built, Meadowbank Stadium had been upgraded; for once, costs had not been counted. It seemed as though the city had reached a high point for prosperity and success.

'For the first time, I feel we might be looking at a peaceful future,' Bobby said to Malcolm and Lindsay one evening at supper.

'Oh, don't say that!' cried Lindsay. 'Don't tempt fate!'

'That's completely illogical,' said Malcolm gently. 'There's no one listening to what Bobby says.'

'I know, but I still don't like him to say it,' Lindsay answered with a laugh.

The following day, while putting handkerchiefs away in Gail's drawer, she found a packet of contraceptive pills.

At first she'd thought they were drugs, and had to sit on the edge of Gail's bed. But when she'd read the label she didn't feel much better. Oh, how it hurt, that this was how Gail and Sean had repaid Bobby's and her trust! Sean, of late, had been made quite one of the family. Why, they'd even let him do his studying in Rachel's old studio, because, poor boy, he'd had nowhere he could work at home. Then, Highers over, Lindsay had found them both holiday jobs at Logie's – Gail in Stationery, Sean in Despatch – so that they could have money of their own, and not a word had been said that they were spending so much of their free time together. And now to find this! Lindsay looked down at the packet in her hand. She was shaking with anger and worry, could hardly wait until Gail came home so that she could tackle her.

'Gail, would you come upstairs please?' she called, when she heard the front door bang. 'I'm in your room.'

'What's up?' asked Gail, coming in with lighthearted step. She was wearing the dark dress she wore at Logie's, and looked, Lindsay thought, positively Puritan. As though butter wouldn't melt in her mouth.

'This is what's up,' Lindsay snapped, revealing what was in her hand. 'I found these in your drawer.'

Gail's dark brows drew together. 'What were you doing going through my things?' she asked icily.

'I was not going through your things, I was putting away your clean handkerchiefs.'

'Oh, dear, haven't been very bright, have I?' Gail had turned a dusky red. 'I suppose you're upset?'

'Of course I'm upset! I'm upset and worried and very disappointed.'

'Mum, it's no big deal, there's no need to be worried.'

372

'No big deal?' Lindsay flung the packet of pills on Gail's bed. 'What on earth does that mean? I don't even understand you. All I know is that you've broken our trust, mine and your father's. You told me you were not sleeping with Sean and I believed you.'

'I wasn't – we weren't – while we were studying. We agreed we wouldn't, until we'd finished our exams.'

'And then you just agreed you would? Is that the way people in love go on these days?' Lindsay distractedly put a hand to her brow. 'Where did you get the pills, then? Not from our doctor?'

'Of course not.' Gail picked up the pills from her bed and put them in her canvas shoulder bag. 'Someone put me on to a clinic where they give you advice.'

'And put you on a pill which is still an unknown quantity. It can cause thrombosis, it can cause all sorts of problems, especially in someone as young as you. Yet you chose to take it in secret, without a word to your parents.'

'Well, I knew what you'd say!'

'But don't you care about the risks, Gail? Surely, you do? You're not irresponsible.'

'Mum, the risks are tiny, everyone says so. The point is that it's much better to take the pill than risk having a baby, that would really be irresponsible!'

Lindsay sank into a basket chair and shook her head, as though she could take no more.

'I don't know what to say to you, Gail, I really don't. We trusted you and we trusted Sean, and this is the way you repay us. Seems very hard.'

'Mum, I know how you feel.' Gail put her arm around Lindsay's shoulders. 'But if you think about it from my point of view, you'll understand. I mean, you wanted to have sex when you were young, didn't you?'

'We called it making love,' Lindsay said tightly.

'OK, whatever. But you did and I bet you were worried the whole time, weren't you? And then you had me.'

Lindsay sprang to her feet. 'We will not discuss my love life, Gail, if you don't mind. And if it's of any interest, I've never regretted having you.'

'But you wouldn't want me to have a baby at seventeen, would you? Isn't it better this way?'

'I suppose the truth is, your father and I don't want you to make love at all. Until you're married.'

Gail smiled. 'Mum, times have changed.'

'But what am I going to tell Daddy?'

'Don't tell him anything. He'd just blame Sean and that wouldn't be fair.'

As Lindsay stared at her with worried eyes, Gail suddenly threw off her Logie's black dress and wrapped a cotton dressing gown round her slim figure.

'Do you mind, Mum? I must take a shower, always feel so hot and sticky in that ghastly outfit. Look, please say you're not going to worry any more about the pill. There are far more important things to think about, you know.'

'What things?'

'My Higher results, of course!' Gail's dark eyes were round with surprise. 'And Sean's!'

All was well. When the results came out in August, both Gail and Sean had achieved the strings of A's and B's required to get them into Edinburgh. Furthermore, though Lindsay and Bobby had argued for Gail's living at home, both had been allocated first-year accommodation where they wanted it. In Catherine's Hall.

Chapter Seventy-Six

It was October. Gail had departed for her new life at the university. Lindsay and Bobby were bereft.

'Which is ridiculous, I know,' Lindsay told Will, who had been invited for supper. 'She's only across the city, hasn't even moved away, but we miss her so much, don't we, Bobby?'

'I miss her, too,' said Malcolm.

'Why couldn't she have lived at home?' asked Bobby, giving Will some wine. 'Why this mad dash to get away?'

'You should know,' said Malcolm. 'You were the same, twenty years ago.'

Bobby smiled. 'Suppose I was.'

'Is Gail settling down all right?' asked Will.

'Oh, wonderfully well,' Lindsay answered. 'Of course, she still sees Sean, but they both seem to be working hard. We're pleased about that, aren't we, Bobby?'

'He's got more going for him than I thought,' Bobby admitted.

'You know Gail's in our old house?' asked Malcolm. 'Will, you should see it, you'd never believe the way it is now!'

'What floor is she on?'

'The second. Now was that where the Muirs were? I've been trying to remember.'

'The Muirs and the Erskines,' said Will. 'Or it might have been the Pringles. I can remember Donnie Muir, all right.'

'Funny, to think of Gail in Donnie's old place,' Malcolm mused. 'Wonder what Nina would make of that? Might cheer her up.'

'Oh, she's cheered up, anyway,' said Will. 'Hamish says she's back to her old self now. Quite reconciled to being an Australian again.'

Later, serving coffee, Lindsay apologised.

'It's terrible, Will, we've done nothing but talk about ourselves. How are things with you? Still enjoying your lovely house?'

'Yes, it's everything I wanted it to be, I couldn't be happier.'

Couldn't you? thought Lindsay, but busied herself offering cream and sugar.

'Funny name you gave it,' commented Bobby. 'I mean, Gilbrides.'

'It's short for Gilbride's House.'

'But it's our name.'

'My name. It's my house, I gave it my name.'

'Thought it'd have been The Rowans, or The Larches, or something like that.'

'Or Dunromin?' Will asked, laughing. 'I haven't done much roaming, have I? No, I'm plain guy and I like plain names.'

'You don't get lonely out there?' asked Malcolm, who still thought of Balerno as it had been when he was young, a village far away from Edinburgh, though it was in fact only seven miles from the city. There had been mills in the area since medieval times, using the Water of Leith, making paper, snuff, flax and cork, processing grain. Many had been still in operation in Malcolm's youth, but were now fast disappearing, giving way to new houses and golf courses. Will was under no illusions that his house would be the only one fronting Easterwood Golf Course; several other plots were already for sale, but he felt he was enough in the country to take pleasure in it. When Malcolm added, 'And there's no train now, is there?' he agreed, but said he didn't mind driving to work every day.

'And no, I don't get lonely. I like being out of the city every evening, I like the space. And then James and Steph come over at the weekends.' Will lit a cigarette. 'Gives Sara the chance to do what she wants to do, go out with Nick Ainslie, or whatever.'

Lindsay stared. 'You're a bit behind the times, Will. Nick went back to Annette ages ago.'

'He did? I understood he thought she was too young for him.'

376

'Men never think women are too young for them. I believe they made it up about Eastertime. I'm surprised you hadn't heard.'

'No.' Will drank his coffee. 'I hadn't heard.'

The following Saturday, when Will went to collect the children for their trip to Gilbrides, he found Sara washing her car. She was wearing jeans and a navy sweater, had her hair tied in a ponytail and looked, he thought, at least as young as Annette Ainslie.

'Hi!' She squeezed out her sponge and dried her hands. 'They're waiting for you, Will, just give them a shout.'

He hesitated. 'It's a lovely day, Sara. Do you fancy driving out with us? The leaves are turning, colours should be terrific.'

She didn't jump at the idea. 'I hadn't thought of it.'

'Well, couldn't you think of it? You haven't seen the house since it was finished. I'd like to show it you.'

James and Stephanie appeared, carrying their overnight bags. As they ran towards Will, Sara shrugged.

'OK, I'll come out and have supper with you. If you're cooking.'

'Sausages!' Will said cheerfully. 'But I've got a good nourishing joint for tomorrow.'

'I didn't say anything about tomorrow, Will.'

'No, I'm just telling you. Into the car, you guys – Mum's coming with us.'

'Mum's coming to the house?' The two young faces stared from one parent to the other. 'Coming with us?'

'No, I'm driving myself.' Sara picked up her bucket. 'You two go with Daddy and I'll follow. Must tidy myself up.'

'You look fine,' said Will.

Chapter Seventy-Seven

Will had chosen well to come out of town, Sara reflected as she drove through the countryside ablaze with autumn colours. She really ought to get out more often herself, see the clouds above the hills, appreciate the changes of the seasons. In Newington one scarcely noticed the difference.

'So, what did you think of our own American fall?' asked Will, coming through his birch trees to greet Sara as she parked at his white painted gate. He had changed into jeans and a checked shirt, and looked well and at ease.

Country life suits him, thought Sara, but her eyes, widening, were already moving from him to his house.

'Why, Will, your house!' she exclaimed. 'Why did no one tell me it was so beautiful?'

'We did, we did!' cried James. 'We kept saying and saying, didn't we, Steph, but you never listened, Mummy, you never listened!'

'You said it was different.' Sara was moving slowly up the drive. 'I don't remember anything else.'

She halted to stand gazing at the house that Will had built. One-storeyed, with white walls, dark roof and glittering windows, its lines were so simple, yet so masterly, the house seemed to fit its setting like a jewel in a ring. There was nothing of the rawness that she had expected, nothing of the piled-up cube effect she associated with modern buildings, yet nothing of the traditional, either. The house was truly different, in the way that Will must have wanted it to be different. Dragging her eyes away to meet his watchful gaze, Sara said lightly, 'I'm impressed.'

'Wait till you see inside, Mummy!' cried Stephanie.

Light was the theme of the interior. Everything stripped to the bone in order to make the most of the Scottish day, colour and pattern banished, hardwood floors kept free and shining. Yet there was comfort in the deep armchairs and sofas of the living area, there were books around and pictures, and the kitchen was warm and welcoming, with an Aga purring away amidst the stainless steel and chrome.

'Mum, isn't it terrific?' cried James. 'Didn't I say you'd like it? Because it's so different from our house, isn't it?'

'It's different from everybody's,' said Stephanie. 'In fact, I don't know how Daddy thought of it.'

'It was the architect who thought of it,' Will explained. 'I can't take any credit.'

'Yes, you can,' said Sara. 'You had to tell the architect what you wanted, didn't you? I think you can take every credit.'

'Thanks.' Will looked embarrassed. 'How about a drink to celebrate?'

As the children left them for the garden, Sara and Will pulled up chairs to the kitchen table and toasted the new house in white wine.

'What I'd really like to know, if you don't mind my asking, is how did you pay for all this?' asked Sara.

'I work in a bank, remember? Got a pretty good deal on the mortgage.' Will made a face. 'Even so, I'm probably going to be in debt till the year two thousand.'

'Worth it, though.'

'You really think so?'

'I do.' Sara finished her wine. 'So, where are these sausages?'

'No need to start cooking yet.' Will refilled her glass. 'I want to talk to you.'

Her look was wary. 'Don't give me too much wine, Will, I have to drive home.'

'Do you?'

She drew her brows together. 'Look, what's all this about? We're a little old for playing games.'

'Was there anything between you and Nick Ainslie?' he asked bluntly.

'I don't think that's any of your business. Anyway, he's back with Annette.'

'There was something, wasn't there?'

379

Sara moved restively. 'What does it matter to you? It's over, anyway. Why are you questioning me like this?'

'Because I want to come back to you.'

Sara drew in her breath sharply. 'That's impossible. That's not going to happen.'

'Why? If you're not involved with Nick and I'm not involved with Kate, why shouldn't we be together again?'

Sara's face was expressionless. 'You'll always be involved with Kate, Will.'

'No.'

The definiteness of the one word, the sharpness of his tone, caught her by surprise; then her face changed.

'You've been seeing Kate again?'

'Briefly. I won't hide that from you.'

'So, what's changed?'

'I've learned what's missing between her and me.'

'And?'

'And it's commitment. When we were young, we were truly in love, but even then we weren't prepared to sink our differences. We still aren't.'

Sara's mouth twisted. 'So you think after all these years you'll come back to me?'

'You put those years between us, Sara. I didn't want to leave you and the children.'

There was a long silence in the handsome kitchen. The Aga sighed. Outside, in the blue dusk, the children rode their bikes through the birches, calling to each other.

'We should be starting supper,' Sara said at last. 'It's getting late.'

Will grasped her hand. 'Just tell me – have I a chance? I know you don't feel the same towards me as you used to, but we can salvage something, can't we? I'm not just thinking of the children.'

She got to her feet and walked to the window. She fiddled with the blind, trying to pull it down. Will came up and quietly released it. As they shut out the night, he turned and took Sara into his arms.

'Could we give it a try?' he asked gently. 'I know it's a lot to ask —'

'Yes, it's a lot.'

'But I'm asking.'

She gave a long sigh and pulled herself from him.

'Where are the lights? We can't see each other's faces.'

Will snapped a switch and in the flood of light, their troubled eyes blinked.

'Where would we live?' asked Sara. 'In Newington, or here? Where you probably wanted to live with Kate.'

Colour flooded Will's face, he bit his lip.

'She never saw this house,' he said huskily. 'Only the site.'

Sara shrugged. She found the fridge and took out the sausages. 'Shall we grill these?' she asked over her shoulder.

'If you want me to, I'll put it on the market,' Will said quietly.

'Your dream house?' Sara was opening drawers and cupboards, finding plates and cutlery. 'Surely not.'

'It's not important. Not compared with you and me and the children.'

'You'd better call them in. They shouldn't be out there in the dark.'

'If I call them in, what shall I tell them?'

'That supper will soon be ready,' Sara said coolly.

She held all the cards, he couldn't blame her if she wanted to play them her way.

'Stephanie! James!' he shouted from the back door. 'Come on in. It's nearly supper time.'

The meal was over and cleared away, the plates in the dishwasher, and Sara was fishing in her handbag for her car keys.

'Right, I'd better get off,' she said briskly. 'I'll see you two tomorrow, OK?'

'Mummy, do you have to go?' asked Stephanie. 'There's a spare bedroom, you know.'

Sara's eyes slid away from Will's. 'I haven't brought my night things.'

'I could lend you a toothbrush and pyjamas,' said Will lightly.

'Yeah, Mum, stay,' said James. 'Why not?'

Sara looked from face to face.

'Well, I don't know — '

'Please,' said Will.

'All right,' said Sara.

Their eyes met. Each knew what the words meant. Will took the car keys from Sara's hand and dropped them back into her bag.

'Shall I show Mummy the spare room?' asked Stephanie. 'It's got its own bathroom, all blue, it's got a shower as well.'

'I'll make up the bed later,' Sara told her. 'You go and watch television with James.'

'My bed's already made up,' Will whispered, when they were alone.

'Will, you're rushing me.'

'I am. We've a lot of time to make up.'

'I haven't exactly said I want to try again. It's not going to be the same, you know.'

'No, it's as I say, a salvage operation. We'll take what we can.'

He drew her again into his arms and for the first time in years, their mouths met.

'Do I sell the house?' Will asked breathlessly.

'No, why should you?'

'It would be a measure of my commitment.'

'I don't need it.' Sara looked long and seriously into his face. 'I trust you, Will.'

'Sara —'

'Don't say any more. You weren't the only one at fault in the past, I did my bit to drive us apart. So, let's just make this a fresh start and like you say, salvage what we can. But we mustn't expect too much.'

'No,' Will agreed sombrely. 'I've learned my lesson there.'

That night, Sara did not make up the spare bed and though she used Will's spare toothbrush, she did not borrow his pyjamas. In the morning, bathed in clear country light streaming on to Will's bed, they clung to each other. Will wanted to speak, but Sara laid her finger over his mouth.

'Don't say anything, don't spoil it,' she whispered. 'Let's get up and tell the children you're coming back.'

But the children showed no surprise, only delight.

Of course, thought Will, setting out cereals, they've been expecting it. That was the nice thing about being young. You weren't afraid to expect happiness.

Chapter Seventy-Eight

October colours gave way to November fogs. They seemed to match Madge's mood. Since Jessie's death her natural good spirits had deserted her.

'The tide's gone out,' she told Abby. 'I'm a piece of driftwood left high and dry. That's how I feel.'

'I wish you wouldn't talk like that, Ma,' sighed Abby. 'Plenty of people live to be much older than you.'

'That's what I'm afraid of,' Madge replied. 'Living to be much older than I am now.'

For some time, Gail had been wanting her to come to Catherine's Hall, to see her room and have tea, but Madge had always made some excuse. Seeing the old place again, seeing its changes, no, she'd always avoided that and always would.

'I don't feel up to it,' she told Abby, when another little note came from Gail. 'Besides, you'd never be able to get my wheel-chair in the lift, and you know how badly I walk these days.'

'Yes, I can get it into the lift, Ma,' Abby said patiently. 'Gail's checked and it'll be fine. Come on, now, don't disappoint her this time. She's really looking forward to showing you round.'

With a touch of her old grace, Madge finally yielded.

'Well, if she really wants me to, perhaps I should go. I don't want to seem a disagreeable old woman.'

'You'll never be that,' Abby said fondly. 'And I think you'll enjoy going back, Ma. It'll be nice for you to see some young faces.'

'I suppose it's true, I don't see many young people. Apart from Will's children, of course.'

'And isn't it lovely that Will and Sara are together again?'

That at least brought a smile to Madge's faded blue eyes but she did not forget Kate. You could tell Jessie's granddaughter was happy, just looking at her on the television. She had got what she wanted, and if it wasn't Will, well, he was happy anyway.

On the Saturday afternoon appointed for the visit, Jennie came over from Fife to join them, bringing Mac who was to watch a rugby match with Frankie. Madge had dressed very carefully in a knitted dark blue suit, with her usual amber beads and a navy blue felt hat, and had even used a little lipstick. As Abby helped her into her winter coat, she gave a smile.

'Remember young Annie Lossie, in Mackenzie's Bakery? She was always in trouble, slipping on the lipstick behind Miss Dow's back, then having to wipe it all off again, soon as Miss Dow saw it! Oh, dear, those were different times, weren't they?'

'Yes, Ma,' answered Abby, grunting over the wheelchair she was trying to fit into the boot of her car. 'Jennie, can you give me a hand?'

When the wheelchair was finally in position, Madge was somehow shoehorned into the front seat beside Abby, while Jennie sat in the back.

'When were you last out, Ma?' asked Jennie, as they drove slowly through the New Town towards the Mound. 'Jessie's funeral, I suppose? You should get out more often, it'd do you good.'

'As though I'm not always trying to make Ma go out!' exclaimed Abby, waiting to cross Princes Street at the traffic lights.

'It's too much of an effort,' said Madge. 'When you get to my age, you'll understand.'

But her gaze on the Saturday afternoon shoppers was becoming interested, and as they drove up the Mound and turned into the Lawnmarket, she gave a little cry.

'Goodness, here it is, then, the old Lawnmarket! Hasn't changed at all, has it? Not really. Oh, dear, doesn't it bring it all back? Hurrying up here after work, carrying the bread and mebbe a few teacakes. We used to get them at reduced price, you know, any that were left at closing time. Oh, but I was always in such a state when all the office workers used to come rushing in, keeping us back when we wanted to get away home!' Madge's voice grew faint. 'Worrying about you and Rachel waiting for me, you see, Jennie. You weren't very old, then.'

Jennie put her hand on her mother's shoulder.

'We were all right,' she said softly. 'You did a grand job for us, always.'

'That's right,' Abby agreed. 'Worked harder than anybody knows.'

'We all worked hard in Catherine's Land,' said Madge.

'Well, here it is, Catherine's Hall.'

Abby stopped the car and they looked out at the tall old house that had been their home. The stone had been blackened in their day, the roof missing its slates, the chimneys at crazy angles, and always from one or two windows there would have been washing fluttering, whatever the weather. In silence, they viewed the changes.

'It's been cleaned,' said Madge, at last. 'Look at the colour! I never knew the stone was so pale.'

'The windows have all been renewed, and the roof,' said Jennie.

'And it's been joined now to the houses next door,' Abby pointed out. 'Still got its own entrance, though, and very grand, too. Remember the kids playing at the door in the old days?'

'It's not really so very different,' Madge said slowly. 'Not from the outside. It'll be the inside that's changed.'

'Completely,' said Abby. 'Jennie, if you can take Ma in, I'll find a place to park.'

New steps had been made to the entrance, but there was also a ramp, up which Jennie wheeled Madge, whose heart was beating fast.

'The shops are still here, Ma,' Jennie told her. 'But the sweetie shop's a bookshop now and my old dressmaker's is a coffee shop. Donnie's grocery is still a sort of grocery, though, sells health foods and all that sort of thing.'

'Fancy.' As Jennie pushed her through into the new vestibule, Madge looked at once for the stairs. 'Jennie, Jennie, where's the stair?'

'It's still there, Ma, behind that door, they only use it in emergencies. Here's the lift.'

Young people dressed alike in jeans and casual sweaters came rushing out of the lift when it arrived, but one or two stopped to help Jennie with the wheelchair.

'OK?' they asked, smiling.

'OK,' gasped Jennie, breathing hard. 'Now, what do we want? Second floor.' She pressed a button. 'Pity it wasn't the third, eh, Ma?'

Madge shook her head. 'I'm not sure I could face that, Jennie. Our old home, swallowed up. It'll be bad enough seeing Joanie Muir's.'

There was nothing left of the second floor Madge remembered. In some mysterious way, the small flagged landing had been replaced by a corridor; the two battered doors that had led to the Muirs' and the Erskines' flats had become four, all brightly painted, all holding names in little slots, one of which was Gail's. Out came Gail, at the sound of her bell, looking so like Rachel, Madge's eyes misted and she could not speak.

'Oh, Gran, you made it!' cried Gail, throwing her arms round Madge. 'Oh, I'm so pleased! I knew you'd want to see where I lived, I knew you'd want to see Catherine's Land again!'

She kissed Jennie and together they got the wheelchair into Gail's room, a part of the Muirs' old living room, though it was difficult to recognise. Half of the original windows were still there, and half of the cornice, but the old range had gone and the walls were so smooth and fresh, the curtains so pretty, Madge and Jennie could only shake their heads in wonder. There was a divan bed in one corner, a washbasin in another, two easy chairs and a small table on which Gail had laid out sandwiches and a chocolate cake.

'I'll just fill my kettle in the kitchen,' she told them. 'It's just at the turn of the corridor, there's a bathroom there as well, and two showers. We're really awfully well off!'

'They are,' said Jennie, grimly. 'If only we had had —' she stopped. 'No point in thinking of that now, is there?'

Abby arrived, followed by Sean from his room in one of the converted neighbouring houses. He presented Madge with a bunch of chrysanthemums, bowing over her wheelchair with such a flourish she was quite overcome.

'If your grandmother could see you now, Sean, at university!' she cried. 'Oh, how proud she would have been!'

'The good news is that Teresa's got herself into Telford

386

College,' said Sean. 'She's taking a computer science course, so that's given me a break.'

Gail came back and boiled the kettle, tea was made, Sean borrowed more chairs, and the sandwiches were handed.

'These are cream cheese and walnut, Gran,' said Gail. 'These are ham. And I got the cake from Logie's.'

'Great,' said Sean.

'You've gone to so much trouble, Gail, we do appreciate it,' said Jennie.

'We do,' said Madge. 'And I'm so glad to see everything. I feel a fool, not coming back before.'

'Maybe you'd like to see your old flat, Gran?' asked Gail. 'I know the girls up there, I could take you.'

Abby and Jennie said they'd like to see it, but Madge said if they didn't mind, she'd just stay quietly in her wheelchair.

'Shall I stay with you?' asked Sean, but Madge told him to go with the others, she'd be quite all right.

Alone, she closed her eyes. She could hear distant music – someone's wireless – and the buzz of traffic rising from the Lawnmarket. Familiar sounds. There'd always been a wireless playing in Catherine's Land, from the time it was invented, there'd always been the sound of traffic. And voices, of course. And steps on the stair. No steps on the stair now, because everyone used the lift.

She was beginning to feel rather strange, being back here, in Catherine's Land. As though she were fading. Losing time. Old faces were floating through her mind, some she hadn't thought of for years, some she thought of every day. Archie Shields, the tailor, she could smell his pressing cloths yet! And old Mr Kay, weighing out sugar into blue paper bags, slicing the bacon, oh so slowly. Donnie'd been so much quicker when he took over the grocery. Frankie's mother, the old dragon, selling the sweeties. Hadn't poor dear Jessie run that shop at one time? They'd had to close it in the war, when the rationing came.

Faces were coming so fast now, Madge couldn't keep track of them. Peggy Kemp and Joannie Muir, Marty Finnegan and Ivy Rossie, poor lovely, flawed Lily MacLaren. What had happened to Lily? Dead, like everyone else, but living on in Madge's mind. As Will and Jim lived, and Gramma Ritchie, and quick clever

Rachel. The tears still sprang to Madge's eyes when she thought of Rachel, dead before her time, but she felt she shouldn't weep. If you thought about them, people didn't die, did they? If you thought about the past, it was still with you.

Madge was beginning to feel very tired. Exhausted, was the word. Yes, exhausted. Spent. There was a little pain in her chest, she'd had it before but it had always gone, now it was back, sapping her strength. It would be lovely to sleep, she thought, but if she slept she might not wake. Waves of sleep seemed to be rocking her, lulling her. But sleep was like dying. Sleep then, sleep. Sleep was what she wanted.

'No!' she cried, and sat up, gasping, in her wheelchair.

There were faces around her again, swirling and moving, settling into people she knew. Abby and Jennie, who had unaccountably grown old. And someone who looked like Rachel.

'Rachel?' she whispered.

'It's Gail, Gran,' a young voice answered. 'Have you been sleeping?'

I nearly died back there, thought Madge, in the car going home. I nearly died in Joanie's old flat in Catherine's Land. As Abby and Jennie exchanged comments about the visit, how pretty Gail had looked, how nice Sean had been, wasn't it amazing what had been done with the old house, and so on, Madge wondered to herself, should she have died?

There was nothing left for her to do. Her family, after stormy passages, appeared to have reached harbour. Jennie had found new happiness with Mac, Hamish and Nina were doing well in Australia, Will and Sara were together again. Even troubled Bobby had settled into contentment with Lindsay and had accepted Gail's Sean. So, she wasn't needed. But why should she be needed? Why should she not just take pleasure in these last years she had been given? Worry no more about things to do? The pain had gone, it might not return.

Why, I might even live to get my telegram, thought Madge, though she couldn't imagine it, couldn't imagine living to be a hundred. Still, if she did, it would be a first. No one from Catherine's Land had ever lived long enough to get the telegram from the Queen.

The early darkness had descended, mixing with the fog, but the lights were shining through in Princes Street, and as Abby waited to cross again, Madge could see the floodlit Castle looking down. Strange to think that whatever happened to her, that castle would still be on its rock. Everything would continue just as always without her. But she couldn't really take that in. It wasn't given to people to understand what life would be without them. And if you were still a part of life, you didn't need to.

'All right, Ma?' asked Abby. 'You're very quiet.'

'Just thinking,' answered Madge.

'Not too tired? I thought you were looking pale back there at Gail's.'

'I'm fine,' said Madge, sniffing Sean's chrysanthemums, 'I've had a lovely day.'

The lights changed, the cars surged forward, Abby's with them, driving home.

'Goodbye, Catherine's Land,' thought Madge.

She knew she would see it again.

A Better Love Next Time
Doreen Edwards

A Welsh saga in the best-selling tradition of Iris Gower

Swansea in the 1950s and Florence Philpotts is ahead of her time. Her parents and boyfriend Ken may see her as an impetuous dreamer, but surely there is more to life than the typing pool?

Defying everyone, Florence takes a job as an apprentice hairdresser. She knows she has talent and enthusiasm, but it isn't going to be plain sailing – she has to avoid the unwanted attentions of her boss, Mr Tony, for a start.

Then, in the midst of a glorious local scandal, the opportunity arises to take over the salon. But neither her parents nor the bank will take a slip of a girl seriously. And marriage to Tony's mysterious brother Cliff could be a step too far even for determined, impulsive, ambitious Florence Philpotts...

The Gift & the Promise
Sarah Pernell

A throne is the prize and Saxon Earl Harold and William the Bastard of Normandy are about to battle to the death to gain it. A land and its people are torn apart and forged anew. Eleventh-century England is drawn in all its bloody, violent, turbulent and irresistible colour in a magnificent historical novel.

A gift is given and a favour pledged in return, but the price of redemption may be too high...

Through the story of Norman knight Renaud de Lassay and Saxon Thegn's daughter Ceolwynn, Sarah Pernell recreates a wounded and divided land in a brilliant blend of historical fact and imaginative fiction.

Love & Lies
Chrissa Mills

Who knows what secrets lie behind closed doors?

A newcomer to the village of Great Chessden, artist Justine Donaldson is fascinated by the old manor house, Tixover Grange, and its inhabitants, the hot-tempered Bettina Lamb and her wayward daughter Jacinth. She is also completely disarmed by Bettina's nephew Charles.

Justine's boyfriend George, the Lamb's gamekeeper, tells her of the bad blood between Bettina and Charles. But as Justine falls into Charles' confidence she finds herself torn between the two men.

Then, to Justine's secret chagrin, Charles appears as susceptible to his cousin Jacinth's charms as the next man. Has he been deceiving her all along or is there an ulterior motive behind this startling mismatch?

The Weeping Tree
Audrey Reimann

From the author of *Wise Child*

When Flora MacDonald leaps from the balcony of an Edinburgh reform school she falls, literally, into the safe arms of Andrew Stewart. A sailor on leave in the days before the outbreak of WWII, he might be expected to have the worst of intentions, but he is touched by her bid for freedom and helps her escape.

With such a beginning how could they not fall in love? But the tides of war conspire to part them.

Surrounded by danger on all sides, the one thing Flora and Andrew can cling to is their love for one another. But someone is conspiring to keep them apart, for their own secret, selfish, even murderous reasons... It may be a long time before the lovers' vows made under a willow tree can be fulfilled...

The very best of Piatkus fiction is now available in paperback as well as hardcover. Piatkus paperbacks, where *every* book is special.

The prices shown above were correct at the time of going to press. However, Piatkus Books reserve the right to show new retail prices on covers which may differ from those previously advertised in the text or elsewhere.

Piatkus Books will be available from your bookshop or newsagent, or can be ordered from the following address:
Piatkus Paperbacks, PO Box 11, Falmouth, TR10 9EN
Alternatively you can fax your order to this address on 01326 374 888 or e-mail us at books@barni.avel.co.uk

Payments can be made as follows: Sterling cheque, Eurocheque, postal order (payable to Piatkus Books) or by credit card, Visa/Mastercard. Do not send cash or currency. UK and B.F.P.O. customers should allow £1.00 postage and packing for the first book, 50p for the second and 30p for each additional book ordered to a maximum of £3.00 (7 books plus).

Overseas customers, including Eire, allow £2.00 for postage and packing for the first book, plus £1.00 for the second and 50p for each subsequent title ordered.

NAME (block letters) _____

ADDRESS _____

_____

I enclose my remittance for £ _____

I wish to pay by Visa/Mastercard   Expiry Date: _____
